About the Author

Dennis Carstens has lived most of his life in the Upper Midwest area of America in Minneapolis and St. Paul, Minnesota. He tries to write a story that is thought-provoking, entertaining, and has an overarching theme that is contemporary. He has always been a student of twentieth-century history and an admirer of the British people. His books normally contain a larger than normal number of characters that he uses to tell the story through their actions and dialog. He is not a big fan of novels that are page after page of third-person narration.

Swingate: Life and London When Britain Stood Alone

Dennis L. Carstens

Swingate: Life and London When Britain Stood Alone

Pegasus

PEGASUS PAPERBACK

© Copyright 2025
Dennis L. Carstens

The right of Dennis L. Carstens to be identified as author of this work has been asserted by him in accordance with the Copyright, Designs and Patents Act 1988

ISBN-978-1-80468-082-7

Pegasus is an imprint of
Pegasus Elliot MacKenzie Publishers Ltd.
www.pegasuspublishers.com

First Published in 2025

Pegasus
Sheraton House Castle Park
Cambridge CB3 0AX England

Printed & Bound in Great Britain

Dedication

This book is dedicated to the people of Britain who saved civilization from the tyranny of Adolf Hitler and Nazi Germany. A very special thank you goes to the women of the WAAF, the Women's Auxiliary Air Force of the RAF. These mostly unsung heroes played an enormously significant role throughout the war but especially during the Battle of Britain. Without their dedication, bravery, and sacrifice, it is doubtful that the battle would have been won.

Thank you again,
Dennis Carstens

5.0 out of 5 stars <u>Masterfully written, emotionally captivating, true to life war drama.</u>

Reading Carstens's carefully researched account of life in Britain during their war years brings the tragedy, the strength, the heroics to life for the reader. To forget history is to repeat history. It's been too many years since a novel of this importance has been written. Thank you for bringing this historical tragedy back into our consciousness. Let us not forget the true losses caused by wars.

5.0 out of 5 stars <u>Another page turner by Dennis Carstens</u>

This author consistently writes a "can't put it down book". I am amazed at how he continues to write such great novels. For anyone who is a lover of WWII and the history of same will love this book. It has everything, war, Churchill, romance and yet again...a fabulous ending. Dennis Carsten's books always leave me being very still, and calm, and thinking about what I have just read and so...what more can you ask? Sue

5.0 out of 5 stars <u>Awesome book</u>

I'm a lover of Dennis Carstens lawyer legal books. I took a chance on this one. Not being a history buff or history novel lover, this was truly a complete surprise. Moved by the plot and characters in the book, it took you back in time to the 1940's and World War era. The characters and plot were riveting. I am always at Dennis books and would not miss any of them.

5.0 out of 5 stars **An incredible read!!**

I'd been prepared not to like this departure from Carstens' series of legal thrillers. Once into the book, I was totally captivated. It is truly one of the most moving books I have ever read. Oddly, I'd put off starting the book until being ordered to shelter in place at least for several weeks, thanks to the corona virus pandemic. Our travails and complaints are trivial when compared to the horrors of the Battle of Britain.
An absolute masterpiece.

During the 1930s, the British built the first ever air defense system. It was made up of a chain of radar installations that ran from the very top of northern Scotland down the east coast of England and around to the west coast of Scotland. This was the first electronic early warning defense system ever built. These installations were called Chain Home Stations and one of them was called Swingate.

Swingate was located very close to Dover where the English Channel meets the North Sea. Directly across the twenty-mile Strait of Dover is the French city of Calais. Swingate's proximity to occupied France made it one of the most valuable installations of this early warning radar system and a key factor in the British victory during the Battle of Britain.

When I began to write this novel, it was not my intention to write another history book about the Battle of Britain. In fact, it isn't. There are any number of excellent books on that subject by historians with far more knowledge than mine. I chose the title 'Swingate' as a place name that had a key role in the British defeating the Germans during the battle. The above explanation of what Swingate was, is for informative purposes. I believe that very few people alive today would recognize the name Swingate and its significance. It is also a representation of what the Chain Home stations were and did and how they and the people who serviced them, mostly women, helped save civilization.

Dennis Carstens

Author's Note

As of this writing, I am the author of ten previous novels. They are a series of legal mystery/courtroom dramas known as the *Marc Kadella Legal Mysteries* available on Amazon. I am a retired lawyer and have enjoyed writing them and the positive results achieved.

For at least a couple of years, I have wanted to try something different. I have always been a bit of an amateur history buff, especially the American Civil War and the wars that have been labeled World War I and World War II. In reality, those two wars are essentially a single war with a twenty-year timeout to rearm and reload.

This novel is a fictionalized account of the lives of two people during the World War II Battle of Britain and the bombing campaign by the German Luftwaffe during what came to be known as the London Blitz. The two main characters are fictitious. They are an American named Jeffrey Bartlett and a British woman named Catherine Hartley. They meet and fall in love in London amidst the backdrop of the year during which Britain stood alone and saved civilization.

When it looked as if the sensible thing to do would be to make peace with Adolf Hitler and Nazi Germany, the British people steeled themselves under the leadership of the British Bulldog, Winston Churchill, and persevered against enormous odds. The world owes this small island nation a debt of gratitude it can never repay. A simple thank you seems woefully inadequate, but it is extremely heartfelt. I only hope, in my limited way, I have created an interesting, entertaining and accurate account and given the British people a little justice.

Thank you again,
Dennis Carstens

Also Available on Amazon:

The Marc Kadella Legal Mysteries
by
Dennis L. Carstens

Previous Marc Kadella Legal Mysteries:

The Key to Justice

Desperate Justice

Media Justice

Certain Justice

Personal Justice

Delayed Justice

Political Justice

Insider Justice

Exquisite Justice

Cult Justice

PRELUDE

On September 1, 1939, Adolf Hitler started the most destructive, devastating global event in world history. World War II began when two million German soldiers, along with thousands of tanks and airplanes, crashed across the Polish border. Before the war was over, sixty to seventy million people, including Hitler himself, would be dead.

Since coming to power in January 1933, Hitler had bullied his way to conquest. He had regained former German territory occupied by the Allies following World War I, while the Allies meekly stood by. Then he simply grabbed the independent German-speaking nation of Austria; all of this without a peep from France and Great Britain.

On September 29, 1938, in Munich, Germany, Hitler hosted a meeting with the leaders of France, Britain and Italy. In their desperate effort to avoid another catastrophic European war, the leaders of France and Britain gave the German Führer everything he wanted. In the interest of appeasing the monstrous Hitler, Neville Chamberlain, the Prime Minister of Britain and Édouard Daladier, the Premier of France, almost groveled at Hitler's feet. Without the leaders of Czechoslovakia even being invited to attend on behalf of their own country, France and Britain gave Hitler a significant piece of Czechoslovakia known as the Sudetenland. This was the last opportunity the Allies would have to prevent the cataclysm that Hitler would unleash in less than a year.

When Chamberlain arrived back in England, before an ecstatic crowd, he waved a piece of paper, the agreement with Hitler, and proclaimed it to be 'Peace in our time.' In reality, since Hitler derisively called it a mere scrap of paper, the Munich Conference would be the guarantor of another, more horrible war than World War I and the war Chamberlain hoped to avoid.

While Chamberlain was wrapping his arms around Hitler's ankles to give him whatever he wanted, Winston Churchill was sounding the alarm. In fact, ever since Hitler came to power in 1933, Churchill was almost alone at warning the world about the new dictator of Germany. Winston Churchill was one of the few people who could see Hitler for what he was.

Within a few months, the Nazi dictator tore the Munich Agreement—peace in our time—to shreds and swallowed the rest of Czechoslovakia. Finally, this act slapped the scales from the eyes of Chamberlain and the French.

Hitler's next target was obviously Poland. Both the British and French quickly made guarantees to the Poles, guarantees that would prove impossible to keep. If Poland was attacked, Britain and France would declare war to protect them, come to their aid and finally stop Hitler. This would prove to be a fool's errand.

Within a few weeks after launching the attack on Poland that started the global conflagration, Hitler's modern army and air force had crushed the outdated, overmatched Poles. The Nazis occupied half of Poland, and their partner in crime Josef Stalin, the leader of the Soviet Union and a socialist mass murderer of millions, sent the Russian army to occupy Poland's eastern half.

During the early days of Hitler's invasion of Poland, despite having entered into a treaty guaranteeing their assistance to Poland, the British and French still waffled. They sent notes to Hitler demanding that he stop the invasion and withdraw. After two days of being ignored by Hitler, Chamberlain and Daladier finally developed a backbone, albeit reluctantly. On September 3, both countries declared war on Germany. This act of defiance by the British and French amazingly stunned the German Führer. He was totally shocked that the two countries he held in utter contempt would actually keep their word to the Poles.

With the destruction of Warsaw and occupation of Poland, there followed a six-month period of inactivity. While the British built up their army in France, the French army, the largest in Europe, did little more than stare across the border at the lightly defended German fortifications. There was some fighting at sea by the belligerent navies but nothing on land in Western Europe. In fact, with most of the German army in Poland, the French could have walked to Berlin and won the war. Hitler would quickly prove the French had no stomach for a fight.

On April 9, 1940, the fighting briefly flared up. Realizing that the British had designs on Norway, Hitler made a preemptive strike. Most of Germany's iron ore came from Sweden. It was shipped to the far northern port of Narvik, Norway. From there, it was transported by ship along Norway's coast in Norwegian waters to Germany. If the British could cut off the Germans' source of iron ore, Hitler's war machine would grind to a halt for lack of steel.

Once again, and certainly not for the last time, the British and French moved too slowly. Hitler sent his Blitzkrieg—Lightning War—army and air force, accompanied by his navy, into Denmark and Norway. The British and French tried to drive them out. But through poor planning and leadership, they never had a chance. Again, in just a few brief weeks, with the total acquiescence of the Danes and Norwegians, Germany was victorious. They would occupy the two neutral countries until the end of the war. Following the events in Scandinavia, a quiet war settled over Western Europe once again while the British and French sat and waited. The bloodied British and French rescued what soldiers they could from Norway then waited for Hitler's next move.

Believing they had won World War I by brilliant strategy, leadership and tactics, the Allies' generals decided to fight that same war again. In fact, they had won not by great leadership, but by exhausting the Germans. Nevertheless, the Allies decided they would again fight a defensive war, exhaust the Germans, and win the war the same way. It was their brilliant plan to make the German army smash up against the Allies defensive fortifications and simply mow them down.

All they needed was to have the Germans cooperate. Except, the Allies neglected to inform Hitler's generals to perform their part. Instead, the Germans, having lost World War I by attrition fought in the trenches of France, had devised a totally new strategy for fighting this war.

The French had built a magnificent line of fortifications along its border with Germany. This line, the Maginot Line, would prevent any German army from breaching the border and getting into France. The line itself, however, was not long enough. It did not cover the border between Belgium and France the rest of the way to the sea.

What the Germans planned was militarily brilliant. They left a small force in front of the Maginot Line to keep those French soldiers in place. They then sent a large force through Holland to the north then into Belgium. This was done to pull the British and French, sitting along the French border with Belgium, northward into Belgium to meet them. Then the bulk of the German Army would smash through the weakly held French line at Sedan,

France, behind the British and French now moving into Belgium. That main German force, after easily punching through the French lines at Sedan, would wheel northwest and cut off the British and French in Belgium and have them trapped between the Germans to the north and south.

On May 10, 1940, Hitler unleashed his army. Unlike the Germans who did not cooperate with the plans of the Allies' generals, the British and French did exactly what the Germans wanted. The Germans attacked Holland and Belgium, both neutral countries, and the British and French drove north into Belgium to go after them. The German tanks of the main force roared through the 'impenetrable' Ardennes Forest at the confluence of Belgium, France and Luxembourg with ease. They took Sedan on May 12, crossed the Meuse River on the 15th, turned their tanks northwest and reached the English Channel cutting off the British and French on May 20, exactly as they had drawn it up on a map. For all practical purposes, the French were finished.

The British Expeditionary Force, along with a few French divisions, were driven onto the beaches at Dunkirk. Beginning on May 26 and lasting through June 4, the British pulled off what history would label as the Miracle of Dunkirk. Using small civilian-owned boats to get to the beach, 330,000 British and French soldiers were rescued and brought back to England. It was a miracle, but it was also a catastrophe.

The fighting in France continued for a short while but the end was inevitable. By mid-June, the French Government realized their situation was hopeless. They requested an armistice, a formal ceasefire, which was signed on June 22, 1940. The Battle of France was officially over. The Battle of Britain was about to begin.

BOOK ONE

Jeffrey
and
Dunkirk

INTRODUCTION

My name is Jeffrey Bartlett, and this is the story of how I came to report on the Battle of Britain. I am a reporter for the *New York Gazette* newspaper. More accurately, I am a dilettante who discovered I had some writing skills while partying my way through college and ignoring what could have been a very good education at Columbia. My father is Wilson Bartlett, a man I respect and fear but mostly adore. My mother is Abigail Bartlett whom I also adore. Mom is Mom, but make no mistake, Dad is Dad.

Anyway, after I earned my degree with an unremarkable C-plus average grade, Dad sat me down and had a serious man-to-man talk. It was what you would now call a 'Come to Jesus' moment. He reminded me of the Trust Fund set up by my forebears and that, as the trustee, he had control of it as long as he lived. And if he died, he had younger siblings, my uncles, whom he could name to take his place as trustee to prevent me from getting my hands on the dough, if Dad believed that was necessary. This may have been some form of insurance Granddad, or Dad, I am not sure who, set up as protection against patricide.

"The long and the short of it," the old man said, sternly looking me in the eye, "is you're going to get a job. You can live a wealthy lifestyle off of the interest of the trust—I'm okay with that—but only as long as you work a full-time job doing something constructive."

While he was making this little speech, I tried to interrupt a couple of times, but he stopped me.

"I know you're a young man and you're going to want to"—here he got an uncomfortable look on his face—"I guess the expression is, sow your wild oats. Believe it or not, I, uh, did a bit of that myself, before I met your mother, of course."

I feigned a look of shock and said, "Why Dad, I would have never—"

"Shut up, smartass," he said, and we both laughed.

"I'm going to get a job, one you might not approve of, but I've sent inquiries for employment to every newspaper in the city. I'd like to be a reporter," I said.

He looked at me, nodded his head and said, "You're right. That would not be my first choice for you. But if that's what you want, I know the publisher of the *Gazette*. If you'd like, I'll give him a call."

And that is how, much to my mother's dismay, I became a newspaper reporter; probably the wealthiest one in America, but then someone has to be.

For all of us, there are dates in our personal history that are forever etched in stone in our memory: your birthday, your children's birthdays, your wedding anniversary maybe, Christmas and so forth. For me, there are the normal ones, although I have been known to forget a birthday, including my own. There are also three from my time reporting back for the *Gazette* to America about the Battle of Britain that shall be, literally, etched for eternity in my consciousness.

The first date would be May 10, 1940. It was the day the German Army attacked the armies of Belgium, France and Great Britain in Western Europe. By a historical coincidence, that was also the day Winston Churchill became Prime Minister of the British government and began his march toward his destiny to save Western Civilization.

Most importantly for me, May 10 was also the day I met her. It was the day I met Catherine Hartley, Lady Ashland; the day I will hold in my heart for eternity. That is the day I discovered what being in love felt like: horrifying, mystifying, life-shattering and marvelously, magically wonderful all at the same time.

The second date would be July 10, 1940. It was on this day, following the surrender of France, that the Luftwaffe, the German Air Force, first attacked England in what would become the Battle of Britain. It started with one hundred and twenty bombers and fighters striking a British shipping convoy in the English Channel. A short while later, seventy more bombers dropped their bombs on the dockyard installations in South Wales. This could only be described as a very modest beginning compared to what was to come.

The third date I will hold onto through eternity is not nearly as historically significant as the first two. However, it is of utmost importance to me. Sorry, but I am not going to reveal it until the end of this tale. Don't try guessing what it is; I doubt you'll be able to.

ONE

April 10, 1940

"Yes, Mother, I'm listening," I say for the third or fourth time. It is a more or less normal Thursday morning, and I am dressing for work. I have the phone cradled under my chin against my left ear. I am listening while I try, for the third time, using a living room window for a mirror, to get the knot in my tie the way I like it.

Mother is making her first call of the day. It is seven thirty a.m. "I don't know why you can't settle down, find a nice girl and start to lead a normal life," she says.

"Yes, Mother," I reply now for the fourth or fifth time.

"What does that mean, 'Yes, mother'? You're not listening," she repeats. "When are you going to settle down with a—"

"Nice girl," I say. "I have looked everywhere and can't find one," I tell her. "At least none that will have me," I add. We have had this conversation so many times, I should simply get it recorded and send it to her.

I feel a pair of feminine hands on my shoulders. I cover the phone's mouthpiece to kiss my new friend as she takes over the job of fixing my tie.

"I know a dozen girls, beautiful, charming, intelligent that would jump at the chance. Why, your own newspaper listed you as the third most eligible bachelor in New York," she says into my ear. I have heard this line at least two dozen times.

"They did? Only third? I'm going to have to try harder. Goodbye, Mom. Say hi to Dad. I'll talk to you later," I say and abruptly hang up the phone.

"Your mother calls at seven thirty in the morning?" my lady friend asks.

I chuckle and say, "I have a great relationship with my parents. She's desperate for grandchildren. She may have to wait for one of my brothers or sisters. There are four of them behind me. You're already dressed, coiffed and ready to go home?"

"Yes," she replies. "I'm an early riser. Besides, I sleep lightly, and you woke me."

"Sorry," I reply.

The lady's name is Patricia Wells, and we met the previous evening at an Upper West Side cocktail party. She is a striking, slender blonde who caught my eye immediately. Two bottles of champagne later and she was on me in the back of the taxi like a Doberman on a T-bone. Or maybe that was the other way around. Memories can be tricky things.

"I need to go," I say as I slip on the suit coat she is holding for me. I turn around, put my hands on her waist and seductively say, "You can spend the day here if you like." Then I kiss her softly on the neck.

"Down big boy," she sighs. "I should get home before my husband."

I take a step back, startled with this revelation and ask, "Husband?"

"Oh"—she laughs—"don't be so surprised." She takes a step back, tilts her head slightly to the right and gives me a serious look. "You mean, you really don't know who I am?"

"Um, Patricia Wells?" I sheepishly answer.

"And my husband, Edgar Wells?" she asks.

"Really?" I say with a surprised look on my face. "Edgar Wells of Granite State Publishing? The owner of—"

"Too many businesses to remember," she flippantly replies. "Yes, that Edgar Wells. Or, more appropriately, Queen Edgar."

"Um, queen as in…?"

"Queer as a jaybird," she replies.

"Seriously? Edgar Wells is—"

"A raging fag," she says. "Oh, I don't care. I've known for a fact for several years. I suspected it all along. I mean, I know that men are attracted to me. Edgar never seemed all that interested. After a week of marriage, we began sleeping in separate rooms."

"How long have you been married?" I ask. I put two cigarettes in my mouth, light both with my gold Cartier lighter, a gift from a different married woman of my acquaintance.

"Eleven years. Oh"—she continues as she inhales a long drag of smoke and sits down on the couch. While we are talking, we have gradually moved into the living room. I take a chair matching the sofa to her right—"it's been fine. He doesn't want children. He's fifteen years older than me."

"How old are you?" I warily ask since I know Edgar Mills is over fifty and I am twenty-eight.

"Thirty-six," she replies with a sly smile.

I looked at my watch and say, "I really should get going. I have to get to work."

"What do you do?"

"I'm a reporter, a journalist with the *Gazette*," I reply, knowing what she would say, what everyone says.

"A reporter, really? Why for God's sake? Do something useful like clean stables or sweep the streets."

I laugh heartily at this, then she says, "Your family has gobs of money. Why are you wasting your time?"

"I found out in college I'm a pretty good writer," I tell her. "Besides, I can do something I enjoy and still live well," I say spreading my arms and looking around my eight-room apartment overlooking Lincoln Square. "I'm quite comfortable here."

She puts out her cigarette, stands and walks with me toward the door. When we get there, after she slips on her shoes, I help her into her coat.

"Can I get you a cab?" I ask.

"I'll call for a service downstairs," she says.

"Have the doorman do it," I say.

"That's what I meant."

"Can I see you again?" I ask with an expectant look.

"Oh, poor baby," she says and puffs out her lower lip. "I don't think my mother would approve. She's a good friend of your mother."

"Who—" I start to ask.

"Nancy Swinton," she tells me.

I roll my eyes toward the ceiling and tilt my head back. When I look at her, she has a huge smile on her face, a beautiful smile, and I almost laugh. "I can see the resemblance," I say. "You're Nancy's daughter? I remember you from, what…"

"Twenty years ago," she says.

I laugh and say, "Yes, the two of us together would be a bit of a shock." I mean about my mother and her oldest, dearest friend. "I'd still like to see you again, anyway."

"You're a darling young man and, I must admit, a terrific lay. Love the stamina of you younger guys," she admits. "Well, I'll think about it."

"Maybe a date," I say. "Dinner, a show."

"That would be novel."

"We can still ride down together. I don't think we'll get caught this morning."

I slip into a light tan trench coat—it has been raining all week—grab a matching hat, then open the door for her. I don't know it now, but I will never see her again.

As I said in the Introduction, my name is Jeffrey Bartlett. I am the twenty-eight-year-old, Columbia-educated son of Abigail and Wilson Bartlett. On my mother's side, we are distant relatives of one Roger Sherman, a long-time-ago resident and representative of Connecticut and a signer of the Declaration of Independence.

As high toned as that sounds, it is Dad and his side of the family that have the money. Grandad Oliver Bartlett found a surefire opportunity back in the 1880s in a little company called Standard Oil of Ohio. He even became a friend of its founder, John D. Rockefeller—or at least as much of a friend as anyone could be of that ruthless curmudgeon.

In the 1920s, two of his sons, Lewis and Robert Bartlett, my black-sheep uncles, added significantly to the family fortune. The apples falling not too far from the tree, the brothers saw a good investment themselves from what they would both describe as an exhilarating experience, bootlegging.

Not satisfied with simply bankrolling the gangsters, they rolled up their sleeves and dug right in with them. Later, in weaker moments, their tongues lubricated by alcohol, they would regale us kids with what were, I came to hope, wild tales of their adventures. I suspected there was more truth to them than Grandma would have approved of.

I was born in 1910, July 8 to be precise. I am the oldest of five: three boys and two girls. My sisters, now twenty-two and twenty, are sandwiched between two older and one younger brother, including myself. When I look back on my childhood, after living in Manhattan and working as a reporter, I am staggered by my good luck. The poverty, despair and hopelessness that can be found in this city are almost breathtaking and certainly heartbreaking.

As bad as that is, I fear worse is on the way. The war drums have sounded across the pond. How bad will it get, and will we be able to stay out of it?

I leave my houseguest with the building's concierge and go onto Ninth Avenue. Of course, I have my own car, but traveling in Manhattan is best done by taxi. Besides, the cabbie that waits for me every morning is a professional.

"Good morning, Frank," I say to the doorman who holds the building's front door open for me. Another daily ritual. "How's everything?" I continue inquiring about his family.

"Good morning, Mr. Bartlett. They're fine, sir," he replies. Months ago, I gave up trying to convince the man to call me by my first name.

Frank hurries under the building's canopy to beat me to the curb. By the time I get there, the cab is waiting for me. As Frank holds the door for me, I slip him a five-dollar bill, and he taps the bill of his cap. Another daily ritual performed.

"Good morning, Dutch," I say to the cabbie. "Thanks for waiting."

I light a cigarette and open the window two inches as he replies, "My pleasure, Mr. Bartlett. Right on time, again."

"Am I getting to be that predictable?"

"We all have our routines," Dutch answers.

"Good point," I agree. "Obviously, I need a vacation."

"Don't we all?" Dutch asks.

For the next fifteen minutes, I silently listen to Dutch give me a rundown of the coming baseball season. Being a Manhattan cabbie, Dutch has the scoop on every team in the Major Leagues.

"Bet the farm on the Yanks," Dutch says. "No question, they'll win it all again this year." This would make five years in a row.

"Hard to bet against them," I agree.

We are on Barclay at Church Street, a couple blocks from my destination, Park Row. While waiting for the red light, Dutch drops a bomb on me. "What's with this Hitler guy? You think he might be a little crazy?"

"He just might be," I reply. "But he might be crazy as a fox, though."

"What does he want with Denmark and Norway? What did they ever do to Germany?"

This question grabs my attention and I spring forward, place both hands on the back of the front seat and ask, "What are you talking about? What's happened to—?"

"Ain't you heard? It was on the radio this morning. Hitler invaded both Denmark and Norway early this morning," Dutch tells me.

Too stunned to reply, I simply stare through the windshield at the cross traffic on Church. Everyone was expecting the war to heat up now that spring is here, but this is a shock. Norway and Denmark are neutral nations. Is Hitler crazy?

The car starts forward, and I snap out of it as Dutch says, "I guess you ain't heard."

"No, no, I didn't have the radio on this morning," I quietly reply.

We ride the final few blocks to the Gazette Building on Park Row—informally known as Newspaper Row—in silence. Dutch stops at the front door. I grab my umbrella and open the door to get out. I then catch myself and realize I have not paid the man. Instead of giving him the normal ten-dollar bill, I peel off a twenty for the three-dollar ride.

"Whoa! Thanks, Mr. B," he says.

"Thank you, Dutch, for the news."

I hurry across the wide sidewalk and into the building. I barely acknowledge the elderly guard stationed at the door as I hustle to the elevators. The Gazette Building was built in 1889. It is a five-story designed specifically to be a newspaper business. My desk, the office where I work, is on the fourth floor; one floor down from the corporate and publisher offices.

"Morning, Carl," I say to the elevator operator.

There are four elevators each with its own operator. At this time of the day, Carl will hold the car until it is full as employees scurry to get to work. A long six minutes after getting on, I am finally able to get off the elevator on my floor.

I hurry to my desk, take off my raincoat and hang it, my hat and my umbrella on a coat rack. By this time, I can see other staff and reporters making their way to a conference room where my boss, Earl Stanton, is standing by the conference room door. When he notices me, he raises his left arm and anxiously waves at me. I quickly cross the room to join him and the others crowding into the small room. There are almost twenty people crowding into a room big enough for maybe ten. Half the people in there are smoking, and the room is already foggy from the smoke.

"Morning, Earl," I say.

I like Earl Stanton. He is a smart, no-nonsense newspaperman. I have grown on him the past few years. When I first came to work for him, he admitted later that he did not like me one bit; the rich, dilettante kid playing at being a reporter. It took a while, but I eventually won him over with good quality, hard work.

"What's going on?" I ask.

"You heard about Norway and Denmark?" he asks.

"In the cab," I answer.

"We're putting out an extra this morning. It's all hands on deck," he says.

Earl's boss, the paper's managing editor, Marty Fowles, is conducting the meeting. For the first ten minutes, he reads from a sheet of paper a list of assignments for the staff. When he finishes, it is hard not to notice my name is the only one that has not been mentioned. This would also explain why so many of my colleagues are looking at me with quizzical expressions.

"Anybody know why the Germans would go after Norway and Denmark?" Mel Johnson, a reporter asks.

I wait three or four seconds to see if anyone else will respond before saying, "Iron ore. The Germans get their iron ore from Sweden. It is shipped by rail across northern Norway to a seaport; I can't remember the name. Then it's transported by ship down the west coast of Norway, in Norwegian waters, to Germany. Without iron ore, the Nazi army wouldn't last long."

"How do you know that?" Earl asks me.

"I picked it up at a party at the British consulate a couple of months ago. A British naval officer and a Brit diplomat were talking to a Norwegian. The Norwegian was trying to get the British Navy to do something about this. Apparently, Hitler beat them to the punch."

"You get invited to the right parties," Mel Johnson says.

"Sometimes," I reply.

"Okay," Fowles says. "Any more questions?" He waits for a moment, and when no one says anything, he continues, "Let's get at it." Fowles then looks at me and says, "Jeff, come with me and Earl."

A couple of the reporters, friends of mine, look at me again. I simply shrug and follow Marty and Earl to Marty's office.

"Have a seat," Marty tells me, gesturing at a chair in front of his desk. "We have something else for you. We got word this morning that our London correspondent, Dennis Byrne, was killed in a car accident yesterday. They say it's the blackout. Traffic accidents at night have increased drastically. Anyway, Earl and I and the international editor, Paul Carlson—do you know him?"

"I've met him," I reply.

"Anyway," Marty says, "we kicked around the problem of whom to send to London, and we came up with you."

"Me?" I say, very surprised. "I have no experience with—"

"It's the same job," Earl says. "Plus, your work is good. You're comfortable with important people—"

"You're single, no kids and can leave right away," Marty adds.

"It's a good opportunity, Jeff," Earl tells me.

"Have you been to London?" Marty asks.

"Yeah," I reply. "Several times."

"That helps too," Marty says. "You know your way around the important part of the city."

"All right," I say. "I'll see about booking passage today."

TWO

April 15, 1940

"You have the suite number for me, and I'm all set?" I ask the ship's porter and his partner.

"Yes, sir," he replies. "We'll have your luggage stored in the storage compartment and the ones you want in your room before you get aboard."

"Great. Thanks," I say, then peel off two twenty-dollar bills and give each of the men one.

They thank me, nod and wheel the luggage carrier toward the ship. I watch them go for several seconds then turn to my right to admire the ship.

The S. S. America is about to leave on its maiden voyage, its first crossing of the Atlantic to England, and I have booked passage. The ship is a beautiful 723-feet, over 26,000-tons, first-class ocean liner with a crew of six hundred and forty-three. I have traveled to England and Europe several times but never aboard anything like this.

I turn back toward my parents who are standing on the pier waiting for me. Dad holds a small, hard case in his left-hand, my personal Remington manual typewriter that I would not trust to a porter. I will carry it aboard myself. Having a first-class ticket and a suite, we are allowed to drive Dad's Packard station wagon onto the pier. We are on Pier 92 directly across from DeWitt Clinton Park on the Hudson. I check my watch and find we have less than an hour until the scheduled departure.

"You tip them too much," Dad admonishes me again. "You young people are too frivolous with money."

"That's because I didn't have to work for it," I reply with a sly smile.

"Exactly," he grumbles.

"Stop it," Mom tells us both. She looks at me and adds, "That's your father's way of saying he's going to miss you."

"I know, and I'll miss both of you. Well, I should get aboard," I say to my parents.

I look at Mom who actually has a tear in each eye. This morning was the fourth straight of early sub-freezing temperatures. Mother, ever the worrier, steps up and pulls my coat lapels together because of the cold. She looks up at me, removes my light gray fedora and uses her gloved hand to push back my hair.

"Did you pack enough warm clothing?" she asks.

"Yes, Mom. This is now the third time you've asked. I'll be fine," I say smiling at her.

"England can be so cold and wet, even in the summer," she reminds me.

"I'll be fine," I repeat. "I promise to eat my vegetables and not spoil my supper with cake and ice cream—well, maybe once in a while."

This brings a smile from the old man.

"And don't drink and carouse around. And watch out for sinful women," Mom reminds me.

"All right, now you're getting a little carried away," I tell her. "There are limits to what I'll promise," I reply, sneaking a peek at my old man who is suppressing a laugh.

"Oh, stop it," she admonishes me with a playful slap on my chest. She reaches around my neck to hug me, and I hold her for a few seconds.

We release each other, and she stares up at me again. A sob escapes her mouth, then a heavy sigh. She places the hat back on my head and kisses me lightly on the lips. "My baby is all grown up and going off," she wistfully says. "Please be careful."

"I will, Mom. I promise. I'll try to get away and come home for a visit in the fall. Don't worry too much."

"And write every day," she says while poking me in the chest with a finger.

I smile and turn to my father. Unlike most of our peers, our family is not afraid to show affection. I put out my hand to shake, and Dad places the typewriter in it. He then gives me a warm embrace which I return.

"I'm proud of you," he tells me. "I've always been proud of you," he continues. He reaches inside his topcoat and retrieves a thick envelope.

"I have plenty of money," I say as he shoves it inside my coat pocket.

"You'll need cash," he says. "Especially for that carousing around you're not supposed to do and I know nothing about."

"That's probably true," my mother interjects. "On our wedding night, I had to give him instructions."

Dad laughs as I say, "I don't want to hear this!"

I look at my dad one last time and say, "Take care of the girls." I turn to Mom and say, "Take care of the boys." Of course, I am referring to my brothers and sisters.

For the first three days of the voyage, it is routine to the point of dull and boring. There are very few unattached females traveling to England. With the war about to heat up, this is no surprise. Most of the passengers are married couples, businessmen, a good number of junior diplomats and a smattering of journalists. I make the acquaintance of a few of them, but I am mostly interested in the diplomats. I guess there are at least fifty on board from a half dozen countries. Several are British, going home after being rotated out of Washington. None of them are very anxious to be leaving the safety of America.

The third evening out, I am invited to the captain's table for dinner. Of course, this is supposed to be quite an honor, which makes me wonder why I was invited. I arrive at the main dining room ahead of the appointed time of seven p.m. Fortunately, I have a tux to wear that was not stored in the hold of the ship, so I am able to dress for it.

The other guests of the captain are already here. When I arrive, introductions are made, and we take our seats. It is then I find out about my invitation. A man, roughly my father's age, along with his wife and daughter, are seated directly across from me. They are the Butlers from Trenton, New Jersey; the husband, Hunter, wife Claire and daughter Jean.

"I know your father," Hunter says after cocktails are ordered. "We went to Yale together."

"Interesting. I thought I knew most of Dad's friends, but he doesn't talk about Yale too much."

"At least not in front of your mother," he says, then lets loose an annoying laugh.

Seated to my right is an older, extremely unattractive, short, plump woman. Her name is Alexis Colby. After the comment from Hunter Butler, a man I do not believe for a moment is a friend of dear old Dad, I strike up a conversation with Alexis. She is widowed for the third time, and each time she adds more money to the pot. She is sailing to England thinking she might move there.

"You do know there's a war on," I say at one point.

"That crazy Hitler will get what he wants on the continent, and it will soon be over," she lightly replies. "As long as we stay out of it."

"Exactly," Hunter jumps in and says. He raises his cocktail in a toast, and Alexis Colby joins him. "No American boys are going to fight and die in Europe this time. The Frenchies and the Brits got themselves into it, and they can get themselves out of it," Butler says.

I look across the table, smile slightly at the man and say, "You do realize the man seated in between Captain Kelley and your lovely wife is a member of the British government? Perhaps we shouldn't be so quick to offend."

"Oh, come on now, Jeff, my boy. I meant no offense. I hope the Allies win, but we need to stay out of it," Butler replied.

"It's all right, Mr. Bartlett. That does seem to be the overwhelming sentiment in your country. We'll manage, I'm sure," the British man says. His name is Hamilton Tarnage, and he is an assistant deputy under-secretary of something or other I am told; or something along those lines.

After that isolationist exchange takes place, the rest of the meal passes in banal conviviality. I spend most of the time avoiding Buffoon Butler by chatting with the thrice-widowed Mrs. Colby and Butler's daughter. Her name is Jean, and she is a rather shy, not quite pretty nineteen-year-old. At one point, I notice her father making unapproving faces at me. Apparently, he is quite protective of the girl. This, of course, causes me to lean a little closer and turn on the charm even more.

After dinner, I politely adjourn to a more raucous setting. Most of the journalists on board and single British men have commandeered a bar on the Promenade Deck. It is almost two a.m. before I manage to fumble out of the tux and stumble into my bed.

The big ship shudders just enough to wake me. My eyes feel like they need to be opened with a can opener. My head has a dull pain in the back, and my mouth tastes like an old boot. There is a clock on the wall that reads 7.40 a.m. although it might be 8.40. We were supposed to cross a time zone line during the night, which I assume we did. I neglected to close the curtains on the suite's portholes last night. Because of this, there is a gray light coming through them. While still lying in bed, I look through the portholes and see it is a cloudy morning. My bladder is so full I am in pain.

When I finish with the toilet and clean my sordid mouth, I decide to take a look outside before going back to bed. At first, I do not notice it because I am looking overhead checking the weather. When I look down at the ocean, I see two- to three-foot waves and something in the water. I watch it for several seconds before realizing what it is. Less than a quarter of a mile out on the ship's starboard side is the low-riding form of a German submarine. It is what they call a U-boat.

I watch the menacing looking sub for almost two full minutes. This close, I can clearly see the U-48 painted on the tower. It is both sleek and ominous looking, like a black sea predator leisurely swimming on the surface as if toying with its prey. It is almost tiny compared to the big ocean liner, but there is no doubt which is in danger. There are also at least five or six men, officers and sailors, in the tower obviously watching us.

By now my headache is gone and there is no way I will be able to sleep. I shave and shower faster than I have ever done. Before dressing, I find my life preserver on a shelf in the closet and try it on. Satisfied I will be able to quickly get into it if the need arises, I leave it on the bed.

"What do you think?" Guy Williams asks me.

Guy is another member of the British Embassy in Washington being transferred home. The two of us, along with a growing crowd of at least two hundred, are standing at the rail watching the U-boat.

"I think that big old American flag flying off the stern is saving our asses," I tell him. "At least I hope so."

"Yes, I concur. Besides, if he meant us harm, he could have done so by now," Guy replies.

"And probably would have," I say in agreement.

The crowd along the rail is mostly quiet with everyone likely thinking the same basic thing: *what is he up to?*

"Good morning, Jeff," I hear a female voice say behind and to my left. I turn to the source and almost fail to recognize her.

"Jean?" I say, making it sound like a question.

"Yes, you remember," she replies, then pats me on the shoulder and smiles as she steps to the rail.

It is the young, shy, dowdy girl from the captain's table the previous evening. This morning her hair was down and below her shoulders, and she is wearing some makeup, dressed in tan slacks, stylish shoes, a blue blouse and a woman's trench coat. The look makes her appear several years older and extremely attractive.

"Surprised?" she asks. "I always look better not dressed as a farmer's wife with my hair up. The farmer's wife look keeps father happy. Do you have a cigarette?"

While I light a cigarette for her, she asks, referring to the submarine, "What do you think he's up to?"

"Probably waiting to hear back from Berlin with instructions about what to do," I reply. "I doubt Herr Hitler wants to drag America into this, so I guess before much longer he'll move off; at least I hope so. Besides, I'll bet our captain has sent his position to the British Navy."

I could hear Guy next to me clearing his throat and tugging at my coat sleeve. I figure he will not stop until I introduce him.

After the 'pleased to meet you,' Jean says quite sullenly, "I wish he'd shoot and get it over with."

"You do not," I say with a laugh. "You're not that desperate to get away from your father."

She looks at me, blows cigarette smoke into the wind then says, "Take me dancing tonight."

"Did your father bring a gun?" I ask.

"If he won't take you dancing, how about a handsome, charming Englishman?" Guy says.

"He will," Jean replies. "But I'll keep it in mind."

She gives me her cabin number, and we are set for eight o'clock.

I still look a little skeptical until she says, "Relax, I'm nineteen." She puts her mouth to my ear and whispers, "And I haven't been a virgin for a while now."

At that moment, the U-boat sounds its horn, the men on deck come to attention then salute us as the boat turns to starboard to sail off.

THREE

April 22, 1940

"We've stopped," Jean whispers in my ear. We are in my cabin, both comfortably asleep, when the ship's engines stop.

Not to brag, but I have slept with my share of women, and Jean Butler is the lightest sleeper I have ever known. She is also incredibly soft and warm and gives off an arousing, almost intoxicating scent from lovemaking. Some poor man is going to become her slave someday and probably soon. If it could be bottled and made into a perfume, women would rule the world. Come to think of it, maybe they should take a turn at it. They could not do worse than men have.

I lightly groan in an attempt to speak, then take a deep breath and reply, "We're in an area known as The Solent. It's the sea between the Isle of Wight and the southern coast of England. The ship will lie here for a while then make its way up into what's called Southampton Water to reach Southampton after sunrise. What time is it?"

Jean rolls off me to look at the clock. After a few seconds, she curls back into me and says, "It's either twelve ten or one ten. Did we cross another timeline?"

"Yes," I answer. "It must be one ten."

She climbs back on top of me and purrs, "Once more, then I have to go back to my cabin."

I have finished what I thought would be my last American breakfast for a while and am standing at the starboard railing. My personal concierge has been in to help me pack a short while ago. He has also taken charge of making sure all of my luggage will be transferred to the train station.

It is half past ten on a cool, blustery, mostly sunny Monday morning. I stand at the rail wearing a hat and overcoat with a dozen or so of my fellow passengers as we come into port. The big ship is being carefully guided into the dock position while most of us silently smoke. From here, having been to Southampton several times, I recognize and clearly see the yellow, three-story Southampton Terminus. This is the train station that has served the city and the dock area for over a hundred years. It is also where I will board my train for the trip to London's Waterloo Station.

"Good morning," I hear a man's voice behind me say. I recognize the voice as belonging to Hunter Butler, Jean's protective father.

I hesitate for a second before turning around, more than half expecting to find the man holding a pistol. "Good morning, sir," I pleasantly reply.

His wife was to his right, and the lovely Jean was behind and to his left. Jean is sporting a very mischievous smile and raised eyebrows that only I can see.

"Well, we made it," Butler declares. "No more submarine scares."

"Where are you off to?" I ask. Of course, Jean has told me, but I thought I would innocently ask.

"Edinburgh," he replies.

Being an obnoxious American, he butchered the word by pronouncing it 'Eden-burg' instead of 'Edin-burrow.' Jean places a hand to her mouth to stifle a laugh.

"We're stopping in London for a couple of days," he says. "I have some business to attend to. Then it's on to Eden-burg."

"Daddy, while you're taking care of your business, perhaps Mr. Bartlett could show me London. I'm sure he's been here before."

"What about your mother?" 'Daddy' asks, driving a stake of horror through me at the thought of dealing with the missus for two days.

"Oh, I need two days to recover from this awful seasickness," her mother replies.

"I'm not sure I approve," her father says. "I mean—"

"Oh, come on, Daddy. Mr. Bartlett is a complete gentleman. I'm sure he won't mind," Jean says. When the old man turns to me, Jean gives me a sassy wink.

"My pleasure," I say. "She'll be in very good hands."

On the train, I find that, fortunately, the cheap Hunter Butler has paid for second-class train tickets to London. I have a first-class compartment to myself for the two-hour train ride. The parents are sound asleep within minutes, and Jean sneaks off to sit with me in my compartment. I pay the extra fare for her when the conductor comes around.

"You little vixen," I say to her when the conductor leaves. "You are going to Edinburgh, and I am going to work. I have a job to do here."

"Don't be angry," she says sticking out her lower lip. "There's a war on, and my father is an idiot. Of course, we'll have to get in it. Hitler is a monster, and America will have to beat him."

"That's very prescient," I say.

"Oh, a big word for a young, silly girl," she replies.

"You're probably right," I agree, ignoring her negative comment, "about America having to get in it to beat Hitler."

"So we're all going to have to grab life where we can," she replies.

She looks at me with mischief in her eyes, locks the door, then pulls down the shades over the compartment's interior windows. When she finishes, she pulls up her skirt and straddles my lap. "Well?" she says with a playful smile.

"Aren't you going to pull the curtains for the exterior windows?" I ask.

She leans down and kisses my neck, then whispers in my ear, "Let the cows watch. They won't mind."

We part, Jean and I, as do I and her parents, at Waterloo Station. They have rooms at Claridge's, which surprises me. The old man would not pay for a first-class train ticket. Now they are going to one of the more upper-class hotels in the city.

I find my luggage and arrange to have it transported to my hotel, The Ritz. I am told it is one of the hotels where correspondents stay and is in the center of the news and information network. Plus, having stayed there a couple of times before, I know it and the area quite well. I pay the two men transporting my luggage fifty American dollars each from Dad's money or, more accurately, the cash he slipped to me on the dock in New York. That gets them moving. It is likely more money than they make in a week.

I find a cab, and typewriter case on my lap, he drives off. Waterloo Station is only a couple of miles from the hotel, but it is on the south side of the Thames, and being midday, traffic is slow. This gives me a chance to watch the people moving about. From here, London looks nothing like you would expect a war capital to look like. The last time I was here was almost three years ago. From my vantage point, it appears as if nothing has changed.

"I thought there was a war on," I say to the driver.

"We 'ear it'll be 'eat'n up now that spring's 'ere," the man replies. "We'll show 'itler and his crew wot's wot."

I have not heard that accent since the last time I was here, and it takes a bit of decoding. I am pretty sure it has something to do with Hitler and the war.

"You're from America," he says, more of a statement than a question.

"Yes, how did you guess?"

"By your accent," he replies. "Not from around 'ere. Been 'ere before?"

"Yes, several times. Great city. Beautiful city and wonderful people," I lie. Londoners are famous worldwide for being snooty and snobbish, especially to each other. The class system is alive and well.

"Well, sir, 'ere's your 'otel," he says as he pulls up in front.

Carrying my typewriter in its case, I walk through the front entrance on Piccadilly. What immediately strikes me is the normalcy. The Ritz is still displaying the full luxury, opulence, old-world charm and class it always had; more than most Londoners will ever see in a lifetime.

Well, I think, *they are the ones at war. At least I'll be comfortable.*

I check in at the front desk, and the concierge acts like I am his long-lost brother and he could not be happier to see me return. Of course, I cannot remember him at all, which likely means he does not remember me, either.

My luggage, every piece of it, is here in the lobby and already loaded onto a luggage carrier. A bellboy who looks to be at least ten years older than my dad guides me to my suite. The *Gazette* has paid for a single room. Since I know I will be working out of it, I pay the difference for a corner suite with a close, pleasant view of Green Park on one side. At the corner is a more distant view of Hyde Park. All in all, it is an extremely comfortable home for however long I will be here.

I have a quick lunch and go out into the city. I spend most of the afternoon walking around the perimeter of Hyde Park. The weather, for London in the spring, is quite good, and I find hundreds of people out in the park. Most of them—I spend a good deal of time talking to the Londoners—are quite casual about the war. The general belief is pretty much what my hack driver had told me earlier: once the real war starts, our boys will hand it quickly to the Germans; the war will be over before summer.

The next morning Jean Butler appears right on time. At eight a.m. she strolls into the hotel restaurant looking for me among the diners. She is a lovely girl, and I have to smile at my initial impression. Knowing what she is really like, she is already giving off a sexual aura from forty feet away.

We have a quick breakfast of toast, bacon and eggs that I told her is a standard British breakfast. She does not buy a word of that, mostly because it is ordered from the American menu. After finishing our meal, we leave to see London.

This morning is a much more typical London day weather-wise: gray, cool and a little wet. Even though she has been on the New York subway many times, Jean wants to ride the Underground. We go into Green Park station across the street. Within a few minutes, our train arrives.

Londoners are nothing like the people of New York. The train is quite crowded and when we try to get on, no one moves to make room for us. Instead, they stand like cattle as we literally push them aside to get aboard. Try pushing anyone aside on a New York subway. You'll be lucky if you don't elicit gunfire. Londoners not only don't mind, they don't even look at you. We arrive at Trafalgar Square in a few minutes and a third of the travelers exit, including Jean and me.

"Trafalgar Square is the name for a great naval battle. Lord Nelson, the guy on top of the monument—"

"Defeated the French and Spanish and established Great Britain as the world's preeminent power for over a century," Jean says, finishing the lecture for me.

"Oops, sorry," I say.

"Not bad for a silly girl," she adds sarcastically.

"Okay, I apologize. I didn't know—"

"You just assumed I was an uneducated, flighty-headed American."

I look at her as she smirks at me, and I say, "I apologize. Are you going to bust my balls all day?"

"No, I'll let it go. But I am going to give them a good workout later."

I laugh and say, "You are a naughty thing."

She laughs and says, "I just like to say things like that to get a reaction. Where to?"

"10 Downing Street is a block or so down there," I say pointing down Whitehall.

"What's 10 Downing Street?" she asks.

"It's the Prime Minister's residence," I answer, then realize she is pulling my leg. "You're not going to do this to me all day, are you?" I ask.

"No," she replies. "I'm done. Let's go see if Chamberlain is home."

After 10 Downing, we spend the entire day hopping on and off buses. London has a long and storied history, and there are an enormous number of things to see and do. The most noticeable sight paying homage to the war is the number of uniforms and sandbags. In the heart of Westminster, there are uniforms everywhere. In a way, they are a comforting sight. At least the British Army, Navy and Royal Air Force are busy taking the war seriously. The civilian government is also, it seems. Any building of even minimal consequence is surrounded, at least up to the second floor, by a built-up wall of sandbags.

By three that afternoon, we both need rest and food. We take a cab back to the Ritz. In the still crowded main restaurant, our meals arrive, and I have barely started eating when Jean pushes her empty plate aside.

"I'm done. Let's go," she announces, her eyes tilted up.

I look at the clock on the bedside table and it is almost nine. The sun is down and the room very dark. There is a blackout in force and the streets are also completely dark. I roll to my left and snuggle up against her naked back and butt. She is giving off that irresistible, delicious scent again, and I can feel myself becoming aroused. So does she. She purrs like a big cat, then rolls to her right to get on top of me.

"I don't want to go," she says afterward.

We are lying side-by-side holding hands and smoking cigarettes in bed. I have an ashtray on my stomach for us.

"You have to go," I say trying not to make it sound like an order.

"Why?" a question I knew she would ask.

"Because no matter what you might be thinking, you're not in love with me," I say.

"How do you know that?"

"I'm old and wise," I answer.

She laughs heartily at this, then calms down and says, "What you're really saying is you're not in love with me."

I stub my cigarette out and hand her the ashtray. I roll over on my side, lean on my left elbow and kiss her. With my nose touching hers I say, "No, to be honest, I'm not in love with you. I'm terrifically attracted to you and terribly fond of you, but that's not love. Besides, Jean, my darling, there is a war on, and it is about to explode. You need to go home."

"I know," she says as a single tear trickles down her face. "I'll miss you."

"And I am not just saying this. I will miss you a lot. And I'll think of you," I add.

"I'll write to you," she says, "care of the Ritz."

"Please do," I sincerely answer, although we both know it will not happen.

She reaches over and places the ashtray on the bedside table. She then wraps both arms around my neck and pulls me down once more.

FOUR

April 29, 1940

Dear Mom & Dad,

I'm really sorry I have not written before this. I have been extremely busy, etc.

Since you know by now, the ship didn't sink, I guess you probably realize I made it. Although, and I should not tell you this, we were shadowed by a German submarine for a couple of hours the third day out. That was interesting. I guess the Führer isn't in a big hurry to get into a war with Uncle Sam.

I have been spending quite a bit of time on buses and in the Underground meeting Londoners. Except for the buildings with sandbags, the anti-aircraft guns in the parks and the uniforms, it hardly seems like there is a war on at all, and everybody has the same optimistic attitude: "When the real war starts, the Germans will be quickly whipped." I have filed two articles about this that you may have read in the Gazette.

Today, Monday, a couple of American colleagues and I are meeting with Ambassador Kennedy. Dad, you probably know him. He's Joe Kennedy of the Boston Kennedys. He has been open and accommodating about his views and allowing reporters to interview him. It is no secret what his views are. He believes appeasing Hitler was the correct policy. And he is totally against America getting involved in the war.

On the whole, London is still London, and I am having a grand time. The weather, for London, has been mostly good, and the people are very upbeat. I will file a story about my Kennedy interview tomorrow. Watch for it.

My love to All
Jeff

I am sitting uncomfortably in the back of the cab between two other reporters, David Morgan, the correspondent for the *Washington D.C. Clarion* and Charlie Dolan of the *Philadelphia Dispatch*. Both are okay guys I met at the Savoy. The Savoy Hotel, about a mile from the Ritz where I am staying, has become the center of the journalist set in London. In the basement is a classy bar and restaurant named the American Bar. This, quite naturally, attracts the Americans which is where I met David and Charlie.

We obtained an audience with Ambassador Kennedy for this morning. Like I said, David and Charlie are both good guys, affable and happy drunks. My discomfort in the back seat is from Charlie's girth. Charlie, who never saw a meal he did not like, all five feet eight inches of him, is pushing two hundred fifty pounds. David is not a small man nor am I. Fortunately, the cab ride from the Ritz, where they picked me up, to the American Embassy is less than ten minutes. As we pile out of the cab at the front gate of the American Embassy, I tell the cabbie to wait for us. Having given him a two-pound tip, the man eagerly obliges.

We are on the list to see the ambassador, and the ramrod-straight marine quickly allows us entrance. We check in at a security desk once inside, and barely two minutes later, a very attractive British girl arrives to escort us. Rumor has it that with the wife and Kennedy brood back stateside, Old Joe is enjoying the company and comfort of several young, pretty, local girls.

Having been around wealth my entire life, I am the only one of us who is not awed by the ambassador's office. The young secretary, Helen, holds the door for us. David and Charlie stare wide-eyed at the surroundings while we wait for the ambassador.

"You were expecting a closet for the American ambassador to the Court of St. James?" I ask.

Before they can answer, Ambassador Kennedy makes his appearance through a side door. We introduce ourselves, and the ambassador, an affable host, seats us in comfortable leather club chairs in front of a cold fireplace.

For the next hour, we take turns trying to ask questions. Once in a while, he actually allows a question to be asked, then he goes into a long soliloquy giving us his personal views on whatever subject he chooses, even if it had nothing to do with the question. The general tenor of the rather one-way discussion is that Joe Kennedy does not believe it would be so bad to let Hitler have Europe; bringing order and stability to the continent, a major trading partner of America, would be good for business. At one point, he all but admits it would be especially good for his business, liquor importing.

Toward the end of the allotted hour, he pauses for a moment to wipe his glasses clean. Given the opening, I decide to leap.

"What about the Jews? What about what the Nazis are doing to the Jews?" I ask.

When I do this, both David and Charlie noticeably sit up and stiffen.

The ambassador smiles, puts his glasses back on and asks, "You're Wilson Bartlett's son, I hear. Is that true?" He uses an obviously patronizing, condescending tone which I can't help but find annoying.

"Yes, Ambassador," I reply. "But what about the Jews? We're hearing ghastly stories of human rights abuses…"

He waves it off with a flip of his right hand as if the question is a nuisance. "Propaganda by the Allies," he says, giving me a toothy smile. "We had the same bullshit during the last war. It is designed to get people angry. Oh, I'm sure there have been some abuses; there were during the Great War, too. But I have met these so-called terrible Nazis, and believe me, they're reasonable people, businessmen. Once the war is over, things will settle down. You'll see, young man. I'm sure your father feels the same way.

"The important thing now is for the French and British governments, especially the British, to make peace. Accept German hegemony in Europe; it's the smart thing to do. If the war goes on, the British could lose their empire. Then where would we be? No, the real enemies are the socialists, the Russians. Make peace with Germany and Herr Hitler will take care of that problem for us."

While he is prattling on about this. I am taking down shorthand dictation as fast as I can. So are David and Charlie.

Kennedy looks at his watch, smiles and says, "Look at the time, boys. I really must go. It's been grand and come back soon."

We all rise, and he genially leads us to the big, oak double doors.

"Just remember, boys," he says as he stands with the doorknob in his hand, "the important thing is that we stay the hell out of it. No American boys should die again fighting a war that is none of our business."

"Well, thank you for your time, Mr. Ambassador," each of us say in one form or another as we shake his hand and leave.

"What do you think?" Charlie asks me.

We are standing outside the gate smoking while a light drizzle comes down. It appears our cabbie has tired of waiting and, with tip in hand, has left us. What had looked like a pleasant spring day was turning cold and wet.

"Personally," Charlie continues, "I think his attitude is dangerous. Hitler will not be satisfied with Europe. And he won't let up on the Jews. I've read that piece of horror of Hitler's *Mein Kampf*, and I think he means what he says in it. He's going to bring a tyranny like no one has ever seen on Europe, Russia and especially the Jews."

I watch Charlie closely while he says this. Sure, I have not known him for very long, but he seems like a joyful man. This is a side of him I have not seen before. David is also intently watching him.

"Well," I finally say—as I flip the remnant of my cigarette into the street and pull up the collar of my raincoat—"his attitude is the overwhelming sentiment of the American public."

"I know," Charlie says. "And I'll tell you something. It won't be much longer before we, I mean us reporters here in London and Paris, will be doing everything we can to change their minds. Mark my words."

Surprisingly, our cabbie is back and apologizes for the wait as we pile in. It is a short but very quiet ride back to the Ritz.

For at least the twelfth time, I yank the sheet of paper I was typing on, out of the typewriter. Frustrated, I crush it and toss it toward the wastebasket by the desk. It rims out and lands on the floor.

I am sitting at the table in my suite. I use it to work on, rather than the desk because it provides more space. I silently stare at the typewriter trying to get my head in the game. I owe the *Gazette* an article about the interview with Ambassador Kennedy. My problem is being objective about it. I am having a lot of difficulty not telling the American people that their government's representative to Britain is a damn fool, that this man believes the way to deal with an insatiable monster is to keep throwing meat at it hoping someday it would have enough and then not want to eat you.

I light another cigarette—the ashtray is almost overflowing—then toss down the rest of my tea. I turn toward the wastebasket and shake my head. Lying on the floor around it are nine or ten crumpled-up balls of paper I had tossed at it. Apparently, my basketball skills have noticeably eroded since college.

The phone on the desk rings, and I stand up to answer it. Not having been out of the chair for two hours, my back has stiffened. I stretch it as I walk to the desk.

"Hello," I answer.

"How's your article coming?" I hear Charlie Dolan ask.

"It's not."

"Mine either," Charlie replies. "I'm going to set it aside and try again tomorrow. What do you say we meet at the Savoy?"

"I don't think so, Charlie. I'm going to get this done so I can get it to the ministry first thing in the morning. I want it sent tomorrow.

"Sheehan called me earlier," I say referring to a well-known American correspondent. "He asked me if I had heard about the rumors that the House of Commons is serious about a no-confidence vote against Chamberlain. You hear anything?"

"Yeah, I have, from a couple of sources," Charlie replies. "They tell me it's likely to happen, but it will take another week or so to round up the votes."

"You think it will happen?" I ask. A vote of no-confidence by Parliament's House of Commons against the Prime Minister would bring the government down. With the war in Western Europe about to become a real war, this could be a catastrophe.

"No, I don't. From what I've heard, the Conservatives will stand by their man and defeat the vote. But I also hear it might force Chamberlain out. We'll see. Listen, Jeff, if you change your mind, drop by the Savoy. We'll be there until late."

"Don't wait for me," I reply.

It takes me until after eleven p.m., but I am finally able to come up with a fifteen-hundred-word report about the interview. I finish proofing it for the third time. Satisfied that it is an objective story about Kennedy's opinion and does not read like he is a Nazi-lover, I put it away.

I make a cocktail for myself, the first one of the day because I don't drink while writing. I turn off the lights in the suite—the blackout is in force—then open the curtains. There is a half-moon in the cloudless sky over the city. It provides enough light to make out a lot of the buildings, mostly in silhouette. I stand looking out the main windows in the living room, sipping my drink and smoking, and feeling a little melancholy knowing most of my countrymen feel the same way as Kennedy. I decide my next report will be an account of Polish refugees in London.

Even though I have only been here a week, I have discovered that there is a significant Polish refugee community. All of them, or so it seems, are anxious to seek out reporters, especially Americans, to tell their stories. I have met several, some civilians and some former soldiers, including three civilians from Warsaw. If their stories are even half true, the Germans must be defeated. The common questions they all have are, "Where is America?" and "When will America rescue us?" It is clear these people are not waiting for Britain, France or Russia; it is America they are looking to. Many of them plead with me to please tell President Roosevelt what monsters, murderers and thieves the Nazis are so he will come to save them.

I finally go to bed about midnight. Lying there, it occurs to me how much I miss Jean Butler. Or maybe it is that scent she gives off.

FIVE

May 7, 1940

Dear Mom & Dad,

Sorry about not writing for a while, again. There is so much activity here. I have made contact with several military sources, and the feeling is the war is about to take off.

Anyway, I wanted to get off a quick note. My guy who flies them to America for us is waiting here in my room. He is a steward on the Pan Am Clipper out of Southampton. When he gets back to the States, he mails letters for us at $20 each. I think he has a pirate for an ancestor.

Heading to Parliament today. There's going to be a big row there. The opposition is going to force a no-confidence vote. From what we are hearing, it will likely fail. But Chamberlain might be forced to resign anyway. Word is that if that happens, the next PM will be either Lord Edward Halifax (likely) or Winston Churchill (probably not). I took a flier and bet a hundred pounds on Churchill. We'll see.

All my love to everyone,

Jeff

I squeeze into the press section of the gallery of Parliament next to David Morgan and an Englishman named Clive Burke. I met Clive a few days ago, and I immediately took to him. He's a rarity in Britain, an affable man willing to pick up a check for a meal. He seems to have some great sources and the inside scoop on everything. Or maybe he is a lot of talk. At any rate, he is a great guy and very likeable. Clive is a reporter for one of the tabloids. I think it is *The Daily Express* though I will not swear to it—a little too much to drink the night we met when he first told me.

It is Clive who told me there is going to be a no-confidence vote against Chamberlain today. He also assures me Neville Chamberlain will survive it easily. But he also tells me, if he does not survive it, then his good friend, Lord Halifax will succeed Chamberlain and become Prime Minister. Plus, I hear King George VI is a very good friend of both Chamberlain and Halifax. Just to be contrary is why I bet a hundred pounds on Churchill.

We have taken our seats at one thirty p.m. It is more than an hour later before the session begins. We are five rows back from the railing overlooking the floor. I have an excellent view of the front where the Speaker will sit. I will have a very good view of the action, if it ever gets started.

At quarter of three, everyone is called to order and some preliminary items are dealt with. It is during this time that I catch my first glimpse of her: a young woman, seated in the first row at the rail overlooking the chamber. She holds a reporter's notebook and pencil indicating she is there as a reporter. A woman reporter at that time in London, I am told, is a very rare sight. At first, I am only curious about a female reporter being allowed into Parliament. Then I look around and notice three or four more. The sight makes me smile—almost laugh actually—at this tiny crack in the wall of Western Civilization.

I look again at the woman by the rail just in time to see her head turn to look in my direction. She is wearing, what Americans would call, a white flapper hat with a stylish red ribbon and a small red rose sewn on. She has light brown hair cut just below her ears, blue eyes and the prettiest, classic British oval face and delicate chin. I see her for only one or two seconds, but I feel like I have been stabbed in the heart. For the next five minutes, while the speakers drone on, I cannot stop looking at her. I finally snap out of it, smile and think, *Get ahold of yourself. She's just another girl.*

The boring business discussion lasts until about ten minutes of four o'clock. At that point, one of the Conservative members—I later learn it is Captain David Margesson, the Government Chief Whip—moves for adjournment. This was agreed to, and I think that means they are done for the day. Instead, there begins the discussion concerning the conduct of the war or, more specifically, the Norwegian Campaign which has been grossly mishandled.

While all of this is going on, every chance I have, if the crowd between us allows, I sneak a peek at her. There is one more time when she turns so

I can see her for several seconds. When she looks away, I continue staring until I realize I am not breathing.

Chamberlain speaks first and tries to downplay the defeat in Norway. He starts off by claiming all British and French forces have been successfully withdrawn. Further, British losses were light compared to those of the Germans. While I watch, I cannot help thinking the PM is trying to put lipstick on a pig. It did not work.

Almost immediately, before Chamberlain finishes, the criticism begins by Labor Party members. It becomes so bad that the Speaker has to stop the interrupting members to allow Chamberlain to finish. Given the level of animosity from the opposition and what I would call the BS coming from Chamberlain, I believe he is, for all practical purposes, already finished.

In an attempt to placate Labor, he informs them that Winston Churchill, already First Lord of the Admiralty—head of the Navy—would take on a greater role in the conduct of the war. This seems to satisfy much of the opposition, which I find strange. It is my understanding that Churchill was the main motivator behind the Norwegian adventure that turned out so badly. British politics seems to be a strange business, at least for an American.

The next two speakers are the leader of the Labor Party, Clement Atlee and the leader of the Liberals, Archibald Sinclair.

Atlee goes first and roundly criticizes the conduct of the Norwegian campaign. He reminds Chamberlain and Churchill of their confident boasts about the outcome. They had painted a rosy picture to gain support for it that did not come to fruition. Atlee finishes by claiming there is widespread belief that winning the war is going to require new leadership. This claim comes with an eruption of enormous support from the opposition side of the floor.

Sinclair takes his turn and speaks critically by bringing up specific instances of poor planning, supply and leadership. This is expected. He is also given a loud cheer of support from the opposition side of the floor.

The most significant speeches made during the day's debate come from members of Chamberlain's own Conservative Party.

Retired Admiral of the Fleet, Sir Roger Keyes, in full uniform, gives an impassioned speech on behalf of the Navy. His criticism is that the officers and sailors of the Royal Navy are extremely unhappy. To a man, they believe, or so Keyes claims that the military, especially the Royal Navy, conducted the campaign boldly, professionally and with exceptional courage. It was the political leadership and interference, again so Keyes claims, that doomed the expedition. Campaign itself was handled boldly by the military, especially the Royal Navy, but for the poor political leadership, it would have succeeded easily. Again, the leadership of the Government is to blame and must be changed.

Finally, a former Conservative cabinet minister Leo Amery gives, what I believe is, the most blistering and eloquent attack of the day. After a long recitation of the facts, he places it in historical context. Amery makes the statement of the day. He passionately quotes Oliver Cromwell telling the so-called Long Parliament three hundred years before, "You have sat too long here for any good you have been doing. Depart, I say, and let us have done with you. In the name of God, go."

The opposition lets loose its loudest and most sustained explosion of support heard during the debate. The session ends for the day without a vote on the no-confidence motion. They will be back at it tomorrow, May 8. I am told there will be a vote that day for certain.

I am up until midnight poring over the history books. By the time I finish, I know more about Oliver Cromwell and the English Civil War than I had ever wanted to. I also believe Amery's quote of the legendary Cromwell will be the final stab through Chamberlain's heart. Within a day, maybe two, Britain will have a new Prime Minister to head the government and fight the war. I am also more convinced it will not be Halifax. It will be the British Bulldog Churchill.

When I finish my research that night on the history of Oliver Cromwell, I almost collapse on the bed. I manage to get under the covers, but the day has been so excitingly stressful I am not sure I will make it. Within a minute I am falling into sleep when I bolt upright into a sitting position. Breathing heavily, I stare out into the darkness wondering if my mind is playing tricks on me. An instant before sleep comes, her face, as clear as it could be, appears in my mind.

"What is wrong with me?" I quietly ask myself out loud.

I forgot to close the curtains in the bedroom the night before. It is barely six a.m. when the light coming in the window awakens me. I lie in bed for several seconds while my head clears, and then it happens again. That lovely girl's face appears in my mind even more vividly than the night before. After a minute or so, when I become fully awake, she disappears.

I pick the suit I had worn yesterday from the bedroom floor. I neatly fold it and place it, along with the other clothes I need laundering, in the hall. I then head for the bathroom. I figure as long as I am up, I may as well get moving. I have to get my story from yesterday filed with the censors and sent to New York. Then I need to go back to Parliament. The vote is sure to take place today.

It seems that people are barely one short step above sheep. The same small mob of reporters returned to the gallery overlooking the house floor. I look around and almost laugh. Everyone, or so it appears, is back and in the same seat they occupied yesterday, myself and my two companions included. Of course, I look for her, and there she is. She is again occupying that same ideal place at the railing. She has her notebook and pencil and is wearing a stylish, elegant light gray jacket and skirt, one that a working woman her age would not be able to afford. The flapper hat is gone and replaced by a small black hat. From my vantage point, she looks lovelier than the day before.

The debate begins with a speech from a member of the Labor Party, Herbert Morrison. In the American Congress, especially the Senate, there is a well-established tradition of decorum. You simply do not make personal attacks on fellow representatives or senators. In the British Parliament, somewhat to my surprise, apparently no such understanding exists.

Member Morrison gives a scathing account of the government's conduct. He goes back to 1931 and reads off a list of the gross mishandling of foreign affairs up to 1939. And he is not shy about naming the culprits. He points his wrath directly at Chamberlain especially as Prime Minister. Also included are the Chancellor of the Exchequer John Simon and Secretary of State for Air Samuel Hoare. It was Hoare who has allowed the Royal Air Force, I am told, to be greatly surpassed by Hitler's Luftwaffe.

Morrison makes no bones about it. These three must go if the war is to be won.

Sitting in the gallery listening, I find myself wondering about one man in particular who escapes Morrison's fury. Lord Edward Halifax is never mentioned. As Secretary of State for Foreign Affairs at the time of the Munich Agreement, he too is culpable for the problems Britain now faces.

Chamberlain rises when Morrison finishes and throws down the figurative gauntlet. Morrison has made a motion demanding a vote on Chamberlain's fitness to continue in office. Chamberlain, for all practical purposes, seconds the motion. He proclaims that he has sufficient friends to prevail and welcomes the opportunity.

"Did he just say what I think he said?" I whisper to my British colleague Clive Burke.

"Yes, he did. He just handed the opposition the rope to hang him and dared them to use it," Clive whispers back.

David Lloyd George, a lion in British politics for fifty years and the Prime Minister during the First War, speaks. He essentially agrees with Morrison and argues persuasively that Britain is in the worst strategic position in its history. During Lloyd George's speech, Winston Churchill interrupts him. Churchill tries, unsuccessfully, as head of the Royal Navy, to take full responsibility for the loss of Norway. It does not work. Lloyd George with a loud chorus of members in agreement, refuse to allow it, insisting the Navy has acted as well as it possibly could.

Finally, it is Churchill who concludes the argument on behalf of the government. Despite being one of the two men who will replace him, Churchill speaks with his usual eloquence and passion to save Chamberlain.

When he finishes, there is a motion for a vote. The number of votes on behalf of Chamberlain total two hundred and eighty-one. Those opposed, two hundred. Chamberlain has survived the vote. *Or did he?* I wonder. Of the members who normally support the government, forty-one had voted with the opposition. Another sixty had not voted by abstaining. Chamberlain's victory is, in fact, devastating. The margin is very thin and the opposition among his normal supporters has sent shock waves through the government.

***

We are filing out after the drama of the day. I have a feeling I have just witnessed a significant historical event. And I have a deep foreboding about what it means for the conduct of the war. Could Britain win with Chamberlain?

"Well," I say to Clive, "I guess Chamberlain survived."

Clive looks at me and shakes his head. "We'll see," he replies. "But I doubt it. His position is very weak. I don't think he'll last more than a few days. He'll resign if he can get Halifax to take his place. That's your story to report to the States."

I am looking to my left while listening to Clive. I see her moving with the crowd across the emptying seats. "Who is she," I ask Clive, "that woman wearing the black hat?"

Clive looks at her then says, "That is Catherine Hartley, also known by her married name, Lady Ashland. Her husband is Captain Arthur Ashland. I'm not sure what his number is—somewhere between the fifth and tenth Earl of Ashland."

The crowd is still moving slowly but making progress.

"So she's married," I say, trying not to sound as disappointed as I feel.

"Yes, she is. They have a title, but from what I've heard, well—"

"What?" I ask.

"I'd rather not say," Clive replies.

We get into the outer hallway almost to an exit when she looks directly at me. Absolutely no doubt, we make eye contact and hold it for two or three seconds—but for me an hour. She parts her lips in a small smile then turns and goes through the exit.

David Morgan, my friend with the *Washington Clarion* gently takes my right elbow. I am continuing to stare though she is now gone.

"Hey, we're going to the Fox & Pony," he says. "You coming?" He is referring to a comfortable pub in Mayfair we have discovered. Pleasant atmosphere, good food and people who seem to be enthralled by Americans.

"Um, yeah. Yes, let's go," I mutter.

We have finished our meal and are enjoying the afterglow when I go back to my mystery woman. "Okay, Clive. I'm not letting you off the hook. What is it about Lady Ashland you don't want me to know?" I ask.

He frowns then fumbles around obviously stalling while filling his pipe. I continue to stare while David looks back and forth at the two of us.

Clive lights his pipe then finally replies. "It's not about her. As you have clearly noticed, she is a lovely woman. It's about her husband. He seems to be, or rumor has it—although I've yet to witness it myself—not the most faithful husband. They, the Ashlands, have a lot of money," he continues with what will prove to be British understatement, "and he likes the London nightlife. He's also quite fond of what you Americans refer to as working girls. Right now, he's across the Channel with the Army awaiting the Germans."

"I get the feeling you're holding something back," I say.

"Rumor has it, and this is unsubstantiated, he may be a bit of a bully toward his wife."

My heart sinks with this news. To think anyone could harm her leaves me insufferably sad. So I change the subject. "What does she do?"

"She does some reporting for the BBC. They probably had a dozen people in the gallery today. They will all turn in a report, then the editors will use them to cobble together their story. I've been told she is quite good. Excellent even."

"Why the interest?" David asks.

"She's an attractive woman. I was just curious about her," I reply.

"Uh-huh," David says, his lips curled up and eyebrows raised.

SIX

May 10, 1940

Dear Mom & Dad,

I'm sure by now you've heard about the no-confidence vote of the House of Commons on the 8th. Chamberlain survived it, but yesterday there was a growing chorus in the government, loud whispers, calling for Chamberlain to resign. These whispers have grown into shouts. It is unlikely he will survive the day.

Halifax or Churchill? That's the question. Don't know if I mentioned it to you before, but I have a hundred pounds on Churchill.

Now for the big news which you will have heard by the time you get this letter. The German army has invaded both Holland and Belgium. I had lunch today with a British colonel and a major. They were both delighted that Hitler has attacked the way he has. The army's attitude is: "Now we've got them. They're doing exactly what we want."

Personally, I'm not so sure. They seem a little too optimistic; almost cocky. So far, Hitler has never done exactly what the allies have wanted, and the German army and Luftwaffe have performed brilliantly. They are not being led by fools.

I'm off to hang out at 10 Downing Street. We should know by the end of the day who will be the new PM.

Love to Everyone,

Jeff

When I wake up this morning, I sit on the edge of my bed for over fifteen minutes, and all I can see is her. Her name, I now know, is Catherine, Lady Catherine Ashland. And I feel rotten thinking about her, a married woman, and I don't know why. Maybe it is because her husband is in France about to fight the Germans for the freedom of Europe. Although, the thought of him being a philanderer and abusive toward her takes the sting from my conscience.

While I shave, I look at myself with curiosity. "When did you start to care about a woman's marital status?" I literally say out loud to the man in the mirror. "Why is this one different? Besides, Clive says her husband is an abusive ass." I carry on this discussion with myself while I shower and dress. Finally, it occurs to me how strange this would appear if anyone saw it.

I am adjusting the leather strap on my watch when the phone rings. "Have you heard?" I hear the voice of Charlie Dolan ask without even a hello.

"No… maybe. What now?" I ask.

"The Germans have invaded Holland, Belgium and Luxembourg," he explains. "They've kicked off and the game is underway."

"So much for respecting neutrality," I reply. "That's five neutral countries: Norway, Denmark, Holland, Belgium and Luxemburg. I wonder when the people back home will realize that we will have to deal with this madman."

"There's a briefing for the press at eleven o'clock at the War Office," Charlie says. "I've lined up lunch with a couple Brit officers at the Savoy for afterwards. You coming?"

"I was going to hang out at 10 Downing this morning," I say. "Any news there?"

"The chorus for Chamberlain to go is getting louder. The betting is, he'll be gone by the end of the day," Charlie replies. "You want to get a bet down?" I pause for a moment, long enough for Charlie to ask if I'm still on the line.

"Yes, I'm still here. No, it seems a little—I don't know—crass, to bet on something like this. There's a war on. This is incredibly important." I'm not sure why, but I don't want to admit I already have a bet down.

"Yeah, that's a good point. Anyway, are you coming here or going to 10 Downing?" Charlie asks.

"I'll come to the Savoy. We can get some breakfast, then head over to Downing Street for a while," I answer.

Charlie has never been one to turn down an invitation to eat. He readily agrees.

I exit the hotel on Piccadilly, expecting to find a cab. The doorman informs me most of them are already busy in Westminster transporting scurrying government officials and military personnel between government buildings. He offers to call one for me but warns me it could be a while. I look down the street and see a bus heading my way. In my travels around London, I have taken many buses and the Underground. The bus I see coming will get me within a couple of long blocks of the Savoy.

I thank the doorman whose name I have forgotten and hop aboard the bus. I look over the crowd—it is standing room only—and grab a pole. The bus lurches forward. I stagger slightly, regain my balance and look over my shoulder toward the back. It is then that I notice her.

At first, I am not sure. She is crushed in between two larger women on a bench facing the side of the bus. Engrossed in a book, a novel by the look of it, she pays no attention to the crowd around her. I notice she is wearing the same white flapper hat with the red ribbon and rose that she wore the first time I saw her. I stare for almost two minutes before I realize I am doing it. I blink three or four times, turn my head to the front and miss seeing her look at me with a tiny smile.

I check my hat and trench coat at the Savoy's dining room entrance. A hostess leads me to the table where my friends are waiting. Both Charlie Dolan and David Morgan are already there.

"We went ahead and ordered for you," Charlie says.

I laugh and say, "Thanks for being so considerate, Charlie."

"Hey, if you don't want it, I'll eat it."

"I know, you will." I laugh again. "Any news?" I ask.

"I've talked to a couple of Conservative MPs who tell me that yesterday the Conservatives did not want Chamberlain to resign; at least a lot of them. And they told him this. What they wanted was a restructuring of the government."

"With or without Churchill?" I ask.

"Churchill would have to stay," Charlie says, and David concurs.

"Apparently," David continues, "Chamberlain said he would stay only if Labor would come into the government. Otherwise, he would resign. We hear Chamberlain met with Clement Attlee, the head of the Labor Party, later in the day to discuss it."

"And?" I ask.

"Attlee said 'No,' and the other Labor leaders backed him; at least that's the word," David says.

"Chamberlain will favor Halifax, his good friend, over Churchill," Charlie tells me. "I heard a good joke about that, replacing Chamberlain with Halifax," he continues. "The reasoning goes like this. If you're going to get rid of the organ grinder, why replace him with the monkey?"

That brought a good chuckle and our meals.

Later that day, the four of us—we had been joined by Clive Burke at the Information Ministry when we went for the briefing at eleven—along with our two army officer friends, exit the Army-Navy Club onto Pall Mall. We have been served an excellent lunch and Colonel Bright and Major Caulfield have shared their military wisdom with us. The two officers' presence was not a coincidence. My colleagues and I all agree they were sent to push the military's propaganda on us for us to report. If it is not obvious from our meeting, a quick look around the dining room confirms it. There are at least another dozen groups of correspondents sitting with Army officers also being fed the army's propaganda.

We are spoon fed what the military wants us to hear for over an hour. It is the same basic drivel we received earlier from the War Office briefing. It is a little too pat, a little too convenient and much too overconfident. We all agree something is not quite right. Afterwards, we part company from our military hosts, and the four of us decide to go back to 10 Downing to wait for news.

"We'll never get a cab," Charlie grumbles. Because of Charlie's enjoyment of food, he is not fond of walking.

"Let's go," David replies. "We'll walk slowly for you, Charlie."

We go about two blocks without speaking when I break the silence. "All this talk from our lunch companions and the press briefing earlier at the War Office sounds a little too confident; this business about the Germans doing exactly what they want them to do. What if they're wrong? What if the Germans are doing what the Germans want to do?"

"That Maginot Line," David speaks up, "we've been hearing for years that it is supposed to be impregnable. I had no idea how short it was." David is looking at Clive Burke when he says this.

We were shown a map of France at the briefing. The line of fortifications, the so-called impregnable Maginot Line, runs from Switzerland to Luxemburg. The brigadier giving the briefing, a man who looked to be at least seventy, assured us the Germans would break their army to pieces smashing into it. "Unless, of course," the old gentleman conceded, "they decide to go around it. But"—he assured us—"the British and French are waiting for them to do just that."

Clive says, "I'm sure they've taken that into account. At least, I hope so."

"I don't pretend to be a military genius," I say as we walk along, "but what if they come through Luxemburg and Southeastern Belgium? If the French and British go north into Belgium, could they be cut off?"

"You heard the brigadier," Clive replies. "They believe to come through Luxemburg and Southeastern Belgium they will have to go through the Ardennes woods, and the Ardennes are too thick for tanks."

"I hope somebody told the Germans that," Charlie says.

"Yes, rather so," Clive quietly replies.

We turn the corner from Whitehall onto Downing Street and come upon a mob of reporters. They are mostly hanging about waiting for news. We make our way through the crowd to several colleagues we know and ask if they have heard anything. All they have are the same rumors we have, that Chamberlain was about to resign; nothing on who might succeed him. The betting line definitely favors Halifax. I remembered my bet. I have a hundred pounds at five to two odds against Churchill.

There is a black government car in front of the famous door, supposedly to take Chamberlain to Buckingham Palace. We have been there for ten to fifteen minutes waiting. Quite suddenly, with no fanfare at all, the door opens, and Chamberlain comes strolling out. He is formally dressed and looking quite serious.

The mob surges toward the car and questions are shouted, all the same theme:

"Have you resigned?"

"Halifax or Churchill?"

Chamberlain stops briefly before getting in the waiting automobile. The corners of his mouth go up in what looked to be a painful smile. He lifts his bowler and tips it, then without a word, gets in and leaves.

"So you're buying tonight," Charlie says then lifts his scotch and soda in a mock salute.

"Why should tonight be any different than most nights?" I sarcastically reply.

"I thought you said placing a bet on this would be too crass," Charlie says.

"It is," I reply. "Unless you win."

We are in the basement of the Savoy celebrating the news. As if a bunch of hard-drinking journalists need an excuse to celebrate. The news is out and now official. Chamberlain has indeed resigned and has recommended to King George VI that Winston Churchill should succeed him. There is a rumor going around that the King fainted. We are all pretty sure this is exaggerated.

We push two tables together, and there are between ten and fourteen of us seated at it. It varies as they come and go. I am sitting at one end with a good view of the bar. It is quite crowded tonight. Included are three Ministry of Information officials in attendance. They are each making the rounds of the tables answering what questions they can. What everyone wants to know is: what will Churchill do? Of course, these poor fellows have no better idea than anyone else.

"Churchill scares a lot of people," Clive tells our end of the table. "He has a reputation of being an impulsive decision maker and an adventurer."

"Gallipoli," I reply, referring to a disastrous Allied campaign against Turkey in the first war.

"Exactly," Clive agrees. "But he's probably the best man to rally the nation. I guess we'll see."

We receive the news in the afternoon barely in time to get off a wire to New York. The story I submit is barely fifty words. It includes the rumor, since confirmed, that Lord Halifax had declined the position. Hopefully, the *Gazette* staff in New York have enough information about Churchill to fill out the article.

Sunset this Friday night will be between eight thirty and eight forty-five. That is the time for the blackout to begin. It is not illegal to be out after the blackout begins each night. It is just dangerous. Traffic accidents have risen dramatically since the blackout was imposed.

I look at my watch and it reads almost seven thirty. I am quite tired from the long day and decide I will leave soon and catch a cab or bus. I finish my drink then look across the bar. Sitting with a crowd at two tables pushed together, her left side to me, is Lady Ashland in the flesh. And there is an empty chair right next to her.

Having consumed enough alcohol to make me quite courageous, I rise to my feet and start after my quarry. I have not covered half the distance when a good looking, young man slips onto my chair. Obviously, he is someone she knows. They quickly become quite engaged in conversation.

With an odd feeling of both regret and relief, I stop dead in my tracks. I watch them for a second or two. She wears a lovely smile while looking at him. Dejected, I turn around to go back to my table. Of course, I turn back at the exact moment she looks at me. Seeing my back to her, she frowns, sighs and slightly shakes her head.

I am standing under an umbrella I have borrowed from the Savoy. I am feeling quite glum and dejected. The rain is coming down a touch harder than when I first left the Savoy which does not help my mood. I am beginning to wonder if meeting Lady Catherine is simply not to be. I feel like a schoolboy rejected by a sympathetic female teacher.

Four others are waiting with me across the street from the Savoy for a bus to come along. I have taken this bus many times from here back to the Ritz and know it well. I check my watch again and frown knowing it will be at least ten more minutes.

After seeing Catherine and missing my chance to meet her, I left right away. I know I was very early for the next bus, but I did not feel like sitting back down at the table. My friends are having a very good time, and I know I am not good company right now.

As I stand in the rain, I again try to understand what is wrong with me. Never in my life, even when I was an awkward prepubescent, have I ever felt like this. I have never been shy or felt the least bit apprehensive about introducing myself to a girl and never afraid of being rejected, which has happened my share of times. *What is wrong with me?*

"Hello," I hear a soft, female voice coming from behind me through the noise of the rain.

I turn around and there she is. With two-inch pumps on her feet, she is only a couple inches shorter than me. A foot away, she is even prettier than I thought,—and getting soaked by the rain.

SEVEN

May 13, 1940

Dear Mom & Dad,

I'm sure by now you've heard the news. Chamberlain is out, and Winston Churchill is the new PM. This happened this past Friday, May 10.

I spent the past two days, Saturday and Sunday, roaming London with two other American correspondents talking with ordinary Londoners. We want to get a feel for what they think of Churchill.

For the most part, they are optimistic. Chamberlain is being blamed for the war by not standing up to Hitler before this. We could not bring ourselves to remind them how popular Chamberlain had been for appeasing Hitler. Now they wish he had been tougher. Sounds like Americans.

The war news, so far, is scanty. I believe it is being heavily controlled by the British Government. Some of us are discussing the possibility of going to France to find out things for ourselves. We'll see. I would go if given the chance. Remember, Mom, we're neutrals. The Germans will respect that.

I must confess to a feeling of, maybe not dread but, at least uneasiness. The British military and government people are a little too sure of themselves. All of this 'we've got them where we want them' talk is becoming a little strained.

Churchill is scheduled to make his first appearance and speech to Parliament as the new PM today. He will also announce the formation of the new government. From what we are being told, the new government sounds a lot like the old one. Halifax will continue as foreign minister and Chamberlain will still be in it. I guess we'll see what happens. I'll be there in the press section.

Love to All,

Jeff

I sit at the table in my suite reading and rereading the letter for fifteen minutes. I know what is bothering me about it. Should I tell them about Catherine? I want to but finally decide against it. Mostly because I have no idea what to tell them.

I have heard about infatuation. As far as that goes, I have even heard about being in love. It's just that I have never experienced either, unless I want to count my third-grade art teacher. She was a slinky blonde named Miss Cutter whom I totally adored. I cannot even decide what I am feeling toward Catherine.

After introducing ourselves in the rain Friday night, we spent our first ten minutes together sharing my umbrella. We made little awkward small talk while waiting for the same bus, mostly introducing ourselves and her wanting to know why I am such a coward because I was reluctant to approach her. She admitted she saw me tonight and decided to take matters into her own hands. I must admit to feeling joy that she had.

During the ride back to my hotel, I nervously asked if she would join me for a nightcap. At first, she declined due to the blackout. I assured her the hotel would provide transportation.

The Ritz bar was crowded, but the host—for the price of a ten-pound note—found a quiet, even intimate, table for two. We talked until midnight, mostly about America. Many times, she gave me a little, almost-electrical twinge touching one hand or the other. I tried to steer the conversation to her to find out what I could about her. She was remarkably gifted—or maybe I simply allowed her—at turning it back to me and life in the Old Colonies. She was especially interested in all things New York.

At midnight the concierge fetched a car for her with its headlights almost completely taped. We shook hands as I held the door for her. She said good night as she was getting in. Then she did something that both surprised and delighted me. Catherine stepped up to me, placed her hands on my shoulders and lightly kissed me on the lips, a kiss I just as lightly returned.

Catherine works at the BBC, duties that sometimes require assisting Ed Murrow with CBS Radio. She is on duty both Saturday and Sunday evenings doing this, so I do not have the chance to see her.

She is still at work this morning but manages to find a few minutes to break away and call me. Of course, I am thrilled to hear from her and more so when she says she will be in attendance for Churchill's speech.

Two days ago, while roaming around London, I purchased a large map of Western Europe. It is pinned to a wall in my hotel suite living room, above the table I use to sit at for work. I am using it as a reference for the war news. With colored pencils, I mark the progress of the two sides as best as I can from the news we are allowed.

On Saturday the 11th, we are informed the Germans have crashed through the impregnable—or so we are told—Ardennes Forest at the confluence of the borders of Belgium, France and Luxembourg. By Sunday afternoon, they put tanks across the Meuse River and are attacking Sedan, the same place where the Prussians soundly crushed the French in 1870.

On my map, I have arrows pointing north into Belgium from the border with France. These show the route the British and French forces are taking to meet the Germans. I also have arrows pointing south in Holland and Belgium to show the path of the Germans as they head toward the British and French in Belgium.

Even though I am not a military expert of any caliber, a blind man can see a potential disaster coming. By looking at my map, it is obvious that if the French are unable to stop the Germans at Sedan, this war may be quickly lost. If they punch through the French lines and drive the French army back, they can turn north to cut off the British and French in Belgium.

Yesterday, David, Charlie and I had lunch with Major Caulfield, our source of military information. When I asked him about this, he chuckled at my amateur map reading. We used the tablecloth and a pencil to draw it up. He then assured me that first, the French will hold at Sedan. If they do not and the Germans drive north to the coast, the Germans' flank will be terribly exposed to counterattack from the south.

When the major left, we discussed his explanation. Of course, he is correct in his belief the German flank will be exposed. I point out to David and Charlie this is true only if the French are able to mount a counterattack.

I follow my three friends into the press section of the House of Commons gallery. Clive is in front leading us to four seats together. While he does this, I am looking over the crowd of reporters searching for a sight of Catherine. Despite being early, we end up sitting quite a bit farther away than the last time. That time we were seated in what Americans would call the 'end zone' if comparing it to a football stadium. We had a clear view of the entire House floor laid out directly in front of us. Today we are up on the right-hand side, around the corner behind the opposition benches.

The good news is we will have a clear, frontal view of the new Prime Minister when he speaks. The bad news for me, once we take our seats, is I see Catherine—once again, she is along the railing very close to where she was when I first saw her the last time we were here—and she is too far to see me.

Before arriving, we stopped in a nearby pub seeking information. It was very crowded with reporters, military officers and junior government officials. These are members of the permanent government; the bureaucrats who run things.

Today's speech is Churchill's opportunity to share his policies with the MPs. In the pub, the rumors were going around as fast as the wind. Some of them claimed that after a short war, Britain and France will make peace with Hitler if he promises to leave Britain and France as they were before the war. In other words, let Hitler have the rest of Europe.

We found an empty table completely devoid of chairs. Clive and I muscled through the crowd back to the bar. It took almost ten minutes, but eventually we made it back with four pints of Guinness. At the table next to us were five men, also standing, arguing quite vigorously over the peace rumor. Two of the men were junior army officers. They seemed quite bitter and certain that the rumor was true. Within a few minutes, we became aware that one of the civilians, a man who looked to be almost forty, is a member of the foreign office. He was taking the brunt of the soldiers' wrath.

With the crowd the size it was, we couldn't hear much. Without staring, we tried to eavesdrop as best as we could. The one word the soldiers repeated loudly and derisively was the name Halifax. I managed to hear one of the men, a major, say it loud and clear several times. "It's your damn Halifax. He's the same appeaser as his pal, Chamberlain. They'll throw away Europe to Hitler, and then we'll have a damnable mess to deal with."

I was standing next to Clive, and he heard this statement as clearly as I did.

"Well, Clive, what do you think? Is the major right?"

"No," he firmly replied. "Oh, that bit about Halifax and Chamberlain is accurate, all right." Clive took a swallow of his beer, then continued, "Winston is not going to make peace without a real fight. You'll see. Winnie wants to be a war PM and he's got it. You'll see."

The benches on both sides of the House are starting to fill. As uncomfortable as these hard, wooden seats are, I do not wonder why people would choose to arrive early. History is being made. While we wait, there is a definite buzz through the floor and the gallery. Everyone is trying to guess what policies Churchill will propose.

I spend the time ignoring the noise and look at Catherine hoping she will see me. In this sea of faces, it will be very difficult to spot any one person in particular. While I watch her chat and laugh with the people around her, I become a bit disappointed that she does not appear to be trying to find me.

We have been here almost two hours watching the House members trickle in and take their seats. Above them, across from us, is the reserved section for the members of the Upper Chamber of Parliament, the House of Lords.

I feel a poke in my right side then turn to look at David, the source. He points across the empty space above the House floor at a dour looking, mostly bald gentleman sitting at the railing looking down. "Halifax," David says.

"Yes, I see him."

Of course, I have seen any number of pictures of the major players of this government crisis. Halifax always looks like, to me, a man with little or no joy or happiness in his life. Charlie had once remarked that he has the face of a man suffering from permanent constipation. Not exactly the most flattering thing to say about such a high-ranking government official.

Churchill arrives, shakes several hands on the Conservative side of the aisle then takes the PM's seat—the British Bulldog personified.

Two to three minutes later, wearing the traditional dress including a white, powdered wig, Speaker Edward FitzRoy, a Conservative, calls the House to order. There follows ten to fifteen minutes of traditional gibberish that I do not understand. At long last, the right Honorable Winston Churchill, His Majesty's Prime Minister, arises to address the House.

I have heard Churchill speak a couple of times before but never concerning anything this serious. He slowly, quite dramatically, steps up to the House Table and places the pages of his speech on it. He reaches up and grabs a suit lapel with each hand. He very quickly makes it abundantly clear what his policy will be.

"If you ask, what is our policy, it is to wage war by sea, land and air with all our might," he begins while looking over the crowd with his stern, determined expression.

A short while later, after informing the nation of the difficulties that lie ahead, mincing no words, he speaks the line that I believe will solidify the man for eternity:

"I have nothing to offer but blood, toil, tears and sweat."

I am sitting on the bench. The press section is as quiet as an empty church, absolutely mesmerized by the man and his words. It is a relatively short speech, barely lasting four minutes, I am later told. But it also leaves no doubt that a new man, with a new attitude, has taken charge. Gone are the days of appeasement, dithering and rumor. There is no one in attendance who doubts that Britain will stand up to Hitler and his Nazi gang, alone if necessary.

He continues, "You ask, what is our aim? I can answer in one word: it is victory, victory at all costs, victory in spite of all terror, victory however long and hard the road may be; for without victory, there is no survival."

No one moves, not a piece of paper rustles. I don't know if anyone was breathing. He finishes with a line I believe means even more than the 'blood, sweat, toil and tears' line. A call for the nation if not the entire civilized world—America—to join him.

"Come then, let us go forward together with our united strength."

I rise up from my seat at the table, pick up a fork and tap it against a water glass. We are in the American Bar in the basement of the Savoy. It is crowded with reporters and abuzz with everyone talking about the same thing: Churchill's speech to the House earlier today.

I am only trying to get the attention of my tablemates. Again, we have pushed two tables together and crowded around them. Instead of the dozen or so people at my table going silent, the entire bar turns to look at me. From my time in London, I know almost all of them and am quite friendly with most. Between that fact and the two scotch and sodas I have quickly consumed, I am not the least bit nervous.

"As an American," I begin, "I, of course, must remain neutral."

This brings a smattering of laughter since no one in this room is neutral and does not pretend to be.

"To my British cousins," I continue, "it appears the man and the hour have met."

I stand silently waiting for the roar to die down before continuing. "To Winston Churchill, a man who can certainly turn a phrase, and the British people, I wish you godspeed and good hunting!"

The entire place erupts again as I clink glasses with several of my tablemates. I take my seat and watch another man at the bar call for quiet. He holds up his glass and starts to speak as a voice whispers in my ear. "That was quite good, for a Yank. I'm impressed."

There is no need for me to look. I will remember her soft, sultry British accent forever. I look anyway just to see her smile.

"Hello, Yank," she says smiling at me.

"Hi," I reply. "Let's find you a chair."

Catherine is with two other people. One is a pretty girl a year or so younger than her. The other is a young man no older than twenty. The girl's name is Patricia, and she tells me the young man's name, which I immediately forget. Four people are leaving from a nearby table, so we quickly grab it and join it with ours. Catherine sits very close, and I can feel the warmth rising in my face. It takes less than a minute to realize the young man is infatuated with Patricia, and she is taking full advantage of it.

The blackout will be in effect in less than an hour. Despite that, during the time remaining until the blackout occurs, almost no one leaves.

There is a grand piano in the bar, and the piano player is playing his normal soft music. Catherine literally drags me onto the small dance floor near the piano. "I looked for you at Parliament, today," she says as we slowly make our way around the dance floor.

"I was there," I reply. "I found you sitting along the rail. How do you do that? How do you always get such a choice seat?"

"Oh, it's not so difficult," she says. "I just hike my skirt a bit and show the old boys a little leg. They're too busy looking to notice me slipping past."

I laugh heartily at this, look at her and in mock seriousness say, "So you just act like a street tart for them."

"Yes, nothing to it. You should try it some time."

"I doubt I would have quite the same effect," I say and laugh again. "Let me take you to dinner tomorrow evening at the Ritz. I'll pick you up in a cab."

"Yes," she quickly agrees. "Six o'clock and you had better be on time."

Despite the blackout and my poor dancing ability, we dance until ten thirty. There are several cabs out front when we leave. Patricia and her admirer get in one first.

As Catherine starts to get in, she stops, puts a hand on my chest and kisses me lightly on the lips. "I'll see you tomorrow, and we'll talk about anything you want," she says.

They pull away and I find two men I know who live at the Ritz. We share a cab being driven by a man with an obvious death wish. Gratefully, we pile out at the hotel's main entrance.

We find out the next day that two people, male reporters, were not so lucky. The cab they were in was in an accident. One of the men, someone I know, was killed along with the cabbie. The other reporter, a man from Brazil, was seriously injured. He will be in the hospital for a month. The blackout has claimed more victims.

EIGHT

May 14, 1940

Dear Mom & Dad,

I apologize for the tenor of this letter. It will likely seem as if I am angry and depressed. If so, it is because I am.

Yesterday, several hundred German bombers raided a defenseless city in Holland, Rotterdam. The news, the truth about it, is a bit sketchy at this point. Tens of thousands of buildings and homes were destroyed. Reports are that at least a thousand civilians are dead including women and children, and there are claims of a hundred thousand left homeless. My Polish refugee friends who were in Warsaw when the Germans bombed them believe every word of it. There must be at least some truth to it.

At the time I am writing this, it is early afternoon here. Before you get this letter, you will know about this: Holland surrendered today. They were able to resist the Germans for barely four days. Soon, I am sure, we will hear stories of Nazi atrocities in Holland. And now it is Belgium's turn. God help them.

The word is, and this has been verified, that the Dutch Queen Wilhelmina, her family and the government have escaped. They were rescued by a British warship and are on their way to England. I feel a little better for having been told that and it being verified.

As for me, I am well and very busy. I need to get a report written for an article typed and sent. Almost forgot. I have a date tonight with a lovely British woman. I have been so busy that this is my first since I got here. Relax, Mom, not a lot of time for carousing after all.

Love to all,
Jeff

I pull the chair out for Lady Ashland as she sits down. We are at a table for two by a window in the main dining room of the Ritz. A small orchestra will start up soon, and Catherine will have an excellent view of it. My back will be to it, but I would rather look at her anyway. The music starts earlier than it did before the war because of the blackout.

I was very prompt picking her up at her house in Fulham. I was expecting a small cottage. Instead, she is in a four bedroom, eight-room manor complete with at least the two servants I saw. On the way back to the Ritz, she explained they are a married couple, no children, who have been with her family since decades before Catherine was born.

"Are you a little glum tonight?" I ask. She looks stunning. In fact, I am extremely flattered because she must have taken considerable time to get ready.

"I'm sorry," she replies. She leans forward, takes my hand and quietly whispers, "The war news, what little of it we receive, is not good. And it seems to be a day or two late. It's a little frightening."

"I know," I quietly concur. I move my hand. It is turned so I am now holding hers to, hopefully, make her feel a little better, a little safer.

"It's the news about Rotterdam," she continues. "Have you ever been there?"

"No," I reply.

"It is—was a beautiful city. And those poor people. I can't help wondering when it will be our turn."

"You look absolutely lovely tonight," I say. It is true, and more importantly, I am hoping to take her mind off the gloomy war news.

She gives me a smile and says, "That's very kind, Jeff. But I know what you're up to. You're trying to change the subject."

I smile back and admit it. "Yes, but you do look lovely tonight, and I'm sure you know it. And now, Lady Catherine, the last time we were here, you learned pretty much everything there is to know about me. You also studiously avoided telling me anything about you."

"You noticed," she says with a shy smile. "It's all very boring."

"I will be the judge of that," I say.

"Very well," she says with a sigh. "My father is a solicitor, what you would call a lawyer, as was his father, who became a highly respected judge, and so on, back several generations of solicitors and judges. I could never keep track."

"I want to know about you," I say.

"I have two brothers, one older, Alex and one younger, Tom. Alex is a pilot with the RAF and is somewhere in France. Tom is in the Navy on board a rather large ship; I don't know where it is currently stationed. Alex is what you would call a Lieutenant; Tom is a sub-lieutenant; and I love them both dearly and worry about them every day.

"I went to boarding school at the Dorset School for Girls. I was admitted to Cambridge in 1934 at age nineteen. I studied English Literature for two years but did not earn my degree."

"Oh, boy, she's smarter than me," I joke.

"Don't feel bad. Most of us are. We just pretend not to be, so we won't hurt your fragile feelings," she replies. "My family is what would be called upper-middle class. We are quite comfortable but hardly wealthy. Mother is a bit proper and not very affectionate. I swore by the time I was ten, I would not let society do to me what it did to her. She and her generation were not allowed the opportunities I have. She accepted it; others refused and after the First War, things began to change. I suppose it was simply too late for her. In fairness, she does have a loving husband and a good provider. That's about it," she says, trying to end the subject.

I hold up her left hand and tap the ring while giving her an inquiring look. "That's not quite all of it," I say.

"No, I suppose not," she says with a heavy sigh.

The waiter comes, and she tells me to order for both of us, which I do. I wait until he brings the champagne and fills a flute for each of us. I make a toast for the safety of her brothers and a quick end to the war.

"Lord Ashland?" I ask.

She is silent for a minute while she thinks about what to tell me.

I finally say, "You can tell me all of it. You must know I am terrifically attracted to you and will respect your marriage."

"I met Arthur through my father," she begins. "It was almost four years ago. Father was his lawyer and was representing him on a manslaughter charge. Arthur had been in a car accident in which a nineteen-year-old girl was killed. She was a passenger in Arthur's car.

"Father convinced the jury, an all-male jury, that the woman driving the other car was to blame for the accident. I later learned that was a lie.

Arthur was drunk and absolutely at fault. Among his numerous flaws is a taste for alcohol and young women. I was only nineteen myself at the time and very stupid.”

“As are we all,” I say.

“I was thoroughly smitten by him. He is quite handsome, educated and can be very charming, especially when he is after his quarry, young women. He is also thirty-four now. My parents were, to say the least, quite displeased when I told them we were going to marry. Of course, Father knew what he was like, knew he was responsible for that girl’s death. Mother more quickly warmed to the idea of having a title in the family. Plus, he does—or at least his family does—have a lot of money. I have no idea how much and I don’t much care.

“Within a month of planting me in the family estate in Ashland, I rarely saw him. He prefers the London nightlife to the life of a country squire. To make matters worse, his mother and other family members resented me as a non-aristocratic interloper.

“His father, Arthur the fifth or sixth, I’m not sure which, liked me a little too much. He has the same problem with a fondness for drink that his son does. Many nights I had to literally throw the old sot, half-naked, out of my bedroom. I complained to his philandering son about this once. He laughed and told me to give the old boy a try; said I might like it.”

“What a godforsaken ass,” I say.

“Fill my glass, please?” she asks.

I pour more champagne for her and notice her eyes have become moist with tears. While she takes a sip, I say, “If this is too painful, you can stop.”

“No,” she says with a heavy sigh. “There’s more and I want you to know. It was about this time that he told me he had brought a venereal disease, gonorrhea, into my bed. He brushed it off as a minor thing telling me he was cured and I should see a doctor. Of course, I had been infected. I was treated, quite painfully, and cured. But because he had kept it from me for many months, I am no longer able to have children.” With that revelation, she pours the rest of the almost full glass down and empties it.

“I’m sorry, Catherine,” was all I could think to say.

Our meals arrive, and we eat in silence. I have no idea what to say to ease her pain. If I could, if he was here, I would drag this fool into the street and beat him into a hospital.

"I told him I wanted a divorce the next time I saw him," she finally continues. "He actually laughed and said that was not possible. He would never agree. I threatened him with a scandal and..." She pauses and looks down at the table.

I can see she is upset and embarrassed. I take her hand again and say, "If this is too painful—"

"No, I'm all right," she says and tries to smile. She draws a deep breath and continues. "He assaulted me. Hurt me physically, badly. Then he told me he would destroy my family and me if I tried to get a divorce. I ran away. I went home, and he came for me. Father stood up to him and got him to essentially pay me off. That was toward the end of '38.

"I got a job at the BBC in the typist pool under my maiden name. After just a few months, I was promoted to assistant reporter. As much as anything else, it was likely because my typing wasn't up to the level required by the typing pool."

"I doubt that," I say and laugh at her little joke.

"I was assisting a man named Stan Worthing. Stan was a nice man but a little too fond of food and drink. We were covering a fire when Stan had a heart attack and died. I finished the story, and they gave me Stan's job.

"I also used some of the money from Arthur to buy the house in Fulham. And his family sends me money every month which I promptly give to a Soldiers and Sailors charity. About once a month I receive a visit from him reminding me we are still married and I am to do nothing to sully the Ashland family name. Imagine him telling me not to sully the Ashland name. Anyway, that was part of the settlement."

"What!" I say a little too loudly. "The arrogance, the ego of this man!"

"I'm sorry if I've upset you," Catherine says. "I keep busy, but..."

"What?" I ask.

"I've met this handsome, dashing American whom I seem to have grown quite fond of." She smiles and says, "It's getting late. I should go."

I sign for the check and walk her to the exit. It has just turned dark, and there are still quite a few buses and cabs running. She has her right arm through my left as we exit the hotel. I have offered to take her home, but she insists that I not do so claiming there is no reason for both of us to run the risk of the blackout. This is hardly what I wanted to hear.

She pulls me off to the side, turns and faces me. I put both arms around her waist and she buries her face in my chest and holds on to me. "Can you be patient with me?" she asks.

"Of course," I whisper.

"I've not been with anyone outside of my marriage at all. I'm still married, and I feel like I am cheating even though I know how ridiculous that must sound, considering the way Arthur has treated me."

"Actually, it does, but I'm okay. I have a feeling you're worth waiting for."

Catherine looks at me, and I see the blood has rushed to her face. She puts a hand behind my head for the first truly passionate kiss we have shared.

NINE

May 16, 1940

Dearest Mom & Dad,

The news is sketchy. We all believe the government is hiding the truth from the public. I believe there is a catastrophe in the making.

Two days ago—we always find out these things a day or two after the fact—or perhaps yesterday, Sedan fell. Find a map of France, locate the Meuse River at Sedan and you will see the danger. The Germans have punched through the French lines north of the Maginot Line.

I am not supposed to know this, but the French and British forces in Belgium have begun to retreat. This is from an impeccable source. I hope he is right. If the Germans, who have broken through at Sedan, turn north, it will be a race between them and the British and French to the Channel. If the Germans get there first, the war is probably lost.

Churchill is flying to France today to consult with the French government on their battle plans.

On a personal note, I have met a pretty, wonderful girl. I may even be in love. Can't know for sure, but I've looked up the symptoms in a medical book and it seems I have them. The medical book had nothing in it about a treatment or cure. I'll just have to see how it plays out. Don't say anything to the single girls in New York. Let's not cause a riot. Calm down, Mom; don't start buying baby clothes for the grandchildren.

All kidding aside, I find the experience to be quite wonderful, if somewhat frightening.

All my love,

Jeff

Churchill is back from France, and the rumors we are hearing are not good. The four of us, Clive, Charlie, David and I, have spent the entire day going from the War Office to the Ministry of Information and to 10 Downing, as have the entire journalist corps.

We ate lunch at the Army and Navy Club with Major Caulfield again. He is not very forthcoming with honest information. He is his usual cheerful, optimistic self. He does admit that the Germans have broken through at Sedan and have turned north. This news is the reason for the major's optimism. Again, he tells us, "We have them right where we want them."

Off the record, Caulfield tells us that the British and French in Belgium are retreating. Yes, he actually tells us this.

The major tells us that the Germans turning north from Sedan are open to a catastrophic defeat. In confidence, he says the French are amassing a huge army of reserves to their south, on the Germans left flank—at least a million fresh soldiers. Combined with the half a million British and French coming down on their right flank from Belgium, the Germans will be crushed between them.

"We're hearing rumors that there are no French reserves in the South to attack the Germans," Clive says.

While Clive and the major converse, I am looking around the dining room and I see a lot of Army officers dining with civilians. I recognize most of the civilians as either government employees or reporters. I make a mental note to get together later with some of the reporters to get their impressions.

Earlier this morning I submitted a seven-hundred-word article to the *Gazette* in New York. It passed through the censors without a single correction—most unusual. I think I understand why. It was another piece of fluff, propaganda really. It was based entirely on information fed to us by the Ministry of Information. I received this before what I suspected had occurred.

Yesterday, while Churchill was in France, the War Department admitted to a minor setback of French forces at Sedan. However, they continued, it appeared the Germans had fought themselves to exhaustion.

Their supply lines were overextended, they were having great difficulty moving through the Ardennes and were stopped. It turned out that none of this is true.

An hour after I sent my article to New York, I happened to run into a War Department civilian that I know. We went for a walk along the Thames near Parliament, just the two of us. He swore me to secrecy then told me the truth.

John is an older gentleman—I will leave his last name confidential—who has been in the permanent government for many years. He explained that the Germans were running hard to the north from Sedan. They paused for a few hours then took off. The British intelligence says they are being led by a General Guderian. John says this Guderian wrote a book about tank warfare. The British Army has studied the book and the man himself extensively. They, the Germans, are doing exactly what Guderian proposed. and it is working brilliantly. It is now a race to the Channel, and John believes the Germans are going to win it.

Caulfield, wearing a smug smile and a closely cropped British officer's mustache, casually butters a piece of bread. Knowing he is about to lie to us, I am resisting the urge to reach over—I am sitting to his left—and slap the smirk off his face.

"Clive," he begins while chewing a bite of bread, "you're old enough to know better than to believe rumors."

I can no longer restrain myself. "Why is it that the rumors generally prove to be true while the official information must be—what's the word?" I ask my tablemates.

"Clarified," Charlie is the first to answer.

"Yes, that's it," I sarcastically say. "The official reports are clarified a day or two later."

"First of all," Caulfield says as he puts down the butter knife and looks at me, "you're exaggerating. But more importantly, during wartime, information is always fluid as events unfold."

"Oh, well, that's probably true," I seemingly agree.

May 19, 1940

I am sitting at the table in the living room of my suite. Room service left five minutes ago. They removed the tray of breakfast dishes and left a second pot of coffee. It is barely eight a.m., and I have been up for three hours. In the past two, I have shaved, showered, dressed and am sitting where I am now.

I light another cigarette and pour myself more coffee. I smoke and sip while alternating my gaze between my typewriter and the map on the wall. This must be what is known as writer's block. My head feels like a void. I have not had a single thought about what to write. I look again at the sheet of paper in the typewriter. The only things on it are the word London and the date. I have an article to submit for tomorrow's paper and have no idea what to tell them.

That is not factually true. I know exactly what I should tell them, what I would like to tell them. The problem is not really an empty head. The problem is, what will I be allowed to tell them? I again lean back in my chair and stare at the map of Western Europe I have pinned to the wall. "That's what I should tell them," I quietly say.

The lines on my map are clearly telling the story. All day yesterday there was an information blackout in this city. Early on, there was a rumor, later confirmed, that Churchill would make his first radio broadcast to the nation. It is now official. At nine p.m. this evening, he will go on the radio and give a speech.

I continue to stare at my map wondering what Churchill will tell them. Because my information is at least a day old, I cling to a small shred of hope that my map is wrong, that the Germans are not winning the race to the Channel. But I must admit to myself at least, that I may be right.

Yesterday, I found out at least part of the truth. The Germans broke through at Sedan on May 15 and barely slowed down. Unless they are attacked and stopped today, they will be at the Channel coast near Abbeville tomorrow or the next day at the latest. The British and French coming down from Belgium appear to have no chance whatsoever to get ahead of the Germans to avoid being cutoff.

On my map, south of the line representing the German tank columns charging north, I have written a large question mark. This represents the French reserves. Where are the million French soldiers Major Caulfield assured us were preparing to counterattack? I no longer believe they exist at all.

I spent yesterday evening at the Savoy with Catherine and friends, having dinner and drinks. We are an item of gossip and good-natured teasing. I don't care and neither does she. While they shared rumors, we held hands under the table like a couple of kids. It was wonderful. That was the best part of a very unproductive day. There was no war news worth mentioning.

Rumors and leaks from government sources were flying all over the place. Most of us are giving little credence to them. We will wait until a day or two after the 'official' news is released. Even the BBC is blocked out of it. Catherine says everyone there is in the dark too. It is generally agreed that if the BBC is blocked out, things must be much worse than we are told.

Around seven, Douglas Williams, an official from the Ministry of Information, stopped by. He is a regular at the American Bar in the Savoy. He is also quite forthcoming and credible. Last night, even he did not have anything to tell us.

I took Catherine home in a cab a short while before the blackout. We cuddled in the back seat and barely spoke a word. I walked her up to her door, and she asked me, point blank, "Are we losing the war?"

"Why do you ask?" I said.

"The atmosphere at the BBC is quite glum. These are people that tend to know what's going on. Morale has dropped like a stone," she answered.

"Well, I don't know any more than anyone else," I replied. "But I do believe there is reason for concern. We'll know more in a few days."

My phone rings as I continue to stare at the map. I crush out my cigarette, thankful for the interruption. I answer it and hear Charlie Dolan on the other end.

"Are you listening to Churchill tonight?" he asks me.

"Of course," I reply. "He's scheduled for nine o'clock. Why?"

"Some of us were thinking of a smaller, more private gathering than the Savoy. David suggested, if you wouldn't mind, your suite at the Ritz. Start gathering around eight, eight-thirty." He then quickly tries to add, "If you don't want to—"

"Not at all, Charlie," I say with a smile, cutting him off. "In fact, I wish I'd thought of it. I'll have the hotel set up a bar, maybe two; one for you and one for the rest of us.

"In that case, better make it three," he says with a laugh.

"I'll make it one and have a buffet set up," I reply.

"What are you doing now?" he asks.

"Trying to write something for tomorrow's paper," I answer.

"Do what I did; send in a telegram and have them do an article about Churchill's speech. I'm sure they'll be listening," Charlie begins.

"Yes, they will."

"Then tell them you'll have an article for Tuesday or Wednesday with reactions of Londoners to his speech. They can do a factual piece about the speech themselves."

"That's a really good idea, Charlie. Where did you get it?"

"Very funny," he replies. "I have a good idea quite often, almost once a month. This is it for May.

"Come over to Downing Street," he continues. "We might as well hang out there."

"I suppose," I reply. "I'll make arrangements for this evening, send a wire to New York, and be along in a while. Wait for me in front of Number 10."

"Eight fifty-five," Clive Burke says from his chair in front of the suite's radio. "I wonder if Winnie has finished writing his speech."

There is a total of fourteen of us gathered in my suite: eight men, all foreigners except Clive, and six women including Catherine. I know all the men but only two of the women, including Catherine. The other is her housemate, Patricia Corning. She arrived with Catherine but has no intention of leaving with her—at least according to Catherine. The buffet has been ravaged and the bar put to good use. We are all seated and anxiously awaiting Churchill.

The rumor mill has it that we are going to get a total cover-up of what's really happening across the Channel. Of course, another rumor has it that we will receive the unvarnished truth. I suspect it will be somewhere between these two extremes. My personal hope is that there really will be a counterattack by the French. I am told by several reputable sources that this is a chimera. There are no French reserves, and no attack is possible.

"Are you serious?" Clark Blane, a reporter from the Chicago Tribune asks Clive referring to Clive's remark about Churchill.

"Oh, absolutely." Clive chuckles.

Clive is seated to my left in a comfortable armchair matching mine. Catherine is on my right, sitting on the arm of my chair.

"Winnie is a notorious procrastinator," Catherine agrees. "I've seen it myself. He makes changes right up to the moment he starts speaking. I'll be quite surprised if he starts on time."

At precisely nine p.m., we hear the voice of the BBC announcer introduce the Prime Minister. Several long seconds pass in silence before we hear the familiar voice.

"I speak to you for the first time as Prime Minister in a solemn hour for the life of our country, of our empire, of our allies and, above all, of the cause of freedom."

It is a relatively short speech lasting less than eight minutes. To me, he walks right up to but does not cross the line of total candor.

Churchill admits that the fighting is not going well, that the Germans are having success mostly due to overwhelming force. But then he continues to insist that the British and French will turn things around. The French will let loose a massive counterattack—a genius for recovery and counterattack for which the French have long been famous, he adds. Then the allies will be victorious.

Everyone in my suite is sitting absolutely still and silent. When the Prime Minister speaks of the French counterattack, I lean back in my chair and turn to look at Clive. He, in turn, has moved to look at me. Without speaking, the communication between us is clear: the British people are getting a polished version of the true situation and a large dosage of hope.

He goes on like this, moving back and forth between the gravity of the situation and giving his people hope—a hope I fear will be very short-lived. He finishes with his usual eloquent flourish.

"Today is Trinity Sunday. Centuries ago, words were written to be a call and a spur to the faithful servants of truth and justice. 'Arm yourselves, and be ye men of valor, and be in readiness for the conflict; for it is better for us to perish in battle than to look upon the outrage of our nation and our altar. As the Will of God is in Heaven, even so, let it be.'"

"The man can certainly turn a phrase," I hear someone say in the silence of the room.

"What do you think?" is the question going around my suite.

For the next hour or so, fueled by patriotism and alcohol, there is a discussion that turns a bit heated. The reality of it is no one knows for certain. Catherine and I barely join in. Clive is also quite reluctant to give his opinion although I suspect I know what it is; it is likely the same as mine. Winnie gave the nation more hope than truth. I guess there is always time for the truth when it really becomes necessary.

TEN

May 21, 1940

Dear Mom & Dad,

The truth has leaked out. The leading elements of the German Army have arrived at the English Channel at a French town Abbeville. It is still not too late, or so I am told. The Germans have not reached the coast in strength. Their lines of supply are strung out behind them and could easily be cut. This is according to my British officer contacts. "How?" I ask. "By the phantom French counterattack that cannot and will not be made?" They reluctantly admit this to be doubtful.

It seems the British needed to be kicked in the teeth to make them realize they are at war. I am at the table in my suite looking at the map on the wall in front of me. A historic catastrophe is about to befall the British, the French are already whipped—and it is staring back at me. There is no chance for the British and French who are cut off in Belgium. I am at a loss to figure out what they can do to save the British Army. We'll all have to wait and see. I fear it will take a miracle to save them.

If you caught Churchill's speech over the radio two days ago, he has some explaining to do. He lied. He knew the French could not possibly attack in time, or at all. The word from the British in France is that French morale, both the army's and the government's, collapsed with the defeat at Sedan.

To finish with a more optimistic tone, I am fine. In fact, I think I have put on a few pounds. The people of London, at least until today, are still carrying on with good cheer. I am thoroughly impressed by them.

Keep writing and let me know what people are thinking at home. Not the politicians, the real people. Ask the doormen, the cabbies and the bartenders. They hear everything.

Again, all my love,

Jeff

I have just now finished my letter to my family with today's date. The bellboy has picked it up and will get it to the Pan AM Clipper steward for delivery. My friends and I have a breakfast date at the Savoy. An official from the Ministry of Information is going to be there, or so I am told. With the war news so up in the air, changing almost hourly, it is a good idea to remain flexible.

Catherine is on a tour of RAF fighter bases with a dozen BBC reporters. Her brother Alex's squadron—I am not supposed to know this—has been recalled from France to a base in England. She is not sure where he will be or if she will see him. She is just happy to have him back in England, safe and unharmed. Of course, I am extremely happy for her even though I will not see her for several days.

The four of us, Clive, Charlie, David and I, spent yesterday roaming around London. We went everywhere by every form of conveyance. We talked to cabbies, pub goers, tube and bus riders. In general—no, that's not right; overwhelmingly, the people understand that the fighting is not going well. They are also amazingly cheerful and optimistic. Churchill does that for them. To be honest, he does that for me, too. They believe the worst is yet to come, but they will carry on to final victory.

I meet Charlie Dolan, by coincidence, on the sidewalk outside the entrance to the Savoy. Charlie has just arrived, and when he sees me step off the bus, he waves and comes after me. Our breakfast meeting is scheduled for ten, and it is a quarter of.

Without even a good morning, Charlie loops his arm in mine and gently pulls me away to talk. Charlie never stops working. When his feet hit the floor in the morning, he does three things. First, he lights a cigarette. Then he rings room service to order coffee and breakfast. With those two chores completed, while still in pajamas, he begins calling contacts he has to find out the latest news. By noon, he has more information than any three of us. Unfortunately, it is mostly rumor and almost all of it is wrong.

Charlie drags me about fifteen feet from my disembarking fellow bus passengers. He stops, looks about furtively—an amusing habit he has—

then begins to whisper to me. "I have it on good authority from the Foreign Ministry," he begins, "that the French are going to ask for an armistice today. An armistice is a ceasefire—"

"I know what an armistice is, Charlie," I say.

"—to begin negotiating," he finishes as if I had said nothing.

"Where is this coming from?" I ask.

"Confidential source," he replies.

"Uh-huh. Let's go in and see if we can get some real news."

May 21, 1940, 11:00 p.m.

At breakfast this morning at the Savoy, we were informed that the French were counterattacking the German flank at Arras, France. Most of us in the room—the briefing was in a locked banquet room—were stunned by the news. After several seconds of silence, a loud and long cheer went up. I joyously joined in. We spent almost the entire day together receiving news reports direct from the battlefield. It seems the government finally decided to give us the truth as it occurs.

A French force of an unknown size attacked the Germans in the early morning hours. For most of the day, the news was quite gratifying. The French and British hit the thin German line at Arras from two directions. The French went at them from the south and a British column from the west.

The Allies made early gains, we were told later, by pushing the Germans back almost ten miles in two places. Unfortunately, by early evening, the German resistance had stiffened, and the attack had stalled. Then, in order to avoid being surrounded themselves, both Allied columns retreated.

I am at my table in my suite typing up a report for the paper. Most of my colleagues, disheartened to say the least, were still drinking heavily when I left at ten. My report is—I am determined—to be as neutral as possible. I will give my editors facts and let them decide what and how to report. Except, unless they try again tomorrow with better success, the attack at Arras is a significant setback.

Seated at the table, I am again staring at my map. The lines for the German advance are getting longer. As they do so, the area into which the

BEF and French armies in Belgium are being squeezed more and more is getting smaller. At the rate this area is shrinking, it cannot be more than a week to a very optimistic ten days before they will be forced to surrender or be pushed into the sea.

The worst of it is, if the Allies had done a better job, if their generals were as good as the Germans, they could have done to the Germans what the Germans are doing to them. I stare at my map, and even an amateur can see it. If they had attacked with both the armies in Belgium and also south of the Germans, they could have cut off the German advance. It would have been a spectacular victory. Instead, their dithering and the Germans' efficiency may have sealed the fate of the BEF, French and Belgians.

May 24, 1940

The German advance to the sea in France has stopped. We received a briefing at the War Office earlier this afternoon. Once again, the British are showing a large amount of unwarranted optimism. I believe this is a show for our benefit only.

I am waiting by myself on a bench along the Thames for my contact, John, the civilian with the War Department. I have discovered that quite a few of my American correspondent colleagues have a secret source of information like him. All of us suspect the government allows this to provide us with information to be published in America. It is no secret the British want us to come in or at least provide them with the weapons of war. There are only three or four American journalists here who are isolationists. Most of us can see the danger of Hitler and his Nazi horde. Sooner or later, it will be our turn. John and the others like him are feeding us propaganda; but it is accurate propaganda.

I check my watch again and note I am still early. I have been watching the Londoners go by. Once again, I think they are probably wondering why a man dressed in a suit has nothing better to do than sit on a bench across the river from Parliament. The people I see appear to be a little glum and more serious today. The two-day old news they are receiving can no longer mask the truth. Turning toward Westminster Bridge to my right, I see John approaching. I check my watch and smile at his punctuality. A British gentleman, it would horrify him to keep someone waiting.

"There is no point in trying to paint a rosy picture," John says after he sits down, and greetings are performed. "We are in serious trouble. The attack on the Germans at Arras failed. But then, you knew that. Did you know there was another French attack on the German lines yesterday?"

Before I can reply, he continues. "It was along their lines between Amiens and Péronne," he says. "Once again, the French were badly beaten. Do you know the Germans have stopped?"

"Yes, I do," I reply. "Why did they stop?"

"It could be for any number of reasons."

"How long?" I ask, then feel foolish asking as if this man would know.

"Temporarily," John says. He crosses his legs, shifts to his left to look at me then continues. "The belief is they are catching their breath, so to speak. They've had such astonishingly fast success that they have outrun their own supplies and infantry. Fortunately, the French seem to have placed enough petrol stations across the country to keep the German trucks and tanks moving along."

"They've been getting their fuel at French gas stations?" I incredulously ask. "Why didn't the French army destroy them?"

"Apparently, no one thought to do it. The Germans have probably used that up as a source of petrol. They are stopped, waiting for supplies. Two, maybe three days and they will be on the move again."

"Now what?" I ask.

"The army in Belgium, including the French and other allies, have already begun the final retreat. They are going to Dunkirk, a city on the coast of France near the border with Belgium. There is a great row taking place within the war cabinet. Several of the members, led by Halifax and Chamberlain, are pushing for a negotiated peace agreement. The word is Winston has dug in his heels and won't even consider it. The Royal Navy is preparing an evacuation plan for the men in Dunkirk. Winston is going to give that a try."

"Will it work?"

"No. They will be extremely fortunate to get even ten percent of the men back to England."

ELEVEN

May 27, 1940

Dear Mom & Dad,

The British, French and Belgian armies are trapped. I am having trouble writing this because it is too difficult to even imagine, not so much that the German army has accomplished this but, the ease in which they have done so. The fighting began on May 10, barely seventeen days ago. From a strictly objective standard, it is the single greatest feat in the history of warfare. Nothing even close to it has ever been accomplished.

I have been told that the Germans have surrounded a half-million men in and around Dunkirk, France. They are completely cut off with their backs to the sea. That's the bad news. The potential good news is that the Royal Navy, with cover from the Royal Air Force, has begun an evacuation. More bad news—there really is no good news—I have spoken to several military sources. They all agree the Navy will be lucky to evacuate even ten percent of the men and none of their equipment. If that is true, the war is over, and Hitler has Europe.

It is beginning to look like Britain will soon have little choice but to ask for an armistice and negotiate a peace agreement. Personally, given Hitler's history of making and breaking treaties, I believe a peace treaty with Hitler is a fool's errand. He will abide by it as long as it suits him. When it no longer does suit him, he will invade Britain.

In all of this gloom, there is still a tiny glimmer of hope. It almost sounds foolish, but the Navy and the government have called for all civilian boats that can cross the Channel and carry troops to report to help with the rescue. The Navy does not have enough shallow draft boats to get close enough to the beaches for the men to wade out to the boats and climb aboard. It is hoped that the civilian crafts can get to the beach and bring the men out to the larger ships or even carry them back to Dover.

I wish the news was better. Personally, I'm fine. I'm still seeing Catherine, the girl I wrote about before. We're both very busy and don't see each other as much as we would like. Did I mention she's a writer for the BBC? They are extremely busy.

This is it for now. Take care of my sibling friends whom I miss and love.

All my love,

Jeff

May 28, 1940

I had a great deal of difficulty falling asleep last night. I finished an eight-hundred-word report for the paper and got it to the censor. It should go out this morning. It seems like the censors are being less strict about what we can report. Apparently, it is time for the unvarnished truth, especially to America. From the feedback we are getting, it is falling on deaf ears back home. The attitude is still: "The French and British got themselves into this mess, they can get themselves out of it." Except, Hitler is a ravenous tiger with an insatiable appetite. Sooner or later, we will have to deal with him.

I tossed and turned in bed thinking about the boys on the beach at Dunkirk. They are waiting to either be killed or captured. Finally, around one a.m., I decided I must do something, whatever I can, to help them.

"I have already talked to David," I say into the phone. "He's in, Charlie. He was going to call Clive, and I said I would call you."

It is the morning of the 28th, and I am on the phone with Charlie Dolan discussing my plans.

"Have you told Catherine?" he asks.

"No, and I'm not going to. She'd throw a fit. No. I'm going to find a boat; I'll rent it if I can or buy it if I have to, but I'm going. Do you want an adventure to tell your grandchildren?"

Charlie is a divorced father of three with whom he has a poor relationship. He has said many times, when he is in his cups, that if he survives the war, he will patch things up with them. I hope he does.

"Yeah, sure, but, um, I don't know…"

"What's the problem, Charlie?"

"Well, I, uh…"

"Spit it out."

"I can't swim! In fact, I'm scared to death of being on the ocean and drowning. On top of it, I get horribly seasick on small boats. There, now you know."

"It's okay," I reply. "That's nothing to be ashamed of. It's all right. I guess I'll see you in a couple of days. I'm supposed to meet David here in a little while. I should get going."

"Be careful," Charlie says.

I step off of the elevator to find the lobby at the front desk empty. I can see three men, the concierge, a front desk attendant and bellhop talking together. As I approach, the concierge, a genuinely affable man, comes over to me.

"May I help you, Mr. Bartlett?'

"Maybe, Mr. Fowler," I say. "I'm looking to rent or buy a boat, something that can make the trip to Dunkirk."

"I doubt you'd have much luck finding one," Fowler says. "But Edward here might be able to help you," he continues.

Edward is Edward Hughes the other front desk attendant. He has joined us. "I'm looking for two or three men to help crew my father's boat," Edward says. "Not to offend, sir, but do you have any experience on the sea?"

"Yes!" I reply quickly. "I've been sailing on the Atlantic, off New York, New Jersey and Long Island since I was a kid. When can we go?"

"Ah, *hmm*," the bellhop, a youngster too young for the army says trying to interrupt.

"I told you, William," the concierge says, "I can only spare one of you."

"It's not a sailboat, sir," Edward says, "It's a forty-four-foot motorboat with an onboard motor."

"Great, even better," I say, getting excited.

"I can handle the boat including the mechanical problems. I'll need help getting the lads on board once we get there," Edward tells me.

"I've done my share of piloting and navigating. Whatever you need me to do. And I have a friend coming who wants to help. Do you need more?"

"No, I don't think so. Three should be enough. I suggest more suitable clothing, sir. It's going to be cold and wet," Edward says.

"Deal," I say as I reach across the desk and shake the man's hand. "On one condition. May name is not 'sir,' it's Jeff. And my friend's name is David."

"I'm coming," I loudly say for the third or fourth time. I have just about finished dressing when I hear a loud, insistent pounding on my suite's door. I am wearing heavy, brown, corduroy winter pants and wool socks. As I walk to answer the door—the impatient pounding has started again—I pull a heavy turtleneck over a long-sleeve undershirt.

I barely get the door unlocked when a wild Tasmanian devil—or something close to it—almost knocks me out of the way. I try to open my mouth to say hello when the look on the devil's face stops me cold.

"What the bloody hell do you think you're doing? Have you gone mad? You're a neutral for God's sake! You want to get yourself killed in a war that isn't yours?" Catherine pauses, her left index finger three inches from my face and wearing a look I haven't seen since I was ten and broke my mother's favorite antique vase.

Catherine noticeably draws in a breath, so I try to say something. I am not sure if I even manage to speak the first word before she starts in again. It's the same basic tirade about neutrality and getting myself killed. I realize she needs to vent so I stand silently and take it. I can see when she is finished because her eyes begin leaking tears.

"Stop it," I whisper then put my arms around her and hold her while she cries.

"Bad enough I have to worry about my brothers," she quietly says in between sobs. "Now this. Bloody damn fools, the whole lot of you."

I hold on to her silently for a minute or so until she catches her breath and settles down.

She finally looks at me, grabs the back of my head and kisses me as hard as she can and holds it as long as she can. "Promise me you won't get killed. Promise me you'll come back to me," she whispers.

"I promise I won't get killed and I'll come back," I answer and kiss her forehead.

Catherine is looking through the open bedroom door when she says, "There's the bloody bed right there." She looks at me and says, "We have unfinished business in there that I've let go too long. If you don't come back, I'll feel guilty about that and never forgive you."

"With that as an incentive, you can bet I'll be back," I say and smile.

"They're waiting for you downstairs. I never would have thought Charlie would be the sensible one," she says.

"He can't swim and gets seasick, or he would go too," I tell her.

"Can you at least swim?" she asks.

"Oh, geez," I say with a worried look. "I didn't think of that. Is the water really deep?"

"I won't sleep until you're back. Why are you doing this?" she asks again, the tears coming once more.

"I can swim extremely well."

"I know but why…"

"We have to get the boys back, at least as many as we can. They are the only trained soldiers Britain has. Hitler is about to knock off France. When he does that, he can invade any time he wants to. If we leave the British army on the beach at Dunkirk, we're going to be in a lot of trouble."

"You could go back to America."

"Not without you. Besides, if that happens, he'll come after us sooner or later. I have to go. I have to do what I can to help," I say.

"I know," she finally agrees. "Did you pack a bag? It will be a few days. Throw some dry underwear and socks in a bag. Quickly."

By the time we reach Dover—the center point of the rescue—and get docked, it is after two p.m. Edward, our captain, has gone off to get instructions. In the meantime, David and I are taking on provisions. We are being told most of the men at Dunkirk have not had rations, or maybe even water, for several days. We have loaded several five-gallon cans of water and a couple hundred pounds of biscuits. It will be at least something for them until we get them back. We have also taken on forty to fifty Royal Navy life preservers.

"Ahoy, anyone on board the Isabella?" we hear a voice saying, coming from the dock. David and I are both below deck storing provisions. We go topside, and a British naval officer is standing there.

"There you are," he happily says when he sees us.

"What can we do for you, sir?" I answer, deliberately not using his rank because I'm not sure what it is.

"Americans! What the bloody hell…?" he starts to say but is smiling.

David jumps in. "We were out on a fishing cruise, then all of a sudden, our guide decides to stop here. What's going on?"

The officer laughs and says, "That's good. Whose boat is this?"

"Edward Hughes," I answer. "He's checking in with whoever's in charge and getting instructions."

At that moment, another officer, a little older and with another stripe on his shoulder, arrives. "That's a good one, Peter."

"Yes, it is, sir," the first officer replies.

"What is?" I ask.

"To believe that someone around here might be in charge. If you find out who that is, be a good chap and let us know, won't you?" the senior officer says.

Turning serious, Peter, the younger one asks, "What we'd like to know is, how long before you're ready to go?"

I see Edward coming down a set of stairs and point at him. "Here's our captain. You should ask him."

Edward arrives, and the three of them converse for a couple of minutes. A moment later, Edward is back on board.

The younger officer says, "Pull around toward the rear of those other boats out in the harbor. Stay with them, but if you get separated, take the northern route. Best to just follow the boats ahead of you. Do not, I repeat, do not, go directly across the Channel to Dunkirk. Too many mines."

"Go north past the cliffs then make a sharp right toward Ostend. Do you know it?" the senior officer asks Edward.

"Yes, I know it exactly. I've sailed it many times," Edward replies.

"When you reach Ostend, stay at least five miles out and sail south to Dunkirk. You'll get there in about three hours. You can't miss it. The whole place is on fire. At that point you just sort of get in line and go either to the beach or the east or west mole, the breakwaters. Good luck, godspeed. And you two gentlemen be very careful. We don't want to explain how we managed to get a couple of Americans killed."

"We would hate it if you had to explain that also," I answer him.

TWELVE

May 28, 1940

Off the Beaches of Dunkirk

Dear Mom & Dad,

It was originally my intention to wait until this was over to write to you. Something in the back of my mind must have warned me before I left. Otherwise, why would I have brought along writing material?

By the time you receive this, hopefully this will be over and I will be back in London safe and sound. Without trying to seem too maudlin, if I am not back, if I am missing or dead, please know your son died trying to do some good. He gave his life for a worthy cause.

We arrived off the coast of France at Dunkirk shortly after six p.m. We are among hundreds of small boats waiting their turn to go ashore. We have been waiting for about an hour and will be heading in shortly.

I am writing because I grossly misjudged the danger. The city of Dunkirk looks to be the entrance to hell. It is completely ablaze. There is still plenty of daylight and the Germans are taking advantage of it. Their planes are everywhere, and we can see the artillery shelling on the beach. Amazingly, the men on the beach are standing in line waiting to get on board a boat. They appear to be quite calm while the Germans bomb and shoot at them.

Our captain has a good pair of binoculars on board. We are sharing them watching the evacuation and as lookouts for German planes. The evacuation seems to be going smoothly but slow. In the meantime, there are German planes overhead, and they are terrifying. About ten minutes ago, one of them dove down onto the boats and dropped a bomb. It landed about two hundred yards from us with a huge roar. Fortunately, he missed everything and only managed to throw up a large column of water. Scared the hell out of David and me.

I finish my letter, address an envelope and put it away. I'll mail it tomorrow. Now that we're moving, I feel a lot better. Much calmer. I ask David about it, and he agrees. Our captain smiles and tells us that is quite normal. We're experiencing a feeling of doing something, of going at the enemy. And we're no longer sitting ducks.

Edward tells me to take over the steering, which I do. He is standing next to me in the wheelhouse looking through the windshield with the binoculars. David is standing behind us.

"There's a soldier on the beach dead ahead who looks to be signaling to us," Edward tells me. "There's a long line of soldiers on the beach leading into the water directly ahead."

"The one with the boat starting to back up to pull away?" I ask.

"Yes, that's the one. Head for that spot. Stay to the left of the line.

"David, can you get up on the bow and keep an eye in front for any rocks or sandbars? Try to gauge the water's depth. We want to get in as close as possible," Edward tells David.

"Will do," David replies.

At that moment, two German airplanes, fighters, scream directly overhead heading toward the beach. They are to our left going away from where we plan to land, barely fifty feet overhead.

"Messerschmitt 109s," Edward calmly says. "Some of our boys are about to catch hell. Stay on course, Jeff."

With David up front as a guide, we cruise toward the beach. When we are about fifty yards out, Edward takes the wheel. He slows the boat to barely walking speed while David and I prepare for our guests. The bow softly slides onto the sand. We are in about five feet of water. We are also right next to the men in the front of the line.

We have a small, wooden ladder to attach to the gunwale to plant it over the side for the men to use to climb aboard. David has done this and is helping them while I am pulling guys up and over the side. While we are doing this, Edward is holding the boat steady.

All of a sudden, the man who was waving us in climbs up on the bow of the boat. He comes back to the wheelhouse and jumps down. By the look of him, he must be in his late forties. He is wearing a tan beret, sporting a huge mustache, and looking as tough as saddle leather. He has a sergeant's three stripes and, I am later told, the insignia of a Regimental Sergeant Major. He could be wearing a dress, and you would still know he was in charge.

While David and I continue to help soldiers climb aboard, the sergeant major and Edward converse. After a couple of minutes, he climbs back on the boat's bow, jumps into the water and calmly wades back to the beach.

Then, we hear it. A German fighter plane like the two who went by a few minutes ago, is screaming right at us. He is flying with his engine almost shut off, gliding, to be as quiet as possible. By the time we notice him, he is less than a hundred yards away. I see him coming and his wing guns are winking fire as he races along the beach. All of us on board, including Edward, drop to the floor. Those alongside in the water dive under the boat, the men still waiting on the beach, sprawl helplessly onto the sand.

The attack—I will be told later, it is called 'being strafed'—lasts barely three or four seconds. When I stand up, I look around, and everyone on board is unharmed. I have no idea how he missed us, but he did. The men on the beach are not so lucky. Of those who were waiting in our line, at least a dozen are lying face down in the sand. These poor devils will never get up.

Then I see the sergeant major who was on board a moment ago. He is calmly walking up and down the line getting the men back in order. He is also reloading his pistol. Instead of diving for cover, he pulled out his handgun and stood on the sand emptying the gun at the plane. With men like that to lead them, the British might whip Adolf after all.

We have taken on forty-one soldiers. They are everywhere. Any space on board has a soldier filling it. They are seated on the bow, down below and on top of the wheelhouse. In fact, I fear we may be overloaded. Edward is pushing the engines, trying to get us clear of the sand. Before long, a small mob of soldiers, patiently waiting their turn in the water, wade over and help push us free. When this is done, a cheer goes up from the men on board who are waving back at those still on the beach. I find their discipline to be astonishing given the circumstances.

While Edward gets us turned around and pointed seaward, I make an announcement. David and a couple of soldiers have carried water cans and sacks of biscuits up from the gallery. They also have three bottles of brandy to pass around.

"We have water and biscuits for you," I announce. "We'll pass them around for you to share."

"Why, you're a bloody Yank!" one of the men, a corporal, sitting about five feet from me says.

"Yes, I'm afraid so. If that offends you, we can let you out here and you can wait for the next boat," I say.

This elicits a roar of laughter and a mock, horrified look on the corporal's face. "No, no," he holds up his hands and says. "I'm quite comfortable right here."

"What are you doing here, sir?" one of the men asks.

"Well, we were on a fishing trip, and the next thing we knew, we were pulling you fish out of the water," David answers him.

"We're newspaper reporters from the States stationed in London. We just wanted to help," I say.

Fortunately, the weather cooperates, and we make it back to Dover at midnight. We dock the Isabella, and as our weary cargo disembarks, each of the men make a point of shaking our hands and thanking us. While they are disembarking, I spot the corporal I had the exchange with.

"Corporal," I say as I gently tug his arm. "A word please."

"Yes, sir," he replies.

I remove the envelope with the letter to my parents in it and show it to him. "I was wondering… We're going back tonight and probably several times. This is for my parents. Would you post it for me, please?"

He knew what it was. He knew I was saying goodbye, just in case.

"Of course, sir. But you'll be writing them again when this is over," he answers me.

I hand him the letter and a five-pound note. He refuses the money. We wish each other well and he goes off into the dark.

We make one more trip that night. Edward navigates with instruments; the man is an excellent sailor. We take the same northern route back and arrive around four a.m.

Once again, we are waiting our turn to go ashore for a load of soldiers. While we wait, we are mesmerized by the fires of hell. It seems the entire coastline is ablaze. As bad as it looked yesterday in the light, it is many times worse at night. The smoke pouring into the dark sky is barely visible. But below it, the flames are both terrifying and oddly beautiful. Like watching a train wreck, I suppose; it is horrible, but too difficult to look away.

I am standing in the steering house with Edward, watching the shoreline for a signal for us to go in. David is asleep below on a bench seat. "Were the trenches worse than this?" I ask Edward.

Edward remains silent. During my time in London, I have met many older men, the fathers of these boys on the beach, who are veterans of the Great War. I have yet to meet one who was really there and spent time in the trenches who is anxious to talk about it. From what I know, that is almost universally true of all soldiers on all sides of every war. I don't press Edward for an answer. Instead, I am just about to relieve him, so he can get a little more sleep.

"I believe the trenches were worse," he finally replies. "There was no relief from it. No hope. The lads on the beach," he continues, nodding his head toward shore, "know we're here. They know someone is coming for them. In the trenches, even when we were relieved, we didn't really go anywhere. We would pull out and go back to a quiet trench for a couple of weeks. Those weren't much better. It's hard to compare, though. I haven't been where these lads have been the past few weeks."

A small boat pulls up alongside, and Edward goes to converse with an army major. He comes back and takes the wheel again. "We'll follow him in. There will be a boat on each side of us going in. Keep an eye on them, will you, Jeff?"

"Sure," I reply.

We are less than a mile out this time. With the darkness, the German Luftwaffe is not flying. This trip should be safer. As we start in, there is a huge explosion about a half mile on our port side. It is worse than the bombs and scares the hell out of me. I look at Edward who seems as calm as a churchgoer.

Off to our left, I see the fire and smoke coming from the side of a Royal Navy destroyer. It was hit amidships by a torpedo. As we make our way to shore, I watch the ship break in two and go down. The realization that there is a German submarine on the loose in the area does not comfort me. Fortunately, our little boat is too small to shoot at and too hard to hit. I try not to think about the men on board the destroyer who were killed and those who are drowning. It does them or me no good.

We are loaded again with a full contingent; thirty-seven this time. The same sergeant major who came aboard last evening is still directing traffic. Somehow his presence is reassuring that things are going well.

As we pull away and head out to sea, we go through a similar routine about our being Americans. I can understand their surprise. I only hope they think well of us. David is carrying around one of the water containers. I am handing out biscuits. We are out of brandy. The men are very thirsty and hungry but almost too tired to drink or eat.

A man in his mid-twenties, a sergeant leaning against the stern wall, takes a biscuit. He gently pulls me in close and whispers to me. "Sir, that man over there, the one to the left of the wheelhouse door…" he says.

I take a quick look to see who he is referring to. He is a hatless man in a private's coat and appears to be asleep. He also appears to be a little old to be a private.

"Okay," I whisper back. "What about him?"

"He's an officer, a captain, and I was there when he was ordered to wait until the last of the regiment was off the beach before he went on board."

"And?" I ask.

"At least half the regiment is still waiting on shore. He disobeyed a direct order and is guilty of desertion in the face of the enemy. Sir, that is a capital offense."

"Yeah, I guess it is. I'm not sure what I can do about it," I say.

"You can report it. Put it in the newspaper if you have to," the sergeant urgently says as he holds my right arm tighter.

"It would be best for you to report it," I say.

"That won't work," he replies.

"Why?"

"He has a lot of connections. And money."

"Tell the man who gave him the order," I say.

"I would but unfortunately Colonel Houle, the regimental commander, was killed in an air attack ten minutes later. He was a good man. Not like this cowardly sot," the sergeant says.

"What's your name and outfit, Sergeant?" I ask the man.

"Sergeant Reggie Gordon, sir. Eighth Battalion, Nottingham Fusiliers."

"All right, I'll remember it," I say. "Who is he?" I ask referring to the deserter sleeping by the door.

"His name is Ashland, Captain Arthur Ashland. He's an Earl; he likes to remind us poor commoners."

"That name sounds familiar," I quietly say mostly to myself.

A moment later, I remember the name. I quickly stand up as the blood rushes to my face. I drop the box of biscuits and don't even notice it. I am glaring with contempt at the man by the wheelhouse door. The thought of grabbing him by the throat and throwing him overboard enters my head. I am clenching my fists and having difficulty breathing.

"Are you all right, sir?" I hear the sergeant's voice. He has stood up and is watching me with a look of concern.

He does not know, and I cannot tell him, but a visceral hatred is all but consuming me. The coward who has deserted his post in the face of the enemy is none other than Lord Arthur Ashland, Catherine Hartley's abusive, despicable husband.

THIRTEEN

June 3, 1940

Dearest Mom & Dad,

By now, hopefully, you have received my brief telegram. I'm sure it has brought you great relief.

I am back in my hotel suite. Operation Dynamo, the codename for the Dunkirk rescue, is complete. Except, I have heard rumors that an attempt will be made to bring out more French troops. They'll have to do it without me.

Since our first trip across the Channel on the afternoon of the 28th, we have been going nonstop. Snatching a couple of hours of sleep here and there, living mostly on cigarettes and strong coffee have left all three of us exhausted. And probably several thousand others.

In the seven days we—David, our boat owner Edward Hughes and I— were involved, we made a total of nineteen trips. Best guess is we brought back almost seven hundred soldiers ourselves. The preliminary reports claim we rescued over three hundred thousand British and French soldiers. The authorities were hoping for forty to fifty thousand. It's being called the Miracle of Dunkirk. Maybe, but it was also a military disaster. Possibly the worst in history.

Well, Mom, Dad, I'm glad to be back. It was an amazing adventure; one I will remember for the rest of my life. Exhilarating and horrifying. But be assured, I'm fine. Not a scratch. You can yell at me later about whether or not I should have done it. I believed it was the right thing to do before I left and am even more certain of it now. We may have helped save England.

I need a shave and a shower. I haven't been out of these clothes for a week. They need to be burned. Good night.

All my love,

Jeff

I have finished shaving and am staring at the old man in the mirror. His entire face is sagging, and his eyes look like a raccoon's. A quick shower and then fourteen hours of sleep.

The quick shower turns into almost twenty minutes. Between being too tired to move and how wonderful the hot water feels, I let it pound on me. My entire body aches, but I have never felt so good. It is a great, even historic thing we did. The faces on the men and the weary look in their eyes as we brought them on board will be with me forever.

I use a heavy, terry cloth towel to dry myself. Even the towel feels good. I feel as if I am scraping a week's worth of crud from my skin. I dry my hair and slip into a warm bathrobe. I go into the main part of the suite instead of exiting into the bedroom. One more cigarette before I collapse.

While lighting the smoke, I notice a light coming through the bedroom door. I think for a moment, trying to remember if I left a light on. Convinced I did not, I pick up the fireplace poker and quietly, silently walk to the bedroom. Slowly, I push back the open door to get a better look. The lamp next to the bed is the one that is on.

"Hey, sailor," I hear a familiar voice coming from the bed. "Home from the sea?"

I feel a catch in my throat and am close to tears. The relief upon seeing her releases the stress, tension and fear of the past week. I step into the room and stop just to look at her. She is lying under the covers on the far side of the bed. I see her clothes neatly folded and placed on a chair in the far corner. She is obviously quite naked.

"I don't think you'll need that. I'm really not that dangerous," she says, referring to the poker in my hand.

"I've never been so happy to see anyone in my life," I manage to stammer.

Next to me, is a writing table with an ashtray. I crush out my cigarette then turn back to the bed. Catherine has pulled back the blankets inviting me to join her. I was right; she is completely naked, and I cannot help staring.

"Don't stare," she says. "You'll make me feel self-conscious."

"You're the most beautiful woman I've ever seen, far more than I had imagined. I'll never want you to wear clothes again," I say, still staring.

I let the robe I am wearing drop to the floor. Beneath it, I am also naked. I crawl in with her while she watches me.

"*Hmm*, you're not so bad yourself, sailor," she says.

We wrap ourselves around each other. She smells and feels fabulous; soft, warm, and sensuous. I bury my face in the crook where her neck meets her shoulder. She purrs like a big cat and squeezes me a little harder.

"What did you say your name is, sailor?" she asks.

I laugh and say, "I didn't. I forgot, was I supposed to pay you before or after?"

"After," she says, smiling and softly kissing my face. "I charge by quality of performance," she says with a smile.

Catherine is lightly brushing my face with her fingers while looking at me with a more serious expression. "Are you really here?" she asks.

"Yes, I told you I'd come back," I quietly reply.

"I could barely function," she says. "I was so worried. But now that you're back, I'm incredibly proud of you. You were right. It was the correct thing to do."

She clamps her mouth on mine, and our tongues almost wrestle with each other. This goes on for a couple of minutes until she pulls away. It is obvious I am not becoming aroused. She notices it, too.

"Tired?" she asks.

"Exhausted," I say, barely able to keep my eyes open.

"Then sleep," she says.

"Sorry," I weakly reply.

"Don't be. I've never been happier than I am right now. Sooner or later, we'll manage it," she says.

"Sooner," I say.

I am unaware of it but there is a break in the clouds outside. Because of it, a ray of sunshine comes streaming through my bedroom window and hits me in the face. My eyes open, my head snaps back, and I cover my eyes with my hand.

I lie on my back while my eyes shift around the room. It takes a minute until I fully realize where I am. When I do, I look for her, but she is gone. *Was I dreaming?* Then I realize, no, the other side of the bed has been slept in. I grab her pillow and hold it to my face. Her scent reassures me it was not a dream. She really was here and spent the night.

I set the pillow aside, sit up and notice the chair where she had placed her clothes is empty. I look at the wall clock, ten fifteen a.m. Then I remember I fell asleep on her, too tired to make love.

"We're going to fix that before the day is over," I say out loud.

I find a note and a still hot pot of coffee on the table I use to write on.

My Darling,

Sorry, I had to go to work. Winnie is giving a speech today. A report to Parliament about Dunkirk. Get your butt in gear. You need to be there.

Good luck for me, you barely snored at all. We have unfinished business to attend to.

I am so happy you're back safe and sound!

All my love,
Catherine

I put her note back on the table, pour a cup of coffee, light a cigarette and say, "Okay, get your butt in gear."

On my way to meet my friends, I send a cable to my employer, the *Gazette*. They have not heard a word from me in over a week. I briefly explain where I have been and promise to send the full story in a day or two: a lengthy first-hand account of the Miracle of Dunkirk.

I am feeling significant ambivalence about writing up my Dunkirk experience for publication. Was it proper for an American journalist to help a belligerent country we are supposedly neutral toward? Will the paper want to publish it? Will the government raise hell about it? This last question makes me smile. Tweaking the government's nose sounds like an excellent idea. The rest, well, I'll see what my bosses think.

On the sidewalk outside the International Cable Office, it takes less than a minute to flag down a cab. I give the cabbie my destination, then sit back for the short ride.

"A Yank, eh?" the man asks me.

"Yes, I am," I answer.

"When will you be leaving?" he asks.

"Leaving? Why would I leave?"

He swings his head around, looks at me with a puzzled expression, turns back and says, "Why, the Germans will be droppin' in any day. That's all anyone's talkin' about. Nothing much to stop an invasion."

I had not thought about this before. The idea, without thinking it through, must seem inevitable. Having been on the English Channel for the past week, the idea of invasion in a few days sounds absurd.

"There's plenty to stop them," I reply. "That moat you call the Channel is not as easy to get across as a river. I don't think the Royal Navy and Air Force will sit idly by while it happens."

"That's an excellent point, sir," the cabbie says looking at me in the mirror. "I hadn't thought of that."

"They may try it, but it will be a while and it won't be easy," I say.

The cabbie lets me out on Whitehall and Downing. I give the man a generous tip and he thanks me profusely. It occurs to me that may be why all Brits think Americans are rich. I am sure we must over-tip entirely too much.

I nod and say hello to the bobby watching the opening to Downing Street. It again amazes me how lax their security is. How easily a Nazi agent could walk up to the PM's home, wait for him and shoot him. Maybe the Brits are a little too civilized.

I find my friends milling about in the crowd. The normal gathering, which is usually mostly the press, is augmented by a huge number of the curious. The talk of imminent invasion is spreading through London like wildfire.

David is with Charlie and Clive, and they vigorously wave as they see me approach. Charlie throws his arms around me, pinning my arms to my side. He lifts me off the ground and squeezes so hard my ribs ache.

"Welcome back, you damn fool. God, I'm glad to see you," Charlie says.

"Thanks, I think. Next time try not to fracture any bones," I say then look at David.

"My back and ribs will be sore for a week," he says with a big grin.

Clive puts his arm around my shoulder and kisses me on the cheek. "Magnificent!" he says. "What you and the others did is historic. When the war is over, this will be why we won."

"All I did was ride in the boat and help the boys climb aboard," I say.

"Stop it!" Clive says with a smile. "I've never been so proud of anyone as I am you two. Let's find a pub, have a bite, a pint, and you can regale us with your heroics."

"Heroics. I'm just glad I brought along extra underwear," David says.

This elicits laughter and Charlie asks me, "Did you go through several changes of underwear, too?"

"No," I reply. "In fact, I had the opposite problem. I was scared shitless the entire time."

As the waiter walks off with our dishes, the four of us sit in silence. No one is quite certain what to say. For the past hour, David and I gave Charlie and Clive a report of each day. When we finally started talking about it, I quickly realized that most of the time was not very dramatic. The vast majority of the time was spent routinely traveling back and forth between Dover and Dunkirk. Of course, there were many moments of sheer terror involved as well.

My personal favorite part was our very last trip. We had gone ashore very close to the same place each time. The amazing sergeant major in the tan beret with the large mustache was there every time, the one who calmly emptied his pistol whenever a German plane went by. Apparently, the man needed no sleep or nourishment.

Edward began backing away from a mostly empty beach when I saw the sergeant major. His hands grabbed hold of the bow point and he pulled himself aboard, the last man to leave that section of the beach. I climbed out onto the bow—once again crowded with soldiers—and welcomed him aboard. He looked down at me, unsmiling, and said, "Let's not make a big thing of it, Yank."

When I told our table this story, they laughed and shook their heads in amazement.

Clive asked, "Did you get his name?"

"No, unfortunately. He went below, and by the time I got down there, he was sound asleep. I didn't have the heart to wake him. And I never did get a chance to ask him his name."

While we eat, I tell them about Catherine's husband. David, of course, already knows. This is the reason the four of us went silent until the waiter cleared the table.

"You have got to report this," Charlie demands.

"Maybe they'll hang the bastard. That would solve Catherine's marital problems," David added.

"Report it to whom?" I ask Charlie. "I have the name of the man who told me but nothing else."

"Nothing will come of it," Clive says. "They will not want to court martial a member of the House of Lords after the debacle that just happened. Your sergeant would find himself transferred to some place such as Singapore and that would be that."

"You're probably right," I reply.

FOURTEEN

June 5, 1940

Dear Mom & Dad,

Your cable was waiting for me when I got back to the hotel last night. It was wonderful. Thank you for your support of my foolishness. Except, if Dad were my age and here, I know he would have done the same thing. The apple probably doesn't fall too far from the tree.

Churchill's speech to the House of Commons yesterday may have been his best one yet. I was in the press gallery, and it brought tears to my eyes. Looking down on the members, I could see many of them openly weeping.

I don't think it was broadcast live. If you get a chance to hear it, do so. The long and the short of it is, Winnie threw down the gauntlet at Hitler's feet. He made it clear his policy is to fight to the death. Or at least until he can get America in it. It was stirring, and I thought it would give the British a morale boost. At least I thought so until we got back to the Savoy afterward.

While there, we heard from a number of British sources that the support for the war is sagging. At least among the ruling class. Halifax is already raising hell about it, or at least it is rumored that he is. Making peace has more support than I would have thought. When will these idiots learn? Hitler cannot be appeased. Sorry, but that's the reality too many will not face. Fortunately, Winnie is not one of them.

I'm going to spend time today gauging support among real people. I'll write again soon and let you know what I find.

Love you,

Jeff

Along with the cable I received from my parents, there was another one waiting for me last night. It was from Earl Stanton, my boss at the *Gazette*. They want me to drop everything and write my Dunkirk story. He does not care how long it is. They will run it as a series. No detail is too small. And he wants it by Friday for Sunday's paper. Today is Wednesday.

If I do what I want, interviews of Londoners today, I will have this evening and tomorrow to write up the story for the paper. That creates another problem. Just before last night's blackout, Catherine and I were leaving the Savoy. The idea was to go back to my hotel suite and finally spend a romantic night together. Except, as we were leaving, an intern with the BBC arrived with a written order for Catherine to return immediately. She called an hour ago and is still there. I absolutely promised her dinner, a show and back here tonight for sure. Even if I wanted to, I cannot back out now.

"Good morning, Jimmy," I say to the Ritz doorman. "Looks like we're in for another lovely day."

James 'Jimmy' Martin is a sixty-year-old doorman who, according to him, was badly wounded in the Boer War in 1899. He has been with the Ritz since 1903 and is an institution unto himself. Every cabbie in the city knows Jimmy.

He has his back to me standing at the curb when I start to speak. He hears me, turns and limping from his war wound, hurries toward me. "Good morning to you, Mr. Bartlett, sir," he says with genuine exuberance, even more than usual. "Please, sir, allow a grateful Londoner to shake your hand."

Slightly embarrassed, I allow him to pump my arm.

The old guy actually has tears in his eyes. "I heard what you, your friend and Edward did. We all heard about it, sir. God bless. We're all so very proud of you."

He finally releases my hand, and I quietly say, "Thank you, Jimmy. I've heard from quite a few of the staff. I appreciate it, but all we did was help the boys into the boat."

"Nonsense. You helped save civilization. How are the lads? How is their morale?" he asks.

I think about this for a moment before answering. "Difficult to say. On the whole, not very good. Don't be mistaken. They took a historic whipping and they know it. Plus, they were all very tired, thirsty and hungry. But their discipline was outstanding. I was amazed by it. No pushing, shoving or fighting to get ahead in the lines. They all calmly waited their turns.

"Let me ask you," I continue, "what are you hearing?"

"Invasion," he quickly sums up the one-word concern. "I know better, but people out there"—he waves an arm indicating the city—"have it in their heads the Hun will be dropping in any minute."

"Are they for making peace or fighting?"

"Fight, sir. Absolutely."

I look across Piccadilly and see the bus I want heading my way. I thank Jimmy and hurry across the street to catch it.

On the bus ride, I introduce myself to several riders. It again makes me smile at the enthusiasm they have meeting an American. Most of them will tell me how much they would like to visit their one-time colony.

My ride only lasts about fifteen minutes, enough time to chat with my co-riders and get their opinion. Before we go a quarter of a mile, most of the people on the lower level have crowded around me. A little more than half are men. The rest are women with a few children.

I am tempted to tell them I was at Dunkirk, but I'm not looking for adulation. Instead, I simply strike up a conversation. There is no lack of determination on their part. It's all: "Let the Huns come, and we'll show them."

A young girl, pretty and quite precocious, speaks up for them all loud and clear. "We're with Winston! We'll fight them on the beaches, the streets, the landing areas, wherever we have to. We will never surrender!" she says, concluding with a look of determination and stamping a foot on the floor.

The entire bus, including the driver, erupts into a raucous cheer. The applause turns her face red and brings several riders down from topside to see what the ruckus is about.

When the cheering dies down, I say to the girl, "I believe you. I wonder, could I get your name? I'd like to use it in my next report to my paper in New York. I'll make you famous in America."

She is less than two feet from me, and everyone has circled around us, crowding in. She looks up at her mother who nods and says, "Go ahead."

"Abby, sir, Abby Perkins," she replies.

As I write it in my notebook, I ask, "And how old are you, Abby?"

"Eleven, sir. Almost twelve," she quickly adds.

I make a note, lean very close to her, smile and say, "Twelve it is. And thank you, Abby Perkins."

I meet up with my friends, and we spend most of the day traveling around London. Several times, even with Clive as our guide, we become lost. We converse with at least two hundred people, and it is unanimous; Winnie has gauged the pulse and mood of these people perfectly. All of them expect an invasion and very soon. And all of them say they will fight to the bitter end and never surrender.

Around four p.m., we are on a bus when I notice where we are. I ask, "Aren't we about a half mile from the US Embassy?"

Clive answers, "Yes, why?"

"You want to drop in and see Joe?" David asks, referring to Ambassador Kennedy.

"Sure, why not?" I say. "Won't hurt to try."

We jump off the bus to walk the short distance to the embassy at Grosvenor Square. As we are walking along, Charlie asks of no one in particular, "Will the people of London feel the same way two or three months after the Huns have dropped in?"

"That's the question, isn't it?" Clive replies.

"What do you think, Jeff?" David asks me. "What if the Nazis do to some of the cities of England what we saw at Dunkirk?"

"I was just wondering the same thing," I quietly reply.

"How bad was it?" Charlie asks.

"Like a scene out of Dante's *Inferno*," David replies, "Maybe worse because it was so real."

"I'll tell you what," I say, "hell like that would be hard to take,"

We are stopped at the front gate, this time by a baby-faced Marine. We give him our names, the names of our newspapers and honestly tell him we do not have an appointment. He keeps us waiting for a few minutes while he calls to check. When he comes back, he hands us our passports and Clive his ID. "Do you know the way in?" he asks.

We assure him we do, and he politely waves us in. Five minutes later, we are ushered into the ambassador's office. Before we have taken two steps, the familiar man with the round, black-framed glasses and fetching grin is headed our way.

"Hello, boys. Good to see you again," Kennedy says as he shakes our hands. "How are your parents, Jeff?" he asks.

"Fine, sir," I reply. I have been around enough politicians to know they work on remembering names.

He holds out his hand to Clive and says, "I'm sorry, I don't believe we've met."

"Clive Burke, sir. *Daily Herald*," Clive perfunctorily replies. Clive has met his share of faux charming politicians, also.

"Come in, boys, come in," he jovially says. "Pull up some chairs," he continues as he sits down behind the big desk. "What can I do for you?" he smiles and asks.

"Well, sir," I begin, "Thank you for taking time out to see us. You must be very busy."

"Oh, yes, I suppose so. But most of it, even with the war, is pretty dull, boring and routine. I guess you'd like to know what I'm thinking the British should do now?" he asks.

Clive, as are we all, is well aware of Kennedy's attitude. Clive won't take offense.

"Two words: make peace," Kennedy says as he slaps the desk with an open hand. "They got kicked out of Europe. They can still keep their empire, most of it at least, and we can do business with the Germans."

He then goes off on a fifteen-minute soliloquy about the war. France is done. Any day they'll ask for an armistice. They'll make a deal. The British can do the same. He goes on for a while about the British Empire and how little of it they will have to give up.

"Churchill made it perfectly clear yesterday. All that rot about fighting all over the damn country and never surrendering, well, boys, that's a lot of hooey. His policy is to hang on until he can get us into it. And I'll tell you, despite that clique of interventionists around Franklin, it won't happen. Congress is dead set against it. And I'll tell you this, it's the Russians Hitler is after. And I say, let him do it; he'll clean them out for us." Kennedy spends another fifteen minutes on the Red Menace of Russia, then finally shows us out.

We are out on the street, and no one speaks for almost two minutes.

Finally, Clive breaks the silence. "He's candid about what he thinks," Clive says.

"A little too candid. I hear from people back at the paper in Washington that Roosevelt wishes he'd shut up," David says.

"What's worrisome," I say, "is that he may be right."

FIFTEEN

June 6, 1940

Dear Mom & Dad,

How about a little light news this time? Catherine and I finally got an evening off together. We had dinner at Claridge's, then took in a play. We saw a musical comedy called Present Arms. It is about three old soldiers from the Great War who find themselves back in uniform in France. It is mostly about their competition for women. This includes a French girl they knew in the war and became reacquainted with. You might remember Evelyn Dall from the New York theater. She had the female lead and was quite good. It was a nice break from the war news.

My reporter friends and I spent yesterday touring around London on buses and the tube. We met with a couple of hundred ordinary Londoners, people who are not politicians or in the government. Without a single dissenting voice, maybe they were too afraid to speak up, all were with Churchill: fight the Germans anywhere and everywhere. I am sure they mean it, but I wonder how many would be willing to stand up to the hell I witnessed at Dunkirk.

They are expecting the Huns to drop in any day. Invasion is on everyone's lips. Crossing the Channel with the RAF and Royal Navy in the way will not be simple. If they come at all, it will not be soon.

We (the guys and me) stopped and met with Joe Kennedy again. Of course, he is urging the British to make peace. He's entitled to his opinion, but again, I believe it is a fool's errand. No piece of paper Hitler signs means anything to him. Sooner or later, people had better realize that. Winston does now. Before this is over, I think we will be very glad he is in charge and not the appeasers, Chamberlain, Halifax, Kennedy et. al.

Time to go. The Gazette is looking for a day-by-day account of my Dunkirk adventure. They want it by tomorrow. So I better get at it.

London is quiet. No bombs or Germans marching about. I am fine. I figured I should make that clear.

Love to all,

Jeff

"Are you a good son?" I hear Catherine ask over my shoulder.

I look up at her standing behind me in my bathrobe, smile and say, "You shouldn't read other people's mail."

"I just read the last part," she replies.

"Good morning," I softly say to her as I put my arm around her waist and gently pull her onto my lap.

She puts her arms around my neck, kisses my cheek and purrs. "Ready for another go round?" she whispers in my ear.

I turn my head, look her in the eyes while I stammer, "I… no… yes, okay, but… I, uh, really need to work. But, oh… what the hell…"

Catherine laughs, kisses me and says, "I'll let you off the hook, for now. I'm late, and I need to get moving. I'm glad I brought some clothes." She stands up, bends down, kisses me again and says, "Besides, three times last night,"—she wiggles her eyebrows—"I'm impressed."

"Are you kidding? I barely got started," I say.

She laughs again—a beautiful, delightful laugh that warms my heart—and says, "You may want to be careful what you're bragging about. I may expect you to deliver someday soon."

As she starts to walk away, I give her a light swat on her behind. She ruffles my hair and walks away humming a tune from last night's show.

While she showers, I dig in and start banging away on my typewriter. The account of my Dunkirk escapade is coming more easily than I thought. The more I type, the more I remember. When I reach the moment of my seeing Catherine's husband, I stop. I light a cigarette and sit back contemplating what to put down. I am tempted to name him explicitly. Then I remember what I have learned about British libel laws. With only the sergeant's word naming his Lordship, it could get me in a lot of trouble. I decide to include the incident but not use any names at all.

"Why did you stop?" I hear Catherine ask.

I turn and see her walking toward me. She is dressed, adjusting an earring and ready to go. For several days, since I saw Arthur on the Isabella, I have been trying to decide whether or not to tell her. So far, I have been leaning toward not telling her. What good could possibly come of it? On a whim, I make my decision.

"I was thinking about something," I say. "Please, sit down. I need to tell you something."

"So serious," she says as she pulls a chair out and sits down.

"It is," I say. "I had an incident on one of the trips back from the beach." I take barely two minutes to tell her about her husband. When I finish, I sit quietly awaiting her response. She surprises me a little.

She lightly shakes her head, then says, "I can't say I'm surprised. It's too bad you didn't chuck him overboard. But then you'd be in trouble. I'm not surprised the drunken sot is a coward. Bullies normally are, aren't they?"

"Yes, they are," I say. "Especially those that abuse women. They know they are weak and try to compensate."

"What are you going to do?" she asks.

I explain to her my conversation with David, Clive and Charlie, and their consensus, especially my British friend Clive's, that nothing would come of it. "Are you upset I told them?"

"No," she says. "Not at all. Why should I be? It has nothing to do with me. But I'm afraid I agree with your friends. It's unlikely the powers that be would want the scandal the court martial of a peer for cowardice at Dunkirk would bring."

"If he stays in the army, sooner or later his cowardice will catch up with him. In fact, it is likely to get him killed," I say.

"That would be a shame," Catherine sarcastically adds.

"Unfortunately, he is likely to get some others killed before then."

"That's all too true, isn't it?" she quietly says.

"Let's think about it. Maybe we can come up with a way to get him to resign or, at least, keep out of any future combat."

Catherine looks at me and silently nods her head three or four times. "Yes, that's a thought. Bring the boys in on it, too," she says.

"I have to go," she stands and says. She bends down and kisses me.

I pull her into my lap for a much more passionate one.

"I have to go," she repeats when it is finished.

"I love you," I whisper.

"It's about time you said it," she says with a grim look. "What is wrong with you people? Even when it is obvious to everyone else, you still don't want to admit it."

"I just did, you know," I say while she sits up, still on my lap.

She looks at me then says, "All right. We'll leave it at that for now. But I still want my question answered. What is wrong with you people?"

She stands and I hold her by the wrist and ask, "Well, are you going to say it?"

"I'm still trying to decide," she breezily says.

"See, this is why we are so reluctant. We know we're going to get our heart ripped out of our chest and treated like a trophy," I say and feign pouting.

She tilts her head to look at my face, frowns, then leans down with her mouth next to my ear. "I love you, too," she whispers.

"I knew it all along," I say. "You couldn't help yourself."

She loudly laughs, swats me on the shoulder and kisses my cheek.

"Can you meet for lunch?" I ask.

"Call me later. We'll see," she replies then heads to the door.

I watch her leave, and when she opens the door, she turns and blows a kiss at me which I pretend to catch.

SIXTEEN

June 18, 1940

Dearest Mom & Dad,

Once again, my apologies for not writing sooner. Hope you were not worried. I'll do my best to avoid stunts like Dunkirk in the future.

As I am sure you are aware, the Germans occupied Paris a few days ago, June 14. In a little more than a month, Hitler's army has accomplished what the Germans tried to do for four years in the Great War. First, he drove the British off the European continent. Then, barely two weeks later, he has captured Paris and, in the process, defeated the largest army—the French—possibly ever assembled.

Churchill along with several senior cabinet members and British army officers, was in France the past few days. I was with them. I was one of four correspondents allowed to tag along. We got back last night, and I wrote my story for the Gazette this morning. I doubt that it will make it past the censors, but I have to at least try to tell the truth.

I'm sure you are certainly aware that Mussolini declared war on France on behalf of Italy on June 10; a sure sign that the French are all but beaten. Hitler's lackey, Mussolini, waited until France was beaten before stabbing her in the back. The little coward is trying to bite off a piece of the French carcass like the sleazy hyena that he is.

Winnie was on the plane to France the next day. He met with the French leadership in a French château near Briare on the 11th and 12th, then in Tours on the 13th before flying back.

Churchill did all he could to instill some backbone into the French. They are whipped and they know it. It is expected that any day now, the French will ask for an armistice. When that happens, Britain will stand alone, although I overheard two British generals agree that they believe that will be for the best. They both believe the Brits will be better off if they cut themselves loose from a failed, defeatist ally. We shall see.

My news, short and sweet. I am fine, back from a quick trip to France. The talk here is still of imminent invasion. I am skeptical. If they try to, it won't be for at least a couple of months. By then, hopefully, the Brits will be more prepared. It does feel like the dark days of Dunkirk are over. That's all for now.

All my Love,

Jeff

I have just finished addressing the envelope when I hear a knock on my door. When I open it, I am not surprised to find my clandestine courier from Pan Am. Looking over his shoulder, I am surprised and delighted to see Catherine walking toward me. I invite the Pan Am steward to come in. After all this time and the number of letters he has delivered, I still don't know the man's name.

I hold the door for Catherine as she enters the suite. Seeing the man politely waiting, she looks at me with a quizzical expression.

"A letter home," I say.

I go to the table and pick up the envelope. As I hand it to the man I ask, "Dollars or pounds?"

He looks at Catherine, and in his obvious American English says, "Um, no offense, but the way the war is going, U.S. dollars please."

Catherine, feigning indignation, stomps a foot, throws her head back and says, "O ye of little faith."

The poor man turns beet red in embarrassment and starts to apologize.

Catherine laughs, pats him on the shoulder and says, "I can't blame you."

"I'm sure you'll win," the man quickly says, "but not for a while."

"Probably true," she agrees.

I pay the courier with a U.S. twenty—I'm still spending Dad's cash— and send him on his way.

"What was that about?" she asks after he is gone.

"He works for Pan Am, a steward on the clipper out of Southampton. He makes a lot more money delivering illicit mail back to the States than he does on his job."

"Take advantage of it now," she says as she lights one of my cigarettes and takes a seat at the table. "Word is the French are signing an armistice any day. When that happens, the German air force will get serious about coming after us. Your postal service may end."

"Hello," I say as I bend down to kiss her.

She returns it and says, "I'm glad you made it back." Picking up a glass carafe, she asks, "Is this orange juice? Where and how are they getting it?"

"I don't know," I reply.

Catherine downs a large swallow from the glass she has filled. "My God, that is good. As long as you can get it, have it delivered."

"Yes, your Majesty," I say as I respectfully bow my head.

"Shag off," she says, then drinks some more.

"You know, I think your language has gotten worse. You're seeing a little too much of Charlie and Clive."

"Yes, and not enough of you. Are you done rushing back and forth to France for a while?"

"It appears so," I say. "Are you working today?"

"I'm going to Winnie's speech in a while. Aren't you?"

"Yes," I tell her. "Can you get me a good seat next to yours?"

"No, sorry. I told you, you have to flash the old boys a little leg to get the railing seat. I've seen yours and it won't work. Mind you, I like them but…"

"Are you working tonight?" I ask.

"Yes, I am," she says crushing out her cigarette. "I've got a bit of an odd duty to help with. There's some French general in town. He fled France on a destroyer and refuses to accept the surrender that's coming. The BBC, at the request of Winnie, is going to let him broadcast a speech to the people of France. I hear he's going to tell the French people not to quit, to resist the Germans."

"What's his name?"

"Charles de Gaulle. Have you heard of him?" Catherine asks.

"Yes, he was at Tours," I say. "Very tall man, six-five or six-six. I have heard he's pretty full of himself and sees himself as the next Joan of Arc, the next savior of France."

"The next savior of France will be American soldiers carrying the Stars and Stripes," Catherine says.

"Alongside their British cousins," I add.

"There's Catherine," Charlie says pointing toward the gallery entrance to Parliament.

Catherine sees the four of us, Charlie, Clive, David and me, waiting to go inside. She is in the midst of a crowd of journalists and excitedly waves at us. The mob is pushing her inside, and she blows me a kiss from the doorway.

Charlie looks me over and with a puzzled expression says, "I don't get it. What does she see in you?"

"I have no idea," I say.

"Especially with me available," Charlie continues.

"That's an excellent point," I sarcastically agree. Charlie's a great guy and an outstanding friend. But physically, he won't replace Tyrone Power or Cary Grant in the movies any time soon.

***

We have been waiting for almost three hours for Churchill to speak. The gallery, except for the section reserved for the House of Lords, has been full the entire afternoon. For almost an hour, the members have been in attendance, and so far, the only thing happening is routine business, business that I find almost incomprehensible.

Churchill arrived a few minutes ago, greeted the members seated directly behind him, then took his seat. He has been waiting patiently.

"So, any time now?" I ask Clive who is sitting next to me.

"Yes," he agrees. "Should be soon."

"Do you understand what has been going on down there?" I ask.

"Some of it," he says with a laugh. "Mostly minor business that even the members don't care much about."

"What do you think he'll say?"

Clive pauses for a moment thinking about the question. "I think Winston Churchill is about to give the speech of his career, a speech that you will tell your grandchildren about with tears in your eyes at your good fortune to be here in person to have witnessed."

"Shh, here he goes," David quietly says from Clive's right.

I look at my watch and make a note of the time on my notebook: precisely 3.46 p.m. GMT, June 18, 1940. I have never done that before. There is something about what Clive just told me that rings true.

For the next thirty-six minutes—I have timed him—Winston Churchill holds the attention of the free world in the palm of his hand. At one point, during a pause, I glance around the gallery, and not a single person is taking notes. We are all mesmerized.

Our cabbie lets us off a block away from the Swedish Embassy. I am with Clive Burke, and we are both dressed in formal evening wear. Like most of the month, the weather is dry and warmer than usual. This evening is proving to be quite pleasant.

I received an invitation to a formal reception at the embassy. It was my intention to surprise Catherine with it, but her duties with the French general and his speech canceled my plans. I asked my friends, and Clive was the quickest to take me up on it. Besides, these events can oftentimes produce quality information—or salacious rubbish.

We are more fashionably late than most of the guests. A very charming, quite attractive, blonde woman with a Swedish accent escorts us into the reception room. Clive's tongue was almost dragging on the floor behind her. I, because of my commitment to Catherine, barely notice her; at least that is going to be my story, and I am going to stick to it.

The reception is being held for the new chargé d'affaires. The chargé of any embassy is a professional diplomat who is really the one who runs it. The blonde I barely notice, leads us to the end of the reception line. She flashes a smile that left spots like a flashbulb in my eyes, then wiggles her hips as she walks away. I, of course, continue to barely notice her. Clive tells me about it later.

"Have you ever been to Sweden?" Clive quietly asks me.

"No, in fact I haven't," I answer.

"Half of the population looks like her," he says. "The other half are men who could be her twin brother—best looking people on the planet."

"I had not noticed, and make sure you tell Catherine that," I say as I watch her escort more people in.

We make it through the reception line, then make a beeline for the open bar. While we wait for the bartender to make our drinks, Clive pokes me gently. "Over there," he says when I look at him.

I turn my head in the direction he is looking and see Ambassador Kennedy. "Who is that he's with?" I ask.

"The young woman or the two people he is talking with?"

"The young woman I assume is one of his numerous nieces visiting from the States," I say. "Who are the two men?"

"I believe one of them, the shorter one, is the ambassador from Spain. I think the other one is an aide and the ambassador's very close friend," Clive replies with a wink.

"Thank you," I say to the bartender as he hands us our drinks. I drop a five-pound note in the large snifter being used for tips.

"That's too much," Clive says. "You damn Yanks are always trying to make us look cheap."

"He'll remember me," I say. "Let's go say hello to Joe."

We walk toward Kennedy and his 'niece'—a long-legged, auburn-haired young woman—and when we get ten feet from him, the Spaniards slide away. The 'niece' is clinging to his arm with a bored expression.

"Well, hello," Kennedy says when he sees us. He reaches toward me with his right hand causing the 'niece' to let go. "Jeff, good to see you again. And Mr. Burke, glad you could make it."

He does not bother to introduce the 'niece,' and after a minute, she sets her glass on a waiter's tray and excuses herself. For a niece from America, she has an unusually distinct British accent.

"How did you like Winston's speech today?" he asks us both. "I assume you were there, as was I."

"Incredibly inspiring, Mr. Ambassador," I say.

"Yes, he certainly is," Kennedy agrees. "You disagree, don't you, Jeff, that we should stay out of it?"

I think about a diplomatic answer then say, "I wish we could, Mr. Ambassador, but we aren't going to be able to. Hitler isn't just a menace to Britain."

"You may be right," Kennedy admits. "You just may be right. I hate the thought of American boys dying in Europe again," he soberly adds.

I see him look across the room before he says, "Excuse me fellas. I need to say hello to some people. Stick around. We'll have a drink together."

Clive and I watch him walk off as Clive says, "That man is absolutely insufferable."

I chuckle and say, "He's not so bad. He just says what most Americans believe—"

I stop when I see them. Walking away from the reception line are two British army officers. That, in itself, is hardly unusual; there are probably a couple of dozen in this room. These two catch my eye because one of them is Major General Sir Dalton Floyd, Deputy Chief of War Plans. With him is a lieutenant colonel whose sighting turns me to ice. It is the recent Captain Arthur Ashland apparently promoted jumping two spots up the ranks. On his left breast pocket is a shiny new medal. On his arm is a comely young woman, at most twenty-years-old.

"It's a good thing you don't have a gun," Clive whispers to me.

"Yes, it is," I agree. "How did that bastard get promoted, and what is that medal he is wearing?"

"I don't know about the promotion, but I do believe the medal is the Military Cross. It is one of the highest awards for valor that we have. There are only a couple higher than that."

I watch the arrogant coward with his latest young concubine trail the general for a few minutes. Clive goes to the bar to get fresh cocktails while I remember Dunkirk.

"Here," Clive says then hands me a glass.

"Thanks. I think I need some air," I say.

"You want some company?"

"No, not right now. Thanks," I reply.

I am standing at the granite balustrade of the embassy's first floor balcony smoking and sipping my drink. Clive must have told the bartender to make it straight whiskey. There are fifteen to twenty people out here. It is a large terrace, and I am off by myself. I finish my cigarette then hear the voice from behind me.

"So you're the bloody Yank who's been shagging my wife," I hear him say.

I turn around, and he is smugly smiling at me.

"Don't worry old boy, I don't much care what she does. I do wish she'd be more discreet, and with a Yank, no less. Well, there's no accounting for taste."

"Like you and your trollop du jour," I toss back at him.

"It's different for men, especially men in my position…"

"You're everything I have heard you are and a lot less. Or lower I guess would be more accurate," I say.

"Watch yourself, Yank," he snarls. I have hit a nerve which makes me smile.

"Do I look familiar to you?" I ask.

He is slightly taken aback by the question and is no longer showing anger.

"I'm not surprised you don't recognize me, but I recognize you. Not because of Catherine. No, I was on the boat. The one that saved your sorry ass at Dunkirk. I also know how much you deserve your promotion and your shiny new medal.

"You see, Arthur"—I say his name derisively intentionally leaving out his title and military rank—"I was told by a witness that your regimental commander, a Colonel Houle, ordered you to stay and be the last man of the regiment off the beach. You disobeyed his order, didn't you?"

He stares at me, the color drained from his face and the arrogance gone, at least for the moment.

"Not exactly the act of a man deserving an award of valor for heroism."

"It's a lie and you can't prove it. Houle's dead. He never gave me any such order, and you had better be aware of British libel laws," he says.

"I know British libel laws. And I know how protected you are. But I also know, and so do you, how much you really deserve that medal. Desertion in the face of the enemy… You, sir, are lower than whale shit, and we both know it."

SEVENTEEN

June 19, 1940

Dear Mom & Dad,

We were all in attendance at Parliament yesterday for Churchill's latest speech. It was rebroadcast to the States last night, and I hope you heard it. If not, whatever you have to do to get a copy of it, Dad, do it. It will go down in history as one of the greatest speeches of all time. Of that, I have no doubt.

Winnie quoted the top French general, Weygand, as saying the Battle of France is over. The Battle of Britain is about to begin. He spoke of its importance not just for Britain but civilization itself. It is not hyperbole. He meant it and it is true.

He ended with a paragraph that will one day be his epitaph. It is already extremely popular that it is in the newspapers. It is being called Churchill's 'Finest Hour' speech. If you have not heard it, this is verbatim, how he ended it:

"But if we fail, then the whole world, including the United States, including all that we have known and cared for, will sink into the abyss of a new dark age made more sinister and perhaps more protracted by the lights of perverted science. Let us therefore brace ourselves to our duties and so bear ourselves, that if the British Empire and its Commonwealth last for a thousand years, men will still say, 'This was their finest hour.'"

You have probably heard by now, a hero of the Great War, Phillipe Petain, has taken over as Premier of France. This was two days ago. The first thing he did was request an armistice. This surprised no one.

When we were in France, the leadership, both civilian and military, not only were whipped but they looked it—with one exception. Last night a French general, a very junior one who fled France and refused to surrender, broadcast a speech to France via the BBC. Catherine was there when he did it.

Our small caravan of six cars stops on a hill overlooking the English Channel. We have been on the road since nine a.m. and it is after one. We have stopped on a cliff that, we are told, is on the coast near Dover. To our left, approximately a mile from us, is a small building with four tall metal towers. They look like some type of radio antennae.

David and I walk down to the edge of the cliff. I have a pair of high-powered binoculars we use to scan the sea and the opposite shore. From here, it is barely twenty miles to the coast of France. Even without the binoculars, we can see the French coast. With the binoculars, we can clearly see small German navy boats cruising along the shoreline. Including drivers, there are more than twenty of us in our entourage. After ten minutes or so, almost all of them, including Clive and Charlie, have joined us. We are passing the binoculars around. I light a cigarette—it is fairly windy on top of this cliff—and hold my lighter for David.

"It doesn't look like much of an obstacle from here, does it?" I say to no one in particular.

"Don't kid yourself, it is a damn difficult piece of water to get across," a man I don't know replies.

David and I both jerk our heads to the right, Clive and Charlie did not hear the man because of the wind. Shocked, we both stare at the man without speaking.

"Mike Burns," the man says with his obvious American accent.

He is in his mid-thirties, has a full head of sandy blonde hair, and is about six feet tall and trim. He is in an off-the-rack sports coat and slacks.

David and I introduce ourselves. He asks if he may borrow my cigarette lighter, and when he hands it back to me, he speaks again.

"Lieutenant Commander Michael Burns, assistant Naval Attaché at the U.S. Embassy," he says. "And you are newspapermen with the *New York Gazette* and the *Washington Clarion*. Your friends are Clive Burke with the *Daily Herald* and Charlie Dolan with the *Philadelphia Dispatch*. And that, gentlemen, is the English Channel, and it will be the graveyard of the German army and most of its navy before they get across it."

"That's comforting," David says.

By now, Clive and Charlie have joined us and introduce themselves to our newly discovered American Navy expert.

"Unless," Burns continues, "the Luftwaffe can gain total air superiority first. It's possible they can, but they are going to have to do it soon."

"You sound pretty sure of yourself," Clive says with a touch of skepticism.

Burns crushes his cigarette underfoot then says, "The U.S. Navy and Marines have been working on this problem for a decade. An amphibious landing against a hostile shore is the most difficult military operation there is—always has been. The British will sacrifice both the Royal Navy, still the largest and best in the world, and the RAF to stop it. And the Germans have a helluva fight waiting for them. They're going to have to wipe out the RAF ahead of time, and it won't be easy."

Burns turns back toward our caravan of cars and points at a large, green tent that has been set up by our British hosts. "In the tent, they're going to serve us some lunch and then give us a lecture on why it won't be easy." He smiles and says, "You'll learn a lot. Shall we go?"

For the next two hours, we receive an almost inedible army lunch and a lecture. The food will, I assume, sustain life. The lecture was absolutely captivating.

The British have invented a use of radio waves to detect airplanes in flight. They call it RDF, short for Range and Direction Finding. To make a long and technical story short, the British are able to detect German aircraft as they take off from their bases in France. They not only spot them, but they can count the number and track them to their targets. This allows the British fighters to stay on the ground until the last minute and be waiting for the Germans before they arrive—an enormous advantage. Of course, this is one of the most highly classified secrets the British have. We are all treated to threats of hanging if we divulge a word of it.

*****

"So, that's what those four tall antennae are all about?" I say looking north toward a small building.

The lunch and lecture are over, and we are outside the tent where it was given to us. The people who came with us and were inside are all milling about. Most of us are smoking and talking in whispers. Why we are all whispering, I don't know; there is no one within a couple of miles of us, and they are the people working in the RDF building. The building is called, we are told, a Chain Home Station. It is one of many spread along the shore of Britain facing Europe and circling the southern shore and around the western shore of the UK: a chain of RDF sites to watch for German aircraft.

"Yes, that's what those towers are for," our Navy friend answers.

The wind has died down which makes using my lighter easier. I light the cigarette of Mike Burns for him then pass the lighter to the others. We, the four of us, are huddled around Lt. Commander Burns.

"Do we have this?" David asks him, meaning America.

"Yes," Burns answers. "We call it radar, radio detection and ranging," he adds. "But the Brits are years ahead of us. We have military and scientific people here trying to get them to let us have their technology. So far, they're a little reluctant. I think if we get in with them, they'd open up.

"Everything you find out here today is absolutely classified and not for publication. But that," he says, pointing with his thumb over his right shoulder at the RDF installation, "is another reason the Germans won't have an easy time invading."

"You said something before," Clive says, "about if they're going to come, it better be soon. What did you mean?"

"Well, two things," Burns replies. "One, every day the British get stronger. I can't give you numbers, but they are building aircraft, especially fighters, as fast as they can. And then there's the weather. Like I said, the U.S. Navy and Marines have been working on this for years. Maybe the most important thing an invasion force needs is good weather and calm seas. After the first of October, the weather over the Channel can get pretty nasty."

"It not only can, but always does get pretty nasty," Clive says.

"So, if they don't come in the next three months, they'll have to wait for spring?" Charlie asks.

"Yes," Burns says. "You can't just put a couple hundred thousand soldiers in boats and send them here. Most of them, even in good weather, won't make it. In bad weather, it will be a catastrophe."

"Well," Clive says looking out over the Channel, "I don't know about you lads, but I thank God for the English Channel."

The remainder of the afternoon is spent visiting several beach areas that are believed to be possible landing zones. We are taken there to be shown the defensive steps the British have taken. Even to my untrained eye, I can tell they are woefully inadequate. Most of what we see could not stop a single German tank. But then, as our British host points out, they will have a difficult time putting tanks ashore.

After visiting the last one, we stop for dinner at a pub in a village a few miles south of Dover. The lieutenant commander, who is not riding in our car, joins us. Apparently, someone with our entourage has gone ahead to warn the pub owner we are coming. He is ready for us and has us all served with a local dish vaguely resembling stew and potatoes. After the lunch we had, it is a gift from heaven.

"Love these old British pubs," Lt. Commander Burns says looking around.

There is a clatter of dishes and tableware and very little conversation going around. I think everyone is getting a little tired and hungry.

"Look at these ceiling beams," Burns continues. "Some of them must be a hundred years old."

"Well, Commander," Clive says, "I feel much better about our chances against the Germans."

"Sorry, you shouldn't," Burns says flicking the ashes of his cigarette into the ashtray. "What we saw on the beaches is a joke. Plus, the German's airborne forces are extremely good. The Luftwaffe could easily drop thirty to forty thousand of them behind the beaches. They could grab a landing strip and hold it while the Luftwaffe flies in another hundred thousand soldiers. They will still need the seaborne landings, but with airborne forces already ashore, it would be a lot easier.

"To be blunt, if the RAF and the Royal Navy don't stop them before the weather turns bad, they can pull it off. Sorry," he says again. "Right now, it's about fifty-fifty they can do it. Hold on until October. After that, you should be okay."

It is after nine p.m. when the cab pulls up in front of the Ritz. Of course, the blackout has begun which normally makes for an interesting cab ride. It has been a long day, and I am too tired to even notice.

On my way through the hotel's lobby, I hear a man's voice calling my name. It is the night attendant behind the reception area. I look at him and see he has a piece of notepaper in his hand, holding it up, waving it at me.

"A message?" I ask as pleasantly as I can when I get to the counter.

"Yes, sir. We took a call a couple of hours ago. The man who called said it was quite urgent," the clerk replies.

Given British understatement, the term 'quite urgent' likely means close to a national emergency. I thank him for it, and as I walk away, I unfold the note and read it.

6:45 p.m.

Mr. Bartlett,

I am Catherine's brother, Alex. There has been a tragedy in the family. She will need you. Please pack a bag and come to the Fulham house immediately.

Alex Hartley

I don't bother to wait for the elevator. Instead, I first turn to yell back at the man behind the reception counter to get a cab for me. He nods his understanding, and lugging my bag, I sprint up the stairs to my room.

I hurry as quickly as possible, throwing enough clothing and toiletries into a small suitcase to last a couple of days. I run back down the stairs, through the lobby and out the front door. It has been less than ten minutes, and a cab is already waiting for me at the curb.

As I climb in the back, I give the driver Catherine's address, toss a twenty-pound note on the front seat and anxiously tell him to hurry.

The front door opens and a man in an RAF uniform is standing there. Alex Hartley, Catherine's older brother, could be her fraternal twin with a slight age difference. He has a sad, worried demeanor to go along with red-rimmed eyes.

"Jeff Bartlett," I say and automatically extend my right hand.

"Alex Hartley," he quietly replies as we briefly shake hands. "Come in please, Jeff."

He closes the door behind us and gently takes my elbow to lead me into the living room.

I set my suitcase down, slip off my raincoat, look at Alex and ask, "Is it Tom?"—their younger brother.

"I'm afraid so," he quietly says.

"Catherine must be crushed. How are your parents holding up?"

"Not well," he replies. "I'm glad you're here. She's been asking for you. I'm needed with our parents."

"I'm terribly sorry," I say. "Tell me what happened," I add as we sit down in separate chairs.

"He was serving on HMS Glorious, a First War battlecruiser converted to be an aircraft carrier. I don't know the full details except Glorious was caught by the German battleship Scharnhorst and sunk on June 8. We just received notice today. She went down with twelve hundreds of her crew, including Tommy," Alex tells me.

"Oh my God! Twelve hundred?"

"Yes, that's been confirmed. Catherine is in her bedroom. Go to her. She'll need you now. Please do what you can."

"Of course, of course," I say. "I am so sorry to meet you like this. I wish I knew what to say."

"Yes, I'm sorry to meet you like this, too. Catherine says you're a good man. I can see that. For a Yank," he adds with a rueful smile.

I stand in her bedroom doorway for a minute watching her. There is a light from a table lamp illuminating her on the bed. Catherine is dressed in slacks and is curled up, her knees almost to her chin. I silently go to the side of her bed and sit down next to her.

"Hey," I quietly say gently brushing her hair from her face.

Catherine opens her eyes, sees me, then gets on her knees and wraps her arms around my neck, her face against my cheek. I hold her like this, expecting tears, but she has no more.

"My Tommy's gone. My little brother, my wonderful, fun, beautiful Tommy, gone forever," she quietly says.

"I know, baby, I know," is about all I am able to say.

EIGHTEEN

June 23, 1940

Dearest Mom & Dad,

First, some bad news which I am sure you have already heard. France officially capitulated yesterday. To rub their noses in it and complete their humiliation, Hitler chose the site of the 1918 Armistice for the ceremony. The Germans even used the exact same railroad car and had it placed in the same spot as it was in November 1918. Who says revenge cannot be sweet? I'm sure Hitler and his Nazi pals are savoring every moment of it.

Now for the very bad news. Catherine received the news that her younger brother, Tom, was killed. He was in the Royal Navy serving aboard the HMS Glorious. Glorious was a battlecruiser converted to an aircraft carrier. On June 8, it was attacked and sunk by the German battleship, Scharnhorst. Glorious went down with twelve hundred members of her crew. At this time, we have not been given the number of survivors, if any.

It is difficult to express how I feel. Catherine, who loved her 'little brother, Tommy,' was all but immobilized for a couple of days. Obviously, she is still in mourning, her grief still almost inconsolable. But she is getting better. We're going to a funeral service for him at the family church this afternoon. It is an Anglican (Protestant) church by the name of St. Mark-le-Bow, a sad affair I am not looking forward to attending.

The war finally hit home for me. A fine young man with a long life to live is gone. He died along with hundreds of other fine young men, swallowed up by the sea. And for what? Already there have been tens of thousands of fine young men and women and children gone forever. And tens of thousands of mothers, fathers, brothers and sisters grievously stricken over their loss, including the Germans. Yes, they started it. But it is the young who are taken.

Before this war is over, there will be millions more who will be sacrificed to defeat Hitler. What a horrible waste. They are not statistics to me anymore. They will no longer be faceless images of soldiers, sailors and airmen. They are sons and daughters, husbands and wives, brothers and sisters. Real people will hurt grievously over the loss of every one of them.

Sorry, I'm getting a little melancholy here. It does hurt. Tom's death somehow makes it more real, more personal, even though I never met him.

Other than that, I'm fine. The war has actually quieted down, but there's still a lot of talk of invasion. I met our assistant naval attaché a few days ago, a Lt. Commander Mike Burns. He is a source of information and insight and seems to be a good man.

He tells us if the Germans try to cross the Channel, it will be their graveyard. Plus, it is his opinion that if they don't come before October, they won't come at all. The weather will stop them. Right now, the weather could not be better. We'll just have to wait and hope for the best. We'll see.

All my love,

Jeff

I am uncomfortably sitting in the front row of St. Mark-le-Bow in Blankford, Sussex. Catherine's brother Alex is, by agreement, sitting between Catherine and me. She is still married and small towns in England are no different than small towns in America when it comes to gossip. The Hartleys have enough to deal with due to Tom's death without vicious whispers about Catherine's affair with a Yank. I totally agree.

The minister—they are also called priests or even 'Father'—is droning on about Tom. This man knew him and the entire family well. Since I was introduced as Alex's friend, he was very nice to me. It seems to be quite the novelty having an American in attendance. Catherine tells me I will be the talk of the town before the day is over. She also doesn't believe we are fooling anyone.

I am trying to pay attention, but I am a little too awed by the church itself. I was told it is over two hundred years old, and the style of architecture helps me believe it. Except, the building doesn't show the wear of a building more than twenty years old, if that. The place is absolutely amazing, a picture postcard of an English country church. Beautiful. Catherine has told me these people take their religion seriously. I believe it. The town is also the image of what you would expect of an English Village.

Blankford, Sussex is a little more than a one-hour train ride from London's Waterloo Station. Because Alex was late, we could not catch the train we originally wanted. When we arrived, we barely had time to make it to the church. I was quickly introduced to Catherine's parents minutes before we were seated with them. Their names are George and Harriet Hartley.

The service ends at two o'clock, and we all walk the few short blocks to the Hartley home. Harriet was amazingly tranquil. For a mother who has lost a son, she is handling herself with incredible aplomb. I already greatly admire her.

Since I am supposedly Alex's friend, Catherine all but ignores me while at her parents' home. I don't know anyone which leaves me sitting by myself observing the scene. At one point, George brings a chair over and we chat for a few minutes. Mostly he is interested in America and slyly getting information about me. I hope I meet with his approval.

Alex needs to catch the 3.40 train to London to be back on time. Shortly after three, he and I gather up Catherine, say our goodbyes and get ready to leave. While the two of them are with their mother, George pulls me aside.

"You're a far better man than that bastard she's married to, that's easy to see," he says.

I'm not surprised he saw through our little charade, but it still leaves me speechless for a moment.

"Oh, come on, lad. Did you think your story about being Alex's friend fooled anyone?" he asks with a nice smile. "Harriet and the other women all think you're damn good looking, too," he adds.

"Well, we tried," I say. "The plan was to not provide the town with gossip."

"Oh, for God's sake, Jeff. That's the least of our concerns," he says with a laugh. More softly he says, "Be nice to my little girl."

"Mr. Hartley—"

"George," he says.

"George," I say continuing, "I worship the ground she walks on."

"I know," he says. "Her mother told me she could see it by the way you look at her."

I see Catherine and Alex coming toward us, obviously ready to leave. I turn back to their father and shake his hand. "I'm terribly sorry about

Tom," I say. "I am pleased to have met you and your lovely wife, sir. Although I wish it could have been under better circumstances."

We are lying side-by-side in bed, naked, holding hands, completely sated from our lovemaking. Catherine crushes her cigarette in the ashtray on my stomach. She picks it up and places it on the nightstand next to her. As she rolls over, Catherine pulls the blankets up with her and crawls on top of me. While she purrs like a contented kitten in my ear, I hold her and savor her scent, softness and warmth.

"Can we stay like this forever?" she whispers.

"Sorry, like most women, you have a bladder about the size of my thumb—"

She pinches my side and gently bites my shoulder.

"Owww!" I yelp.

"Be nice," she says. Her arms are around my neck, and she tightens her grip on me. "Thank you for being here for me," she says.

"That's part of the job, ma'am," I reply trying to imitate Gary Cooper. "And my pleasure. You know, we didn't fool your parents one bit."

Catherine laughs, buries her face in my neck and says, "I knew we wouldn't. You can't stop looking at me." She pushes herself up on her right elbow, looks down at me and adds, "I don't blame you. It's my magnetism. Men can't resist."

"The only one I'm concerned about is me," I reply. "I admit it, I'm lost."

Catherine snuggles against me while still lying on top of me and simply says, "Good."

We stay this way for a couple of minutes, and I feel myself slipping off to sleep. Catherine kisses my cheek and quietly says, "I need to talk to you about something."

"What?" I barely mutter.

"Sorry, you need to wake up. It's serious, and I've been putting it off for a couple of days," she says.

"You figure you have me in the right mood now?"

"Jeff, please," she says, almost pleading.

"Wow, this is serious," I reply as she rolls off me to my left. I push myself up onto my elbows and look down at her, in the dark. A light comes on when she reaches over to the nightstand and turns on a lamp.

"Okay, what's wrong?"

"There's something you don't know about me because, until now, there was no reason to tell you. Oh, don't look so shocked and concerned. It's not a bad thing."

"Okay," I say relieved.

"I'm a member of the Women's Auxiliary Air Force. I'm what is called a WAAF. Technically, I am part of the reserve forces. I was called up to active duty last October and served for several weeks, mostly training. The BBC was able to get me back because the RAF was persuaded that I could do at least as much for the war effort with the BBC than what I was trained for," she explains.

I let my head fall back onto my pillow and silently stare at the ceiling for three or four seconds. "You're going back," I quietly say.

"Yes," she replies.

Still staring at the ceiling, I say, "The BBC is right. You're doing more for the war effort—"

"I don't care," she says. "I don't believe that, and more importantly, it's time I did my duty," she says.

I angrily toss the blankets aside, get up and put on a bathrobe. I turn on the table lamp on my side of the bed, find my cigarettes and light one. Wordlessly, I pace about the bedroom trying to suppress what I want to say. This goes on, the silence between us, for a full minute before she speaks.

"Don't be angry, please. It's something I must do. We'll still see each other. I love you. That has not changed."

I stop pacing while she says this and look down at her. There are tears in her eyes which soften me considerably, but the tears don't stop me. I finally say what I have been trying to avoid.

"You can't make up for Tommy's death, no matter how guilty you may feel."

"How dare you!" she yells back. The tears are flowing now. She sobs and says, "I have to do something. I have to do my part."

"You are," I reply still staring down at her.

Like most men, I have never handled a crying woman well. She turns her head from me and pulls the blanket up to her chin. I am on the verge of melting. I can feel it coming on and am helpless to stop it. Before I even realize it, I have put out my cigarette and am holding her in my arms.

While the sobs continue and the tears flow, I gently rock her and quietly assure her I am with her on this. I'm not, not really, but what choice do I have? I realize I am being selfish, although I don't care. The Germans are going to attack. They already have with sporadic air raids. What if she is assigned to a high-priority target? I push that thought down as deeply as I can, but it won't go away. Not completely.

"When do you leave?" I ask.

We are seated at my dining room table, the one I work at when writing. The map of the Battle of France is still on the wall. It serves as a reminder, as if I need one, of what could come to London.

Catherine knocks the ash off of her cigarette into the ashtray. "A few days," she vaguely replies.

"What's a few days?"

"Next Monday. I have a week. I have to report next Monday at eight a.m."

"Where are you going?"

"I can't tell you that," she says.

"Really? What will you be doing?" I ask.

"I can't tell you that, either," she replies.

"What—?"

"It's a highly classified thing. Please, Jeff, can't you just trust me?"

"Of course, I trust you," I say with a shrug. "I'm just curious."

Catherine stubs out her cigarette, stands up and sits on my lap. She puts her arms around my neck and her cheek against mine. "I'll come back every chance I get and shag you till you're mush."

"Deal," I say smiling.

"Now carry me back to bed and make love to me again."

BOOK TWO

Catherine
and
The Battle of Britain

NINETEEN

July 5, 1940

The dull green British Army staff car turned into the short driveway at the Swingate Chain Home Station a short distance north of Dover. The driver, an army corporal, turned the car to his right to stop parallel to the small building. Before the corporal could exit the car to open the doors for his passengers, an RAF sergeant, who was standing by, beat him to it.

The corporal/driver watched the two army officers walk toward the building with a sense of relief. One of the men, a major general, was a legitimate VIP. The other, a lieutenant colonel, was an arrogant ass who thought he was God's gift to the world. The corporal was relieved to have a break from the demanding lieutenant colonel.

The sergeant ran to the small building while the two men stared at four tall skeletal towers. A minute or so later, the two men reached the door held by the sergeant. The older and senior of the two, the major general, returned the sergeant's salute and thanked him. The younger lieutenant colonel ignored him completely.

Once inside, they were spotted by an RAF group captain, the station's commanding officer, Boyd Robinson. "Good afternoon, sir," Robinson said to General Dalton Floyd. "I see you made it all right."

Floyd returned Robinson's salute, and the two of them shook hands.

"Yes, we made it. This is Lieutenant Colonel Arthur Ashland, my adjutant," Floyd said introducing the two men.

"Welcome to Swingate Chain Home Station," Robinson said. "You're just in time. It looks like Jerry is sending a few planes up, probably Stuka dive bombers. There is an eight-ship convoy entering the Straits. We'll probably see some action."

The Swingate Chain Home Station was one of the first of what the British called RDF stations. A string of Chain Home stations was built before the war along the coast from northern Scotland all the way around the UK to the west coast of England then back north to the west coast of

Scotland. They were the first early warning radar network in the world. During the coming Battle of Britain, they would play a tremendously important part.

The building was essentially a large room where members of the Women's Auxiliary Air Force worked. While technicians manned the scopes to detect the planes, the techs would call out the number, location and altitude of the enemy aircraft. The WAAFs would then position models on a horizontal large map in the center of the room on a table. Others would relay this information by telephone to RAF Fighter Command at Bentley Priory.

Circling the room and slightly above it was a walkway with a railing. There was also a section for a command post—a desk—for the commanding officer and others to oversee the operation.

"Follow me, please, General," Robinson said. "We'll watch from in front. You'll get a better view."

As the three of them walked around to the command post, one of the women below followed the men with her eyes. She was standing almost directly beneath the command station wearing a telephone headset. Catherine Hartley—she was using her maiden name—felt her stomach become nauseous at the sight of her abusive husband. The sight of the lieutenant colonel trailing the Deputy Chief of War Plans rattled her to the point where she wanted to flee. Instead, she concentrated even more than she normally did on doing her job. It was extremely important to relay as quickly as possible absolutely accurate information to Fighter Command. With her back to the three senior officers above and behind her, Catherine could only hope Arthur had not noticed her.

For the next twenty minutes, Group Captain Robinson explained to his two visitors what the various personnel were doing. While he did this, a young lieutenant bounced up the stairs from the floor below.

"Sir," the lieutenant said to Robinson as he handed him a single sheet of paper.

"Thank you, Cal," Robinson said.

He read over the summary report then told General Floyd what it was. "It seems we have a twelve-plane squadron from Calais being joined by twenty-four others out of Cap Gris-Nez. Those from Calais would be Stuka dive bombers, and the other twenty-four are probably Messerschmitt fighters. They'll go after the convoy but what they are really up to is seeing if we respond with our fighters. Essentially, General, the Jerrys are baiting us to come after them. They want to see our tactical response.”

“Will we respond?” General Floyd asked.

“No, I doubt it. Of course, that’s up to Vice Marshall Dowding, but I don’t believe we will.”

“They’ll go after the convoy of merchant ships?” Floyd asked.

“Yes, sir,” Robinson answered. “If you’d like, my people can handle this without me. We can use your car to run over to the coast and watch the show. It’s barely half a mile.”

“Yes, let’s do that. Splendid idea,” Floyd said.

“Um, uh, won’t the planes come after us, I mean, if they see three British officers on the cliff watching?” Arthur Ashland asked with a slight quiver in his voice.

“Not likely,” Robinson replied. “We could bring guns and shoot back.”

“Yes! Let’s do that,” Floyd said enthusiastically with a laugh.

Oh, by all means, Ashland thought, significantly less enthused.

“Martin,” Robinson said, looking at a sergeant, “be a good man and find some glasses and handguns for us.”

“Yes, sir,” the sergeant replied. Sergeant Martin was originally army then switched to the RAF. He had been an outstanding soldier. “Sir, how about if I ride along?”

“We’ll be fine, Johnny; don’t worry,” Robinson replied.

Fifteen minutes later the three of them were standing in ankle deep grass atop the White Cliffs of Dover. Each man held binoculars to his eyes scanning the Straits of Dover where the English Channel met the North Sea. It was a bright, warm, sunny day with only a few fluffy, white clouds in the sky. They could see the eight merchant ships slowly plowing north toward the Thames Estuary. Each ship appeared to be between five and eight thousand tons. They were fairly small cargo ships.

“There’s a destroyer escort with the convoy,” Robinson remarked.

“Yes, I see her,” General Floyd replied.

“She’s searching for submarines,” Robinson added. “Although I’m sure her captain is aware of the threat of aircraft along here.”

Floyd removed his field glasses from his eyes, looked at Robinson and asked, “Has he been warned?”

“You mean of what we know?”

“Yes, of course,” Floyd said.

"No, sir. We do not send out radio warnings to the ships. The Germans will intercept them and figure out how we know this. No, sir, better to leave them on their own than to give away our secret."

"Yes, of course," Floyd quietly agreed. "That makes sense."

A few minutes later, the first four Stukas started their attack. For the next twenty minutes, in waves of four planes each, the dive bombers went after the slow-moving ships. Each plane carried a single 250-kilogram bomb, and not a single hit on any of the ships was scored. The covering anti-aircraft fire from the destroyer helped. Stukas are slow airplanes, and to dive straight down into anti-aircraft fire is extremely unnerving. It certainly would not help the pilot's ability to aim.

"Why don't we have anti-aircraft guns along the cliffs up here and the shoreline?" Floyd asked.

"We've requested them, sir. We've been told they are in the pipeline," Robinson replied.

"Yes," Floyd quietly said. "Everyone is clamoring for their own specific needs. It all takes time, I'm afraid."

While this was taking place, the three officers, even without binoculars, could see the German fighter planes. For the most part, they did little except fly in lazy circles above the convoy. At one point, two of them flew along the cliff past the three men watching—their driver was hiding behind the car—close enough to see the pilots' faces. Arthur Ashland squeezed his eyes shut and held his breath. General Floyd held his revolver up threatening to shoot. The second pilot, seeing this, smiled and saluted.

As the three officers walked back toward the staff car, Floyd remarked, "Quite a show. I'm glad I got a chance to get out of London and see it. What do you think, Ashland?" he asked Arthur.

During the entire time, from the moment they left the Chain Home building. Arthur Ashland had not uttered a peep. He was wiping his brow with a handkerchief when his boss asked for his opinion.

"Oh, um, yes, quite a show, sir," Ashland replied.

"Are you all right, Arthur?" Floyd asked.

"Oh, yes, of course. I was, um, just so worried about the people on those ships. They, uh, well, seem to be so vulnerable; sitting ducks, as it were," Ashland answered.

"Yes, that's true," Floyd quietly agreed. "Well, cheer up, they made it through. How about some lunch, gentlemen? I'm famished."

Catherine and a dozen or so of her WAAF comrades were out back of the Chain Home building. The raid on the convoy was over, and the RDF was no longer detecting any Luftwaffe activity. The women were sitting around what passed for a patio area, smoking, talking and enjoying the pleasant weather.

Catherine was sitting in a small circle with four of the friends she had made. None of the WAAFs knew anything about her marriage and certainly nothing about her husband inside enjoying an officers' meal. In fact, Catherine had literally said a silent prayer that Arthur had not seen her.

Suddenly, the women went silent and the four sitting with Catherine were looking past her. As the women started to quietly stand up, a lump appeared in Catherine's stomach. Fear came over her because she knew who had appeared behind her. The right hand of every one of the women came up in a salute, and they all came to attention. By now, Catherine was also standing and turned around to face her husband. Unlike the others, she did not salute or come to attention.

Lt. Colonel Ashland returned their salute then said, "If you'll excuse us, please, ladies. I'd like a private word with my wife."

The women quickly started walking away, and each of them stole a quick, curious glance at Catherine.

When they were all gone, Arthur spoke first. "It's wonderful to see you, Catherine. And you look splendid in—"

"What do you want, Arthur?" Catherine tersely asked. "I have to get back to my duties."

Ignoring her obviously hostile attitude, Arthur stepped forward and continued. "I knew you were here, and I wanted to see you. Please, sit down. I'd like to talk to you."

By now he was physically close enough and reached toward her right arm. Instinctively, Catherine jerked it away from him, took a step back and then sat back down on her canvas chair.

"What do you want, Arthur?" she repeated more quietly and with less enmity.

"I told you, I wanted to see you, talk to you," he said again.

"Why?"

Arthur retrieved a pack of Players from his blouse pocket, put one between his lips and offered Catherine one. She accepted it, and he used his gold lighter to light both while he thought about a response.

Catherine was leaning forward, her legs crossed, holding the cigarette in her right hand resting on her knee. She wore an uninterested expression while waiting for him.

Arthur exhaled a long stream of smoke, flicked ashes onto the ground then finally replied. "All right. I'll lay my cards on the table, so to speak." He drew in more cigarette smoke before continuing. "I've been a rather bad husband, a cad really…"

"You've been far worse than that," Catherine calmly said.

"Yes, point taken. I suppose you're right," he said.

"You have to see it from my point of view," Catherine said. She flicked the burning end of her cigarette off with a fingernail then field stripped the rest.

Arthur finished his and crushed it underfoot. "Of course, at any rate, the war has made me realize some things, things that are truly important. What I'm trying to say is, well, I want you back. I want to try to make it up to you. Give us another shot," he said with the sincerest look she had ever seen from him—at least since their wedding day.

Catherine sat in stunned silence for over ten seconds, staring at him as if she misheard him. "What? What did you say? Did you say you wanted us to get back together?" she finally asked.

"I knew you'd be taken aback…"

"I'm shocked down to my toes!"

"Of course. But I still believe—"

"Arthur, I am in love with someone else."

"Yes, yes, I know. The dilettante Yank you've been dallying with. You can't possibly think he's right for you. Catherine, whether you realize it or not, you are a British aristocrat. Your flirtation with this man cannot possibly last. You have nothing in common with him; you must see that."

Catherine had straightened up, her back gone stiff with the shock of his news. She leaned forward, looked Arthur squarely in the eyes and slowly shook her head. "If you mean, is he different from you and your half-mad, arrogant family, you could not be more correct. He is decent down to his bones. He is kind, caring, affectionate, and I could go on all day. He loves me, and I am absolutely mad about him. So yes, he is quite different from you."

"Sorry, Colonel," they heard a young man's voice. "The general sent me to tell you he is ready to go."

"Thank you, Corporal," Arthur replied. "I'll be there in a moment."

Arthur watched the young soldier scurry off, before turning back to Catherine. He stood up and looked at Catherine. "I'm not going to just let this go. I have no doubt you and I were meant to be together."

"Arthur, please just go. Go do your duty. I'm sure your general needs his bum kissed. Get on with it," Catherine said.

"Don't be so flippant. You're still my wife," he said, clearly annoyed by her last comment. "I could use my influence and have your Yank kicked out on his arse."

Catherine almost jumped out of her chair, snarled and said, "Do that, you bastard, and I'll desert and go with him."

"I'm sorry. I didn't mean that," Arthur contritely said. "I have to go. Take care of yourself, and think about what I said. We were meant to be together."

TWENTY

July 9, 1940

Dearest Mom & Dad,

Please forgive me, again, for not writing before this. I received your happy birthday cable late last night, and it was a verbal slap in the face. I needed it. I've been moping around for a couple of weeks, and I need to snap out of it. Your cable did the trick. Thanks.

Catherine is gone, sort of. After the death of her brother, Tom, she confessed to me she is a reservist in the Women's Auxiliary Air Force, WAAF. She has been on loan to the BBC. When Tom died, she decided it was time for her to go back on active duty. I tried to selfishly talk her out of it, but she was adamant. She has been gone for a couple of weeks, and I don't even know where she is. She can't tell me.

She writes every day, and the postal service is still operating well. I'm not sure if that helps or hurts. I am, of course, delighted to hear from her and know that she is all right. On the other hand, the letters make me miss her even more. Is that how love always is or am I... I'm not sure what? The truly good news is that she is getting a forty-eight hour pass this weekend. We will have to live a month in two days.

The invasion talk and fear have died down. It is still there, but people seem to be a lot less panicky about it. I'm not sure they should be. I'm hearing from informed sources that the Germans are moving hundreds of small boats to the French and Belgian coast. Obviously, these are to be used to ferry troops across to England. Again, my military friends say the Germans will need to establish total air superiority before they can even attempt an invasion. The Brits are already calling it the Battle of Britain and it has not even started.

There have been sporadic air raids on shipping in the English Channel. My sources—actually, by sources I pretty much mean our assistant naval attaché, Mike Burns—tell me the Germans are really trying to get the RAF

We are about an hour out of London traveling almost directly south. I still have no idea exactly where we are going. Once again, we have been invited along to tour the beaches and various defenses of the English shoreline. I originally begged off. Since Catherine's departure to fight the war, I have not been very good company.

She did manage a phone call yesterday for a birthday greeting. How she knew it was my birthday is a mystery, and she would not tell me. I feel like a love-sick schoolboy, but I can't help it. I am not sure I would if I could. I decided to tag along after talking to Catherine. Hearing her voice and making her laugh cheered me immensely. She still would not tell me where she is, and I did not ask. She only told me that she is safe and well.

The four of us, David, Charlie, Clive and I, are sharing a first-class compartment. It is Clive who convinced me to make the trip. He claims to have inside information about a large convoy that will be making its way to London. There is a good chance we may see some action. Plus, London is very quiet these days.

Clive and Charlie are both lightly snoring, and David's head is drooping. I'm about to join them. I am sitting at a window across from Charlie, silently watching the countryside go by. There is a knock on the door, and someone tries to open it. We have the interior window shades pulled down so we cannot see who it is. The knocking snaps David awake, and he unlocks the door.

Lt. Commander Mike Burns sticks his head in and looks at our sleeping companions. "May we come in?" he quietly asks.

I loudly reply, "Yes, please do." I then reach over, shake Charlie's leg and say, "Hey, we have company."

"What? Oh, who…?" Charlie sputters as Burns enters.

Burns is in civilian clothes and is followed by a trim British Army major in uniform. Clive is also awake by now and is looking over the British officer. Clive recognizes the man and slides over on the bench seat to make room for him. David does the same on our seat for Mike Burns.

"Sorry to wake you, old boy," the major says to Clive.

"It's all right, Oliver. I wasn't really sleeping," Clive replies.

Clive introduces the man to us. He is Major Oliver Evans. He is Regular Army, currently assigned to the Home Guard, he explains. The Home Guard is a volunteer force created after Dunkirk to help fight the expected invasion. Essentially, they are well-meaning amateurs who will be slaughtered like sheep if the Germans ever do arrive.

"How is the Home Guard training coming along?" Clive asks Major Evans.

"Splendidly," Evans replies. "I'm sure just the thought of having to face them will deter old Adolf."

No one laughs at the sarcasm. It is stoic, stiff-upper-lip, British humor. It only serves to remind us that if the Germans do get ashore, the British don't have much to throw at them. Most of the Home Guard don't even have rifles.

"Where are we headed, Major?" I ask him.

"Eastbourne. We'll change to staff cars there and then go to a place called Beachy Head. I'm currently with General Malcolm Hughes. We're on an inspection tour of the beaches and defenses. To be perfectly honest, if it was up to me, you gentleman would not have been invited along; no offense."

"Relax, Oliver," Clive says patting the man's knee. "We will submit our work to the censors. The Nazis won't be coming ashore on our account."

"I guess you've been asked, or more likely ordered, to be our guides and keep an eye on us," Charlie says.

"Well, in fact, yes," Major Evans replies.

"He's okay," Burns says to us, meaning Evans. "It's wartime."

The eight-car train grinds to a halt at the Eastbourne Train Station. We have been sitting continuously for more than two hours, and it feels good to get off the train and walk around. There are two other groups of journalists with British army chaperones. As we stretch, smoke and walk around, I wander off a short way by myself. I stop a few feet shy of the first car just in time to see General Hughes disembark. The general was followed off the train by four men I recognize and know fairly well.

Leading the group with his hat rakishly slanted on his head is the voice of CBS London, Edward R. Murrow. He is followed by three of his 'boys': Eric Severeid, Charles Collingwood and Howard K. Smith. Murrow sees me watching, smiles and lightly waves to me. When he does this, Collingwood and Smith break away and walk over to me.

"It must be rough to ride with the big brass," I joke as we shake hands.

"To tell you the truth, Jeff," Collingwood replies, "I'd rather be back with you guys."

"Amen to that," Smith agrees.

"Ed's idea," Collingwood says. "They treat him like royalty—"

"And we have to tag along. British generals are not great company," Smith quietly adds.

We chat for a couple of minutes until they have to leave. As they walk off, I wave to Severeid then return to my friends.

"Murrow getting the red-carpet treatment?" Charlie asks.

I shrug, then reply, "He earns it. He's the best propagandist back to America there is. His radio broadcasts are turning public opinion back home in favor of helping the British. I, for one, think that's a good thing."

We start the inspection tour with a car ride to a Chain Home Station at Beachy Point. Beachy Point is a tiny, out-of-the-way place whose main attraction is a light house in a larger area known as Beachy Head. The lighthouse is located in the water off the shoreline below the cliffs. The cliffs at Beachy Head, we are told, are also well known as a favorite place to commit suicide.

The Chain Home Station is set back from the cliffs. None of the civilians, except Murrow and his pals, are allowed into the building. We roam around bored for the half-hour or so, then get back in the cars. When we leave, we turn back the way we came and drive bad roads up the coast.

As the day wears on, we inspect six beaches as potential invasion points and four more Chain Home stations. Every one of the beaches leaves us feeling less and less confident. Most have a few anti-aircraft guns and barbed wire in place. Very few have more than a couple of machine gun emplacements or even trenches to hold defending soldiers. Even to my untrained, nonmilitary eye, it is clear the British have a lot of work to do.

"What did General Hughes have to say, Oliver?" Clive asks Major Evans.

We are seated at a large table in a pub in Folkstone. We will be spending the night here, then continuing up the coast to Dover tomorrow. It has been a long day, and we are all tired, hungry and depressed from what we have seen.

"Nothing for publication," Evans says in reply to Clive and his question regarding the general.

"Understood," Clive replies.

"He is quite displeased, to put it mildly," Evans says.

"The Germans will still have to crush the RAF," Mike Burns, the naval expert chimes in. "Unless they get total air superiority, your Navy and Air Force will turn any invasion attempt into a catastrophe."

"I hope you're right, Commander," Evans says.

"And each day that goes by, their chance of getting air superiority diminishes. The U.S. Navy has been working on this for years. Tell General Hughes that," Burns says.

"Yes, he knows. Your naval personnel have made that very clear, as have ours. Still, what we saw today is very disappointing," Evan says.

"It's better than it was a few weeks ago," I say. "You're making progress. There are at least some big guns in place."

We eat supper and spend a couple hours hanging out in the pub. When we finally call it a day, the pub owner sincerely tells us we are welcome back anytime. He has not had a day making this much money in years.

The civilians—with the exception of Murrow's group—along with Lt. Commander Mike Burns, have been driven to a point overlooking the Straits of Dover. We are all watching a large convoy of merchant ships. They are slowly making their way along the coastline as close inshore as they dare travel. Up and down the cliffs, every hundred yards or so, we can see an anti-aircraft gun emplacement.

I am one of the few not staring through binoculars watching the convoy. I am standing off by myself watching as the gun crews take to their stations. Mike Burns joins me and offers me a cigarette. As he lights it for me, he says, "They look more impressive than they are."

"The guns?" I ask.

"Yes, they won't be much help in protecting those ships. It's damn difficult to hit a dive bomber from a shore battery, even one as slow as Stukas."

Charlie joins us and asks Burns, "What is that across the Channel above Calais?" He hands Burns his glasses while pointing at dark specks in the sky.

Burns watches for over a minute and, at the same time, a car arrives behind us. I turn and see Major Evans exit the car and begin running towards us.

"Good, God!" Burns says while still watching. "They're German planes forming up. There must be at least a hundred of them."

He hands the glasses to me as Evans arrives. While I am watching, there is a loud murmuring of voices coming from the others watching the same thing.

"I've come to fetch you," Evans breathlessly says. He was having a little difficulty catching his breath—more from anxiety than exertion. "They're expecting the largest raid yet. More than a hundred planes. There are two more convoys coming in. The Germans are—"

"Starting the Battle of Britain," Clive says who has also joined us.

Evans looks at Clive and says, "Yes, it looks like it. We are responsible for your safety, and I cannot let you stay here."

"I want to stay and watch," I say.

"No. Sorry, but I've been ordered to arrest you and put you in jail if you refuse. Sorry," Evans says again.

"Have they been warned?" Charlie asks, pointing down at the ships.

"Sorry, not your concern. Now we must go."

By this point, most of the civilians have made their way back to the cars. Fifteen minutes later, we are in a sort of patio area behind the Swingate Chain Home building.

The rest of that day is worse than Dunkirk, David and I agree. We can hear the attack, the bombing and the anti-aircraft guns. Unlike Dunkirk, we can only stand around helplessly. At least at Dunkirk we were involved; we were doing something.

Charlie calmly asks Major Evans if it is safe to stay here. "Do the Germans know what those tall radio towers are for?" Charlie asks.

"We don't know what they know," Evans admits. "But we believe it is safer to stay here than be on the road. British Army staff cars might be a very inviting target for Luftwaffe fighters."

So we sit, hour after hour listening to the battle. Rumors start making the rounds about how many ships have been sunk and how many planes have been shot down. We are all veteran journalists who should know better than to listen to them. By the late afternoon, the shooting and bombing have stopped. To be on the safe side, we are ordered to stay put.

Shortly after six o'clock, the back door to the building opens, and a line of women in RAF uniforms begin to file out. While this is taking place, a corporal comes for Major Evans.

As I watch Evans hurry off, I hear a very familiar voice. "Jeff?" she says barely loud enough for me to hear. "Jeffrey!" she yells.

I turn toward the sound just in time to have Catherine run into me.

TWENTY-ONE

July 15, 1940

At the time it began, July 10, 1940, the participants on both sides of the English Channel were unaware of its significance. The large attack on convoys and the bombing of South England ports was the first phase of the Battle of Britain. This beginning phase would come to be known as the Battle of the Channel; Kanalkampf to the Germans.

Adolf Hitler, his mind and eyes already on Russia, was still hoping to make peace with England. Hitler had never wanted a war with Britain, at least not yet. His goal had always been to crush Russia and destroy Bolshevism to obtain Lebensraum—living space—for the German people. The expansion of Germany was to be found in the East. In order to achieve this, Hitler and his generals knew that a two-front-war—one with an undefeated Great Britain and the other with the Soviet Union—must be avoided. A two-front war had defeated them in World War I and was to be avoided at all costs.

Because of his need for peace with Britain, during the Battle of the Channel, Hitler strictly forbade the bombing of London. Hitler's goal was to make the British realize that continued resistance was futile, and negotiated peace was the best way to resolve it. And although the British did not know this, Hitler had no real interest in the invasion of Great Britain.

To bring Churchill to the negotiating table, Hitler unleashed his air force, the Luftwaffe, on British shipping and British ports. The British could not last long without the imports to sustain themselves, especially food and the raw materials for armament production. The Germans were also doing this to draw the RAF fighters out. In the event that an invasion became necessary, total air superiority was absolutely essential. This could only be achieved by destroying the RAF fighter aircraft and pilots.

Catherine yawned while staring out the train's window at the passing English countryside. She looked at her watch, 5.40 a.m., then turned back to the window. The train was heading east into the sunrise. The sun was already high enough to make the scene outside her window visible. The melodic clacking of the wheels was making her drowsy.

Catherine gently placed the side of her head against the window next to her third-class seat. She let her thoughts drift back to the past two days: her forty-eight-hour weekend leave she spent with Jeff. For the most part, it had been the most blissful two days of her life. Catherine could feel the soreness between her legs from the almost-rabid lovemaking. The two of them had spent at least half of her leave naked in bed—even to eat room service meals. By Sunday evening her lover was in a state of near exhaustion, an image that brought a sly smile to her.

The problem that almost ruined it for her occurred this morning as she prepared to leave. Jeff brought it up barely minutes before she left. "I want you to get a transfer," Jeff politely, quietly said. "I'm terribly worried about you. Sooner or later the Germans are going to figure out what those towers are for. When that happens, they'll bomb the hell out of them."

"You're bringing this up now? I have to leave. I have no time to discuss this, and bringing it up now will only make me remember it—"

"Good! That's what I want you to do is remember it, to think about it. I want you safe. If I had my way, you'd go back to the BBC."

"Please don't," she had almost begged. "Don't do this to me. I have a train to catch."

The phone rang. It was the front desk informing them that a cab was waiting for her.

"Let me go to the train station with you," Jeff said after talking to the concierge.

"No," she had resolutely replied shaking her head. She put on her uniform hat and picked up her bag. "No," she repeated. "Let's just—" she started to say.

"Will you at least think about it?" he had calmly asked.

"You're being selfish," she replied.

"Yes, I am!"

He held her tight and kissed her several times. She reminded him she had to go and reluctantly broke away.

"Please, think about it," he said again.

"I will," Catherine finally agreed.

"Hey, we're here," Catherine heard a female voice quietly say and felt a hand gently shake her shoulder.

Catherine's seatmate was one of the women and a friend she worked with named Margaret Brown. There were two other women from Swingate on the train returning from a brief respite.

"Busy weekend?" Margaret asked while Catherine covered a yawn with her hand. The way she said it made Catherine laugh.

She tilted her head to Margaret and quietly replied, "I wore him out."

The two women laughed, then Margaret said, "Let's hope there's a transport waiting."

***

"Welcome back, ladies," Group Captain Robinson greeted the four women returning to duty. "We've been quite active in your absence. It seems clear the Jerrys are getting serious about going after our shipping. Fighter Command has decided it's time to send some of our boys up to engage them. We're likely going to continue being quite busy."

"Yes, sir," all four women replied in unison.

"To your stations, then, please."

The four women started moving off to get back to their duty stations. Catherine took her place under the walkway in front of the group captain's station. Before she could finish attaching her headset, the group captain joined her.

"Catherine," he quietly said.

"Yes, sir," she replied.

"Everything all right?"

"Sir?" she asked with a curious look.

"Normally, I wouldn't stick my nose into someone's personal life—"

"Then please don't," Catherine said.

"Except, your husband has made several obviously unofficial inquiries about you," Robinson said.

"Tell him to bugger off!"

Robinson suppressed a laugh, and before he could reply to that, Catherine said, "I'm sorry, sir. I'll write him and tell him to stop."

"I don't mind," Robinson said with a sincere smile. "You're under my command, and I am concerned for you as I am everyone here. I can handle his calls. I just want to make sure you're all right."

Catherine sighed as she continued to hook up her headset. She looked up at the tall group captain. "We're estranged," she said. "We have been for quite some time. To be honest and between us only, I've met someone else. Arthur doesn't like the idea of me with another man. I don't give a fig what he does or doesn't like."

Robinson smiled again and again asked, "Are you all right?'

"Yes, sir. In fact, I've never been better," Catherine replied.

"They're forming up over Calais, sir," Sergeant Butler told Robinson.

"Very well, Sergeant," Robinson replied. "Keep the information coming."

"They're a bit early today, sir," Catherine said.

"Not really. This is how it's been. We don't have anything coming up to Dover today," Robinson said referring to any convoys in the English Channel. "The Jerrys will head for the Isle of Wight and the area around Southampton. Better get on to Fighter Command and give them a heads up."

"Yes, sir," Catherine said.

"I'm glad you're back. Carry on."

Catherine, with only a few very short breaks, was kept busy all day relaying information back and forth with Fighter Command. At the end of the day, Fighter Command lost one Hurricane fighter shot down. The RAF shot down three German planes: a Heinkel III medium bomber, a Stuka and a Dornier flying boat. At this point in the war, this was a significant day for the RAF. It would not be long before a day with these few aircraft losses would be a very slow day.

Each day, with mild weather for the latter part of July favoring the Germans, more and more Luftwaffe planes were sent up. The targets continued to be, almost exclusively, British shipping convoys.

On July 19, there were nine convoys at sea which created a significant amount of activity. It would also be the worst day of the battle for the RAF. The Germans were able to take tactical advantage of British Defiant fighters and shot down ten of them. German losses, in comparison, were only four total aircraft.

That same day, Hitler went before his puppet legislature, the Reichstag, and gave a significant speech. It would come to be known as Hitler's last 'appeal to reason' speech; a final attempt to bring Britain to the negotiating table. Of course, like all of his attempts to avoid an invasion, Churchill and his war cabinet would spurn the offer with poorly disguised contempt.

The Battle of the Channel went on through July, and at the end of each day, Catherine and her mates almost collapsed from exhaustion. First, there was the stress, tension and pressure they constantly dealt with monitoring the Germans. If that was not enough, their own lives were terribly at risk. Every day, although mostly unspoken, they all expected the Germans to turn their attention on them. How could the Germans not figure out how it was that British fighters knew exactly where to find them? Sooner or later the Chain Home stations, with their clearly visible towers, were going to become targets.

"What did you hear back from Fighter Command about casualties?" one of the women asked Catherine.

Darkness was coming on, and the women were enjoying an after-supper respite. They were back at their barracks, a ramshackle collection of 'temporary' flimsy wooden huts. They were located a mile from the command center.

The question asked of Catherine elicited a sharp look from one of the other women. The questioner looked back with a bewildered expression.

"Oh, I've learned not to take much stock in those early reports," Catherine replied. "I think the pilots get a little excited and miscount the real number. We'll get a more accurate report in a couple of days."

While Catherine said this to the women sitting around with her, one of them whispered something in the ear of the woman who had initially asked the question. Her eyes widened and she got a bit of a startled look on her face.

"Catherine, I'm sorry, I didn't know about your brother and—"

"It's all right, Judy," Catherine said with a weak smile. "Yes, I have a brother flying Spitfires against the Germans. I'm quite worried. It helps to stay busy."

"He's also flying the best fighter plane in the world," one of the other women spoke up. "Our boys are going to stop old Adolf's invasion from ever happening."

"And we're going to help them," Judy added.

Catherine finished her daily letter to Jeff, kissed it and sealed it in an envelope. As she did each morning, she would drop it in the postal box at the hut next door. She said a brief prayer for the safety of herself, her mates, her brother and Jeff. An exhausted Catherine then, literally, crawled under the bed covers and was asleep in under a minute.

July 29, 1940

Group Captain Robinson sensed, more than saw or heard, a buzz of commotion starting up from the floor. He was sitting at his post overlooking Swingate Chain Home Station. Almost instinctively, a sign of his experience, he stood up and stepped to the rail. Directly below him, he could hear Catherine Hartley speaking into her headset. She was relaying information to Fighter Command.

Robinson watched the activity, his hands on the railing, and saw Lieutenant Swanson writing information for him. Apparently, there was more German activity starting up across the Channel. Swanson looked up at Robinson, nodded and briskly walked across the floor. A moment later he was handing Robinson several sheets of paper.

"Tell me, Cal," Robinson politely said instead of reading the report given to him.

"Sir, there is significant activity forming up at the Pas-de-Calais. Looks to be forty to fifty bombers, probably Stuka dive bombers."

"Escorts?" Robinson asked.

"Yes, sir. An equal number of fighters," Martin replied.

At that moment, a senior WAAF joined them from the floor. "Sir," she said addressing Robinson. "They appear to be heading our way, toward Dover."

"Thank you, Section Leader," Robinson replied. "Does Aircraftwoman Hartley have this information?"

"Yes, sir," she answered.

"You may return to your duties," Robinson told the Section Leader.

The distance between Dover and Calais, France across the English Channel is barely fifty miles. Even a relatively slow aircraft such as a Stuka Ju 87 could cover the distance in less than fifteen minutes. There is a significant harbor located at Dover, and on this day, it was crowded with Royal Navy ships and their supporting cargo vessels. This was the target for this particular attack force.

A Stuka typically flies at 13,000 feet and then plunges down on its prey. The aircraft is armed with a 250-kilogram bomb load. As the forty-five Stukas attacked, the RAF fighters appeared overhead to go after their escorts.

The bombers went after both the town of Dover and the ships in the harbor. The worst of the damage was done when the 10,000-ton support ship, Sandhurst, was hit. Among its cargo was a significant amount of ammunition and torpedoes. Courageously, Dover tugboats and firemen fought the blaze pouring tons of seawater onto the Sandhurst managing to avoid a potential catastrophe. While this was going on, other bombers went after the Swingate facility.

"All right, everyone down," the group captain yelled after the first bomb hit.

Of course, they had rehearsed this very thing many times. All of the people working the RDF scopes and telephones were moving before Robinson spoke. Everyone had immediately and calmly dropped what they were doing and took cover.

Catherine removed her headset and dropped it where she was standing. She took three quick steps and scrambled under a sturdy, wooden table with two other women. The next bomb to go off did so barely a hundred yards from the building. A direct hit would likely kill them all. The attack seemed to go on forever, but in fact, lasted only a few minutes. While she was under the table, Catherine found herself and her two companions holding each other. They were also reciting The Lord's Prayer.

Suddenly, it stopped almost as quickly as it started. One moment there were bombs going off and the next there was total silence. One of the women with Catherine, a young girl barely nineteen years old, was crying like a baby. When the bombing stopped, Catherine could hear several others doing so as well. Much to her surprise, Catherine was quite calm. It was over; she survived and was thinking of Jeff.

The Swingate attack of July 29, 1940, did very little damage. A backup transmitter was damaged, an empty barracks destroyed, and a feeder line also received some minor damage. The station itself was back up and operational within minutes. Fortunately, and unknown to the British, the Germans still did not know the significance of the towers and support buildings.

TWENTY-TWO

August 7, 1940

Dearest Mom & Dad,

London is still quite peaceful, and I am fine. I'm still worried about Catherine. She writes everyday so I know she is all right. I'm worried because I sense that she (they) are putting in long hours, and she is overworked. Interesting how eagerly I look forward to getting her letter. Of course, I write to her every day also.

Again, I know where she is but cannot tell you. Someday, when the history of this war is written, her part will come out. Personally, she is a very small cog in an extremely significant part of the machine that defends England. Part of me is incredibly proud of her; part of me is worried sick for her safety; and another part of me is embarrassed and feeling quite guilty about my own lack of involvement. Here I sit in the luxury and safety of London while Catherine is participating and risking her life.

For the past week, the weather has been quite poor for the Germans. The air battle taking place has been mostly confined to the Channel. So far, the Germans are mostly attacking British merchant shipping. They are going after convoys bringing materials and supplies to England via the British Channel. In fact, the British are already calling it the Battle of the Channel.

They, the British, believe the strategy of the Germans is to draw the RAF out for a showdown battle. It is the lynchpin of the Germans' invasion plans. They must achieve total air supremacy if they are to invade.

My British military contacts and Lt. Commander Mike Burns, USN, are expecting a change of strategy from the Germans. The RAF is not 'biting' on the temptation to go after the Germans, yet. They, the British, expect the Luftwaffe to change what they're doing fairly soon. They will start bombing cities and RAF airfields.

As for me, personally, I am actually a little bored. As I said, London is pretty quiet, and we can't get near the war right now. I spend most of my days hanging out at the Ministry of Information. We get daily briefings which are nothing more than propaganda from the government. I add that to what I can get from my military friends and embellish it into an article for the Gazette. Write and let me know if you've read them and how they are being received.

I have taken to walking a lot. Too many lunches and dinners with sources of information. If you have money, the rationing the government has imposed can be skirted. Even in wartime the wealthy are not too terribly inconvenienced. I feel more than a little guilty about that, too. So I walk a lot to keep my weight down. It would look ridiculous to get fat while the rest of the country gets by with much less. I'm also drinking too much. Sorry, Mother. Don't worry. I'm just bored and worried about Catherine.

Enough for now. As always, all of my love. Let me know about my articles in the paper.

Love,

Jeff

The bartender replaces my Bloody Mary with a fresh one while I am addressing an envelope to my parents. The Pan AM service out of Southampton has been stopped due to the bombing. I have a new source: a clerk in the Portuguese Embassy. He takes the letters from Americans and others in the Western Hemisphere countries and sends them to Portugal. His ambassador allows him the use of the diplomatic pouch, likely for a cut of the money. Why not? They are then sent via the Pan AM Clipper out of Portugal. It takes a few days longer but still works.

How the Ritz continues to obtain tomato juice is a serious mystery. Because of my mild hangover and slowly ebbing headache from last night, now is not the time to inquire. I shall simply thank my blessings of having wealthy ancestors. Besides, George the bartender mixes a life-saving Bloody Mary.

While I take a moment to contemplate the previous evening, I allow myself a moment of smug self-satisfaction. The availability of women in this city is astonishing. It makes the social scene in New York seem almost chaste in comparison. Unlike far too many of my contemporaries, almost all of whom are married, I am avoiding the indulgence to the point where I may have reestablished my virginity.

Last night—as I have far too often recently due to Catherine's absence—I spent the evening at the Savoy's American Bar. There appears to be a significant movement taking place among the females of London to shag an American. I don't know what they are expecting. I doubt they will find the experience significantly different than shagging a Brit.

My friends, married and single, are not shy about indulging the British women. They tell me a significant number of the ladies are married themselves. I am no hypocrite, or at least try not to be, so I keep my disapproval to myself. There is something even I find disturbing about a wife with a husband in the military being less than faithful. The war is going to affect an enormous number of things before it is over.

I check my watch while sipping my Hair of the Dog cocktail. It is after eleven a.m., and I am meeting my journalist friends for lunch. I light a cigarette and stare across the bar at myself in the mirror. Frankly, I think I look like hell. I need at least a couple of days of complete sobriety, normal eating and solid sleep. Except, sleeping is sometimes difficult. I am worried about her, and it can keep me up.

I set my cigarette in the ashtray and retrieve her latest letter from my inside suit coat pocket. I read it again—it is barely a couple of paragraphs— then fold it up and replace it. Catherine is fine, but I can tell she is working too much, putting in too many hours. Every day I write and tell her she needs a leave, even forty-eight hours would help. She ignores this which tells me no one is receiving any leaves right now. They are simply too busy.

I take one last swallow of my drink and push the half-full glass aside. I crush out my cigarette and decide I have time to walk to the restaurant. To annoy the British hotel guests seated at the bar around me, I drop a five-pound note on the bar and wave at George before setting off. The Brits hate Americans for tipping the servants.

Clive, Charlie, David and I are seated together in the back row of the room. We are at the Ministry of Information for the daily briefing in which they tell us nothing. A man we know from the American Bar in the Savoy's basement is conducting the briefing. Douglas Williams is a spokesman of the Ministry of Information. He is a good man, an honest man who has become if not a friend, at least a sincere acquaintance.

Today, he is doing his level best to tell us the government's version of the fact that the war has been relatively quiet due to the weather. David is sitting next to me. He is even more hungover from last night than I was. David is unmarried—divorced—and is becoming a bit of a hound. He is in his mid-thirties but looks older because he is rapidly losing his hair. Even David is in demand by the much younger London girls. He left around midnight with a striking brunette. Today he is having trouble staying awake.

I jab him lightly in the ribs with an elbow and whisper, "Those young girls will be the death of you, old man."

David smiles, nods his head once and replies, "But what a way to go. I have to get out of here. Doug is putting me to sleep. I need some air."

We have all been given a single page handout of the briefing's high points. I look past David and see Clive's chin on his chest. Charlie is to my right stifling a yawn. I poke his arm with my elbow and gesture toward the door. Several others are also leaving, which gives us an opportunity to do so as well without appearing too rude.

Charlie is reading the briefing handout and says, "I don't know if I am creative enough to get more than a couple hundred words for a column out of this."

We are on the sidewalk outside the Ministry of Information. I look along the front of the building at the four workmen piling another layer of sandbags against the building.

"What do they know that we don't?" I ask.

"Given the scarcity of the information we just received, probably a lot," Charlie replies.

"Instead of sneaking off with some twenty-year-old doxie, like a couple of others I know—" Clive starts to say.

"You're British; they're not interested," David says.

"As I was saying," Clive says with feigned annoyance, "I spent most of the evening with a couple of RAF officers. The belief is that this so-called Battle of the Channel—Kanalkampf, the Germans are calling it—isn't working for the Krauts. Fighter Command, while not totally ignoring it, is not sending our boys out to fight it out with the Luftwaffe as much as the Germans would like. And they're not having much effect on our shipping. So the thinking is, we will likely see a change of strategy before much longer."

"What do they think?" I ask.

"Bombing fighter bases and cities. I'm sorry to say this, Jeff. I know how worried you are for her safety…" Clive says.

"As we all are," Charlie adds.

"They believe the Germans might go after Chain Home stations," Clive says.

My heart sinks to my stomach with this thought. I do my best to smile and take the news lightly, but I am sure my friends can see through it.

"Those, uh, places," David says, "won't be easy targets. And they are well protected with anti-aircraft guns." David places a comforting hand on my shoulder and continues, "She'll be okay, you'll see."

"Thanks," I quietly say. Then I say, "I have an idea. Let's grab a cab and go see if Joe Kennedy is in."

"Why not?" Charlie replies. "We don't have anything better to do."

It is still a Wednesday morning, and the Ministry of Information is located at the University of London; finding a cab here is going to be a problem. While we discuss this among ourselves, good fortune strikes. A black cab pulls up to the building twenty feet from us. Two British gentlemen—they are wearing bowlers and carrying umbrellas on a clear, cloudless day is how we can tell—exit the cab. The two men are barely out of the cab's doors when we pushy Americans pile in. Charlie, because of his girth, always gets the front seat.

In front of the embassy, as the three of us in the backseat scramble out of the cab, Charlie tells the driver to wait. I march up to the marine guard, introduce ourselves and ask about seeing the ambassador.

"Do you have an appointment?" the marine asks, a three-striper sergeant.

"No," I reply. "We were in the neighborhood and thought we'd see if we could get an interview. Is he here?"

"I can't tell you that," he answers. "May I see some identification, please?" he politely but seriously asks.

I hand him my American passport. He turns and takes it with him into the guardhouse. I can see him through a window as he speaks with someone inside. The other marine walks out and stands silently watching us. Both marines are armed with sidearms. These two are not young kids. They are probably older than me and very serious looking men. While the marine is in the guardhouse and calling inside, we see a very familiar face come out the front door. It is our assistant naval attaché friend, Mike Burns.

While we greet Burns, the first marine comes out holding my passport. "Sorry," he says, "I'm told the ambassador will be busy all day."

The sergeant hands me my passport, then recognizes Burns. He salutes the lieutenant commander saying, "Sorry, sir. I didn't recognize you at first in civilian clothes."

Burns returns the salute and says, "At ease, Sergeant."

"Thank you, sir," he says as he turns to go.

Burns says to us, "You here to see Smiling Joe?"

"We thought we'd try," David replies. "Slow news day. Joe's always good for a quote."

Burns silently looks us over and says, "I'll tell you what. I may be able to get you a story. But if the man I'm meeting says no, then no it is. Deal?"

We exchange looks and nods and each mutter a variation of an affirmative response.

"You can let the cab go," Burns says. "It's only a couple of blocks. We'll walk."

Charlie, an advocate of leisurely living, grumbles about walking.

"Come on, Charlie," I say. "This is London. Everyone walks."

The four of us are waiting in the entryway of a pub while Burns speaks with his contact. We can see them conversing at a table as far from the door as possible. There are no other patrons anywhere near them. Their heads are nodding as Burns explains our presence.

A minute or so later, Burns rejoins us. "He's okay with the four of you joining in. But keep his name out of anything you write, okay?"

We all agree, then join the man at the table. Burns introduces us, and we make small talk until the waiter brings our drinks.

The mystery man is a high-level clerk in the Swedish Embassy, or so we are told, and his English is excellent. Before we are finished with our little clandestine meeting, it becomes obvious he is more than a clerk. He is a member of Swedish military intelligence whose job is to pass along information to the Allies. He even lets slip that he fought the Russians for Finland during the Winter War.

For the next hour, he gives us a detailed accounting of German atrocities. When the Nazis occupied Denmark, as they did with every country, they ordered all Jews to wear a yellow Star of David. The Danish royals stood up to them and ordered all Danes to wear one in defiance. Amazingly, the Germans backed down. Since then, Denmark has served as a transport point for Jews escaping Europe, sort of an Underground Railroad station similar to ones used to help slaves escape the South before the Civil War.

From Denmark, the Jewish refugees are put on small boats and taken to Sweden. Of course, the Nazis are viciously retaliating. The word coming out of Berlin is that the Nazis are planning on rounding up all of the Jews of Europe and shipping them to Poland. It is uncertain what will happen to them, but it is feared the Nazis plan to exterminate—murder—every Jew on the continent.

"That's preposterous," Clive says. "There must be ten million Jews in Europe. Even the Nazis can't kill that many people. It's ridiculous propaganda."

"There have already been tens of thousands of executions in Poland," the Swede says. Before Clive can respond, the man continues, "I've been in and out of Berlin many times. I have come to know them. I have no doubt that is their intention. Read Hitler's book, *Mein Kampf.* He spells it out for anyone to see. And with the clouds of war to provide cover for them, they can do it."

I am up very late writing my article for the paper. After meeting with the Swede, the four of us and Mike Burns discuss the matter very thoroughly. Clive flatly refuses to use what we have been told for a news story. Charlie is wavering but doubtful. David says he will think it over and decide tomorrow but will likely do it. I am in completely.

I read over my notes of the man's tale for the third time. I have been very vague about where I got this information. I have gone back and forth with myself about letting the *Gazette* editors know where it came from. They will likely insist on at least identifying the man as some sort of intelligence operative. I decide I cannot risk even that much. It could cost the man his life if the Nazis get wind of it. Plus, I have promised Mike Burns to let him read it before I send it.

Is his story true? Are the Nazis really out to commit genocide against European Jewry? It is almost too horrible to imagine. But with the stories he had about what they have already done to people with physical or mental disabilities, political opponents, dissenters, I am convinced it is true.

A week after I submit my article to the *Gazette*, I hear back from them: a short, terse cable telling me to refrain from letting the British use me as a propaganda tool. They will not run the story.

TWENTY-THREE

August 12, 1940

"You still haven't told Jeff about the attack?" Susan Compton asked Catherine.

"Of course not," Catherine replied. "He'd be on the next train to drag me away from here."

"I wish someone loved me like that," Sadie Wilson chimed in.

"Sadie, you're nineteen, give it time," Catherine replied after blowing a stream of cigarette smoke into the air.

"And don't be in a hurry. The smooth, charming and good-looking ones are likely the worst," Susan said.

"I think I got lucky," Catherine said with a wistful smile.

Most of the WAAF women of Swingate were behind the building. They were taking a short, mid-morning bathroom and cigarette break. It was a pleasant, mostly clear sunny day. RAF Fighter Command was expecting another busy day today.

While the women smoked and chatted, they were suddenly interrupted by the sound of something screaming in towards them. Before they realized what it was, an explosion occurred about a half a mile away. It was quickly followed by several more.

"We're being shelled," Catherine stood up and, as calmly as possible, told the others.

There was a dozen or so of them, and having been trained for this, very calmly they all hurried back inside.

The shelling was also directed at Dover and its harbor. This went on until the Stukas arrived overhead. Once again, the Chain Home Station itself was targeted as well as the ships at sea and in the harbor. They would later learn that several other Chain Home stations were attacked. Most suffered little damage with the exception of Ventnor. Located on the Isle of Wight, the facility was virtually destroyed. Fortunately, there were few casualties caused by the bombing raids. Swingate suffered minor damage and was off the air for approximately ninety minutes.

"We're off the air, Group Captain," Lt. Swanson yelled up to Robinson.

They could hear the bombs going off by the towers. Unknown at this time to those inside, a cable had been damaged causing the station to go off the air.

"All right," Robinson yelled from his station above the floor, "everyone take cover. There's nothing to be done until this is over."

Most of the women were already under some protective cover. A few, including Catherine, were still at their stations—Catherine, because it was her duty to stay on the phone with Fighter Command as long as possible. Hearing Robinson's order to take cover, Catherine reported the damage into her phone and informed Fighter Command they were off the air. By the time she finished, she and Group Captain Robinson were the only ones still at their station.

"Catherine," she heard Robinson calmly say to her, "get yourself covered up. It will likely be over soon."

"Yes, sir," she replied, removing her telephone equipment.

Catherine crawled under the table with the others while, again—only this time, silently—saying The Lord's Prayer. Death was literally raining down around them. Having been through it before and taking strength from the group captain's steadiness, this time the women were far more composed—probably somewhat fatalistically.

Robinson's prediction was correct. Barely ten minutes after Catherine got under the table, the bombing stopped. Close overhead they could hear the unmistakable roar of a dozen Rolls-Royce Merlin engines.

"Those are our boys! Those are Spitfire engines!" Lt. Swanson yelled.

"Go get 'em," almost all of the women yelled and cheered at the RAF chasing off the Germans.

Even though they could not see them, everyone in the cramped and crowded room looked up at the ceiling. Just the sound of 'our boys' driving off the hated Germans lifted all of them off the floor.

Catherine, as overjoyed as everyone else, crawled out from under the table. She brushed herself off and saw the group captain talking to several enlisted men.

"They'll be going out to assess the damage," Swanson said while both he and Catherine watched.

"I need a cigarette," Catherine said. "And a shot of whiskey."

"Well," Swanson laughed, "you and the others can go for the cigarette, but the shot of whiskey will have to wait."

"Yes, sir," Catherine smiled then walked off to join the others to wait for repairs to be made.

While the women waited outside, most of them wandered away from the main building. The transmitting towers were all unscathed. The area in total looked relatively undamaged. Word came from the damage assessment team that a feeder cable had been damaged and repairs were being made.

"For all the noise they made, they don't seem to be very good at hitting anything," one of the women said to Catherine.

They were about a hundred meters from the main building. Catherine was looking at the towers when she quietly said as if speaking to herself, "They must not know what we're doing here. They don't seem to have targeted our building or the towers. If they had any idea what we do, they would make a massive effort to go after us."

"Be thankful," her friend replied.

"I suppose you're right. Our security must be good. Thank God."

Unknown to Catherine and her mates, the Battle of Britain was about to make a dramatic change. So far, the Germans had been after ships and ports. Hitler and his top henchman, Hermann Goering, the Luftwaffe chief, had reached a decision. If Fighter Command would not make a serious effort to come after them, they would go after Fighter Command.

Goering had designated August 13, 1940, as Adlertag, 'Eagle Day'. The beginning of Adlerangriff, 'Operation Eagle Attack.' This was the code name to destroy the RAF in preparation of the invasion. In order to do this, the Germans were changing their strategy and targeting. They would go after the airbases and fighter planes.

August 20, 1940

"I am so tired I'm going to collapse on my bunk."

Catherine put an arm around the shoulders of the woman who said what they were all feeling. "We all are, Martha," Catherine assured her.

"Oh, I know," Martha contritely answered her. "I don't mean to complain, it's just—"

"Seven straight fourteen- or fifteen-hour days. We've hardly had time to go to the loo," Betsy Halvorson, the women's Section Leader, chimed in.

The women had been transported back to their barracks in army lorries, a godsend to save them from a long walk after another exhausting day.

At least today they had not suffered another bombing attack. Yesterday, a large force of bombers, estimated to be sixty of them, were detected by Swingate. Two of them peeled away and flew south to the Dover area. They dropped their bomb loads on Swingate and the surrounding area causing many military casualties. Fortunately, the Germans again failed to bomb the towers or Chain Home Station buildings.

As they reached the door to their barracks, Catherine reached in her blouse pocket to touch Jeff's daily letter. She was saving it until now to savor the anticipation. It was a great relief to hear from him every day. Even if most of what he wrote was mundane, routine daily trivia. Just to hear from him warmed her heart, to know that there was someone out there who loved her and was thinking about her.

She received a letter at least once a week from her parents. They were getting on as best as they could after the loss of Tommy. And then there were the constant, daily reminders that Alex was up there every day.

The rumors were going about that the fighter bases were catching hell. The German bombers, Heinkels and Dorniers, with clouds of Messerschmitt fighters flying cover, were on the verge of crushing Fighter Command. They were hitting the airfields every day, and the losses were piling up. Or so the rumors had it.

"Are you all right?" Betsy quietly asked Catherine.

Catherine was sitting on the edge of her bunk, clutching Jeff's unopened letter. The tension and stress of the past week was getting to her. Suddenly, out of nowhere, she broke down and started crying. She was lightly sobbing as her shoulders shook and the tears flowed. Fortunately, her friend in the next bunk was outside smoking.

Betsy sat down next to Catherine and gently took her hand. "I was beginning to wonder about you," Betsy quietly said.

"What?" Catherine asked between sobs.

"I was wondering when it was going to get to you. You've been like a rock for the rest of the girls."

"Oh, that," Catherine said, wiping the tears with a handkerchief. "I was thinking about my brother…"

"Oh, no," Betsy said. Everyone knew Catherine had a brother flying Spitfires. "Have you heard—"

"No, no," Catherine quickly said vigorously shaking her head.

"Thank God," Betsy replied squeezing her hand.

"No. No news, which is good. I just worry about him, after what happened to Tom," Catherine said.

They all knew she had already lost one brother. Of course, there was not a single person who had not lost a friend or family member or at least knew someone who had.

"The news isn't really as bad as the rumors. The boys are giving more than they are getting," Betsy said, trying to cheer her up.

"The BBC is replaying Winston's speech to the House of Commons in a short while. Would you care to join me and listen?"

Catherine wiped her eyes again and blew her nose. She weakly smiled at Betsy and agreed to join her. "Let me read Jeff's letter first. That should cheer me up. I'll be along," Catherine said.

"Bring the others," Betsy replied, then stood up to go to her quarters. Being a Section Leader, the equivalent of a sergeant, she had her own room.

Catherine finished Jeff's letter, smiled and kissed it before replacing it in its envelope. Once again, she marveled at his ability to turn a day's worth of mostly monotonous tedium into three pages of interesting prose. Her own letters—she would write a quick one before bed—were barely two or three paragraphs. Of course, she could not tell him much about what she was doing.

By the time Catherine went to Betsy's private room, several of the others were already crowding in. There were some standing in the doorway, and Betsy ordered them to let Catherine inside.

"I made sure to save you a space on my bunk," Betsy told her.

The three girls who were sitting on it squeezed over to let her sit down.

When the broadcast was finished, Betsy turned off the small radio and looked around the crowded room. "Well," she said looking directly at Catherine, "what do you think?"

"I think if he leads us through this, and he will, he'll go down in history as the greatest Prime Minister of all time," Catherine replied.

"What were his words?" one of the girls squeezing through the doorway asked. "'Never in the field of human conflict was so much owed by so many to so few.' Absolutely smashing."

"He may have been referring to the men in the Spitfires and Hurricanes, but he was talking about us, too," Catherine said.

TWENTY-FOUR

August 21, 1940

Dear Mom & Dad,

If you have not heard it, get a copy of Churchill's latest speech. He gave it yesterday to the House of Commons, and it might be his most stirring one yet. I was fortunate enough to again be in attendance. Along with every journalist in London, I am considering writing a book about my experience when the war is over.

What little I learned of history in college, I do remember this. At the beginning of the American Civil War, Jefferson Davis became President of the Southern Confederacy. One of the other rebellious slaveholders—has there even been a less worthy cause?—said of Davis, "The man and the hour have met."

I'm fairly certain I have that quoted correctly. I have serious doubts about the veracity of that statement as it relates to Jefferson Davis. I have no doubt whatsoever about its validity in describing Churchill. He certainly has his flaws, but I believe the man is going to save civilization. And I am not alone in that assessment.

As for me, personally, London is still quiet, and I am quite well. I am more worried than ever about Catherine.

I probably should not tell you this. I have debated with myself for two days about it. But I need to unburden myself. I need to share my heartache with someone and especially someone that I know loves me. The censors would have a fit, but they'll not have an opportunity to review this letter. It will go through Portugal by way of their embassy.

I have been informed by a very reliable source that the place where Catherine is located has become very dangerous. In fact, it has been bombed several times. She is unaware that I know this, so far. I will write her about it and soon.

I feel so very helpless and more than a little ashamed and useless, ashamed of myself and my fellow countrymen. The woman I love and a significant number of other women are risking their lives and America sits fat, wealthy and uninterested. I'm sorry but I feel embarrassed, pathetic and guilty.

Sorry Dad, but it is our war. Tell your fat, rich friends that if we don't help Britain, we will live to regret it.

I don't mean to make you feel guilty. I know you understand this. Please forgive me.

Love to all,

Jeff

I read through the letter to my parents for the second time. Is it too much? I decide that it is not. America needs the unvarnished truth. My paper, the *Gazette*, is not a pro-Roosevelt newspaper. It is not necessarily anti-Roosevelt but our audience—they have data that shows this—is decidedly against intervention. Like any other business, we must give our customers what they want. Of course, my reporting is factual, and I do my best to keep my opinion out of it. However, I refuse to make the Germans out to have moral equivalency with the British. They are monsters and must be stopped.

I place the letter in its envelope and staple two American twenty-dollar bills to it. I'll get it to my Portuguese contact this morning. It should be delivered in New York in three days.

Having finished that letter, I turn my attention back to the one I have been avoiding. Do I write and tell Catherine I know of the danger she and the other women are in? This is the question I have been dealing with and avoiding for two days.

The daily letter I sent yesterday did not contain even a tiny hint that I knew. When I wrote it, I was so angry with her for keeping it from me, I did not dare write a word. I knew if I started in that frame of mind, I would write some things I would regret. Today, I am much calmer. I know she kept it from me to spare me so I would not worry more than I already do.

I am seated where I do all my writing, at the dining room table in my suite. I have stationery in front of me, pen in hand. While I think about the letter, I am staring at a new map I have put up on the wall.

After France so grotesquely, shamelessly, capitulated and surrendered, I took down the map of France, Belgium and the Netherlands. In its place, I have put up an enormous map of the United Kingdom including Scotland and Ireland. I am using it to mark the places the Germans have bombed; except, I do not have the location of any of the RAF Fighter Command airfields that have been hit. That news is being kept secret and withheld from the public.

The whispers—rumors—we are hearing are that Fighter Command is having a very rough time of it. So far, they are holding their own. The German bombers hit the airfields, bomb them, tear up the runways and destroy facilities and planes each day. The RAF manages to patch them up and keep the planes flying, but for how long? They are simply not sure. The word is—rumors again—the Germans are shooting down British planes faster than the factories can replace them.

Along with the loss of airplanes, the damage to airfields and facilities, the Germans are also targeting airplane factories. Obviously, the Germans have a very well-integrated espionage network in England. That must be how the Luftwaffe is finding out where the factories are located.

If all of that is not enough, the attrition of fighter pilots is Fighter Command's biggest concern. The number of trained pilots killed, maimed and wounded is reaching the breaking point. And these are the best, most experienced pilots. Sending green, barely trained men up to take on the clouds of German fighters is likely suicidal.

In other words, I fear it is only a matter of time. The big question we all ask our British sources is, can they hold on until October when the weather turns bad over the English Channel. No one knows.

I light another cigarette—we are all smoking and drinking entirely too much—then look at the blank sheet of paper on the table in front of me. I will write in today's letter and make a vague reference to the fact that I know of the Swingate bombings. Of course, I dare not mention Swingate by name. I will be as calm as possible about it so as not to alarm Catherine.

I am told that the Chain Home stations are under as much duress as the fighter bases. They are not being attacked as heavily, but they are targeted. The personnel operating them are putting in long, stressful days, or so I am told. Catherine has enough to worry about without me adding to it. I will not even ask her about getting a forty-eight or even a twenty-four-hour pass. I know it is impossible right now. My letter must be cheerful, upbeat and positive. And I will swallow my concern for her.

I am almost finished with my letter to Catherine when my phone rings. I smile to myself at the thought that it has Charlie's ring. Of course, it has the same sound as anyone else calling, but I'm sure it is Charlie.

"Hello, Charlie," I answer.

"How did you know—oh, never mind," he replies. "Did you listen to Murrow's broadcast last night?"

"No," I answer. "It must have been about Winnie's speech."

"It was and it was damned good," Charlie says. "I have to give it to Ed; he has a great voice for it."

"Yes, he does," I agree.

"Are you ready to head over to the Ministry of No Information?" he asks.

"I'm hungry," I say. "Let's get something to eat first."

"Excellent plan," Charlie readily agrees. It does not take much to convince Charlie to get a meal.

"Give me ten minutes to finish my letter to Catherine."

"Are you going to tell her you know they were bombed?" Charlie asks.

"Yes, I have, but very calmly, very carefully. I don't want to upset her. She is going through enough right now," I reply. "I'll be along to the Savoy in about thirty minutes."

By the time I arrive at the Savoy's American Bar, my friends are already there and have a table. As usual, the restaurant is crowded. Due to the war shortages of food and virtually everything else, prices are creeping upward. We are even seeing shortages in the nicer hotels, and I think it is about time we shared the pain—mostly items that would be considered luxury goods such as oranges and orange juice, which I have had with breakfast my entire life. But then, oranges are grown in America.

Along with the usual suspects, Clive, Charlie and David, Lt. Commander Mike Burns is at the table. I take the empty chair next to him and greet everyone.

"There's a question I've been wanting to ask you, Commander," I say to Burns. "How much effect will Hitler's blockade of Great Britain have?"

On August 17, Hitler ordered a blockade of the British Isles. Since his navy is no match for the British Navy, I have wondered about the practical impact of it.

Burns begins to explain it as the waiter starts taking our orders. "As a practical matter, not much. Hitler is essentially warning ships from neutral countries plying British waters that they may be stopped and searched. If they are found to be carrying goods to Britain, they may be seized. But legally, neutral ships may not be sunk for trying to run the blockade. The problem Hitler has is he simply does not have the ability to maintain a real blockade. He is warning other countries, especially America, that their ships may be stopped."

"Is he trying to provoke a war with us?" David asks.

"I find that hard to believe," Burns solemnly replies. "Keeping America out of it has to be his number one priority. No, I think he is just sending out a warning."

"And if we don't listen to him?" I ask.

Burns shrugs then answers with, "I guess we'll see. Does Adolf have the balls to start a war with America? I doubt it. If one of his submarines stops a ship flying an American flag, well, we'll see what happens if he does.

"What they're not letting you know," Burns quietly says as he leans forward and looks around for eavesdroppers, "is their submarine attacks on shipping convoys is starting to be a serious concern. The total for July is at least double what the official amount was reported."

"If you report that," Clive tells us, "you'll be on the next ship back to America."

"You mean, the Ministry of No Information is lying to us?" Charlie says with obvious mock seriousness.

"It's wartime," Burns says with a smile. "And I'll tell you something else," Burns says barely above a whisper. "This is not for publication."

By now we are all leaning in anxious to hear what he has to say. It is bad news for sure or he would not be acting like this.

"The RAF Fighter Command is in serious trouble. It's far worse than the government is admitting. In fact, they are on their last leg. The Germans are about to achieve air superiority. If something doesn't change pretty soon, the invasion is likely to happen."

Our food arrives, and after that news, we go silent while we eat. All along we believed the RAF was at least holding its own. Now we are told that is not true. In fact, the British are losing the air war.

Compared to what most people are eating, we have nothing to complain about. Although that does not stop us from complaining anyway. From what we are observing, the people are not suffering too terribly much, yet. Burns has contacts with other neutral embassies, including our own, in Berlin. It seems the German people have never had it so good. Hitler has made it clear that the rest of Europe can starve but the Germans are to be provided for, no matter what.

I am the first one to finish my breakfast and light a cigarette. The Savoy is still able to serve coffee which I enjoy while waiting for my friends. My thoughts at times like this invariably drift back to Catherine. I need to find a way to prevent it, but I cannot help myself. There is a war going on, mostly above us, to prevent the Nazi swastika from flying above the Parliament building. I am guiltily enjoying a very good meal while young men and women are dying to protect us, and my love is in the thick of it.

"Swingate has been bombed," I whisper to Mike Burns.

"I know," he replies. "Several times, in fact. Little damage and few casualties, so far."

"You knew and didn't tell me!" I angrily reply.

He places a hand on my arm and says, "I was sworn to secrecy, Jeff. Besides, what good would it do? You'd get angry and worried sick for her and could do nothing. I knew you'd find out sooner or later."

"I suppose you're right," I say with a sigh.

"If it's any consolation, the Brits don't believe the Germans know what those buildings and towers on the coast are really there for. They haven't made a real effort to go after them," Burns tells me.

"Are you sure?" I ask.

"Yes. In fact," he continues while lowering his voice again, "they believe the Swingate attacks were collateral to the bombing of Dover harbor. They weren't after Swingate at all."

Everyone at the table stares at me while I think about this. I look at my three friends, and they all nod in agreement and to comfort me, at least a little.

"Okay," I finally say. "That does make me feel a bit better. At least they're not a specific target."

I look at Burns and say, "Let me ask you something. Do you think I could get permission to go to Dover? Maybe see her for a few hours?"

"Let me look into it for you," Burns says. "I know some people to check with."

"Thanks," I reply.

TWENTY-FIVE

August 26, 1940

Another long, busy day for the Swingate Chain Home Station. Catherine is riding back in the lorry that takes them to their quarters. It is Sunday evening, and she thinks about God, her parents, their village church and Jeff as they bump along the rutted dirt road. No mail today, but she has a letter from Jeff waiting for her. Too tired to read it last night, she saved it for today, like waiting till the last minute and enjoying the anticipation before opening a special Christmas present.

It is earlier than usual tonight. The night crew, inexperienced a couple of weeks ago, has begun to take over without assistance. That has eased the burden significantly on the day crew 'veterans.'

A meal is waiting for them, and the women discuss the big news while eating. This afternoon, during a slow period, Group Captain Robinson made an announcement that boosted morale and everyone's spirits appreciably.

The day before yesterday, Saturday the 24th, the city of Portsmouth was bombed again. This time, they received the highest number of casualties so far for one city: over one hundred dead and another three hundred injured. And for the first time, London was bombed. The Germans dropped bombs on Oxford Street in the West End. There were no reports of casualties from this attack, at least none so far.

The Group Captain told the crew that Churchill was outraged and ordered the RAF to retaliate in kind. Last night, for the first time in the war, Berlin itself was bombed. This news produced an almost riotous cheer, then a spontaneous singing of *For He's a Jolly Good Fellow* in honor of Winston Churchill. Fine news, indeed.

"Oh my," Catherine said out loud while reading Jeff's letter. She was sitting on her bunk all set for lights out when something he wrote jumped out at her.

"What?" Carla, the woman in the next bed asked. "Bad news?"

"No, not at all," Catherine replied.

Their section leader and friend, Betsy Halvorson, heard them as she walked by. She stopped and asked Catherine, "Good news?"

"Well, sort of," Catherine said. "Jeff is working on getting permission to come to Dover. He wants to know if I could sneak off for a few hours."

"Write him back, tell him yes, and we'll figure out a way to make it happen," Betsy quickly told her.

"I couldn't, I mean, I can't take advantage of everyone like that," Catherine said. "Could I?"

"Absolutely," Carla said. "Then you'll come back and tell us every bawdy detail. Especially the shagging. It's been so long, I might be a virgin again."

By now there were several other women leaning in listening. They all laughed at Carla's remark. A couple of them agreed, and they all affirmed that Catherine should agree to it and have Jeff come. Most of them had husbands, boyfriends or brothers in uniform somewhere. If one of them could enjoy a few hours away from the stress, especially with a lover, they were all for it.

"Wouldn't you help one of us do the same thing?" Betsy asked.

"Yes, of course," Catherine quickly agreed.

"Well, there you have it," Betsy said.

Catherine looked around at the smiling faces and said, "All right then, I'll do it, and bless you all."

August 31, 1940

Saturday was another exceptionally busy day for the crew of the Swingate Chain Home Station, the other Chain Home stations and the entire RAF Fighter Command. It was also a very hard day for them. In the greatest one-day loss so far in the war, the Germans destroyed thirty-eight planes total in the air and on the ground. They also all but destroyed several critical airfields in southern Britain. How many more days like this could Fighter Command handle?

Like everyone else at Swingate, Catherine was having another very stressful day. Since August 13, the RAF had battled the Luftwaffe every day. And if the reports were to be believed, the Germans had suffered far more losses in aircraft and pilots than the British. Yet, every day it seemed the Germans were able to put more planes in the air than the day before. At this rate, or so the Swingate crew were starting to believe, the Germans were going to prevail. As a consequence, morale was creeping downward.

For Catherine, today was both more stressful and exhilarating. According to yesterday's letter from Jeff, he had a ticket for the earliest train from London to Dover for today. In fact, if all went well, he was at this moment checked into a suite at the Grand Hotel in Dover. Just her luck, the Germans would pick today to make such a massive nuisance of themselves.

"Aircraftwoman Hartley," Catherine heard the voice of Group Captain Robinson say from behind and to her left.

"Sir," she said after turning to face him. It was 1000 hours and there was a lull in the action.

"Aircraftwoman Hartley," Robinson said, "you are obviously not feeling well today."

"But I feel fine, sir," Catherine said.

"No, I'm afraid not. I can see it as plain as day," Robinson said. "Section Leader," he said looking at Betsy, "join us, please."

Everyone in the room was looking at Catherine and Robinson. They all knew that today was the day Catherine was to sneak off to spend time with Jeff. It was supposed to be later this evening. All of the women were in on it, and they were all set to provide cover for her. Now it seemed Robinson was going to derail their well-laid plan.

"Hartley, you'll give your equipment to the section leader. She will take over your duties. You are evidently not feeling well, and I am forced to relieve you," Robinson said.

Catherine was in a near panic wondering what this intervention would do to her hope of spending the night with Jeff. "Sir, if there is something I've done or missed—"

"Don't argue with me," Robinson said.

Reluctantly Catherine took off her telephone gear and headset for Betsy Halvorson. Betsy looked every bit as concerned as Catherine.

"Follow me," Robinson sternly said looking at Catherine.

She followed him outside through the front door. When they got outside in the sunshine, Robinson's personal staff car and driver, holding the rear door open, were waiting.

"My driver will take you to your quarters where you will shower and change into a fresh uniform. He has an errand to run in Dover. If you would like to ride along, he'll take you and possibly drop you off somewhere. Oh, and one last thing," he continued more quietly, "he'll be in front of the Grand Hotel at 0700 hours tomorrow to pick you up. Sorry, Catherine, but this is the best I can do."

A stunned Catherine Hartley looked at the smiling driver, then turned back to a smiling Robinson. "How did you—"

"Don't ask," he said.

She put her arms around his neck, hugged him, kissed him on the cheek and whispered a thank you in his ear.

"Enjoy yourself," he said, when she let go and stepped back. "I wish I could do this for all of them."

"Thank you, again, sir," she said then saluted.

I look at my watch for at least the fourth time since I sat down. I don't even notice the time. I look again to find that it is only a little bit after eleven a.m. I was on the earliest train from Waterloo Station to Dover this morning and arrived before eight. After leaving the train, I easily find a cab for the short ride to the Grand Hotel. I was too early to check in, but since doing so, I have had nothing to do but anxiously wait for Catherine. Over and over the same thought runs through my head, *What if something happens and she can't get away?*

I put out my cigarette and hold the watered-down scotch and soda in my hand. I am in the Grand's pub. It is about half full of the early lunch crowd. I should not be drinking on an empty stomach, but there is little else to do but hope she gets away later. I look at my watch again while thinking about getting some lunch. Afterwards, I will take a long walk and explore Dover.

"Hey, sailor, looking for a good time?"

I spin around on my barstool, and there she is! I audibly gasp and literally stop breathing just to look at her. She is more beautiful than I remember: dashing in her blue WAAF uniform, holding a small suitcase in her right hand, her head slightly cocked, her mouth turned up in a mischievous smile.

"Jeff, breathe," she says as she sets down her suitcase.

I step forward, put my arms around her waist and lift her completely off the floor. Her face is above me as I look up at her.

"Hi," I finally manage to say.

"Hello to you, too, Yank," she returns.

By now everyone in the pub is staring at us, the pretty British girl and her American. Catherine holds my face between both hands and kisses me, which I eagerly return.

"I am very happy to see you," I manage to say still holding her off of the floor. "How…?"

"I am very happy to see you, too. Now, put me down and I'll tell you. We're making a scene."

"I don't care," I reply. "Let them watch. In fact," I continue in a whisper, "we could have at it right here for all I care."

Catherine laughs and replies, "Now that would get the girls' blood pumping back at the barracks to tell them about that."

I set her down and kiss her again. As I do, the pub patrons erupt in applause. Catherine's face turns red, and she buries it in my chest trying to hide while she laughs.

I pick up her bag, and she put her arm through mine. As I lead her to a table, I wave at the small crowd. "Thank you, thank you," I say to them. "Glad you liked the show. Come back soon."

This sets off an even louder and more prolonged applause and even a few whistles. Again, Catherine tries to hide behind me.

I take her to a small table for two in a corner by itself. While holding her chair, I lean down to smell her, to get her scent as if to make sure she is really here. I sit down across from her, reach over the tabletop, take her hands in mine and kiss them both. We stare at each other, time frozen but for only ten seconds or so.

"Hello, again, my love," I say again breaking the silence. "You're not going to cry, are you?" I ask.

"Maybe," she replies, the tears glistening in her big, brown eyes as she sniffles. "Can we freeze this moment forever?"

"Sorry, no," I say. "We have business to attend to in our room."

At that, Catherine leans forward and sensually whispers, "Speaking of which, my adorable Yank, I have had an itch for some time now that desperately needs to be scratched. Do you think you can help me with that?"

I also lean forward so that my nose is almost touching hers and reply, "I'm pretty sure I have just the thing to fix that for you."

An hour later we lay naked together, our bodies glistening with a light sheen in the warm room, entwined in each other. We are both lightly dozing, not sleeping but not awake either.

"Twice in less than an hour," Catherine says, almost purring in my ear. "I'm impressed."

My eyes are closed but I smile at her and say, "Our service aims to please, ma'am. Plus, it's been a while."

I am lying on my back, the blankets up to my waist. Catherine is curled up at my side lightly moving the fingertips of her left hand over my stomach. When I say this, she reaches down and grabs my genitals giving me an ominous squeeze.

"It damn well better have been a while," she says as I gasp in surprise. Catherine laughs and lets go. She rolls over on top of me and starts lightly kissing my neck and face.

"Um, maybe, uh, a bit later," I say. "I'm not sure this is going to work."

She looks down at me, smiles and says, "I know. I'm just so happy to be here. I want this moment to last forever."

"That reminds me," I say. "How did you get here so early?"

"Cigarette," she says as she rolls back to my left.

I reach over to the side table, get two from the pack, light them and hand one to her. While we smoke, she tells me the story.

"How did he find out?" I ask when she finishes.

"I don't know. I was so shocked and relieved, I didn't push for an answer," Catherine says.

"Nice man," I say.

She puts out her cigarette in the ashtray I am holding. She exhales a stream of smoke and says, "Actually, yes, he is. He's a good man and a good commanding officer."

"I'm hungry," I say.

"Such a romantic," she replies.

"Let's get a bite then explore Dover. I'd like to go down by the harbor and—"

"I doubt they will let us in," Catherine says. "I'm sure it's a restricted area. There's a war on after all."

"Thanks for reminding me. I'd almost forgotten. We can interview some locals. As long as I'm here, I might as well get material for a story."

Catherine rolls over, sits up on the bedside, looks over her bare shoulder at me and says, "I need a shower. Care to come give me a hand and wash my back?"

She stands and as she walks toward the bathroom, I toss back the covers. I get up and say, "You have some other parts that need my attention also."

The two of us spend the rest of the day holding hands like love-struck teenagers. Catherine, for the first time since her short leave in July, is wearing a civilian dress, shoes and even underwear. We wander aimlessly up and down the streets of Dover. It is a beautiful, warm, sunny day and the war seems to be a distant memory. Except there are a few times when I stop and talk to local civilians about the war. On the whole, their morale is quite good, excellent even.

A little before seven o'clock that evening, we make our way back to the hotel. The walk and the fresh seaside air have made us both hungry again. The bar's pub serves a passable shepherd's pie. Being a seaport, the shortages London was starting to deal with are not as evident here. Sundown in Dover will be around a quarter of eight. The blackout will begin then. Of course, the two of us have only one thing in mind after dinner.

Catherine pushes her empty dishes aside—I have already done so—and lights a cigarette. Leaning on her left elbow, the cigarette in her left hand, she leans forward with a lustful look in her eyes.

"Well, Yank, have you had sufficient recovery time?" she asks.

I crush out my smoke in the table ashtray and reply, "Oh, I'm fairly certain I can accommodate my lady's wishes."

Before Catherine can answer me, the air raid sirens in the city go off. The Germans are paying Dover and its surrounding area a visit.

"Into the basement shelters!" we hear the barman announce. "Please be quick about it, ladies and gentlemen."

The management of the hotel has turned the basement into a comfortable bomb shelter. There are rooms with beds and rooms with chairs. They have even set up several radios for people to listen to during an attack. These things have also been done in all of the hotels in London.

We sit together on a small sofa, holding hands, listening to the bombs exploding off in the distance. There are seven other people, hotel guests, with us in this small room. There are even two young girls, children of a couple staying at the hotel. The husband is originally from Dover, now living in London. We learn they are here visiting his family.

Of the small group, Catherine is easily the calmest. None of the bombs have gone off anywhere near the hotel. Catherine has been through far worse than this several times. Within a short while, the two young girls are sitting on the rug at Catherine's feet while she calmly talks to them. She explains to them what is happening and soothes the youngsters. It is again the harbor being attacked two miles away.

A half-hour after it starts, we hear a significant number of bombs going off to the north. Both Catherine and I know what this means: Swingate and the surrounding military facilities are being bombed. I look at Catherine who is avoiding me.

"They'll be all right," Catherine finally says referring to Swingate.

We can also hear the 'thump, thump, thump' of the anti-aircraft guns. A moment after what would be the last bomb goes off; we hear the screaming sound of a plane going down. It is followed by a large explosion somewhere between the hotel and the harbor.

"We got one," Catherine quietly says.

The next morning the two of us are standing in front of the hotel waiting for Catherine's ride. A few minutes early, the staff car pulls up to get her. While the group captain's driver holds the door for her, we are saying our goodbyes. I walk her to the car and flip my hand to dismiss the driver. At the car door, Catherine throws her arms around me, and we cling to each other for a full minute.

"Thank you for not saying it," she says. "Thank you for not getting on about the bombing last night and how much you worry about me."

"I do worry about you, a lot," I say. "But we had a wonderful time, and I knew it wouldn't help. Please be careful. I love you and don't want to lose you."

"I love you too, and I promise I'll be careful."

***

The next day, now back in London, I find out the casualty report from the attack on Dover. Four civilians died when the Heinkel that was shot down crashed in the city. A small, empty cargo ship was sunk in the harbor with two men aboard, both missing and presumed dead.

The bombing we heard north of the city was the worst: thirteen dead and another twenty-two injured, all military personnel, none of whom were assigned to the Swingate facility.

The Swingate Chain Home Station suffered no damage or casualties. All of Catherine's friends made it through unscathed.

TWENTY-SIX

September 12, 1940

Dear Mom & Dad,

You have probably been reading my articles and listening to Ed Murrow on the radio. If so, you know by now the Germans have been bombing London. The first bombing, back in August, appears to have been a mistake.

What the city is experiencing now began in the late afternoon and early evening of September 7. It has continued every day since. They are after the London docks on the Thames. So far, their main target area is what is called the Isle of Dogs. It is a peninsula almost encircled by the Thames where most of the docks are located. Unfortunately, it's where most of the dock workers and their families also live.

For the first few days, and nights, these poor people were catching hell. Where I am, Mayfair, as I am sure you remember, is several miles from the target areas. In fact, we guiltily go up on the roof of whatever building we are in to watch. We're not supposed to do this. Once the air raid alarms sound, we are to immediately seek shelter.

The hotels, government buildings and more privileged buildings have prepared shelters in them. As you may be able to guess, this is not true of the less affluent areas. The Isle of Dogs and the surrounding boroughs are among these.

There has been a holy row coming from the people who live there. Quite understandable. The government has not done enough to provide shelter for these citizens, and the casualties are mounting. Estimates are a thousand dead already.

The government may have received a reprieve last night. Buckingham Palace and St. Paul's Cathedral were bombed. The King and Queen were in residence at the time; their children were not. Fortunately, the Palace received only minor damage and the Royal Couple were not injured.

This morning my journalist friends and I spent most of the day visiting the dock areas. It seems the Palace bombing has been a morale boost. The attitude is: "We are all in it together after all. If the King and Queen can take it, so can we."

A typical bombing, for me, begins with a trip to the basement shelter of the Ritz. We can hear the bombers overhead, wave after wave of them. Over one hundred on most days. After a short while, some of the more foolish among us (yes, I am among them, but please don't worry) venture up to the roof.

We watch with our hearts in our throats and listen to the bombs going off. It never fails to remind me of Dunkirk. Although Dunkirk, by the time I saw it, was much worse. Still, the fires burn through the night.

We are all tempted to go to the affected areas to see if we can help. So far, the government has requested that people not do this, at least until the fires are out. They have an excellent point. The firemen have enough to do without untrained amateurs getting in their way.

This morning, and I wasn't going to tell you this, we helped remove rubble from damaged buildings. We were helping to look for survivors along with hundreds of other volunteers. Again, I wasn't going to write this, but we pulled out the bodies of a woman and two children. One of the women working with us knew her. The children were only four and two years old. Her husband is serving somewhere in the Royal Navy. I am starting to tear up trying to write this.

I am back. I took a break when I started to cry over the young mother and her children.

My naval attaché friend and contacts we have in the British Military believe Hitler has made a huge mistake. It appears he threw a tantrum following the RAF's bombing of Berlin. Shifting his strategy to bombing British cities (Dover is still a target) has been a blessing for the RAF. Hitler and his fat friend, Goering, must not have realized how close they were to winning. Bombing cities, while horrible for the people, is giving Fighter Command a chance to recover and regroup. If they continue bombing cities, the invasion will not happen.

Writing to you always makes me feel better. Don't worry about me. I'm on the safe end of London.

Love to all,

Jeff

I read through the letter to my parents a second time. Have I told them too much? Have I been too graphic? The censors would certainly think so.

In my articles for the *Gazette*, I am much more circumspect. I describe the bombings and even put in the one for today, the story about the woman and her children. I was a bit surprised the censors let that go through. They must be looking for sympathy and more support from America. I hope it works. I decide to send the article because Americans need to know what is taking place here. Ed Murrow's radio broadcasts are receiving great acclaim, but there are still too many isolationists.

FDR is breaking presidential precedent and running for a third term. The Republicans have nominated Wendell Willkie to oppose him. Willkie is a good man, and under normal circumstances, I could vote for him; except he is an avowed isolationist. I understand the appeal, but it will take America and Britain to defeat Hitler.

I have two maps on my wall now: one of Great Britain and one of the City of London. I am using colored pins to mark the bombings. One area of London is bearing the brunt of it. I fear that will not last.

While I look at the markings of bombings and artillery shelling of Dover, my phone rings. It is Clive Burke with news. Along with London and several other cities, Dover was hit again last night. My heart sinks a bit but then, the air raid sirens start up, so I end the call. Another long night for London.

I head for the shelter, and when I arrive, I find most of my hotel neighbors there. The Ritz is filling up with the elite of London. A number of eminent royals, aristocrats and politicians are moving in. The entire Albanian royal family has taken up residence including King Zog I. A more mediocre group of people, not just the Albanians but most of the rest also, I have never met. At first, I thought they might be interesting and a great source of information. Instead, they have proven to be the most pretentious, self-involved, simpletons imaginable. And instead of being a source of information, they are constantly trying to get information from me. Little wonder I never socialize here, and during air raids, I head for the roof as soon as possible.

I can hear the planes overhead, by now a familiar sound. Once again, they have circled around London to the north to fly east to their targets. They are still after the docks and storage facilities on the Thames. Mayfair is primarily an affluent borough with little industry, apparently, of little strategic interest for the Germans.

Within twenty minutes after I arrive in the basement, I can take no more of my neighbors. Hundreds, perhaps thousands, of people may die in this raid. These self-proclaimed elites care not a whit as long as they are safe. The European class-system is alive and well. Since I can hear the distant explosions of the bombs, I am sure Mayfair is not a target. Once again, I head for the roof.

When I get to the roof, there are five other people already up here, including two women. They are hotel guests of whom I am acquainted. Two of them, a married couple, are well-known theater actors. There are normally three or four more who may still arrive or might be out of the hotel.

On my way up to the roof, I stopped in my room to retrieve my binoculars. Sunset is approaching, but it is still light enough to use my glasses. I put them to my eyes and train them upward. This is a very large raid, at least two hundred bombers and they are still flying past. Most of them are flying almost directly overhead. It is light enough for them to go between Hyde Park and Regent's Park. There are anti-aircraft batteries set up in both parks and are firing away at the planes. We have yet to see any German planes downed by these guns in any raid so far.

Along with two of the men on the roof, I walk over to the east side of the building. Once again, we watch with a mixture of fascination and horror. It is an awesome display laid out before us. As the crow flies, the dock area being hit is about five miles. With the darkening skies before us, the sun almost down at our backs, the area is clearly visible from the fires already blazing. Despite knowing the horror these poor people are being subjected to, we cannot stop watching. This may be the largest raid yet. Hundreds are being killed and injured and many thousands made homeless.

Like Dunkirk, I am watching another scene out of Dante's *Inferno*. The smoke and fire rising up into the sky illuminates the area. Unlike Dunkirk, there are searchlights stabbing the sky finding the occasional bomber. The AA fire and bombs going off create an almost symphonic sound to go along with the lighting. What people do not get from newsreel film of it is the smell. Even from this distance, we can smell the explosions as well as hear them. And in the morning, we will join the rescue efforts and smell the dead and the death. There are times when I wonder if I will ever get the smell, or at least the memory of it, out of my head.

Each night we bear witness to it. I flashback to Dunkirk; the nights when we stood offshore waiting our turn to pick up a load of soldiers. At least then I was doing something, and our cargo was soldiers. Here, again tonight, the targets are civilians: men, women and children, although most of the children have been sent out of the city. It is incredibly depressing and leaves me feeling guilty and helpless.

My rooftop companions are all at least two decades older than me. I consider this when I think about the morning. David, Charlie and I—Clive will probably join us—will make our way to the affected area. By then, the fires should be under control. We can help with the search for survivors; a rewarding task when we find one, a gruesome one when we come across the dead buried in the rubble. The simple truth is my friends on the roof are a little too old or I would invite them. We will be at it most of the day, all morning at least. It is hard, difficult labor which none of us are used to. It gives those of us who do it a feeling of helping, even after the fact.

To their credit, we saw the King and Queen touring the area the day after Buckingham Palace was bombed. Their presence was a significant morale boost for everyone, including us cynical Americans.

As an American, before moving to London, I wondered why the British kept the King and Queen and Royal Family. It seemed to be a rather extravagant, anachronistic, even somewhat silly indulgence. Having lived here for a while, I completely understand it now. Britain has a long and deep history. The Royal Family has been an enormously important, even vital part of that history. They are playing a critical role on behalf of the British people during the current crisis.

September 13, 1940

It is midafternoon, and the four of us, Clive included, are at a table in a pub near the American Embassy. The name of the place, the Cock and Bull, or Dog and Pony, whatever it is, escapes me. How these people come up with these names is a mystery to me. We have had nothing to eat since a quick breakfast very early this morning. The four of us are hungry, exhausted and quite filthy, but feeling very good about ourselves. We have been hard at it helping with the survivor search, even finding several; and no buried bodies. I am sure there are some, but we were fortunate to have missed them.

The brunt of the damage occurred inland from the Thames' docks. Despite it happening on civilian areas, the casualty reports are not as bad as they might have been. The government is working to provide better shelters. They are trying to keep civilians out of the Underground train stations, but no one is listening. It is feared a direct hit by a bomb would kill hundreds crowded into the train tunnels. It seems people are willing to risk it. If I lived there, I would join them.

The pub owner, a bald man wearing his medals from the First War, serves our food. We are filthy and probably smell like sweaty socks but are too tired to care. We have told the owner where we have been, and he is treating us like royalty. The man is especially impressed that three Americans were helping. A couple of his customers make snide remarks insulting to American passivity. He chastises them and threatens to show the two men the door for their rudeness.

The meal itself is some passable, reasonably edible combination of some type of meat and some type of vegetables. As tired and hungry as we are, the meat could have barked at us, and no one would care.

"Hello, gents," we hear the voice of Mike Burns as he approaches the table. He pulls up a chair to sit in between Charlie and David and asks, "So, how was it?"

"Not as bad as a couple of days ago," Charlie answers. Charlie was with me when we found the bodies of the young mother and her children. Neither of us will likely ever forget it.

"What are you hearing, Mike?" I ask.

Burns signals to the pub owner to bring another round of pints for us and himself. We wait quietly while the man delivers, then leaves. When he can no longer be overheard, he answers me.

"Fighter Command is almost back to full strength. Adolf and Fatso Goering have made a huge a mistake. The planes the RAF lost are almost completely replaced. They've had a chance to do more training, and they're getting pilots back—those that were wounded but are now ready for duty again."

"Yes," Clive agrees. "That's what my sources are telling me, too."

Burns lifts his glass for a toast and says, "To the RAF. Never has so much been owed by so many to so few."

We touch glasses, agree heartily and spend the next four hours getting shitfaced drunk. Fortunately, I sober up enough before the attack that night to get to the basement. The weather over London is cloudy with sporadic rain showers. The number of German bombers are fewer than the previous night, and the cloud cover hampers their accuracy. They overshoot their normal target and hit a sparsely populated area.

I am too tired and dealing with a headache to make it to the roof. I manage to write a reasonably coherent letter to Catherine. Before the all-clear sounds, I sneak up to my room and collapse on my bed. It is almost noon before I awake.

TWENTY-SEVEN

September 15, 1940

Catherine placed her daily letter to Jeff in the postal box. Several other WAAFs had also dropped off letters and others were still in line to do so. As she walked toward the lorry filling up with her mates, Catherine thought about Jeff's latest letter.

London was being bombed every day and most nights. Of course, she knew this. Even though the Germans had changed their strategy, Dover and by extension, Swingate, were still targets. Except now it was no longer aerial bombing from planes. The Germans had set up long-range coastal artillery that could reach across the twenty miles from France to Dover.

Yesterday Dover was bombarded for several hours. Mostly the harbor was targeted. For an hour, while their bombers were flying overhead toward London, Swingate and its surrounding area was hit. Catherine and her mates huddled together inside the Chain Home Station during the shelling. These are big guns with 11- and 13-inch-long range shells. Several landed close enough to rattle the building, knock things off of tables and cause dust to filter down on them from the rafters. An 11- or 13-inch shell landing directly on the building would likely kill them all.

Even the soldiers, one of whom was an older veteran sergeant who had served in France in the First War, were also terrified. Being shelled is an extremely horrible experience: the feeling of terror, helplessness and panic knowing that any second a large artillery shell could come through the roof and blow the flimsy building to pieces.

It ended abruptly around 1800 hours. For fifteen more minutes, all the personnel stayed where they were to be sure it was over. The group captain was the first to crawl out. Covered in dust, he looked as frightened and shocked as anyone.

It was hardly the first time and not likely the last that they would endure it. When Catherine came out from under the large table, she looked around the room. A few of the WAAFs were giving each other a hug, but amazingly, no tears, no hysterics, just grim determination.

"Is everyone all right?" she heard Group Captain Robinson ask. "Any injuries that need attending?"

They all looked around at each other then back at the group captain with shaking heads.

"Very well, then," Robinson said. "Let's put the place back together and get back to our duties." He looked up at the ceiling and listened to the sound of the bombers still going by. "Another busy night, I'm afraid," he announced.

At 2200 hours, once again Catherine and her friends wearily climbed into the back of the lorry. As it started off toward the station, the women held hands with each other. This had become a custom a couple of weeks back. It was a sign of solidarity, comradeship and comfort for each other.

As their transport bounced along, Catherine looked over the weary, even exhausted faces of her friends. If they were becoming this worn out, how were the men flying the combat missions holding up, she wondered. And how much more of this could they take?

A couple of days ago, Robinson discreetly told them that the change in strategy by the Germans was a godsend. Two or three more weeks of attacks on the RAF airfields might have won the war. The bombing of the cities, as horrible as it was for the civilians, had given Fighter Command a much-needed reprieve, a reprieve that might end up saving Britain from invasion.

For Catherine, the bombing of London was one more thing to worry about. Jeff's letters were almost casual about it. Of course, he assured her that he was not in any personal danger at all. She knew this since their job at Swingate was tracking and plotting the Germans, then relaying the information to Fighter Command so they could direct the fighters to the attackers. They all knew what part of London was taking the brunt of the bombing.

In his letter two days ago, Jeff let it slip that he and his friends were helping with rescue operations. This meant he was spending time in the target areas risking his life to help. It reminded her of her worries for him during the Dunkirk evacuation.

"Damn fool, Yank. Should be minding his own damn business," Catherine said out loud as the truck hit another hole and lurched to the side.

"What?" the woman next to her said.

"What?" Catherine asked.

"What damn fool Yank? Yours?" the woman asked.

"Did I say that out loud? Oh my God, I'm sorry, Sadie," Catherine said then laughed along with the others who were listening.

"It's all right, love," Sadie replied. "We're all becoming a little daft."

At precisely 0800 hours, Catherine and her mates were all in place and ready for another long day. Since September 7, the Germans had launched daily attacks but mostly in the afternoon and evening. Today was to be different. Beginning in the morning and lasting all day and into the night, the Luftwaffe threw everything it had in an all-out attack on London.

In fact, this day, September 15, 1940, would eventually be given the title 'Battle of Britain Day': the semi-official day that England won the Battle of Britain and would end the threat of invasion. This would go unknown, of course, until after the war was over.

At the time, the Luftwaffe pilots were being told the RAF was on its last legs. Hitler was also told this. It is estimated that over fifteen hundred aircraft in total for both sides went into the air that day. The Germans were hammered by Fighter Command. Estimates of German losses were as high as two hundred planes shot down. The actual total, while never precisely known, is likely closer to sixty, fewer than several attacks that had occurred during August.

The difference this time was the morale of the Luftwaffe was shaken to its core. Having been assured they were winning, the ferocity of Fighter Command's response would cause Hitler to postpone the invasion code named Operation Sea Lion, indefinitely. Of course, the British did not know it at the time. Operation Sea Lion would never take place, and the Battle of Britain was over, won by the British due, in no small part, to the heroic women who operated the Chain Home Stations, including Swingate.

"That was a bloody, long day," the woman walking behind Catherine softly said.

It was, again, 2200 hours. They had been at the duty stations for another fourteen-hour day. They had little time for food and barely enough for quick trips to the loo and an occasional smoke break. And they would be back at the same time and place in the morning.

Standing in line, waiting for her turn to climb into their transport, Catherine almost fell asleep. Her head went down bumping the back of the woman in front of her, which snapped her awake.

"Sorry, Betsy," she managed to mutter.

"It's okay," Betsy said. "It woke me up too."

Betsy climbed up and sat down. As Catherine started up, her legs went weak. She fell back and would have gone down but for the woman behind her.

"Sorry, Carla."

"It's all right. Come on, up you go," Carla said, literally pushing her up to grab Betsy's hand and collapse on the hard, wooden bench.

"My legs feel like rubber," Catherine weakly said.

"No wonder," Carla replied who was now next to her, "You're on your feet talking into that damn phone all day. Tomorrow, we'll get you a chair.'

"That would help," Catherine said.

***

Catherine finished her letter to Jeff and placed it in an envelope. Not a word again about the shelling they endured yesterday. Fortunately, the Germans took the day off today from attacks on Dover and Swingate. Instead, they had turned their guns on a small convoy heading toward the Thames Estuary. Swingate had received a report of just minor damage to one ship.

Catherine pulled her blanket up to her shoulders then tried reading Jeff's letter again, the usual banalities but a joy for Catherine. There were women with her who rarely got mail. A daily letter, no matter how mundane, reinforced the knowledge that someone out there loved her, missed her and was thinking about her.

She was reading it for the third time. This time, she did not finish it. Her friend in the next bunk found her lightly snoring holding the letter to her chest. Carla took it, folded it and put it back in the envelope a minute before lights out.

"May I have your attention, please," Group Captain Robinson said addressing the day shift crew.

Catherine had already assembled her telephonic transmittal equipment. As did all personnel, she turned to face the group captain.

He was standing above them, looking down, hands behind his back with an impassive expression. "First of all, the poor weather conditions of the past several days appear to be over. The relative lull in operations that resulted during that time is likely to be at an end. We can expect a significant increase in German air operations.

"Next, I have been authorized to pass along some good news," he continued, looking down at the expectant faces. "On September 19, Bomber Command flew missions bombing the invasion staging areas on the coast of France and Belgium. We have received intelligence that, as a result, Hitler has ordered the barges and landing craft staged in these areas to be dispersed. This has been verified by over-flights by the RAF."

A murmur went through the crew, and most of the upward-looking faces were wearing a smile.

Robinson continued, "Because of this, I have been authorized to pass along, and this is extremely classified, the War Office believes the threat of invasion has diminished."

A wild, raucous cheer went up. It was the threat of invasion that these people were so diligently working against. Robinson, also wearing a grin, raised his hands as a gesture requesting quiet. It took twenty to thirty seconds, but the room eventually went still again.

"There's more," Robinson said. "We have received intelligence—I'm afraid unverified—that Hitler has postponed the invasion indefinitely."

This time, the cheering was accompanied by hand clapping, foot stomping, whistles and howls that rattled the walls. Several of the women and some of the men had tears streaming down their faces. Catherine, standing directly beneath Robinson, was sobbing almost uncontrollably. The relief was so great her knees felt weak and her legs almost buckled.

Robinson let them go for another minute, then again raised his arms requesting quiet. "Be advised, this does not mean they're not coming. But

Herr Hitler has certainly hesitated. Of course, this has been accomplished through the efforts and sacrifice of a good many people, not least, those of us in this building. You have all been exposed to grave danger, gave enormously of yourselves and played a tremendous role in bringing this about. And I am damn proud of each and every one of you. It has truly been the honor of my career to have worked alongside you through these many thankless hours to bring this about."

Another round of loud cheering, clapping and foot stomping broke out. As it did, Lt. Connors bounced up the stairs from the floor to the walkway. He went directly to Robinson and whispered in his ear.

Once again Robinson held up his arms, only this time he also yelled out, "Quiet please! Quiet! I need your attention. The lieutenant has just informed me that the Jerrys are forming up over Calais. Let's get to it."

In all, the attacking force of Luftwaffe aircraft that day totaled over two hundred. The Germans were becoming less discriminatory in their targeting. Despite the efforts of Fighter Command, most of the bombers made it through to hit London. At least a dozen enemy planes were shot down with a loss of four RAF fighters.

By noon, the morning attack was over and there was a lull. This allowed the support staff to bring up a meal for the station personnel at noon. Catherine was in the first shift enjoying the break.

"That was nice news this morning," her friend Carla said.

Catherine and several of the others were finished eating and enjoying a quick smoke break. They were behind the building in the patio area.

"Boosts everyone's morale," another woman agreed.

Catherine field stripped her cigarette and stood up to go.

"You're going in already?" Carla asked.

"Yes. The lieutenant is handling my phone. I should get back so he can have a quick bite," Catherine answered.

It happened while Lt. Connors was removing Catherine's gear. She was standing next to him when they heard the first ones.

"Incoming shelling!" Connors yelled. He grabbed Catherine's arm and the two of them dove for cover under the table.

Eight or ten 11- and 13-inch shells went off fiercely shaking the building. Connors and Catherine were under the table. His right arm was holding onto her while they laid face down on the floor. This attack was the closest one yet. They could hear screaming coming from the patio area as the next round of shells moved farther off.

"Richard," Catherine yelled over the noise using Connors' first name, "they're outside! We have to do something!"

Catherine tried to get up on her hands and knees, but Connors pulled her back down. The shelling was still close enough to make normal speech too difficult to hear. Instead, Connors put his mouth next to Catherine's ear.

"There's nothing we can do, Catherine. You go out there, you'll be killed."

The shelling continued to move off and after fifteen minutes stopped all together.

"All right, let's go," Connors told her.

Along with most of the people still inside, Connors and Catherine, led by Group Captain Robinson, ran through the door outside. The first shell had landed less than twenty meters from the group of women.

The casualty count would be three dead, seven seriously wounded and the other eight with minor wounds. Among the dead was Catherine's good friend, Carla. She had been sitting in Catherine's normal chair when the shell hit and decapitated her.

BOOK THREE

Jeffrey, Catherine
&
The Blitz

TWENTY-EIGHT

September 27, 1940

Dear Mom & Dad,

I am sure you are seeing the newspaper reports and hearing the radio broadcasts. London and several other cities in England are taking a pounding from the Germans. London appears to be getting the worst of it. As of today, Friday, September 27, the city has endured twenty consecutive days being bombed. So far, Mayfair has gone unscathed, but the Germans are no longer concentrating on the East End dock areas. They are becoming more and more indiscriminate. Civilian casualties are rising.

My journalist mates and I have spent a lot of time in the target areas. Don't worry, it is always after the bombing when it is safe. We help in the search and rescue efforts. This is both rewarding, when we find someone alive, and gruesome, when we pull out dead bodies from the rubble. So far, the morale of the people is still extremely good. If the Germans believe they can bomb England into surrender, they will be disappointed.

I am not sure I mentioned this before. The government has developed a small but effective shelter for people. It is called an Anderson Shelter named for the man in charge of air-raid preparation. It is basically a small hut made of corrugated metal. It is roughly six feet tall, six and a half feet long and five feet wide.

People dig a hole in their yard, place it in the hole and cover it with any number of things. Mostly, they are covered with dirt, and many people plant flowers and vegetables on them. They will snugly hold up to six people. Of course, a direct hit on one will not protect them. But they are quite effective at protecting people from near misses and debris. The English are still a clever and inventive people. These little nests have saved hundreds of lives.

Now, for some interesting personal news. I am not sure I should tell you this, but you'll know soon enough. I received an invitation yesterday

I read through the letter again. Not a word about Catherine. I know she is still on the front line of this wretched war. Every day I spend time thinking about and reliving the time we had in Dover recently. It is both a great joy and terrible sadness. I can't help thinking it may be the last time I see her. It is a dread I cannot shake.

I address the envelope and get it ready for mailing. Mail service, without going through the government is becoming more sporadic, less reliable and more expensive. I am not sure if what I have written will make it past the censors. My newspaper columns contain more information and are more descriptive of the damage and casualties. It seems the Brits want this publicized in America. From the feedback I have received, it may be having an effect on public opinion, especially Ed Murrow's broadcasts.

Ed's voice and descriptions of the carnage are much more graphic than a newspaper article. Plus, the people listening to him do not have to do anything; they merely need to sit in their living rooms in front of their radios. Most nights Ed will broadcast from the roof of the BBC building. The bombs exploding in the background are carried into the homes of America. Hard to match that in a written article that must be read.

Isolationism is still held firmly by the majority of Americans. But their desire to send material support has increased significantly. A great example are the fifty old ships, destroyers, Roosevelt found a way to give them. They will help significantly with convoy escort duty. Hitler may be able to starve England into surrender before he wins by bombing or invasion.

On September 6, Congress passed the first ever conscription law. It is called the Selective Service Act of 1940. It requires all men between the ages of twenty-one and forty-five to register for the draft. I guess that includes me—although I am not sure how I am supposed to do this. Eventually, I will check with the embassy.

Charlie is quite concerned. I don't really believe the army will take a thirty-eight-year-old, married man with a family. Plus, he is not exactly physically fit for the job. It has been a source of amusement for the rest of us. David is considering returning home and enlisting. I think I convinced him to hold off until we actually get in the war.

I fill my coffee cup, light a cigarette and stare at the maps on the wall. I am running out of room on the London map, at least in certain areas of the city, to mark all of the bombings. It seems the dock areas have been receiving more help from the government, or at least less interference. The people have taken over the tube stations despite the government's efforts to stop them.

My phone rings. It is the concierge informing me that my ride is here. Along with the invitation to interview the PM—in reality a command—a car is sent for me. I quickly stub out my cigarette, grab my hat, trench coat and leather folio and hurry downstairs.

Due to the war, except for cabs and government vehicles, traffic in Westminster is barely a bother. The car—a green military one—delivers me quickly to my destination. I have no prior knowledge of where I am to meet with the PM. I assumed it would be 10 Downing. Instead, I am standing on the sidewalk in front of the Treasury Building. It is on Horse Guards Road across from St. James Park.

"Go in the front door, sir," the driver tells me. "Someone will meet you."

I turn to look at the man as he drives off. I shrug, look up at the columned office building and head up the concrete stairs. When I reach the top, the door opens and a handsome man with receding hair, thick black eyebrows and a pleasant smile greets me. I immediately recognize him. He is Jock Colville, the PM's primary assistant secretary. He is also the one who arranged my interview, at the instigation of his boss.

It takes almost fifteen minutes for him to lead me through the Treasury Building, down several flights of stairs and into a rabbit warren of subterranean rooms. As he leads me down the narrow hallways, we pass a small army of scurrying military and civilian personnel. Colville notices that I am looking around in wonder. We pass by a number of offices, doors open and men and women inside working. They all look tidy, cramped and each has at least one bed for its occupant.

"Everyone moves more quickly when the PM is here," Colville says. "Here's my office. Come in, please."

He opens the door for me, and we go in. It is a room smaller than my bathroom at the hotel. Using the word Spartan to describe it would be generous. It has a desk, two small chairs, a very small armoire and a bed. This for the top personal assistant to the number one leader of the British Empire.

We take our seats, and Colville says, "You are in one of the most closely guarded secrets in the Kingdom. These are the offices of Churchill's War Room, the offices where the very top echelon of the British government is conducting the war. Obviously, the Germans would love to have this information. It was Winston's idea to meet you here. Simply being here makes any information you obtain subject to British secrecy laws. If you were to reveal its location, you would be prosecuted and hanged."

"I couldn't tell you where we are even if I wanted to," I reply.

Colville smiles and continues. "You aren't the first to be here and won't be the last to say that. In fact, Winston is the worst security problem we have. His mouth runs faster than his brain sometimes.

"Anyway," he says while taking a quick peek at a clock on his desk, "it's almost time to meet with him. He is a stickler for punctuality for everyone but himself. I'll take you to his office and leave you there. Go in, take a seat in front of his desk and wait for him. He is thinking of thirty or forty things at once. He'll probably be at his desk reading something and making notes. Trust me, he'll be aware of your presence. When he's ready, he will speak. You are scheduled for twenty minutes. If you are dismissed in less than an hour, I will be surprised.

"This office," he continues, referring to his office, "is just around the corner. If I am not waiting for you, come get me. I'll leave the door open. Do you have any questions?"

"Are there any subjects that are off limits?" I ask.

"Of course. Ask anything you want; he'll tell you if he won't answer."

I have been sitting in a hard, wooden armchair in front of Winston Churchill for almost two minutes. His office/bedroom is barely less minimalist than the others I saw. A couple of times he has swallowed some brandy and puffed on a foul-smelling cigar. The only other sounds are an occasional snort and his pen scratching on the document he is reading.

"We're going to win, you know," the man finally says continuing to finish the note he is writing without looking up. He sets the paper in a basket marked 'Out,' removes his black-framed, oval-lensed glasses and places them on the desk blotter.

"Yes, sir, I know that," I reply, while he picks up the cigar and puffs on it some more. I am not really sure I believe it, but in his presence, I will not insult him by disagreeing with him.

"You have your doubts, Mr. Bartlett," he says with his world-famous growl. "I can see it in your eyes."

"Well, I, uh, I suppose I do, at least a little."

He leans back, tilts his head at the ceiling and blows cigar smoke upward. "It's all right, young man," he says now looking straight at me. "If I was sitting in your chair, I would have doubts, too. But I'm not. I'm in this chair, not yours. You can afford to have doubts; I cannot. Therefore, I don't. See how easy it is?"

"Yes, sir," I say, smile and chuckle.

"I believe my mother knows your family. She's American, you know."

"Yes, sir, I do know that."

"Tell me, Jeff—you don't mind if I call you, Jeff, do you?"

"No, sir, of course not."

"You may call me Prime Minister," he says and laughs.

"Thank you, Prime Minister. I will do that. If I may, sir, it's good to see you laugh. I can only imagine how little time you have for amusement."

"I try to find things," he replies. "Tell me, through no fault of your own, you come from the moneyed class of America. What are they saying of President Roosevelt's chances of being reelected?"

"They don't think much of them, Prime Minister. But then, you probably have better sources of information than I do. Personally, I believe he will win easily. Willkie is a good and decent man, but I am hearing the tide is turning on isolationism, at least as far as providing you with aid. Once the election is over, you'll see things start to happen," I tell him.

As Colville predicted, I am there for the better part of an hour. The conversation is mostly about what America can do to help. Even when I manage to get in a question for my 'interview,' he easily swings the topic to what he wants, mostly the same tune he has been singing for the American public: "Give us the tools and we will finish the job."

Just about the time when I begin to sense my time is up, there is a sharp rap on the door. It opens and Jock Colville hurries in carrying a single sheet of paper. Since I am not asked to leave, I remain seated. Churchill puts on his glasses as Colville hands him the paper. The PM quickly reads what is on it, hands it back to Colville and removes the glasses.

"So, they've done it?" Churchill says to his assistant.

"It does appear so, Prime Minister," Colville replies.

Churchill looks at me and explains. "The Germans, Japan and Italy have signed a treaty. We had received information—that is not for publication—that they were going to. The three great threats to civilization have joined hands. In my opinion, Japan will now attack us in the Pacific. Eventually, it will lead to war between the Japanese Empire and America."

With that, my interview with Churchill concludes. He has been a gracious, even pleasant, host. Of course, I am well aware of what he is up to. He wants to use me and all of the American correspondents for propaganda purposes. Despite his outward confidence, the British war aims are quite clear: hang on until Roosevelt can figure out a way to get America in.

Colville guides me back through the labyrinth outside onto Horse Guards Road. The car and driver that brought me are waiting at the curb. Of course, I will write an article as sympathetic as I possibly can. The higher ups at the *Gazette* have been showing more and more affinity for the British of late. I have a good feel for the boundaries and will push them as far as I dare.

The front desk has a telephone message for me when I get back to the hotel. It is from Lt. Commander Burns and it is marked 'Urgent.' He is asking me to call him at the embassy right away. I do not even wait to go to my suite. I tell the counter clerk to place the call and transfer it to me in one of the booths.

The call goes through, I ask for Burns and he answers on the first ring. I have a lump in my throat the size of a baseball until he assures me Catherine is all right. I did not receive a letter from her yesterday, which is not unusual. It did cause a touch of concern, but it has happened before— several times in fact.

"They were shelled two days ago," Burns tells me. "Catherine was not injured. But they did take some casualties, including several dead. I am told one of the women killed was a good friend of Catherine's."

My forehead thumps against the side of the phone booth upon hearing this news. Of course, I am extremely relieved to know she is all right. It is upsetting to hear she has lost a friend and is now dealing with more grief.

"What can I do?" I quietly ask.

"Nothing, Jeff. There's nothing to do. I am trying to get more information. If I do, I will let you know.

"Jeff," he says, "she's in the military, on the front line doing an important job. There's a war on."

"I know. I understand," I reply. "It's just that I can't help her, can't protect her. I feel so helpless, so useless."

"You're not. Keep loving her. That will be enough. It's all you can do."

"I will," I say with a heavy sigh. "Thanks, Mike."

TWENTY-NINE

October 3, 1940

It has been one week since the death of Catherine's bunkmate, Carla Hayes. Catherine has carried on, performing her duties with professionalism, but perfunctorily. There is an emptiness, or at least a hole in her since Carla's death. Her many friends, all of whom were affected by Carla's death and the other two WAAFs, console each other and carry on.

The army has brought in a chaplain to counsel anyone who wants it. His name is Edgar Smith. He holds the rank of captain but has no real authority commensurate with his rank. A veteran of the First War and Dunkirk, the chaplain has seen his share of horror and has helped deal with those who survive it.

Almost all of the women and several of the men have been in to see Chaplain Smith. So far, Catherine has not. The only one she has minimally confided in has been Betsy Halvorson, her section leader.

Three days after Carla's death, Betsy found Catherine outside the barracks after lights out. She was sitting by a tree sobbing uncontrollably. Betsy silently watched her for several minutes before sitting down with her. Catherine, startled by Betsy's sudden appearance, almost jumped up. Instead, Betsy sat down with her, put an arm around Catherine's shoulders and held her.

Finally, Catherine stopped and looked at her supervisor. "That should have been me. That should have been me," she whispered twice.

"Stop it! If it should have been you, it would have been you. That's all there is to it," Betsy told her. "Come on, now," Betsy said. "We're going on night watch tomorrow. We'll be a lot busier. You need to get some sleep."

"I know. I will. Thanks, Betsy," Catherine replied.

The bombing of British cities had not let up. Catherine's crew had been on night watch which meant they were on duty during the worst of it. Every morning when relieved, the women would stagger out like the walking dead—most mornings too tired to eat. Today, the morning of October 3, was no exception.

While Catherine was removing her gear for her day shift counterpart, Group Captain Robinson, on day shift himself, approached her,

"Aircraftwoman Hartley," Robinson said. "I need a word, please."

"Yes, sir," Catherine replied with no inflection at all in her voice.

She followed him up the stairs to the walkway surrounding the floor. He turned to his right and led her into his cramped office. He pointed to a chair next to a small desk, then sat at the desk.

"It has come to my attention, and I have seen it myself, that you have not been yourself since your friends were killed in the shelling," Robinson abruptly started off.

"Is there a problem with my job performance?" she asked with obvious defense.

Robinson held up a hand to stop her and said, "Catherine, don't. My job is to look after morale also. You're not the first one I've had to bring in for a chat. No, you have performed your duties with your normal efficiency. It is Catherine Hartley I am worried about. I like her and don't want her to go away, go into a shell and no longer be you."

By this time, Catherine's eyes were glistening, and she was lightly chewing on her lower lip. "It should have been me," she finally, quietly whispered.

"Survivor's guilt," Robinson said.

"What?"

"Survivor's guilt," he repeated. "You survived something that others did not, and you feel guilty about it. It's very common especially during war."

"Yes, I see. You're right. I feel almost empty," she said.

"You're not alone. Several of the women have it. The ones who were outdoors have it the worst."

"Carla was in my chair," Catherine said. "The chair I always sit in and was sitting in a minute before the shell hit. It should have been me," she said again, only this time almost pleading.

There was silence between them for a minute while Catherine stared with a pleading look on her face. She wanted, needed, someone to remove the guilt, exonerate her for being alive.

"I want you to see Chaplain Smith. From what I am told, he is quite good and very experienced. He was in Belgium and on the beach at Dunkirk during the worst of it. He has seen a great deal of what you're experiencing."

"I don't know. I'm not sure…"

"It can't hurt. I could make it an order, but I won't. Please, Catherine, go see him. And be open and honest with him. Have you heard from Jeff?" Robinson asked.

"I, uh, yes. He, uh, writes every day. I, uh, haven't opened his letters since, well, since it happened."

"Why?"

"I'm not sure. I think I might believe I don't deserve him," she whispered.

"That's it. Go see Chaplain Smith today. In fact, right now. And that is an order."

"But—"

"Catherine, you're a delightful, intelligent, strong woman and a genuinely decent person. The world needs all of those it can get. Let's not lose you. Go, now."

"Yes, sir."

Catherine knocked on the tent pole and waited for a response. She was sure the chaplain was in because she saw a woman she knew leave as she approached. She knocked again, a little louder this time, and received a reply.

"Oh, yes, come in," she heard a man's voice say.

Edgar Smith was a forty-eight-year-old career army chaplain. An Anglican priest, Smith had joined up in August 1914, two years after being ordained. The horror of the trenches opened his eyes to what men were capable of inflicting and enduring on each other. He stayed in, never rose above the rank of captain nor wanted to but administering to soldiers was immensely rewarding.

"Come in, Catherine," the slightly pudgy, slightly balding, bespectacled man greeted her.

"How did you know my name?" Catherine asked.

Smith pointed toward a chair, and Catherine sat down. Smith also sat down.

"The group captain called and said you'd be stopping by," Smith replied with a comforting smile. "In fact, I've been waiting for you, hoping you would come and see me."

There was something about the man, an almost Santa Claus-like aura that Catherine took to immediately. Twenty-six years of counseling casualties had taught Smith well.

Smelling the aroma of pipe smoke in the tent, Catherine, a little nervously, asked if she could smoke.

Smith gave her permission and reached for his pipe. Puffing away, he finally asked, "Well, how are you feeling?"

Catherine paused for a moment then said, "Rotten. I can't help it. Carla was such a sweet girl and a good friend. It should have been me. She was in my chair when she was horribly killed."

For the next twenty minutes, Smith let her talk. Between crying, wiping her tears, blowing her nose and half-smoked cigarettes, she let it all out. When she finished, he sat quietly watching her as her breathing returned to normal.

"Have you told anyone all of this before?"

"No," Catherine replied.

"Not even Jeff?"

Catherine smiled at the reference and refrained from asking him how he knew who Jeff was. Almost everyone did. Any number of people could have been the source.

"No," she quietly said.

"Does he know?"

"I'm not sure," Catherine replied.

"Has he been writing?"

"Every—" Catherine started to say.

"He writes every day, and you haven't been opening his letters," Smith said.

"How do you—"

"Your friends care about you, and they're worried about you," Smith answered before she finished asking.

Catherine cast her eyes downward for a moment then looked back at Smith. The corners of her mouth were turned up in a tiny smile as she said, "And spying on me."

"Have you written Jeff since the shelling?"

"No," she admitted.

He placed his now cold pipe in an ashtray, leaned forward with his elbows on his knees and took her hands in his.

"Catherine, what you are going through is understandable and, in wartime, extremely commonplace. Again, it's called survivor's guilt." Smith let go of her hands and sat back in the chair. "There was an enormous amount of it in the First War. I knew men who were in the trenches when a shell landed. The men next to you could be blown to pieces and, somehow, you would survive. There's no explaining it, no understanding it.

"I knew one man I'll never forget. He was in a shell hole with five other men out in no man's land between the trenches. A German shell landed among them and all five of his companions were killed. This man did not receive a scratch. He was convinced God must have saved him for some great, special purpose. He was killed two days after I met him."

"Please don't tell me we can't know God's plan," Catherine said. "I don't believe God has a plan. I believe we were put here, given a free will and are butchering ourselves while God looks on in disgust at what we've become."

"Perhaps," Smith solemnly said and nodded his head. "But we're not here talking about God's plan. We're here to help you deal with a horrible tragedy. You didn't die. Carla, your friend, and two others did. You didn't kill them. You weren't even there. You simply survived. Many others did as well."

Every day for a week, Catherine would stop in Smith's tent after her shift was over. She would meet for anywhere from a half hour to two hours. Each day she continued to receive a letter from Jeff along with letters from friends and family.

After the fifth day of counseling, Catherine finally opened and read all of Jeff's letters. He knew about the casualties from the September 25th shelling and was worried about her. She could tell, despite his best efforts to remain positive, upbeat and even cheerful, he was becoming worried and angry at her silence.

By the end of the eighth session with Edgar Smith, Catherine was feeling better. When she returned to her barracks, she was startled to find a young WAAF moving into Carla's old space. It took Catherine a long moment before realizing that the war and life were moving on.

"Oh, I'm sorry. I didn't mean to startle you," the newcomer said when she saw Catherine staring at her. Betsy Halvorson, who had assigned the girl to Carla's old bunk, and two others were watching Catherine's reaction.

"This was my friend's space and I, well, I just—" Catherine started to say. "Never mind," Catherine continued, "Welcome to Swingate." She put out her hand to shake and said, "We've been short-handed and it's nice to meet you."

As they shook hands, Catherine said, "I hope you like long hours and stressful work."

It had been a long busy night of bombings of several cities, especially London and Liverpool. Catherine, as were all the women, was being worked to exhaustion. Instead of undressing and crawling into bed, Catherine took writing material out of a small desk drawer.

October 9, 1940

My darling Jeff,

Please forgive me. I am so very, terribly sorry for not writing before…

THIRTY

October 11, 1940

Dear Mom & Dad,

Just finished dinner here in my hotel room. Finally (!) heard from Catherine. There was a letter waiting for me when I got back earlier. I literally raced up the hotel stairs to my room. I was less than two steps inside when I tore it open. The important part is that she is fine! I can't believe how relieved I am. The first time I read through it, I dropped to my knees and wept. Whatever happened to the devil-may-care, number three bachelor in New York.? How painful yet wonderful being in love is. Why didn't you tell me?

Catherine has been receiving counseling from an army chaplain, an older gent who has been at it since the First War. She is suffering from what is called survivor's guilt, a very common experience, especially in wartime. Catherine's best friend was killed, and Catherine survived. She has been dealing with a crushing sense of guilt over it. The chaplain is relieving her of that guilt and getting her to realize it is simply fate and there is no fault to allocate. She is finally feeling blameless and doing much better.

It is 5.50 p.m. and the sirens have started to sound off. It will be sunset soon and the Germans will be back. If so, it will be the thirty-fifth straight day of bombing. Amazingly, morale is still quite good with only occasional cracks.

The government issues daily casualty reports which cannot possibly be accurate. The briefings from the Ministry of Information occur daily in the early afternoon. How can they know what the previous night's raids' casualty figures are that soon? They cannot, but we dutifully report them anyway. In a few days, we will be given a correction.

I'm not sure it matters how accurate the numbers are. Thousands of civilians on both sides have been killed, maimed, wounded or made homeless. From what the Air Ministry and War Department tell us, the RAF is giving the Germans quite a dose of their own medicine. This war may come down to how many civilians die before one side yells, "Enough!"

Time to wrap up. They're pounding on my door for me to get into a basement shelter. There has been some nearby bombing but not much. Rumor has it that Hitler wants to spare the nicer neighborhoods and hotels for his use when they invade, macabre humor. Everyone now believes he missed his chance.

Have to go. Mom, Dad, love you. And don't worry about me. I am quite safe in the shelter and enormously relieved having heard from Catherine.

All my love,

Jeff

It is almost dark and still no sign of the Germans. The sirens are sounding because of what the Air Defense heard from the Chain Home stations. The Germans have been spotted across the Channel and will be along shortly.

One of the hotel staff is back pounding on my door and shouting through it. I am not sure who it is. It's a man's voice that I do not recognize. And I don't care; I am literally light-headed from Catherine's letter. She is safe, relatively speaking, and well—or at least getting better. If I get blown to bits tonight, I will die happy knowing that.

I finish addressing the envelope for the letter to my parents, seal it and post it for mailing. I put on my hat and autumn overcoat. I am not going down to the shelter. My friends and I have other plans, again.

At the front desk, I drop off the letter to America and the one I wrote to Catherine. The one to my parents will be delivered to a postal box in Liverpool. It will be picked up by Pan Am and flown home. Catherine's will be delivered the day after tomorrow. It is quite astonishing how well the postal service is still operating.

While I count the change to pay the postage, I hear a familiar voice behind the hotel counter. "Mr. Bartlett, I do wish you would not pursue this adventure of yours," Howard Fowler, the concierge says.

I smile while I finish counting the postage then look up and hand it across the counter to a young man. "Thank you, William," I say to the clerk. He will make sure my letters are mailed.

"It's not an adventure. I feel it's part of my job," I say.

"Well, do be careful. It would be a serious bother and expense to clean out your suite and send your personal property back to America. And well, I'm sure we would we miss you if the damn Nazis dropped a bomb on your head."

"Thank you, Mr. Fowler. That's very kind of you to say."

He leans on the counter and, in a hushed tone, says, "Not at all, sir. You're one of the few guests who is not a demanding, pretentious boor."

While I chuckle at the truth of that statement, he continues in the same whisper. "Not to be nosey, but if you finally received a letter from Lady Catherine. Is she—?"

"She's good. Much better. She's been receiving some grief counseling from a chaplain. I'm very relieved," I say. The entire hotel staff are aware I have been worried sick about her. In less than an hour they will all have the news.

"That's wonderful, sir."

"Thanks for asking, Mr. Fowler," I say. I would normally call the man Howard but somehow it never seems appropriate. I check my watch and say, "Time to go."

Fowler reaches across the counter, gently grabs my arm and sincerely says again, "Do be careful, sir."

"I will."

I exit the Ritz onto Piccadilly and stand on the sidewalk looking up at the sky over London. It is almost exactly sunset. Still plenty light, enough to see but growing dark. No sound of our unwanted, uninvited aerial guests yet. I am sure they will be along—German efficiency.

I turn right onto Arlington and begin my walk to meet up with the others. Due to the nightly bombings, I likely will not see a bus or cab out and about. My destination is the Savoy where I will meet up with my three friends. Because of Catherine's letter—I have it in my shirt pocket—I am late tonight. Fortunately, it is only a little more than a mile. It is still light enough for me to make it before it is completely dark.

"Here he is," Clive says as I enter the American Bar. The three of them have a table near the entrance with a fourth chair.

"We were a bit worried," David adds.

"Got a letter from Catherine," I happily reply while taking the fourth chair.

"And?" Charlie expectantly asks.

The three of them have been as worried about her as I have. Although she is my lover, our little group has more or less adopted her.

"She's good," I say. "Or at least better," I add looking over the relieved faces. "She's been receiving counseling from a chaplain, a man named Edgar Smith. He's been in the army since the First War. She has survivor's guilt. Her best friend was killed during a shelling. And Catherine was in the same, exact chair her friend was a few minutes before it happened."

"No wonder," Clive says. "I've seen cases of this; even did a story about it a few years back. Some men never get over it, never come to grips with why someone else died and not them."

"Does that sound like what she is dealing with?" David asks.

"Yes, I think so. She was very apologetic about not writing sooner. Her letter seemed pretty upbeat."

I reach in my shirt pocket and retrieve the letter. It makes its way around the table, and all agree it is very encouraging.

I return the letter to my pocket and David asks, "Okay. Where to tonight?" He is looking at Clive while asking.

Being a Londoner, Clive has been our guide. For the past three nights, we have gone into stations of the Underground to experience what ordinary people are dealing with. We have all written up daily articles for our respective papers. I received a cable yesterday. The management of the *Gazette* was unusually effusive in their praise. Without regard for my safety, they are demanding more.

The previous evening, having spent the day helping clear rubble, we stayed in the East End. An hour before the blackout would begin, we went to the station at Canary Wharf. Believing we were early; we were quite surprised to find it already full. The four of us spent an hour carrying food and water down into the station. When the sirens sounded, we managed to squeeze in. It was a long night and a nightmare to live through.

The Germans did not come until almost midnight. By then the station platform was so crowded no one could move. The atmosphere had been lively, almost gay. There were small groups playing guitars and singing popular songs providing a little entertainment. Many of the people were friends and neighbors sharing their sacrifice. A significant number had become friends while being in the shelters, some of whom were people who had never met before.

There were a lot more men than I expected. Clive later explained that they were likely dock workers, stevedores who were needed for loading and unloading the cargo ships. The army is not taking them, yet.

There was one young woman, who looked no older than twenty, with three small children—two still in diapers. She was sitting on the fringe of a larger group of women all with children and no men. Before the bombing started, I managed to make my way to them. I found an empty sliver of the platform floor and sat as close as I could. For an hour, I interviewed them— or, at least, got their story.

They were all women whose men were off serving in the military. There were more than twenty in total along with, perhaps, almost fifty children of various ages. Three were already widowed and more or less getting by on the charity of the rest. The young one with three little ones, the one who had caught my eye, was quite pretty, but up close seemed many years older than the twenty-three she was. She was also one of the more fortunate ones.

Her husband is part of an anti-aircraft gun crew stationed in Hyde Park. Her name is Rosie McGuin and they are from Ireland. Sean, her husband, and his crew, she proudly told me, shot down a German bomber. They hit it over Hyde Park, and it crashed in Green Park. Everyone on board was killed.

As she told me this story, many of the others who had obviously heard this before, crowded around. When Rosie reached the part where it crashed with all loss of life, the others all smiled and laughed, and a few applauded. Rosie told me when this happened, and I claimed that I may have seen it go down. True. I remembered the sight of a German Heinkel crashing in Green Park right around that time. This revelation made me an honored guest among them.

Unfortunately, less than ten minutes later, the bombers came over. Until they left, we all huddled together, most of us quietly praying. If a bomb did hit, it could kill us all.

Last night's bombing, while we huddled down in Canary Wharf, was enough excitement for a while. Plus, we later found out that almost fifty died outside the shelters and tube stations in the subsequent fires on the East End. I can still smell the stench of burning bodies.

Tonight, Clive decides to move into a more upper-middle class neighborhood to see how those a bit more affluent are coping. From where we currently are, Waterloo Underground is just across the Thames. We will try there tonight.

Unable to find wheeled transportation—a single-horse carriage filled with people passed us—we hurry to get across Waterloo Bridge to the south bank. We reach the Waterloo Underground after eight p.m. It is almost as crowded as Canary Wharf was the night before. The only noticeable difference is this crowd is better dressed. Charlie is the first to notice an abundance of single women.

The young woman I met last night with three small children, Rosie McGuin, was the subject of an article back to New York. I wrote eight hundred words about her, even using her real name. I promised a copy of the paper to her when it comes out. I hope she will still be alive to read it.

Tonight's raid, the thirty-sixth night in a row, is relatively light, I would later learn—only fifty to sixty German bombers. Fighter Command would also claim seven shot down before they arrived over London. How accurate is this? Who knows? According to German propaganda, London should be burned to the ground by now. According to the British, Berlin must be engulfed in flames.

Waterloo Underground is about a quarter mile from the Thames. Before we hear the first plane arrive, we hear the thumping sounds of the anti-aircraft guns. They have been strategically dispersed throughout Greater London. Of course, the largest concentration is along the Thames.

When we hear the guns that must be coming from Hyde Park, David and I go up to the entrance of the Underground. No bombs yet, but we know they are coming, although this side of the river has not been hit as heavily as the north side, especially the Isle of Dogs. There is a significant number of wharves and ships loading and unloading. At least some of the German bombers have circled the city and are flying east to their targets. The ack-ack—the name the gunners have given to anti-aircraft fire—is moving from west to east along the river.

David and I are sitting on the top step at the entrance to the station. There are four wardens with us. They are men and women whose job it is to get people into the shelters. They have tried to make us go back downstairs, but we refuse. Muttering, "Crazy Americans," among other things, they finally give up. In fact, they have joined us. We want a front row seat for the bombing we believe will be on the other side of the river.

About a mile off, in the beams of search lights, we can see bombers flying along. They are using the river as a guide and seem to be flying very slowly. It is an awesome, incredible and terrifying sight all at once. When a searchlight hits a plane, it stays with it to guide the gun crews. The shells are bursting all around them but seem to be having no more effect than a mosquito to an eagle.

Along this part of the river are piers and docks. A quarter mile before Waterloo Bridge, they begin dropping their bombs. I notice four or five planes veer north, and soon I hear bombs exploding away from the river. At the same time, I hear David speak. It is the first time any of us has said a word since we first saw the German bombers.

"What are these two doing?" David asks of no one in particular.

"They're comin' right at us!" one of the wardens yells.

There are twenty or so stairs on the first flight downward back into the Underground. Without another word, the six of us begin sprinting down them. How we all manage to get down without someone falling is a minor miracle. We turn the corner at the landing just as the first bomb explodes. We continue running down as the explosions get closer.

The two planes dropped seven bombs each. The last one explodes in the street fifty meters from where we were sitting. It rains rocks, dirt and asphalt down into the stairs but otherwise does little damage. I finally had a real experience of being bombed. If I never have another, I will be extremely grateful.

We spend the rest of the night at Waterloo Underground. Charlie has the time of his life interviewing young London women. What he learns is they are unashamedly on the prowl for sexual partners. The attitude is, "We could die tomorrow." They have a point.

After running down from the bombing, when I start to breathe normally again, I interview several of these women myself. In the morning—we do not help with the search for casualties—I write two articles: one about my experience being bombed, the other about the loose morals of London's youth.

I shower and am about to get some sleep when my phone rings. It is Mike Burns from the embassy. Dover and the surrounding area, mostly the harbor, have been shelled again. No casualties at Swingate. I sleep quite poorly until four p.m., then prepare for another night in a different tube station.

THIRTY-ONE

October 12, 1940
Swingate Chain Home Station

When Lt. Commander Mike Burns reported no casualties from the latest Swingate shelling, he was not completely accurate. There were no serious casualties. One of the lorries, returning empty after dropping off some of the crew, was hit. An 11-inch shell landed a few feet from the back of the truck and exploded. It tore the vehicle in half and flipped it over onto its side. The driver, a young soldier, miraculously escaped serious injury. His left wrist was broken, and he received a good assortment of scrapes, cuts and bruises. The private spent a pleasant few days in the hospital, then went on leave to let his wrist heal.

"May I have your attention, please?" Group Captain Robinson said to his team members on the floor.

He was standing on the walkway at his station looking down at the crew. It was after noon of October 12. Today's bombing by the Germans was finished. At least there was a lull. It would be odd for them to make another attack this late. The crew members were slowly making their way to where the group captain looked down upon them. In fact, a few of them knew what was coming and had surrounded Catherine.

When they were all assembled, Robinson began: "There are times when one's duty is required that is not only a pleasure but an honor.

"Today, it is my honor to single out two of you for an extremely well-deserved promotion. Now, of course, typically promotions are earned because of the soldiers, sailors and airmen who serve with the recipients, and they are a significant factor in these promotions being awarded. Sorry, that seems to have been a long-winded way of saying all of you helped these individuals to earn them."

With that, Robinson, followed by Lt. Connors, went to the stairs and down onto the floor. The two men walked to the center of the gathering and stood before Catherine.

"Section Leader Halvorson, would you come forward and stand next to Aircraftwoman Hartley, please?"

Betsy was standing in the back, and the group separated to allow her to pass through. Neither she nor Catherine had an inkling of what was coming.

"Section Leader Halvorson," Robinson continued when she had reached the front of the group.

"Sir," she sharply said and snapped to attention.

"It is my honor and privilege to inform you that, due to your leadership, it has been decided that from this point forward, you shall wear the rank of Senior Section Leader, the equivalent of Flight Sergeant."

Both Robinson and Connors came to attention and saluted. An obviously surprised and mildly embarrassed Betsy Halvorson, while the others also came to attention, returned their salute. Lt. Connors stepped forward and handed her the insignia of her new rank, three stripes with a crown, and shook her hand.

Connors returned to Robinson's side, who looked at Catherine and said, "Aircraftwoman Hartley. It is my honor and privilege to inform you that due to the leadership you have demonstrated on multiple occasions, you have been promoted to Section Leader with the equivalent rank of Sergeant."

A totally shocked and stunned Catherine was barely able to come to attention and return the two officers' salutes. Connors went forward and gave her the new insignia, the three stripes of a sergeant. With a huge grin, Connors also shook her hand as he had done with Betsy. At this point, a huge cheer went up from everyone. All of them were genuinely happy, and they all believed the promotions were well deserved.

Catherine Hartley had been born into an upper middle-class family. On top of that, she had married into British aristocracy and was technically a countess. She was also a trend breaker, having gone to university and served as a serious journalist for the BBC. None of that compared one bit with how proud she was to have earned the three stripes she would sew onto her uniform sleeve.

Catherine spent the rest of her shift training her replacement Joyce Darby. Aircraftwoman First Class Darby was quite capable and needed little training. In fact, she had spelled Catherine at the post several times when Catherine needed a break. Betsy would be moving up the stairs onto the walkway. Catherine would be taking her place on the floor.

The rest of her shift was spent roaming around the floor receiving hugs and genuine congratulations. Even though she knew everyone and how to do their job, she took time to sit down with each and have it explained to her. If, for some reason, one of them became incapacitated or they were short-staffed, it would fall to Catherine to take their place.

While she did this, it occurred to her that never before had such responsibility been thrust upon her; lives depended on her. While she worked the phones, she was simply passing information along to others to make decisions. Now she was in a position where the lives of others could very well depend on the decisions she made. Toward the end of the shift, she was very concerned and having doubts that she was up to the job. Fortunately, the night passed quietly.

A couple of hours before their shift ended, Betsy Halvorson took her outside for a cigarette break. "Well, what do you think?" Betsy asked.

"Betsy, I had no idea the amount of responsibility you carried. I'm not sure—"

"Of course you can," Betsy said. "If I didn't think so or the group captain didn't think so, you would not have been promoted. They're a good crew. Relax. Let them do their jobs. Most of the time you'll be bored for lack of anything to do. During those times, spell them. Take their place and let as many as you can get an extra break in. It will keep them fresh for when the real action is on. I'm staying on. If you have any questions, don't hesitate to ask. I felt the same way when I was first promoted. You'll see. You'll fit right in."

The back door opened and one of the women came through it. "Betsy, that convoy is moving up the Channel and we're seeing activity above Calais," she said.

"Don't tell me," Betsy said. "Report to Section Leader Hartley."

"Oh! I'm so sorry," she said. "Section Leader Hartley—"

"Let's go, Connie. Time to go back to work," Catherine said. She put her hand on Betsy's shoulder, smiled and thanked her.

There was an eight-ship convoy that Connie had referred to. It had originally been part of a thirty-ship convoy from Canada and America. The others had split off for Liverpool and Southampton. It was likely that a German U-boat had spotted it during the night and sent a message. A group of German aircraft was forming up above Calais. Swingate called it in to Fighter Command HQ at Bentley Priory.

A short while later, Swingate reported the flight of German aircraft as an unescorted group of a dozen Stuka Ju 87 dive bombers. Fighter Command scrambled six Spitfires with overworked and weary pilots who easily drove the Germans off. None of the ships were damaged nor any of the Spitfires. Those overworked and weary British pilots shot down two of the attackers and damaged one other.

Catherine had calmly and professionally handled her first attack. By the end of it, she was feeling much better about her ability. Plus, she saw up close how efficiently the crew handled their duties.

As she was getting ready to leave, Betsy Halvorson stopped by and chatted for a minute. Betsy also told her that Robinson wanted to see her for a minute. When she told Catherine this, she had a mischievous look and sneaky smile on her face.

"Yes, sir," Catherine said to Robinson's back.

He was on the overhead walkway bent over his desk signing a document. When he heard her, he stood and turned to face her.

"Yes, Section Leader Hartley," he replied using her new rank. "You need to know that Betsy Halvorson has earned a forty-eight-hour pass, and she will be leaving in a short while."

"She certainly deserves it," Catherine said.

"Yes. Anyway, you may have to carry a bit more the next couple of days. I have all the faith in you, and you will be fine," Robinson said.

"Yes, sir," Catherine replied but without much conviction.

"Catherine, you'll do fine. Trust me. Plus, my driver is standing by to take Senior Section Leader Halvorson to the train in Dover. He is also going to drop you off at the Grand Hotel. I'm afraid I went behind your back and made contact with a gentleman of your acquaintance. I am told he has arrived and is at the hotel. Sorry, but I can only give you one night. The corporal will pick you up at the hotel at 0700. A reward for your promotion."

THIRTY-TWO

October 14, 1940

Dear Mom & Dad,

I have been sitting at my dining room table for over thirty minutes staring at the wall and this paper. I have a story to write, and I'm having a great deal of difficulty with it. I finally gave up. Instead of the story for the Gazette, I thought I would try writing you. I probably shouldn't since what I have to write about is pretty awful.

Last night shortly after midnight, a German bomb hit an Underground station in Balham. Balham is on the north side of the Thames a few miles from here. The bomb went through the street and into the Underground station before exploding. A No. 88 bus traveling in the blackout was unable to stop in time and fell into the crater on top of the people who had been seeking shelter from the bomb that hit them.

Early this morning, before six o'clock, my British friend, Clive Burke of the Daily Herald, called. Clive has sources everywhere. One of them called him with the news and he called me. We met up at the Savoy and took a cab to Balham. By the time we arrived, there were already hundreds of rescuers crawling over the debris.

To help out, we shuttled coffee, doughnuts, breakfast, food, etc. to the rescuers. We stayed until early afternoon, then the civil authorities ordered us away. By then the body count was over fifty and rising, mostly women and children. There were hundreds of people down there, and the description of the carnage was horrible. I may never get these memories out of my head, especially the smell. Photos cannot convey the awful stench of burning bodies. Sorry, if I'm being too graphic.

According to the War and Air Ministries, the RAF is giving it right back to the Germans. I feel good about that, although I shouldn't. The German civilians being killed, maimed, injured and made homeless are no more guilty of this horror than are the British citizens.

This is going to be a very different war. I fear the civilian citizens will bear the brunt of it along with their cities and homes. It will cost the lives of millions before it is over. Sorry again, but America needs to wake up.

We met a group of Polish and Czech refugees yesterday. They always ask the same questions: "Where is America? Why doesn't President Roosevelt rescue Europe? Only America can save the world." These poor people believe FDR is their savior and only America can stop Hitler and the Nazis. All they know is that when we entered the last war, it meant defeat for Germany. They are probably right. Where is America?

Now that I've made you as depressed as I am, I'll give you some better, lighter news. Catherine has been promoted. She was promoted to section leader. It is the equivalent of a sergeant in the army. She told me all about it when I saw her in Dover two days ago. As part of the promotion, she was given a short pass.

She says she has never been as proud of anything as the three stripes she wears on the sleeves of her blouse. From what I have been told, it is a bit of a rarity for a woman to be promoted so quickly. I can't help but feel proud of her also.

Well, Mom and Dad, I still feel like hell, but I have to write my article. I'll be sending in a photo of the bus sticking out of the hole in the street. They really need to put that on the front page.

All my love,

Jeff

***

David Morgan and I are in tuxedoes waiting for a cab. We are standing in front of the Ritz enjoying the evening weather. It is still mostly cloudy but not raining. No Germans overhead, yet. We have been invited to a cocktail party at the American Embassy. Charlie was also invited but begged off. Clive was not invited. He has written a couple of unflattering articles about Ambassador Kennedy. In one, he called Kennedy a defeatist and made reference to his well-known antisemitism. Old Joe is careful what he says for publication, but the rumors are he has little sympathy for the plight of the Jews under Hitler.

We received the invitation several days ago, and I had forgotten all about it until David called to remind me. I was writing my article for the *Gazette* at the time. I almost canceled, then remembered that the embassy is a good source of political information especially after the guests have lubricated their tongues with alcohol. American journalists get invited to a lot of these.

The evening doorman for the Ritz waves down our cab and it stops before us. The doorman holds the door for us, and David says, "Here we go. Lighten up. We'll have a good time."

"Catherine is being shelled every day. I'm not supposed to have a good time," I reply.

David opens his mouth to speak but waits until we are inside and on our way. "I'm not sure what to say about that," David says.

"Sorry, I shouldn't have said it. Have I been rotten company lately?" I ask.

"No, not at all."

"Liar," I say with a smile.

"No, really. You're worried about her. So am I and so are the others. We adore Catherine. You know that. If I could get her out of there for you, I would."

David saying that rings a tiny bell in my head. I am not sure what it means but it is noticeable, nonetheless.

It is only a five-minute ride from the Ritz to the embassy. Under normal circumstances we would have walked. But I am not walking the dark streets of London in a tuxedo. That would be inviting an attack.

With the war and the blackout in place, crime is starting to go up dramatically, especially low-level street crime. Muggings are becoming more and more common and brazen. The upper classes are demanding that the police round them up, put them in uniform and ship them off to North Africa. There is fighting going on there against the Italians. The hope is, of course, that London's criminals will be promptly shot as soon as they arrive.

We are standing in the embassy's small ballroom admiring the crowd. A waiter walks by with a tray of champagne flutes. David takes two and hands one to me.

"Must be a vintage Kennedy imports himself to the States," I say after taking a swallow.

"And he overcharges the embassy for it," David adds.

I see Joe Kennedy across the room. He seems to be doing his best to charm a beautiful woman with the Spanish Embassy chargé. The man she is with, the Spanish chargé, is a well-known homosexual. Kennedy must like his chances with her.

"Hey, guys," I hear a familiar voice say. It is our Naval Attaché Mike Burns. He is dressed in his dress blues, and the women are eyeing him up.

"I'm thinking about taking over one of the bars and getting drunk on the U.S. taxpayer," I say. There are three bars, and all of them are doing a steady business. There must be almost a hundred people already in attendance.

Grosvenor Square, where the American Embassy and several other embassies are located, has been spared by the Germans. Of course, the Germans know exactly where it is and are avoiding it intentionally, especially the American Embassy. Hitler would like nothing better than to keep America neutral. Our entry into the First War tipped the balance to the Allies and brought about Germany's defeat. If anything, America is vastly more powerful now than it was then.

With recently being the exception, since Catherine was posted to Swingate, I have been something of a regular at these embassy parties. My three journalist friends and Mike Burns have as well. I have adhered to my vow of celibacy even as my friends have not. I'm in love, and there isn't anyone else that interests me.

"Before you go anywhere—" Burns starts to say.

"Oh, wow," I quietly say cutting Burns off.

I am looking over the crowd. Quite a few of whom are British Army and Naval officers. Twenty feet from Joe Kennedy are four British officers, one of whom is Field Marshall Lord Gort. He was in command of the British Army at Dunkirk. It is no secret that Churchill thinks very little of the man and will not appoint him to anything important. Gort is talking to another man, a general I know, Major General Dalton Floyd. With Floyd is his aide, Lt. Colonel Arthur Ashland. The fourth man is a British colonel of whom I am unacquainted. He is obviously with Gort.

In military circles, Gort is known as a mediocrity who rose through the ranks the old-fashioned way by using political and family connections. Floyd is anything but a sycophantic climber. Word is that he will one day be a significant commander in combat before the war is over. This amuses me because the thought of seeing more combat likely terrifies Arthur. Why

Floyd would stoop to associate with the disgraced Gort is a question for another day. I am determined to have a word with Catherine's nominal husband.

"Don't do it, Jeff," Burns says.

"Do what?"

"Go after Ashland. He's not worth it."

"Relax," I reply. "I'm not an idiot. I just want to talk to him. But I could use a drink first."

I lead the way toward one of the three bars set up in the room. It is the one nearest to Joe Kennedy. He is still standing at a window next to the bar's end to my left. Kennedy does not notice us as we step up to the bar and order drinks.

While we wait, I cannot help but overhear Kennedy clearly say, "Well, of course, it's unfortunate what is happening to Europe's Jews, but one must remember, they brought it on themselves." This is the first blatantly antisemitic statement I have personally heard him say. I am a little surprised but not much.

"Absolutely," the Spanish chargé heartily agrees in almost flawless English. He is an almost comical figure. Barely five feet three inches tall—the beauty he is with towers over him—he is decked out in a bemedaled uniform. "They have been asking for this for centuries," the man adds.

"Yes," Kennedy agrees. He gestures to a male aide hovering nearby before adding, "Still, unfortunate."

Kennedy bends down slightly and whispers in the woman's left ear. She smiles seductively then takes the aide's arm who leads her away.

The Spanish chargé clicks his heels together, bows to Kennedy and wanders off with her.

"Well, hello boys," I hear Kennedy say to us.

We now have our drinks and move to the ambassador. He finishes his highball and orders another.

"How are you, Jeff? And you David?" he asks shaking our hands. "Commander," he says to Burns with his politician's smile, "you look great in that uniform. You should wear it more often."

"I just wear it to help me get laid," Burns replies.

This elicits a hearty laugh from Kennedy who says, "Mind if an old man borrows it sometime?"

"Mr. Ambassador," Burns starts to reply, "I seriously doubt you need any help."

"Ah! Very good, Mike. Flatter the old man," he says, laughing. "Listen boys," he continues, fresh drink in hand, "I have to circulate. Jeff, call and set up a time for an interview and bring your friends, even that British chap. I don't hold a grudge for long."

"I'll do that, Mr. Ambassador."

We find an unoccupied, stand-up table to lean on. Burns holds up his glass and proposes a toast. "To Ambassador Joseph Patrick Kennedy. May we be rid of him and soon."

We click glasses, take a drink then David quietly says, "So, the rumors must be true."

"I don't know any more than you do," Burns says.

"Bullshit," David replies.

"Okay, maybe I do, but it is strictly off the record. Word from Washington is Roosevelt has had enough of him. He's been keeping Kennedy here so he wouldn't run against him and to help with the Catholic vote. Once the election is over, Kennedy is gone. I've even heard he'll be called back home before the election to help Roosevelt."

"Roosevelt doesn't need the help," I say. "He'll win easily."

"Probably, but so what. Pretty much the entire embassy staff has had enough of him. He's a nice enough guy, pleasant and affable. But his attitude toward the war is not shared by many people."

The three of us notice the ambassador slipping into an unoccupied side room.

"The stairs in back through that room go upstairs. Little does he know his Spanish senorita is both a high-priced prostitute and very likely a spy working for the Germans."

"Wonderful," David says.

"Joe doesn't talk out of school to women. He knows better, I hope," Burns says.

At that moment, I see Arthur Ashland go through a pair of French doors out to the balcony area. David sees this too.

"I have to go—" I start to say.

"Don't," David says, grabbing my arm.

"Relax," I tell him and smile. "I need to talk to him is all. I'll be right back."

"Hello, Colonel Ashland," I say to his back.

Arthur is standing by the balustrade smoking. He turns around at the sound of my voice. When he sees who it is that spoke, he almost snarls. "What do you want? What's your name, again?" he arrogantly asks as if he doesn't remember my name.

"Stop it, Colonel. It should be beneath you to act like this. Besides, your arrogance and condescension have no effect on me."

"It is certainly beneath me to speak to you," he says.

I am two feet from him and suppress the urge to put my fist through his face. Instead, I say, "Then just listen, for a moment. I need to see you, privately. I have a favor to ask. It's about Catherine and her safety. If she ever meant anything to you, please allow this."

He silently stares at me for a moment wondering what I want. He takes one more long drag on his cigarette. Next to him is a plant holder filled with sand to use as an ashtray. Arthur bends down, shoves the cigarette into the sand, then straightens up and looks at me. He is at least three inches taller and twenty pounds heavier. But we both know he is, at heart, an arrogant coward.

"All right," he finally says. "Do you know where my office is located?"

"Yes," I say, although I don't, at least not specifically. I know the building which will get me close enough. In our little game of 'mine's-bigger-than-yours,' concede nothing.

"Call and make an appointment for 1000 hours the day after tomorrow. Don't be late. I'm an important, busy man."

Arthur stomps off before I start laughing. This man trying to act tough is too ludicrous. But I got what I wanted. Now all I have to do is suffer through the indignity of a meeting with him.

THIRTY-THREE

October 15, 1940

Catherine was the first one to climb down from the back of the lorry. She stayed there helping each one of the women down. Her first days as section leader and she was fitting right into the job. The important word of her new title was leader. Lead your people. Look out for them and act as an example. She was taking to it like a duck to water.

The last of the crew was out of the lorry and waiting for Catherine. There were three of them, the others having gone ahead.

"Nice to be back on day shift," said Francine.

"It is," the others agreed.

Catherine was looking at the cloudless sky over the Channel. A beautiful mid-October day, normally one to be enjoyed but not likely today. The weather report called for a calm, cool day, partly cloudy, mild temperatures and light wind—a perfect day for flying.

"They'll be coming," Catherine said. "Too nice. We'll be busy today."

Francine put an arm around Catherine's shoulders and said, "Have I told you how good those stripes look on you?"

"No, you haven't," Catherine replied. "But please, feel free. Never hurts to flatter the new boss."

"They look wonderful, new boss, Section Leader Hartley," Francine barely managed to say without laughing.

By now they were at the back door to their building. One of the women held the door as Catherine said, "Go on, the lot of you. Get to your stations."

Before she went in herself, she felt a tug on the back of her blouse. "Can I have a word, Catherine?"

"Certainly, Lois. What is it?"

"Can we go to the patio?"

Catherine looked at her watch and said, "Well, make it quick."

Since the shelling that killed her friend Carla, Catherine had been unable to sit in that chair. In fact, she had moved as far from it as possible. They went to where she now normally sat and found chairs.

"Okay, what is it?" Catherine smiled while asking.

"I don't know what it is, but I have a terrible feeling. I'm not sure how to describe it. Something bad is going to happen today," Lois said.

Catherine took both of Lois' hands in hers and said, "I have that feeling at least twice a week. The others do too."

"Really? I mean, I've never…"

"That surprises me," Catherine said. "And you know what? Something bad does happen every day. We deal with it."

"I mean something bad to us, here, today."

Catherine released the girl's hands, patted her on the knee and said, "It might. We can't worry about that. That's what they pay us for. When the war is over and we've won, we'll all know we did our part."

"Section Leader Hartley," Catherine heard the voice of Connors behind her.

"Sir," she turned and replied.

"We have three separate, small convoys moving up the Channel today," Connors told her.

"Yes, sir," Catherine replied. "I saw the report before leaving yesterday. Sir?"

"Yes, Catherine," the young lieutenant replied.

It was the worst kept secret at the Swingate Chain Home Station how terribly smitten Lt. Richard Connors was with Catherine. She used to get good natured teasing about it until she angrily put a stop to it. He was several years younger than her and a romance between an officer and a rank was strictly forbidden. Plus, Connors knew about Jeff.

"Why don't they form up into one convoy? Wouldn't that make more sense?"

"Bloody hell if I know," the lieutenant replied. "Ours is not to reason why."

"Let's hope we're not the six hundred riding into the Valley of Death," Catherine said, laughing.

"Section Leader," Catherine heard several voices almost in unison call out for her.

"It appears we're getting started," Catherine told Connors as she walked away.

The first of the convoys, nine cargo ships, was being escorted by a single Royal Navy frigate. A frigate was a slightly smaller destroyer-type ship. They were designed for anti-submarine warfare which made them invaluable for convoy escort duty. Along the coast of Britain in the English Channel, German submarines were a constant source of attacks usually combined with aerial bombings.

"The first of the convoys is getting close. The Germans are forming up over Calais," the closest woman told her.

"How many?" Catherine asked.

"A squadron," the woman said.

"Yes, I make it an even dozen," the WAAF at the next scope to their left agreed.

"Make your report, Molly," Catherine calmly told the first woman who had spoken, the senior of the three. "Best we wake up Fighter Command right away."

Catherine was telling Molly to inform the WAAF on the direct phone line with Bentley Priory, Catherine's former job. A long day was about to begin.

****

The first wave of attack aircraft struck when the first convoy was twenty miles from Dover—a dozen Stukas accompanied by four Messerschmitt fighters. They went into their attack dive in three waves of four planes. The accompanying frigate, HMS Duke of Amboy, opened fire on the closest planes. There were a dozen shore batteries within range, and they also opened fire. The cargo ships went into their routine of zigzagging to avoid the bombs and any torpedoes that might be fired from a submarine.

The Stukas dove in staggered flights. The first group dropped their bombs on the leading cargo ships. Each plane was equipped with a high-pitch siren that screamed on the way down. The screaming terrified the people they were attacking. Each plane carried a single 250-kilogram bomb under the fuselage. Additionally, they also carried a 50-kilogram bomb under each wing. Each plane dropped all three bombs simultaneously then peeled off skyward for the run back to France.

The first wave scored two hits. The lead plane hit a cargo ship with a 50-kilogram bomb that did little damage. The third plane hit the second ship in line amidships with its 250-kilogram bomb. It exploded three decks below and split the ship in two. It sank so fast that the rescue boats were only able to find three survivors.

The second and third attack waves went in with minimal results: a couple of hits with the smaller bombs and three near misses with the larger ones. The lesson learned was the Germans were getting better. Their tactics and bombings were improving.

Two of the Stukas were hit by anti-aircraft fire from shore. One was in the second wave. As the pilot flew off, a stream of smoke trailed behind him. He would make it back to Calais having suffered minor damage that would be quickly repaired. The second one hit was the first in line of the third group. As the pilot pulled up after dropping his payload—all misses— he flew directly into the path of an anti-aircraft shell. The shell exploded on impact, almost disintegrating the small plane. The pilot never knew what happened.

Thus, it went for the rest of the day. When the first convoy reached Dover, the young captain of the British frigate turned the ships loose and went south for more convoy duty.

The second and third convoys fared slightly worse than the first. Each lost another ship although most of the sailors were rescued. The Stukas kept coming, and of the seventeen ships that made up the last two convoys, in addition to the two that were sunk, nine others received bomb hits that killed another twenty-two sailors and injured over fifty.

Just as the last Stuka was flying off—one of four more trailing smoke—the second to last ship exploded. A torpedo hit it and tore the stern from the main body of the cargo ship. Somehow it managed to stay afloat— the larger part—for thirty minutes. A half-dozen sailors were killed, the rest rescued.

For the next four hours, the Duke of Amboy, joined by the destroyer HMS Plantagenet gave chase dropping depth charges and firing hedgehog spigot mortars at the U-boat. Hedgehog mortars were small bombs fired into the air in groups of up to twenty-four at a time. They were set to explode at the depth where it was believed the sub was.

The U-boat was rocked badly several times and developed an oil leak. This led the British to believe the U-boat had been sunk. It was not. The captain, showing nerves of steel, settled the boat on the sea floor and waited out his pursuers. Despite their belief that the U-boat had been sunk, the two British ships stayed for almost two hours searching for it. While they did this, they continued to drop depth charges and fire hedgehog mortars. They came close several times and rocked the German boat severely. Eventually, the British gave up.

With half his crew unconscious from lack of air, the captain managed to sneak back to Calais. His boat needed extensive repairs and was eventually towed to sea and scuttled. For his bravery, the captain received the Knight's Cross from Hitler himself.

Catherine looked at her watch when she noticed the first members of the evening shift crew had arrived. It had been a long, tense day. In addition to the convoy attacks, the Luftwaffe had launched raids on five cities other than London. This fact explained why the RAF had not flown sorties over the Channel to help the convoys. They were simply stretched too thin.

"Thank God this day is over," Catherine quietly muttered to herself.

"Amen to that," Molly replied.

Catherine, as section leader, was always the last one relieved. It took her a while to bring the evening shift section leader up to date. While she did this, two German Messerschmitt 109s flying along the coast flew directly over their building. They were so low the men and women outside could see the young faces of the pilots in the cockpits.

"Been a while since one of them did that," Catherine said to her counterpart as she looked up at the ceiling.

"Okay, I guess you're relieved, Catherine," the woman said.

"Thanks, Peg. I hope you have a quiet night."

When Catherine reached the exit, she found the WAAF, Lois, she had spoken with before the shift.

"Catherine, I want to apologize for being such a bother. I don't know—"

"It's no bother, Lois," Catherine cheerfully replied. "It's part of my job. Feel better now that the day is done?"

"Much. Thanks," she replied.

From above they heard the voice of Group Captain Robinson calling for Catherine. "A moment before you go, please, Section Leader," Robinson said as he leaned over the railing.

"Certainly, sir," she replied.

Catherine looked at Lois and said, "You go ahead, I'll meet you in the lorry. Save a place for me."

"Yes, I will. Thank you again."

Lois went out the door, and Catherine went up the stairs to meet Robinson. She took two steps toward Robinson when she heard the shells screaming in.

"Incoming!" several people yelled.

Everyone in the building dove for cover as eight shells landed outside behind the building. It was over as quickly as it started. One short burst of shelling, probably called in by the Messerschmitt pilots. One of the shells hit a power line. It would be repaired and back online in less than an hour.

There was, however, one casualty. Lois Storm was caught halfway between the building and the transport. When she was found, there was not a single wound on her body. One of the shells exploded close enough to kill her from the concussion alone.

THIRTY-FOUR

October 16, 1940

Dear Mom & Dad,

You're probably shocked to get another letter from me this soon. No, there is nothing wrong. I just wanted to drop you a quick note while it is still fresh in my memory.

I went to an embassy party last night with one of the guys. Lots of interesting gossip. Seems Ole Joe Kennedy is finally on the outs with FDR. Or, from what we heard, FDR has finally had enough. Rumors have his demise being quite imminent. In fact, he probably won't last until the election. He is an extremely affable and pleasant man, charming at the very least. And I can tell you, firsthand, he is not a stupid man, very intelligent, in fact. Why he cannot, will not or refuses to see the menace that is Hitler and the Nazis, I cannot understand.

Rumors of his antisemitism have been around for years. There is no shortage of that among his class. Sorry, Dad. I know you personally don't have a bigoted bone in your body. But a lot of your contemporaries do. And don't let them tell you the atrocity stories coming out of Europe are exaggerated. They're not. If anything, they are not as bad as what is really happening.

I've been trying to read Hitler's book, Mein Kampf. It's a lot worse than you may have heard. Anyway, Hitler says he's going to rid Europe of the Jews, and I have no doubt he means it. Even if he has to round them up and murder them.

Last night, I overheard Joe Kennedy talking to someone, a beautiful woman, but that's a story for a time when Mom's not listening. He, Kennedy, told her that the Jews have brought it on themselves. I heard him say it myself. Later, I had the chance to talk to him alone and he repeated it. He had been drinking and his tongue was alcohol-loosened, but he said it again. And he said a couple of other antisemitic things.

There will be a lot of people with blood on their hands if Hitler massacres the Jews. Time does not permit me to list them all now. Kennedy is the most visible and prominent American. There is a large number of Britons, especially among the aristocracy, who are far worse and more vocal than good Old Joe. In fact, I find Kennedy's antisemitism to be pretty mild.

We spent a good part of today helping with rescue work again. I'm going to try to get a few hours of sleep before the sirens go off later.

Love,

Jeff

October 17, 1940

It has taken me three attempts to get my tie correctly tied. I am looking in the mirror and not seeing myself. My mind is completely preoccupied with what I am doing this morning.

I have been mentally wrestling with my decision. Each time I reach the same conclusion: I will grovel on my hands and knees begging, if that is what I must do to get Catherine to a safer place. It could infuriate her to the point where it might be the end of us. So be it. I only care about her safety. I will do whatever I can to bring that about.

My ride—a black cab—is waiting for me on Piccadilly. The Ritz doorman, Jimmy, is holding the door for me. I slip him a five-pound note for which he will certainly chastise me later. Entirely too much, he will claim. I have learned that by simply being pleasant and a little generous, I receive first-class service anytime, day or night.

The ride to the War Office in Westminster is barely fifteen minutes. The arrogant ass I am meeting will be annoying enough. No need to give him an excuse by being late. As the cab pulls away, I check my watch. 9.40 a.m.

I have been waiting in an uncomfortable wooden chair for almost twenty minutes. It is in a nice, walnut paneled suite, part of the War Plans Department. There are three offices in front of me, side-by-side. These are for staff officers. The Deputy Director's office is to my left. It is a large, corner office overlooking Horse Guards Square.

A very pretty young woman was at a desk in front of the office I wanted. She is a member of the Auxiliary Territorial Service, the women's branch of the British Army. On her desk facing me is a plaque with what I assume is her name, Sub-Leader C. Parker. It seems there is something about my presence that causes her a little anxiety. Every minute or two she steals a quick glance at me. The last three times I smiled at her, and she blushed a bit.

My appointment with Corporal Parker's superior is for ten a.m. I know he will sit in his office staring out a window if he must just to make sure I wait for him. Sure enough, at ten fifteen, Catherine's husband comes out to fetch me. Before he does, he places a document on Corporal Parker's desk. He leans over her, his left hand on her left shoulder, his face and mouth practically attached to the poor girl's right ear. He takes a long minute to point out something on the document. I cannot hear what. The buffoon is practically drooling into her ear, and I am very uncomfortable watching this. By the look on Corporal Parker's face, she is on the verge of fleeing. And I am sure this behavior is standard.

His Lordship, Lt. Col. Arthur Ashland finishes harassing the pretty Corporal Parker, straightens his blouse, looks at me and says, "Yes, well, Bartlett, isn't it? Let's hear what you want and get this over with."

With that, he turns on his heel, goes through the open door to his office and sits at his desk. I suppose I should be grateful he did not shut the door on me.

I take a very comfortable leather armchair in front of his desk. For the size of the office and his modest rank, the office furniture is way above his pay grade. It is almost certainly purchased with his own money.

"Let's get to it," he abruptly says even before I sit down. "What do you want?"

I am tempted to say, "A little adult-like civility," but I am sure that is beyond him. Instead, I say, "I want you to use your influence to get Catherine transferred. You know where she is, and I am sure you know she is in constant danger. I want her some place safer."

Ashland leans back in his chair with an indifferent look on his face and brushes some invisible lint off of his left arm. He then steeples his fingers under his chin while waiting for me to continue.

"If she ever meant anything to you, please, do this," I say.

He breathes in heavily through his nose, pulls up tight against his desk and places his forearms on the blotter. I think it is evident that he expected this. It is probably my imagination, but it seems as if I can literally smell the arrogance, conceit and hatred this pampered fool must have toward me. I don't care. I will throw myself at his feet if that will achieve what I came for.

"And why should I do this? We all have our duty to perform. She is performing hers, and rather well from what I have been told," he says.

This last sentence tells me he has been kept informed about her. I grab this straw and cling to it. "Then you do still care about her, at least enough to be kept informed," I say.

This statement catches him off guard. His eyes shift back and forth as he tries to think of a way to refute this. It only lasts for two or three seconds, but it was there.

"I merely want to make certain she does nothing to sully the Ashland family name, make sure she does her duty honorably," he proclaims.

This statement shocks me. This man, if there were real justice, would have been tried for cowardice in the face of the enemy for his conduct on the beach at Dunkirk. I am sorely tempted to throw this in his face, but it will serve no good purpose.

I start to speak but he beats me to it. He picks up a several page document from the desktop, tosses it to me and says, "I knew that's why you wanted to see me."

I look at the document's title. It is a transfer order. It is all filled out and ready except there are no signatures on it.

"I'll tell you what I'll do, Bartlett. As you can see, I have already prepared a transfer order. Yes, I know the people who can do this. I have already made arrangements for it, and it requires several signatures. The necessary names and their ranks are already filled in. I need only present it to a good friend of mine, and Catherine will be out of Swingate for good in less than forty-eight hours."

I take a minute to scan the document more carefully. Catherine's name even has her new rank on it. When I check the signature lines and names, I almost swallow my tonsils. One of them is Air Vice Marshall Keith Park. He is the commanding officer for all of RAF Fighter Command 11, the sector in charge of defending London and all of Southeast England. The man's equivalent rank is that of a three-star general. His signature on a transfer order will not be questioned.

A tiny alarm goes off in my head. Something is wrong. This is too easy. Is that all he wanted, to see me plead a little? I doubt it.

"What's the catch?" I ask.

"The catch, as you say, is simple. Catherine and I were meant to be together. If you want her brought back to a safer posting, you will break it off with her and pledge never to see her again."

I stare at him for a while as he leans back with a nasty smirk on his face. "She won't be fooled by that," I finally say. "She'll figure it out in less than a second."

"Not if you tell her you've met someone else, that her long absences made your feelings for her die and you've been sleeping around. There's plenty of it available. Some of your American friends are taking full advantage of it. You can convince her.

"If you need additional incentive…" he continues again coming forward up against his desk. He picks up another document and again tosses it to me.

I recognize it as another transfer order. It is also completely filled out including the signature lines. The same names and ranks are on it for signing. Catherine's name is again filled in as the transferee.

"This order is your only option. Again, I have made arrangements with a friend. You either agree to my one condition and she is transferred to safety, or the one you are holding will be executed and she will be on her way to a posting in Singapore. And I will use my influence to prevent you from going there. One way or another, your little affair with my wife is over. Checkmate, Mr. Bartlett."

I sit stunned for several minutes trying to understand what I have done. If I had not come here, she would be no worse off than she is now. I cannot agree to tell her I have found someone else. The thought of hurting her like that is a dagger through my heart and soul. It would kill me and hurt her insanely. Instead, the blood rushes to my head, and in a fury, I leap to my feet.

"You sonofabitch, I'll—" I start to say leaning on his desk.

"Don't do anything stupid. You know about the young woman, her friend who was killed in a shelling several weeks ago," he says, while I glare at him. "I doubt that you have heard… It happened again, a very similar situation. Another one of her crew members was killed by a shell. She had been waiting to go out with Catherine. Instead, Catherine sent her out ahead and a German shell killed her."

Shocked, I slump back in my chair. I watch him, trying to decide if he is lying or not. I realize it does not matter. Either I walk away from her or she goes to Singapore, literally half-way around the world. I am crushed, beaten and defeated. He has power and the will to use it. I have love, and he will use that, also. If this is what must be done to protect her, then there is no decision to make.

"You win. I'll do it," I hear myself quietly say.

"Good. Now get out."

In the outer office where the secretaries are, they are all gathered around Sub-Leader Parker's desk. As I open the door to leave Arthur's office, I hear the women scatter back to their desks.

THIRTY-FIVE

Group Captain Robinson was using a lull in the activity to go through his official correspondence. He was at his desk in his small office along the walkway above the station's floor. There was a one-foot square board on the building's exterior wall. One of the ranks had made it for him and cut a hole in the wall, since there was no window in his office. The board was to cover the hole and could be swung aside to allow some fresh air in. It also allowed Robinson to smoke in his barely cubbyhole-sized office without suffocating.

Daily he received ten or twelve official communications. Usually, they were from Fighter Command HQ at Bentley Priory. They were the normal, routine communications created by every military since, probably, the Trojan War. This day was no different. Using his sharp letter opener, he quickly went through the pile. There were eleven official envelopes in all. Each envelope had to be stamped with the date received then stapled to the document or letter. These would then be stored in a locked file cabinet in the office.

The board covering the hole in the wall was pulled back allowing sunshine and fresh air in. He could hear the women in the patio area but was too far away to make out what was being said. He wholeheartedly approved of this. His people should be able to relax without fear of being spied upon.

Robinson lit another cigarette then looked out through the 'window' for a minute or so. He was down to his last envelope and in no hurry to finish. Picking up the envelope, he neatly slit it open. He opened the folded document and started to read. Within seconds his heart sank to his stomach.

Catherine read the document for a second time while Robinson patiently waited. When she finished it, she looked at him with a puzzled expression. "I, uh, um," she began, trying to speak. "I don't understand, sir. Is it something I've done?"

"I was wondering if it was something *I've* done," Robinson replied.

"No, of course not. I don't have the faintest idea where this comes from or why."

"As to whether or not it was something you did, certainly not. This is not something I requested. Apparently, you have a fan at Uxbridge. It could be just that. When you were on the phone to them you must have impressed someone," Robinson said.

"Well, can I turn it down? What if I simply tell them I'm not interested, that I want to stay here?"

"I'm afraid the military doesn't work that way, Catherine," Robinson said with a smile. "We all go where and when they tell us."

"Well, then I'll resign and stay on as a civilian."

"I'm afraid that won't work either. You can't just decide to quit in the middle of a war. They'll charge you with desertion and hang you," Robinson replied.

"They will not," Catherine replied and laughed.

"No, you're right, they wouldn't hang you, but you could go to prison," he agreed, laughing to himself at the thought of the army hanging her.

"Yes, sir," she quietly replied.

The two of them sat silently for a while, Robinson fighting off the feelings he never acknowledged before for this subordinate.

Catherine checked her watch and ruefully smiled. "I have an appointment to keep with Chaplain Smith," she said.

"Very good," Robinson said. "You have your transfer and travel orders. Be careful with them. I'll have my driver take you to the train in Dover in the morning. The first one to London leaves at 0830 hours. You can make connections to Uxbridge at Waterloo Station. Try not to overdo it this evening when the ladies throw you a going away party," he said.

They both stood up and Catherine said, "I'll pack tonight so I'm ready in the morning. I don't know how I'm going to say goodbye to everyone."

"A lot of tears, I'm sure. You can stay in touch with your friends, you know. We will all like to hear from you."

"Of course," Catherine replied. She neatly folded the orders and placed them in a pocket. She started to come to attention and salute. Halfway through it, she stepped forward, wrapped her arms around Robinson's neck for a hug, then kissed him on the cheek.

"Thank you, Lady Ashland," Robinson replied, choking back tears. "I shall miss you tremendously."

The train leaving Dover the next morning pulled out of the station only fifteen minutes late. There were a total of six cars, two for passengers and four carrying freight. The Dover docks worked around the clock as did the trains running out of Dover. Most of them had no passenger cars.

Catherine, in the second car back from the coal-fueled locomotive, sat silently watching the English countryside roll past for the first half-hour. She was trying to deal with and understand her ambiguous, confusing and ambivalent feelings. She was not quite able to understand how she could be both sad and happy to be leaving. If she was only going on a short leave to see Jeff, that would explain it. But she was leaving many friends permanently. How could she be both sad and happy about that?

There was also the hangover she had to deal with. There was plenty of alcohol at her going away party, but Catherine had minimally indulged if at all. Apparently, living an almost abstemious lifestyle for several months had weakened her consumption ability. Remembering she had one more day before reporting, she smiled at the thought of this evening with Jeff and friends. It was then she remembered the letter from Jeff.

When Catherine returned to the barracks, word of her transfer had already swept through the place. Being a military facility, there had been personnel changes before. Most of them had been by request of the transferee for any number of reasons. Catherine's had been the lone exception.

The party started almost immediately upon her arrival. It started with hugs and tears then almost angry questions about why she was doing this. Catherine, of course, had no answer to that question since she was not the one doing it.

For once the Germans were a bit cooperative. The only attack on London—forty-second straight day—was a light one later in the evening. By the time the party began to die down, Catherine was too tired to read Jeff's letter. And too busy this morning as well.

The train continued to roll along as she reached inside her WAAF blouse to retrieve the letter. With no letter opener available, she tore it open as neatly as possible.

October 15, 1940

Dear Catherine,

There is no easy way to tell you this, so I must be blunt and brutally honest. I have met someone else. I suppose I could give you the usual palaver about long absences, I didn't mean for it to happen, etc. These things are probably contributory factors or, more likely, lame excuses. Please be absolutely assured it is not about you or anything you did or did not do. In fact, my love for you was real. There will always be a place in my heart for you.

Do not hate me. That would only serve to assuage my guilt. I am not a good enough man to deserve that.

There is really nothing more to say. Be careful in your duties. Know that I wish you all the happiness life can offer. You deserve at least that.

Jeff

For the remainder of the trip back to London, Catherine sat staring out the window. Three young men, all in uniform, tried to make contact with her for obvious reasons. She simply ignored all three, not so much as even acknowledging their presence.

While the wheels clacked along on the rails, her mind was almost a total blank. Catherine did not and simply would not accept this by way of a brief letter. She knew Jeff well enough to know this cowardly missive was not how he would do this.

***

For two nights I have not slept. For two days I have not eaten. Catherine probably received my letter yesterday. With that realization, I feel that I should crawl in a hole.

There is nothing to be done. When I received word from her husband that the transfer was done—a note from him delivered to my room—he made it crystal clear. If she transferred and I told her the truth, he could easily have her sent anywhere in the world. And he would do it. I am to act surprised at her transfer and deny any involvement. To get her out of harm's way, I must let her go. I am more certain than ever I am doing the right thing.

My friends have been calling, and I have been making excuses. Last night Mike Burns called. He received word that several of the Chain Home stations were again targets of German bombers. One—he would not tell me which but assured me it was not Swingate—was hit hard. It will be offline for several months. Casualties for the one destroyed—he is certain the numbers are accurate—were seventeen killed and another forty-plus injured. Many of the injured are critical with loss of limbs and several will probably die.

It is now afternoon, and I am still in a t-shirt and pajama bottoms. I have not shaved, showered or dressed again today. I know what I did was right, but I do not want to be a martyr. Sacrifice my happiness for her safety? I would do it again without hesitation. It is not my pain I am having trouble dealing with; it is hers. I am certain I hurt her. Perhaps after the war is over, I will get another chance: an opportunity to make it up to her.

I have been living on coffee, brandy and caffeine—and self-pity. It is getting a bit better. At least I am starting to feel like cleaning up and going out. I don't know how I will be able to face my friends.

There is a sharp knock on the door. I have ordered more coffee and cigarettes, so I assume it is room service. When I open the door, she pushes the cart inside and almost knocks me down.

"Here's your room service, sir. Not much of a meal," a furious looking Catherine fiercely says to me.

I don't know what to do. I don't know what to say. I simply stand there looking at her.

"You, you bloody damn coward!" she yells. "Tell me to my face! Don't hide behind a simpering, sniveling, cowardly letter!" This last part, she says almost snarling at me while holding my last letter two inches from my face.

I am speechless, totally at a loss for words. I am also hungover, tired and probably reeking of, well, two days of stench.

"Well! I'm waiting," she yells, still holding the letter in my face.

"There's nothing more to say," I finally find the courage to tell her. If she doesn't get out of here soon, I am going to melt. I know Arthur. If that happens and I confess to her, he will have her on a transport to the other side of the world.

"Really?" she quietly asks dropping the hand with the letter in it. "Where is she? You look like you've been whoring for several days. Where is she?"

"Not here," I simply reply.

She stops, her shoulders stooped, her wrath momentarily vented, and says, "I thought you were a better man than this. I find this hard to believe that you could be such a coward. Tell me I was wrong. Tell me this is who you really are, then look me in the eye and tell me you don't love me."

"Catherine, I think it would be best for you to go now," I again quietly say.

"Best for whom?" she asks.

"For you," is all I can say.

THIRTY-SIX

October 20, 1940

Dear Mom & Dad:

The latest news—no longer a rumor—from the embassy is Old Joe will be leaving to go back to America any day. He is supposed to go back to help out his good friend, FDR, get reelected. Then he'll be back to take up his duties. The first part, the part about the election, is probably true. The second part is unlikely.

FDR is rumored to have had it with him. His negative/defeatist attitude is giving the president fits and undermining his policies. Joe still believes England should make peace with Hitler. I heard a story that during the Dunkirk Crisis, Churchill and Halifax were at each other's throats. Halifax was insistent upon making peace. Rumors have it that the two old gents almost came to blows. Finally, Churchill nailed it. He was supposed to have screamed across the table, "You cannot make peace with a tiger, when your head is in the tiger's mouth!"

I cannot verify it, but it does sound like Churchill. And he is absolutely right. In fact, we cannot make peace with Hitler at all.

During the times that I interviewed Joe Kennedy, I found him to be an affable, charming and intelligent man. Why he can't see this about Hitler I can only guess. On the other hand, there are many other very prominent people who believe as Kennedy does or have in the past, including the briefly tenured former king, Edward VIII, the older brother of the current king, George VI.

Enough of this maudlin rumormongering. The bombings continue. People are becoming both tired of it and accustomed to it. They are heartened by the news that the RAF Bomber Command is giving it right back at them, at least that's what we're told. I had an opportunity to speak with several officers, pilots and copilots of British bombers. They admitted they have no idea how effective their attacks are.

Quickly, I am fine. The bombings go on. The war goes on, and people on both sides are killed every day. I must admit, it is both fascinating and horrifying. Robert E. Lee was right. He supposedly said, "It is well that war is so terrible, or we would grow too fond of it."

See Dad, I did get something out of college.

All my love,

Jeff

Catherine slowly walked out of my hotel room and out of my life. I could not even bear to look at her as she left. When I heard the door click shut, my knees finally gave out. Looking back on it now, a couple of hours later, I am surprised I was able to hold it together as long and as well as I did. The look on her face when she burst in on me was enough to drop me to my knees. And when she called me a coward, she hit the nail right on the head. I can only hope that someday she will learn the truth and be able to forgive me.

When I hit the floor, I fall forward and cross my arms under my face. I lie like this until I run out of tears. Not for myself. I deserve all of the pain I have to endure. I hurt her. I hurt her worse than the abuse her husband inflicted upon her. I will never forgive myself.

So, this is what a broken heart is like. The more I realize it, the more I understand what a thoughtless, insensitive snob I have been. I think back on my life in New York, and it finally dawns on me that I have inflicted this on at least six or seven, maybe more, kind, caring, decent young women—beautiful girls whose only sin was confessing love to me. I casually tossed them aside without giving it a thought. Is my self-inflicted, shattered heart the price I must now pay? If so, it isn't enough.

I am off the floor sitting at the table where I work. I am hunched over, my arms on my thighs, a blank look on my face. I am staring at the wall but all I can see is the pain on her face, a look I have seen before from others. What a horrible person I have been to inflict that kind of pain as callously as I do. I cannot imagine ever forgiving myself for any of it. At this point I begin to understand that I am simply wallowing in more self-pity. This realization makes me even more ashamed.

"Open the door!" I hear a loud voice yell and the sound of pounding on my door. It snaps me back to reality where I don't want to be. There is a momentary, silent pause then more pounding and yelling. This time I recognize the voice. It is Charlie Dolan, my hefty colleague from Philadelphia.

Before I can yell back at him to tell him to go away, I hear a key in the lock, and the door opens. I am sitting with my back to him. I hear him take several steps, then Charlie and the bellhop who unlocked the door for him stop.

"Jeff! Are you all right? We've been worried…"

"Go away, Charlie," I mutter.

"You can go; I'll take it from here," I hear him tell the bellhop. There is a rustle of paper as Charlie tips the young lad. Then the door closes behind him.

"What the hell is your problem? Sonofabitch! Open some windows. It stinks in here," he says.

I sit quietly while Charlie moves about opening curtains and windows in the living room and dining area. When he finishes, he sits down next to me to my right.

"The concierge told me you haven't been out for two days. We've tried calling, but you won't answer. He also told me he saw a pretty young woman in a WAAF uniform leave a few hours ago. He said she had an uncanny resemblance to one Lady Ashland. She also had tears streaming down her face. What did you do?" he asks, more of a demand than a request.

With this I finally turn my head and look at him. "I ripped her heart out and tossed it away," I quietly admit.

He closes his eyes momentarily, shakes his head and asks, "Why?"

So I tell him everything, all of it. When I finish, there is a silence between us while he absorbs what I have done.

"You had no right to interfere in her life like that," he finally says.

"I don't care if I had the right to do it or not. I did it; it's done. She's out of harm's way. She is safe and that's all I care about."

Again, there is a silence between us.

"I don't know if that is the most selfish thing I've ever heard of or the most loving," he says.

"It doesn't matter. It's probably both, but mostly selfish," I reply. "I think I'll get cleaned up—"

"That's a start," Charlie says.

"—get a bite to eat and wait for the sirens. Then I'll go down to the docks and wander around with my arms extended trying to catch a bomb. That would make me feel better."

Charlie laughs and says, "At least you're getting your sense of humor back. We'll go out and get you drunk—"

"I've had enough to drink the past two days to last a month. No, I need to get busy, to stop wallowing in self-pity. She's alive, safe and unharmed. I knew what I was doing and the price I would have to pay. It's done, and now I have to live with it."

I push my chair back from the table. I look at my friend for a moment then say, "I'm glad you're here. I needed someone to come by and talk to. Where are David and Clive?"

"Working. They have jobs to do, remember?"

"Yes, so do I, and the sooner I get back at it, the better."

The phone on the table rings and I answer it. I hear a familiar male voice and, without a word, simply hand the phone to Charlie. It is David, but I don't tell Charlie that. "Here, talk to him," I say as I walk toward the bedroom and bath. "Tell him we'll meet at the Savoy."

"That's not the end of it, you know," Clive tells me.

We are in the American Bar in the Savoy's basement. It is getting close to the blackout time and the bar is rapidly filling up. There is a story going around about today's raid. The Germans came in at midday, a couple dozen Heinkel bombers. Douglas Williams from the Ministry of Information is here. He is a good man and a regular here at the American Bar. He assures us today's attack did little damage before the RAF drove them off. No more than fifty dead and fewer than three hundred injured. The RAF claims six bombers were shot down and at least three more trailing smoke as they ran off.

When I hear this, I cannot help thinking, *Is fifty dead and three hundred injured now considered a light raid?* Not very light for those who died and those who are injured. Some of the injured are likely maimed for life. This is now characterized as a good raid, a British success. Worse, I realize it is. We are not receiving many daylight raids any more. It is a safe bet the Germans will be back in greater force tonight. Then, only fifty dead will likely sound even better.

"Catherine left," Clive continues saying, "but she knows you were lying. Catherine is nobody's fool. She knows something is not right, and sooner or later, she'll find out what it is."

"I hope not," I reply.

"What if she ends up back with that bastard?" David asks, referring to her husband.

"There's nothing I can do about that," I say.

"Where is she being transferred to?" Clive asks.

"I don't know," I reply. "Ashland wouldn't tell me. He just assured me it was a very safe place."

THIRTY-SEVEN

October 21, 1940
RAF Uxbridge

Catherine stood smartly at attention before the desk of the man she was reporting to at Uxbridge. His name and rank was Wing Commander Glenn Clark-Hoverfield. He was in charge of personnel at Uxbridge. He was also a nasty, small martinet who washed out of flight training. This consigned him to a desk job and a career that had reached its apex.

"Well," he said after standing and pulling down his blouse at the waist. "I must tell you, Hartley," he continued as he walked around the desk, sat down on the front and looked up at Catherine. "I must tell you, Hartley," he repeated, an odd habit he had with subordinates, "I am extremely displeased. Extremely displeased."

Catherine remained at attention, impassively staring straight ahead. She had been warned by the clerk she originally checked in with about him. Being given a heads-up, Catherine was determined not to get on his bad side. It happened she had no choice in the matter.

"I should have been informed of your transfer ahead of time. Informed ahead of time. Why wasn't I?"

Catherine remained silent thinking his was a rhetorical-type question. Obviously, it would not be up to her to inform him ahead of time.

"Well, speak, Hartley," he demanded.

"Sir, I'm sure I have no idea. I did not know that would be my responsibility," Catherine replied.

"Are you trying to be clever, Hartley?" he snidely asked.

"No, sir. Not at all," she replied.

"Humph," he grunted through his nose. "We did not request a transfer of your rank. How did this come about?" he asked. "How did this come about?" he repeated.

"I'm sure I have no idea, sir. I simply go where I'm told," Catherine replied, barely hiding the contempt she was feeling for this little man.

Clark-Hoverfield reached back across his desk and pressed a button on his intercom. A female voice responded, and Clark-Hoverfield abruptly said, "In here."

In a few seconds, a young WAAF of enlisted rank appeared. Catherine would learn her name and rank as Aircraftwoman 2nd Class Dorothy Bremel. Bremel snapped to attention next to Catherine.

"Do we have an appropriate place for Section Leader Hartley, Bremel?"

"Yes, sir. She can bunk—"

"I don't need specifics. Show her to her quarters. To her quarters. You're dismissed," Clark-Hoverfield said with a lazy wave of one hand.

The two women saluted, which he ignored, smartly turned, and Bremel led Catherine out. Catherine's personal gear, two suitcases, were in the outer office. Bremel grabbed one and hurried out of the building. Having already met Bremel and the other assistant for Clark-Hoverfield, introductions were unnecessary.

"I have your assignment papers," Bremel told her as they walked toward the women's barracks. "You'll be in a room with Senior Section Leader Wynona Graves. You'll like Winnie. She's older, in her late thirties, and looks tough."

"Will she mind me dropping in on her?" Catherine asked.

"No, not all. Oh, damn. I just realized, I left my cigarettes in my desk," Bremel said.

"I have some," Catherine said. "Do you want to stop?"

"Do you mind? Among other things, the old bugger doesn't drink or smoke. So we can't smoke in the office. Here's a bench we can sit on."

"Will the little tyrant time you to see how long you're gone?" Catherine asked, handing Bremel a cigarette. Catherine took one for herself then used her lighter to light both.

"Probably. Who cares? I should tell you; you've been assigned to Group Captain Sidney's crew. They're on the day shift now. After we drop off your gear, I'll take you down into the operations room. You can meet the group captain and Winnie Graves. Group Captain Sidney is all right, a good officer who treats his people with respect."

"Good. How do you like your job?" Catherine asked.

"The job's fine. It's my boss who is a complete horse's arse."

Bremel led Catherine into the bunker's entrance and down the seventy feet of stairs to the operations room. Unlike the Chain Home stations, Uxbridge, which became known as the Battle of Britain Bunker, was completely underground. Inside was a room somewhat similar to Swingate. The most obvious difference was the lack of RDF—radar—sets to monitor incoming aircraft. Instead, there was a huge table in the middle of the room. On it was a scale map of the Group 11 responsibility area, Southeastern England including London.

On one wall was the Order of Battle of Group 11 airfields. A giant display board, the width of the room, covered the entire wall. This was used to keep track of each of the Fighter Group's twenty-five squadrons. A series of lights recorded the state of each unit: those on standby, those aloft, those that had sighted the enemy and, finally, at the top, red lights for those 'engaged,' that is, in action. Directly opposite this wall overlooking the room was an observation platform. This is where the senior officers would sit and watch the action below.

When Bremel led Catherine in, there was an almost total lack of activity. Group Commander Sidney was next to the table talking to a subordinate.

"Sir," Bremel said coming to attention and saluting the group captain, as did Catherine. "May I introduce Section Leader Catherine Hartley. I believe you're aware of her assignment," Bremel said.

"I am indeed," Sidney said returning the salutes. "Welcome to Uxbridge, Section Leader," Sidney said to Catherine. "We can always use another hand. Although I must admit your transfer comes as a bit of a surprise. From what I heard you were doing splendidly at Swingate. Several of the women are well acquainted with you having worked the phones with you."

He turned and loudly said, "Senior Section Leader Graves, a moment please."

A woman in her mid-thirties, stocky with short brown hair turned to them and walked over. "You must be Catherine Hartley," Winnie Graves said, smiled and extended a hand. "Winnie Graves."

"My pleasure," Catherine replied.

Bremel saluted Sidney again then left. As she did, Sidney turned Catherine over to Winnie Graves. Catherine's first day in her new posting— there were only a couple of hours left—was beginning.

October 22, 1940

Catherine slipped seamlessly into her new position. This second day was mostly quiet. The bombing raids would start up later and carry on into the night—the forty-fourth straight day of London being bombed. Later that night, Liverpool would be bombed for the two hundredth time. Since Liverpool was not in the area covered by Group 11, it was not the immediate responsibility of Uxbridge.

Catherine and her mates, several of whom she was already acquainted with by phone, had a relatively leisurely day. They spent the day mostly monitoring RAF Fighter Command patrols.

Toward late morning, there was a flurry of activity in the observation area. An officer came in and went directly to Air Vice Marshall Park, the commander of Group 11. Park was seated on the observation platform with several senior officers. The man whispered something in Park's ear, then straightened up. Park looked up at the young officer who brought him the message then also stood up. As he did this, the other officers looked at Park expecting to go with him.

"Stay where you are," Park could be heard telling them.

He followed the messenger out of the room and up the seventy feet of steep stairs to the outside. When they reached the top and exited the bunker, Park found a visitor waiting for him.

Catherine was stationed at the side of the map table facing the exit door. She was holding a long stick with a squared end. This was used to slide squadron designators on the large map. Even on a slower than normal day the WAAFs doing this duty were kept busy. As a result, Catherine failed to notice the short, stout, mostly bald, cigar smoker come through the door. Despite his annoyance at being surprised by the visit, Air Vice Marshal Park was guiding Winston Churchill around. Park, as did almost the entire military hierarchy, hated these pop-in visits, which were frequent, from the PM. Churchill saw himself as a military expert. Because he believed this, he was never shy about giving his advice to those in command.

Uxbridge, being less than twenty miles from the heart of London, was a favorite of Churchill's. Fortunately for Park, the PM had been too busy of late. Winnie's last appearance was on September 15. He had received intelligence of massive German raids for that day. Churchill had arrived early and stayed late. September 15 would become the day the Battle of Britian was won. Possibly sensing the significance, Churchill visited and had the good sense to stay out of the way.

Caught up in her duties, Catherine did not notice the entire room go silent and come to attention. As she was sliding the last block she needed to move into place, she heard a familiar voice. Catherine had a headset on and was uncertain of what she heard. She straightened up, noticed the others all standing still when the voice spoke.

"I said, hello, young lady," Churchill repeated.

Catherine turned to her left and there he stood. Startled by his sudden appearance, she blurted out, "Oh my God! Its Winnie!"

Before she realized she had used the name people normally used, Churchill was heartily laughing. Even the normally stoic Keith Park could not completely prevent a loud laugh and large grin.

"I mean, Prime Minister, sir. I'm so sorry…"

"It's all right, my dear," Churchill said. "I needed a good laugh. And besides, I get called a lot worse than that in the halls of Parliament on a daily basis."

"I'm so sorry," a red-faced Catherine said again.

"Don't be," Churchill said as he touched her elbow with his empty, right hand. "What is your name, child?"

"Section Leader Catherine Hartley," Catherine replied.

"Well, Section Leader," Churchill said in his familiar growl, "you go about your duty, and don't let me get in your way."

"Thank you, Prime Minister. It was very nice to meet you, if somewhat startling," Catherine replied more calmly.

For the next hour, Churchill, followed by the Air Vice Marshal and two lesser officers, wandered around the room. The women at the table map and on ladders working the squadron board did their best to keep working. Churchill, oblivious to the nuisance he was making of himself, felt free to interfere as much as he wished. A few times he took one of the chairs along the wall. He would sit quietly, puffing his cigar, for a minute or two. Suddenly, he would notice something, jump up and scurry to what he had seen. The WAAFS did their best to appease him and still go about their duties—impossible with Churchill. His was an inquisitive mind, and being the Prime Minister, he was difficult to ignore.

Above the floor, seated in one of the observation chairs was a courtly looking old gentleman in the uniform of a British field marshal. He was a South African by the name of Jan Smuts. He was also one of the few close, personal friends of Churchill and perhaps the most influential. While he watched Winston with a mixture of amusement and apprehension, a civilian bent down, spoke in his ear and handed him a note. With that, Smuts stood and went to the floor to fetch his friend.

"Yes, Smuts, what is it?" Churchill growled.

"It's time to go, Winston. You told me to watch the time. It's after twelve, and you have meetings beginning shortly," Smuts reminded him.

"Can't we put them off?" Churchill asked, a common question he used to avoid people he did not want to deal with.

"No," Smuts emphatically said, a common answer to Churchill's request.

"What is this?" Churchill rhetorically asked. He put the cigar in his mouth and read the note Smuts had been given.

"Oh, I see. Well, interesting. I shall have a word," Churchill said.

He went to where the Air Vice Marshal was impatiently waiting for his uninvited, unwanted guest to leave.

"Air Vice Marshal, I would like a word with one of these women," Churchill said.

"Yes, Prime Minister. Anyone in particular?" Park asked.

"Yes," Churchill replied. He unfolded the note Smuts had given him and read the name. "I need some air," Churchill said. "Perhaps she could come outside for a few minutes?"

"Certainly, Prime Minister," Park replied.

***

Hurrying up the stairs, Catherine literally held her hand in front of her mouth to check the smell of her breath. Halfway up she laughed at the absurdity. As a cigar smoker, Winston Churchill probably could not smell much of anything. She reached the top, then hurried outside. The weather was pleasant, partly cloudy and almost 17 degrees Celsius—a fine, autumn day.

She found Churchill waiting for her, and when she approached him, he smiled slightly and said, "Lady Catherine, I presume. It's nice to make your acquaintance. Come walk with me."

So, that's what this is about, she thought as the two strolled off.

"Prime Minister," Catherine replied, somewhat embarrassed. "I married into it, sir—the title I mean."

"I know the family," Churchill replied. "Frankly, a useless bunch."

This brought a laugh from Catherine who also said, "Well put, Prime Minister. They are indeed."

"Smuts here tells me you're estranged. Your husband is Lieutenant Colonel Arthur Ashland?"

"Yes, sir, that's him," Catherine answered.

"He's at least doing his duty," Churchill commented.

Catherine did not respond, and after a minute or so Churchill said, "You don't seem anxious to vouch for your husband."

"As you said, Prime Minister, we're estranged," Catherine replied. "Sir, you obviously don't remember but we met before. In fact, a few times, when I worked at the BBC."

Churchill stopped and took a closer look at her. "Yes, I do remember. Well, it's nice to see you doing your duty," he replied.

The two of them, the most powerful man in the British Empire and one of the three most powerful men on the planet and a three-stripe sergeant, strolled along through the grounds of a top-secret military installation. For ten minutes the two of them chatted amiably, Churchill sincerely looking for Catherine's opinion on how the war was going. This was pure Churchill: always curious about what non-politicians were thinking.

They made it back to his car, said their goodbyes and Catherine stood silently watching it drive off.

"Life can take some strange turns at times," she said to herself.

THIRTY-EIGHT

October 22, 1940

Dear Mom & Dad,

Well, it finally happened. Old Joe Kennedy left for the States today. It isn't official. As far as anyone knows, he has not resigned or been replaced. But if FDR wins or loses, no one believes Kennedy will be back.

They threw a going away buffet luncheon for him today. I was invited along with my friends, Charlie and David. Clive, our British pal, is still persona non grata, at least for now. Once Joe is gone, he should be off the blacklist.

Ed Murrow and his CBS 'boys' were there. Ed's a bigger celebrity in this town than any movie star or theatre actor. This is also true of his 'boys,' Severeid, Reasoner et. al. It was amusing to watch the guests almost shun Kennedy to be seen with Ed. I know him well enough that I got a chance to kid him about it.

The London news remains the same: forty-four straight days of bombing, not counting today. It's only five p.m. No bombs yet but we're sure they will be along. Tomorrow we will go out to help with search and rescue efforts. It is still a very grim business, but we are becoming inured to it. Bodies of children still make everyone weep, especially the little ones. Fortunately, those are very rare. Most of the city's children have been removed to the countryside.

We, the entire city's population, are becoming exhausted from it. Literally no one has had a decent night's sleep for weeks. Amazingly, morale is still quite good, but the lack of sleep is starting to show. Tempers are a little short.

I hear the sirens going off. The Germans are stopping by to say hello.

Before I sign off, something unpleasant to pass on. I recently broke things off with Catherine. Maybe I'll tell you why in a letter some other time. For now, just be assured, it was the best thing I could do for her.

Say hello to the siblings. Tell them to continue writing. I look forward to their letters.

All my love,

Jeff

Having taken a cab from the Savoy to the Ritz to pick me up, David and Charlie insisted we take it to the American Embassy. If I had my way, we would walk it. It is only a mile or so, and it will take us longer. Since I am in no hurry to get there—I am in no mood to go at all—why the rush?

"Why are we in a hurry to get there?" I ask as I climb into the backseat with David.

"Free food and booze," Charlie answers from the front passenger seat.

"Ah! Yes, of course. The journalist's mother's milk, hobnobbing with the political class for free food and booze," I say.

"Don't you want to say goodbye to Joe?" David asks.

I think about the question for a moment then answer, "You know, I do. I like him. He's a charming, pleasant man and a source of information. I don't like his views about the war and Hitler, but I do like him personally, although I think Clive is the lucky one."

Our British newspaper friend, Clive Burke, is still blacklisted by the embassy. Apparently, Ole Joe is still smarting about a story in the *Daily Herald* critical of Joe. It also had a photo of him arm-in-arm with a young British beauty—probably another 'niece' Joe is always available to entertain.

"I was joking," David said about my answer to his question.

"Don't you like Joe?" I ask.

"Oh, I guess he's a decent enough guy. These rich guys buying plum ambassadorship assignments doesn't sit well with me," David replies.

"The way of the world, my friend," Charlie says. "Money talks, bullshit walks."

A male host, whose name I cannot remember, greets us and escorts us in. The dining room and adjacent ballroom are more occupied than I had ever seen them. Apparently, the word is out that Kennedy is unlikely to return. The host leaves us at the entryway and wanders off. He did manage to inform us the ambassador is near the balcony doors. We can see him, the familiar round glasses and Joe Kennedy smile. There is a reception line moving slowly as the guests wish him bon voyage.

The three of us, Charlie in front running interference through the crowd, make our way toward one of the bars. David and Charlie order vodka tonics. I am still on the wagon trying to purge the booze from my breakup with Catherine. I order a soda water with a twist. We stand off to the side, a foot from the bar. Charlie is looking for the buffet tables. David and I are checking out the crowd.

"A lot of Brits," David remarks.

"Probably to make sure he really does leave. I'm surprised Winnie himself isn't here to kick his ass out," I reply.

"There's still time," David says, laughing.

"Check this out," I say. I am looking at a tall, bald, gaunt-looking man making his way through the crowd.

David sees who I mean and says, "He must be the official 'glad-to-see-you-go' delegation from the government."

We are watching the man who would be Prime Minister but for Winston Churchill. It is Lord Edward Halifax, the Foreign Secretary. All four of our little gang have placed bets on how long before Churchill fires him. I have already lost my wager. Great country: you can bet on almost anything. Considering that Halifax is smooth oil to calm Churchill's roiling waters, it is a bit of a surprise he has lasted this long.

A few minutes ago, Charlie wandered off to find the food. I look toward the open ballroom doors and see him returning empty handed. My attention goes back to Halifax. He has moved slowly through the room; much handshaking as he heads toward Joe Kennedy. It is rumored, although I personally have not verified it, that the two men despise each other. Odd since both share the same view toward the war. Halifax is widely quoted as having said, "Even more than making money, Joe Kennedy's special gift is self-promotion. Chamberlain can't go to the bathroom without Kennedy." A good line even if it isn't true that Halifax said it—although I have been assured he did.

We continue to watch as Halifax reaches the reception line. Kennedy, the ever-present smile in place, says something to the people in line, then steps around them. He heads toward Halifax at the same time Halifax sees him. I am silently hoping they get into a fist fight, anything to liven the place up. Instead, they reach each other and very cordially shake hands, both smiling cheerfully, much to my disappointment.

"What's going on?" Charlie says as he arrives. David and I are both watching the two old gents.

"Halifax and Kennedy," David says.

"Ah," Charlie replies. "Halifax dropped in to make sure he was really leaving?"

"No food yet?" I ask.

"They're setting it up," Charlie answered.

"We should get in the reception line," David says.

"I need another drink, first," Charlie tells him.

While we are in line to see Kennedy, I notice him. There must be at least fifty British military officers in uniform in attendance. I don't know why, but I can always spot him. Arthur Ashland is in a small crowd near the open doors to the ballroom. Perhaps like two male bears vying for a female, he gives off a scent that only I can pick up. Whatever it is, I am no longer in the competition.

"Well, there you are!" good ole Joe says when we reach him. He is beaming as if we are long lost relatives.

I notice a number of heads turning as we shake hands with the man. Oddly enough, with another twenty or more people waiting in line, Joe takes almost four minutes to chat with us. Always the politician, he knows our next stories back to the States will be about him.

While Joe is prattling on in search of good press, I hear a man clear his throat behind me. I turn my head and find newly promoted Mike Burns— newly promoted to full commander, a big step for a man as young as Mike.

Mike goes with us as we head back to our perch by the bar. When we get there, Mike joins me in having a soda with a twist. At events like this, our naval attaché is on duty and alcohol is strictly off limits.

"Took his time with us. Are we that special?" Charlie asks Mike.

"A little. Don't let it go to your head. He expects good press. Murrow has him alone for a half-hour during the lunch service," Mike answers.

While Charlie and the commander converse, I can literally feel his eyes on my back. I would rather do almost anything else. Except I know protocol calls for me to eat some humble pie. I excuse myself and make my way through the crowd toward him. When I turned around, I saw him quickly look away. He glances at me a couple of times then ignores me until I reach him.

"Colonel Ashland," I say.

He turns and looks at me and silently waits for me to speak.

"May I have a brief word?" I continue.

Again, he does not speak but moves two or three steps away from the people he is with.

"I just want to thank you. I know she is safe, and I know it is you who did it."

"You're welcome," he icily says as if speaking to a servant. "Not another word to me or anyone else about it ever again," he says. He then dismissively turns his back on me and rejoins the other officers.

Having choked down a large slice of humble pie, I head back to my friends. How I loathe that vile fool she is married to. I ponder, *Do I hate him more than I love her?* Absolutely, unequivocally not, I realize. I shall do as I agreed and keep my mouth shut. She is safe, and that is all I care about.

While most of the guests are eating, I wander out to the balcony. It is still a cool, partly cloudy, yet very comfortable autumn day. London can change in a matter of minutes, especially this time of year. I am standing at the balustrade looking out over the embassy garden. I light my second cigarette and sip my soda when I hear it.

"Hello," I hear a very soft, sultry female British accent.

I turn to find an extremely attractive, slender brunette looking up at me.

"Could I bother you for a light?" she asks, holding up a cigarette in her left hand. She is dressed in an almost formal gown, an afternoon dress not an evening gown. She is wearing a smile and an inquisitive look.

Of course, I light her cigarette, and for the next half-hour, we make small talk. It seems my ability to be the charming American is still with me. Under normal circumstances, I would take a shot at this woman without a second thought. She is also quite obviously waiting for me to do so. Her name is Helen, and she has not missed a single opportunity to flirtatiously touch me.

"It's been delightful," I finally say to her. "I must be going."

She reaches behind my head, pulls herself up and kisses me. "Thank you," she says. "It was very nice meeting you. I should probably find my date."

With that, she twirls around and walks off.

THIRTY-NINE

October 24, 1940

Catherine rolled over onto her right side. Her bed, little more than a sturdy cot with a thin mattress, was quite uncomfortable. She had a cure for any potential complaints she might make. She would think about how many others had it so much worse, especially those who had died, been injured or crippled, made homeless and those who were going to die before the war was won—and her brothers, Tommy, taken by the sea, and Alex flying a Spitfire to exhaustion. Complaining about an uncomfortable bed seemed childishly petty in comparison.

There was a small window above the cot where Wynona Graves slept a few feet away. Being noncommissioned officers, Wynona and Catherine were entitled to a semi-private room. Each had a small armoire, a table and chair for writing with two desk drawers.

It was still very dark when Catherine's internal clock awakened her. Thanks to the small window and Catherine's adjusted pupils, she could read the time on her clock. It read 5.52 a.m., a few minutes before six. She yawned and decided to get up. It was early enough for the shower room to be empty or nearly so. As quietly as possible she gathered her clean clothes which she laid out the night before.

Catherine entered the shower room and found two women already showering. "Good morning," Catherine pleasantly said to them.

The two women were next to each under separate shower heads. The closer one, an older woman, turned and muttered 'good morning' back to her. The second one, to Catherine's left, had turned her head, glanced at Catherine then turned back. When the first one said, 'good morning,' the second one mumbled something that sounded like, "Your ladyship."

Catherine stopped and was going to say something, then thought better of it. The woman who said it was a bit of a malcontent, whom Wynona had pointed out to Catherine. The rumor mill had it that these two were a bit more than just friends. Catherine chose the easy path, ignored the remark and went to the shower farthest away from them.

As a section leader, Catherine had been assigned to a specific lorry to travel to the bunker. It was her job to wait until everyone assigned to that lorry was aboard. She was always the last one in. The day before, while she stood next to the queue of women climbing aboard, only two of them greeted her with a friendly 'good morning.' This had occurred the day before as well. Catherine shrugged it off, assuming it was because she was new. With the response of the two women in the shower to her greeting, she was starting to wonder if it was not something more than that.

When Catherine returned to her room after her shower, she found Wynona up and making her bed.

"Good morning," Catherine said as she entered.

"Good morning," Wynona cheerfully replied. "Sleep well? I hope I didn't snore too much."

"Not at all," Catherine smiled and replied.

For the next few minutes, while they straightened out their quarters and dressed for duty, the two women chatted amiably. Wynona was a carbon copy of Betsy Halvorson, Catherine's immediate superior at Swingate.

"Are these two your brothers?" Wynona asked picking up a photo in a frame on Catherine's table. It was a picture of Catherine in civilian dress and Alex and Tom in uniform.

"Yes," Catherine replied. "Alex on my left and Tom on my right. Alex flies a Spitfire. Tommy… well, Tommy went down with the Glorious, an aircraft carrier…"

"Oh, God! I'm so sorry," Wynona sincerely said. To ease the pain in Catherine's eyes, or so she hoped, Wynona picked up the other picture on her desk. "And who is this handsome devil?" she asked.

Instead of easing Catherine's pain, a single tear trickled down her cheek. Without answering, Catherine took the framed photo from her and looked at the picture of Jeff and herself smiling at each other. "Someone I thought I knew," Catherine said, then laid the picture on the desk face down.

She looked at Wynona and asked, "Do the other girls resent me? I sense that at least some of them do."

"Yes," Wynona agreed, "some do. They think you used your influence to get promoted and transferred here."

"I have no idea how my transfer came about," Catherine protested.

"And then Churchill didn't do you any favors when he singled you out," Wynona said.

"I had nothing to do with that," again Catherine protested.

"It looked like you did," Wynona said, "when you saw him and called him Winnie. Some of the girls took that as a sign you knew him personally."

"I swear, it was because he startled me, not because I know him. We met once when I was working for the BBC. That's all."

"Catherine, I believe you," Wynona said. "And to tell the truth, I don't care if you'd been screwing his brains out," she said laughing. "You seem quite good, and I'll take you as that. But you know what bitches women can be sometimes."

Catherine hesitated, nodded slightly and said, "Yes, I suppose."

"The worst of it is, we found out you have a title, Lady Catherine Ashland."

"Oh, damn. I tried to keep that a secret. It's more honorary really, by marriage," Catherine said.

"And…" Wynona said with slight hesitation.

"There's more?"

"Well, that cot you're sleeping in… They expected one of their own to get promoted," Wynona said.

"And how is that my fault?" Catherine asked.

"Do your job. Show them you're a leader. They'll come around," Wynona said.

"I hope so," Catherine replied.

The day shift was, again, quite routine. Catherine stood her station alongside the table map using her stick to position fighter patrols over Southeast England. She noted a medium-sized convoy of a dozen cargo ships heading along the Channel coastline toward Dover. There was a fighter squadron flying cover for it. This gave her a moment to think about Swingate, her duties and her friends. She missed them terribly. Here, at Uxbridge, she was not really needed and felt very unwelcome.

Arthur Ashland replaced the phone in its cradle and checked his watch. He had been on the phone with a schoolmate for almost an hour. Perry Newman could talk the ear off a marble statue. But it never hurt to stay in touch with and on the good side of Baron Perry Newman, the 14th baron of Woodhill Spa. Perry had an uncle, also a peer, who was a very close friend of the Duke of Windsor; the same Duke of Windsor who was, briefly, King

Edward VIII before he abdicated "for the woman I love," a divorced American named Wallis Simpson. Perry was also a good friend of a commoner from whom Arthur was going to seek a favor. Name dropping, a long and honorable tradition, always came in handy, especially when one can drop a name, even indirectly, tied to the current occupant of Buckingham Palace.

Checking his watch after the call with Perry, Arthur decided he did not have sufficient time to make his next call. General Floyd, Arthur's boss, had made it clear he wanted no delays in today's schedule, mostly because he loved these opportunities to get out of the office. Arthur decided the call would have to wait.

He was putting on his tunic, briefcase in hand, leaving his office when Floyd came out of his. In another minute, the two men, much to the relief of their female staff, were in Floyd's staff car, gone for the day.

Their second stop of the quick one-day tour, was the RAF Bunker at Uxbridge. Normally an army general would not stick his nose into the workings of a top-secret RAF facility. There was a significant reason for today's exception. Air Vice Marshal Keith Park and Major General Dalton Floyd had been friends since they were boys; their families were also close.

It was not a coincidence that they arrived just before lunchtime. The Vice Marshal himself was at the car door when they parked. The two men greeted each other as if it had been years since they had seen each other. Of course, senior officers, especially those with the reputation for the stoicism these two had, even now showed little genuine emotion. Park led them into the officer's mess where every officer at Uxbridge, even those on current duty, were at attention. Enlisted personnel there served a veritable feast that lasted almost two hours.

Among several neuroses that Arthur Ashland was afflicted with was claustrophobia. As he followed his boss and Vice Marshal Park down the steep stairs to the bunker, a line of sweat broke out on his receding hairline. He forced himself to breathe calmly which helped keep him calm on the way down.

"Here we are," Park announced when he reached a door. His aide, a colonel who was first in line, held the door open as the boss and his guests filed in.

They were above the floor where the monitoring took place in the observation section. There were chairs for everyone, and Arthur, much to his relief, took the one closest to the door. To Arthur, the door meant 'escape.'

General Dolan was supposed to be on his way by now to his next destination, an army training facility. Wanting to spend more time with his RAF friend, Dolan asked Park to call the base and send his regrets. An aide of Park had done so. As Arthur sat seventy feet below ground, he found himself very much regretting having made the trip. To make matters worse, they were staying even longer.

The room itself was large enough to calm his fear. After a few minutes, Arthur's breathing normalized, and he was able to release the death grip he had on the arms of his chair. It was then that he saw her. A few seats away, Park was giving Arthur's boss a thorough explanation of everything taking place. Arthur ignored them and watched his wife as she went about her duties.

General Floyd seemed totally absorbed by it all even though there was not much activity. Even so, they stayed long past when Arthur believed his boss would care to stay. Fortunately, shortly after 1500 hours, a convoy in the Channel was attacked by the Germans. Two squadrons of Stukas accompanied by a dozen Messerschmitt fighters went after the convoy. Park ordered an immediate retaliation by twenty Spitfires and Hurricanes.

The activity down on the floor quickened. There was a real buzz in the air and the officers observing from above all leaned forward to share in the excitement. To Arthur it was all quite boring: a couple of women climbing up and down ladders on the far wall and along with that a dozen or so pushing small, wooden blocks on the table map. Several times a cheer went up when it was announced an enemy plane had been shot down. Of course, Arthur joined in, but on the whole, he was thoroughly unimpressed.

Because the German planes could not stay long due to fuel, the fight lasted barely fifteen minutes. The final score was RAF, five planes shot down and only one loss. The RAF pilot was able to bail out close to the convoy and would be picked up. The Germans did hit and sink one cargo ship and damage three others.

At 1600 hours, the evening shift arrived. Fortunately, there was little activity by then. That would change later when the Germans made their bombing raids. When Park and Floyd stood up to leave, Arthur did not hesitate. He was first out the door and first up the stairs and out.

"I'm joining Vice Marshal Park for tea," Floyd told Arthur outside the bunker's entrance. "You're welcome to join us."

"If it is all right with you, sir," Arthur started to reply, "I'd like to spend a few minutes with my wife. I assume she'll be up any moment now."

"That's right. Sorry, it slipped my mind that she was here. Was she on duty just now?"

"Yes, sir. She was one of the women at the table. In fact, sir, here she is now," Arthur said seeing Catherine emerge from the entrance.

Catherine noticed Arthur at the same time he saw her. She hesitated for a moment, deciding whether or not to ignore him. She then saw the general with Arthur and noticed Park a few feet away. If she fled, it would surely cause a bit of a scene. Instead, she marched up to Arthur and General Floyd, came to attention and saluted the general.

Floyd returned the salute and said, "Your husband has asked for a few minutes to meet with you. Of course, he has my permission." He turned to Arthur and said, "Very well, Ashland. I'll be a while. Take your time."

Floyd looked at Catherine again then back at Arthur. "She's lovely. You're a lucky man, Colonel," he said. Floyd smiled at Catherine took her hand and graciously said, "It was a pleasure to meet you, Lady Catherine."

"Thank you, sir," Catherine replied.

The two of them found a park bench nearby and sat down together.

"Arthur, I have to ask you, and please, for once, don't lie to me," Catherine abruptly said before Arthur could speak. "Are you responsible for my transfer to Uxbridge?"

"Why would you think that? I have no such power. I'm a very small part of a very large army. I have nothing to do with the RAF," he said.

Catherine, knowing this man was a pathological, almost professional liar, watched him closely. She could not tell so she asked, "Is that a no?"

"Of course, it is," he replied. "I'll admit I'm terrifically relieved that you are here. It is much safer than where you were."

"Except, everyone here, at least the women I work with, hate me," Catherine said. She retrieved a cigarette, but her hands were shaking so badly she could not get it lit. Arthur took the lighter, helped her, and lit one for himself.

"Why are you here, Arthur? What do you want?" Catherine asked with less animosity than she normally felt.

"You know why. I want you back," he replied. "I know I was a terrible husband," he quickly added before she could say anything. "I was a bully and a philanderer and worse. You have every right to hate me; I see that now. But the war has changed me. It has changed all of us. I believe we were meant to be together. Let me make it up to you, please," he pleaded.

"I don't know," she replied. "Arthur, I still love another man and—"

"I need to show you something," Arthur said. He reached inside his army tunic and pulled out a plain, white envelope. "I have been in a quandary about whether or not to let you see these," he said. "Before I do, let me tell you how I got them. I was at a reception with General Floyd two days ago. It was a luncheon at the American Embassy. You may have heard Ambassador Kennedy is leaving and likely won't be back."

"No, I had not."

"Right. Well, your…"—Arthur paused as if looking for the right word—"American friend was there. And he was not alone. There was a photographer at the reception taking pictures of the guests—"

"And you just happened to get pictures of Jeff with another woman. And you just happened to bring them along and just this moment decided to show them to me," Catherine practically snarled at him.

"Yes, I did," Arthur emphatically replied. "You need to know the truth even if it hurts you. I'm sorry, but there it is. I love you. You're my wife. He has obviously moved on. The sooner you believe that, the sooner you can move on also." Arthur stood up then placed the envelope on the bench. "I have to go. Look at them or not. It's up to you. I am truly sorry to cause you more pain." With that, he walked off leaving Catherine alone.

The envelope remained untouched while she chain-smoked two more cigarettes. Fighting back more tears, she finally picked it up and opened it. There were ten photos in all. Nothing really salacious about them; Jeff and a very attractive woman having a quiet moment together. It was obvious from their expressions that theirs was more than a brief encounter at a party. The last picture, the one when they kissed, made that a certainty.

Later, when she was in her room, for some reason she could not explain, instead of burning them, she placed them in a drawer of her small desk. Catherine picked up the photo of herself and Jeff, the one taken at the Savoy that she had framed, and placed it face down in the drawer with the others. During the evening meal which, as usual, she ate at a table alone, she made a decision. She would bury herself in her work. After dinner,

Catherine went out by herself and walked for an hour. She hoped the tears would come, but they never did.

When Arthur arrived back at his office, there was an even dozen messages waiting for him. He went through them and lined them up in order of importance, higher ranking officers to call back first. Then he came to the one he was hoping would be there. Arthur quickly dialed the number and was relieved when the man answered.

"Peter Cumberland," the man answered giving his name.

"Mr. Cumberland, this is Arthur Ashland calling. Thank you for leaving a message."

"You're Lieutenant Colonel Lord Arthur Ashland, a friend of Perry Newman," Cumberland said.

"Yes, that's right. But no formalities please."

"Any friend of Perry's," Cumberland replied. "He called and explained what you want. I made a couple of inquiries around the office, and it seems to be quite doable."

"Wonderful," Arthur said. "How long?"

"It will take a few days, at least, but not long."

"Great news. Is there anything I can do? Anything you need from me?" Arthur asked.

"Not that I can think of. If something comes up, I'll let you know. We need to get together with Perry. Like I said, any friend of Perry's is a chap worth knowing."

"That's kind of you. Please, keep in touch."

FORTY

October 29, 1940

Dear Mom & Dad,

You may have heard the news by now. Hitler's Italian bootlicker, Mussolini, has invaded Greece. Apparently, stabbing France in the back was not enough for the strutting peacock. He has done it to Greece, beautiful, ancient, peaceful Greece. Neutral Greece, who wanted no part of this war. We are told the Italian ambassador to Greece issued an ultimatum to the Greeks at three p.m. By then the Italian army was marching across the border from Albania.

If the Italians win and occupy Greece, this could cause significant problems for the British. The convoy routes through the Suez Canal and the Mediterranean Sea will be jeopardized. It is the Achilles Heel of Great Britain. Their dependence on imports of food and raw materials is of grave concern. If Italy and Germany can cut that off, they could literally starve the British into capitulation.

Shortages are already being felt. Rationing of such staples as bacon, butter and sugar began last January. There is talk of adding other food stuffs to the list. At least this is being leaked out to the public through newspapers by government sources. So far, the reaction has been less than positive enthusiasm. I'm starting to sound like an understated Brit.

Love to all,

Jeff

I have a call to my civilian contact in the War Department, John. I also have a meeting set with Commander Burns and a couple of British army officers. Clive, David and Charlie will also be there. They are also meeting with civilian government sources looking for news. Mike Burns has told us the officers we are meeting are of high rank. This explains meeting in the Army & Navy Club.

I see my source, John, coming down the steps off Westminster Bridge. I am sitting on the bench we normally use along the Thames across from Parliament. I have asked him if meeting in the same place is unwise. He merely smiles and says, "Only in the movies."

I check my watch and smile. The man is more punctual than Big Ben. It is 1.29 p.m.and John will take his seat on the bench when Big Ben chimes exactly one thirty p.m.

"How long will the Greeks be able to hold out?" I ask.

"Against the Italians? Until hell freezes over," he replies. "The fighting is taking place in the worst terrain possible. Heavily forested mountains, hills and deep valleys are not conducive to modern warfare. Plus, Mussolini will find out that Greeks can be ferocious warriors; and they are defending their homes."

"Is that the official word or the unofficial hope?" I ask.

"Both," he says with a smile.

John is the stereotypical image of a British government official: graying hair combed back, neat mustache, Savile Row suit and gold rimmed reading glasses tucked away in his suit's breast pocket. It is a cool, mildly wet day. He is wearing a Burberry and has an umbrella on the bench. While I wait for him to elaborate, he holds a lighter to a pipe, puffing to get it going.

"I agree with the assessment, though. I have spent a bit of time there, where the fighting is taking place. Foolish to attack there. That's the problem with dictators like Mussolini and his boss, Hitler. They come to believe in their own propaganda, that they are infallible geniuses that know more than anyone else. Mussolini orders his army to attack there and then expects them to do it. If they fail, it is their fault, and he will simply have them shot. It will be their undoing.

"We are hearing some talk that Winston is on the rampage. He is already hinting at pulling troops out of North Africa to send as reinforcements to Greece. So far, it's only a rumor," John says with a disagreeable attitude.

"You think that would be a mistake?" I ask.

"Absolutely. We must protect Egypt and the Suez Canal at all costs," John replies.

"What if the Germans attack south through the Balkans to help Mussolini conquer Greece?"

"Then Greece will fall," John bluntly replies. "And if we send troops to Greece, it won't prevent it."

His legs are crossed, and he's sitting to my right. He shifts around enough to face me then takes a moment to light his pipe again. This is a technique I have seen the man do many times. He is stalling while he thinks about the subject and what he is about to say.

"This is not, I repeat, absolutely not, for publication, Jeff," he says.

I have heard this admonition many times. It is usually followed by something, some news or information, received from a clandestine source, probably someone in Berlin spying for the British.

"Certainly," I say.

"We are hearing that Herr Hitler is furious with Mussolini. Hitler has his own plans, and he is in a fit that Mussolini's Greek adventure may disrupt those plans."

"Which are?" I ask only half expecting an answer.

"Russia," he says in a whisper so faint I barely hear him.

John puffs on his pipe while I stare wide-eyed at him.

"Impeccable source," he quietly says in response to the look on my face.

"I have been reading his awful manifesto, Mein Kampf," I say.

"Dreadful," John says. "But it is all spelled out in there."

"You've read it?"

"Oh, yes," John says with a painful smile. He pats more tobacco into the pipe while adding, "Possibly the worst piece of writing ever, but mandatory reading. That's why the military will not want to send aid to Greece. If the Bavarian Corporal has his eyes turned eastward, we must not do anything to dissuade him. Again, Jeff, none of this is for publication."

"Oh, of course. I understand completely. When do you think—?"

"Not before spring. May or June, most likely. You don't start that before winter is finished," he answers.

Across the river, Big Ben strikes two p.m. John takes a few more puffs on his pipe before knocking the bowl on the bench to put it out. He stands as do I. We shake hands and I watch him walk off.

The news about Russia is both earth-shaking and not surprising. They—the Nazis and Communists—signed a treaty, a nonaggression pact, a week before Hitler attacked Poland. Stalin, as monstrously devious as Hitler, waited until the Poles were beaten then he attacked them from the opposite direction. Apparently, Hitler had agreed in their cynical treaty to let Stalin and the Russians have almost half of Poland.

John has just informed me that Hitler used that treaty to keep Stalin fooled while Hitler got what he wanted in the west. In the spring, Hitler will go after Russia exactly like he spelled out in his book.

By previous arrangement, I meet David at the Savoy. We take a cab together to the Army & Navy Club where Charlie, Clive, Commander Burns and two British army officers will meet us.

The four of them are already at a table. The maître d' leads us to them, and I see two familiar faces. They are Colonel Colin Bright and Major Stephen Caulfield. I am a bit disappointed. I was hoping for officers of a higher rank. We have met with these two several times. Both are stolid, a bit tedious and quite boring. I have also found them to be less than dependable. Thus, my disappointment which I manage to hide.

We join them at the table while a noticeable buzz permeates the dining room. Normally this place and British clubs in general are quiet. Today, every table is full, and the words 'Greece, Greeks and Mussolini' are not so quietly spoken at each one. David and I have stopped the discussion, momentarily, at ours.

"The Colonel was explaining to us how much the invasion of Greece will help our war effort," Clive says to David and me.

"Really?" I ask. Having been briefed a bit earlier by my friend, John, I believe I know what the colonel will say. "How so?"

Colonel Bright lights a cigarette, then exhales a long stream of smoke toward the ceiling. He does this as a technique to slow down the conversation to choose his words carefully. "The strutting peacock," he begins, referring to Mussolini, "will find a tougher nut to crack than what he believes. The Greeks will fight hard, and the terrain, the Eyeties"—a derogatory term for Italians—"have invaded will hold them up."

This is almost verbatim of what John told me earlier. Coming from John, I believe it.

"The problem is Winston," Major Caulfield quietly says.

"Oh, how so?" David asks before I can.

The two officers steal a quick peek at each other, then the colonel answers. "Winston Churchill has a well-deserved reputation as an amateur strategist. Usually that means he likes to meddle in military affairs. He is also an adventurer, especially when it comes to the Mediterranean and Middle East."

"You're referring to Gallipoli," I say.

"Yes," Bright replies, "and other things. We're quite concerned that he will strip our Desert Army in North Africa to send help to Greece."

"There are rumors that he is considering this already," Caulfield says with palpable disapproval.

These two desk soldiers continue along this path for another fifteen to twenty minutes. Having heard it before from them, I finish my beer then beg off from ordering another.

"I need to go prepare my story," I say.

Charlie and David both quickly agree. Clive does so a bit reluctantly. He enjoys these little informal get-togethers, mostly for the beer and socializing. I, myself, can't get away from these two insufferable boors fast enough.

"They're right, you know," Clive says when we reach the street. Clive has detected my attitude and is saying this for my personal benefit.

"I know," I say, sincerely agreeing. "I was hoping for someone else this time."

"Let's find a pub," Charlie says. He is standing in the street waving at a cab as he says this.

"How about the Savoy?" I say. "Let's see what others have come up with."

October 30, 1940
RAF Uxbridge

Catherine walked almost casually from her quarters toward the personnel office. She was coming off the midnight shift and was ready for bed. When she arrived at the women's barracks, there was a note waiting for her on her bunk. Winnie Graves entered their tiny room while Catherine was reading it.

"Don't know," Winnie said with a puzzled expression after Catherine showed it to her. "Not sure why the Midget Tyrant would need to see you. Probably a scrap of paper isn't perfectly filled out. He'll want to have you shot for it."

"I'll be lucky if that's all the punishment he'll want," Catherine said.

Catherine stopped at the bottom of the administration building's exterior stairs and looked at the entrance. The shift she had worked had been a busy one. The Germans had attacked multiple cities at the same time. This meant spreading Group 11 squadrons thin trying to defend against all of the attacks. As a result, Catherine was tired and in no mood to deal with the Midget Tyrant of personnel.

"Hello again," Aircraftwoman Bremel pleasantly greeted Catherine when she entered the outer office.

"Why does he want to see me?" Catherine quietly whispered.

"He never tells us," Bremel whispered back. "Have a seat, and I'll check to see if you should go in."

Catherine had barely settled onto the hard, wooden chair when Bremel reappeared. She silently waved Catherine forward to go right in.

Catherine snapped smartly to attention in front of the desk, saluted and while holding the salute, said, "Sir, Section Leader Hartley reporting, sir."

Clark-Hoverfield leaned back in his chair while Catherine awaited his response. After five or six seconds, he casually returned her salute and said, "At ease." He picked up a document, looked it over and reached across the desk handing it to Catherine. "What do you make of this, Hartley?" he asked. "What do you make of this?" he repeated. "Or, should I say, your Ladyship? *Hmm*, your Ladyship?"

Ignoring the nasty little man's snide remark, Catherine simply replied, "I don't know, sir. What is it?"

Clark-Hoverfield silently watched her while Catherine read what he had given her. Finally, he said, "You expect me to believe you don't know anything about this?

"Sir, I don't know what it is. Something about a transfer to the BBC but—"

"You didn't use your influence to arrange this? I don't believe that for a moment. Don't believe it for a moment," Clark-Hoverfield said.

Ignoring him again, Catherine read from the transfer orders, "I'm to leave immediately and report as soon as possible."

"Well, your Ladyship, I still don't believe you did not have anything to do with this. I don't believe you didn't have anything to do with this."

Knowing she was leaving, Catherine finally had enough of the man's arrogance. "Colonel, frankly, I don't give a damn what you do or do not believe." With that, she came to attention, snapped a quick salute, did a sharp about face and marched out of the office.

"Get out! Get out!" he yelled as she slammed the door behind her.

FORTY-ONE

November 6, 1940

Dear Mom & Dad,

Once again, my apologies for not writing sooner. I keep doing that, apologizing for not writing more often. It seems every day is an event of one kind or another. The war interferes with everything. Plus, I am still dealing with a very real personal loss.

Before I get to that, of course we received the news late last night (early this morning) about the election. Not exactly a big surprise. The few Brits I have spoken to so far today are quite pleased with the result. They believe that now that FDR is settled in for another four years, he will be quite generous in his support. We shall see how much Congress agrees with this.

Now the bad news, the terrible news. Charlie Dolan, my friend from the Philadelphia Dispatch, died on Monday, November 4. Two days before that, Saturday the 2nd, we were helping in an area of Vauxhall, across the river from Westminster. It had been targeted the previous night and we were digging for survivors.

An apartment building had been hit with two bombs (only three dead), one of which blew a large hole in the street. The front of the building had collapsed into the hole. Charlie and eight or ten others were in the hole digging for bodies and survivors. I was across the street doing the same thing at another site.

Something sparked a gas main causing a large explosion. By pure coincidence, I was looking directly at it when it happened. Worse luck, I literally saw my friend being blown out of the hole through the flames. I watched, horrified, knowing it was him as he landed on the opposite sidewalk.

David Morgan was with me, and when we got to Charlie, others had extinguished the flames. We got him to a hospital as quickly as possible but there was little hope. He had severe burns over eighty percent of his body.

On top of that, he received a significant number of broken bones and internal injuries from the explosion and being thrown thirty to forty feet.

David, Clive Burke and I took turns with him while he lingered in agony for the next two days. It was the most horrible thing I have experienced so far, and I have seen a lifetime of horror in the past six months. Charlie would float in and out of consciousness. Medicine for civilians is becoming scarce. The doctors did what they could for the pain, but when he was conscious, he was in obvious agony.

Mercifully, he died at 10.47 a.m., officially, on Monday.

His newspaper ran a flattering obituary after his family was informed, how he died heroically helping the victims of Hitler's bombing etc., etc. It's all rubbish. There was nothing heroic about the way my dear friend died. It was a nightmare.

When we are kids in school, the history books paint a picture of death in war as sterile, swift and heroic. It is no such thing. I watched a good man, a kind, caring man, a father of three, suffer through a death we would not put an animal through. It was dreadful.

The three of us, David, Clive and I, escorted his body to Liverpool. We saw to it that he would be transported back to the States. Each of us wrote a letter of condolence to his ex-wife. We lied like hell to her and told her he died quickly without suffering. Why not? What good would come of telling his wife and children the truth?

Well, Mom, Dad, if you're not depressed enough, how about some more? I told you I broke things off with Catherine. The reason was quite simple. I love her more than life. I agreed to leave her if her estranged, abusive husband would use his influence to get her transferred to a safer place. He did so, and I will keep my word. I don't know where she is, but he assures me she is in one of the safest, most secure facilities in Britain.

It is Wednesday morning. Time to get back to work. The PMQ is this afternoon. I can't recall if I told you about this. Maybe you know what it is. If not, here it is. The PMQ is short for Prime Minister's Questions. Every Wednesday, the PM goes before the House of Commons to answer the members' questions. For an American, it seems to be an odd ritual. Imagine the president standing on the floor of the House being hammered with questions. Winnie gives as good as he gets, so it can be quite entertaining.

There is some good news. After fifty-seven consecutive days of bombing, London has received a respite. The last attack was the night of

November 2 into the early morning hours of November 3. The best part is the fires are all under control, and it seems people have gotten some sleep again. The government assures us they will be back. We must remain vigilant, but a few days without sirens, airplanes overhead and bombs going off has had a terrific effect on morale.

Don't worry about me, please. I'm fine.

All my love to everybody,

Jeff

The three of us, now of course without our gregarious friend Charlie, arrive by cab at Parliament as Big Ben is sounding ten a.m. In deference to Charlie who, because of his size, always rode in front, we squeeze into the back seat. Eventually we will stop this, but not yet.

We make our way to the press gallery in time to watch some of what is known as Question Time. Clive has explained this to us. Each day that the House of Commons is in session, an hour is set aside for question time. This occurs every Monday through Thursday. Every department, through its minister or a representative, must take questions from the members of Parliament. It can become quite heated, at times.

Clive tells me—I believe he is pulling my leg, but he assures me he is not—that the space between the members' galleries on the floor, is slightly more than two swords length. This is for obvious reasons from days of old.

Today's question time is quite congenial, boring even. Of course, all of the questions pertain to the war. Since mid-September when it seems the Battle of Britain was won and invasion talk lessened, the members have calmed down considerably.

There is a mild buzz taking place in the gallery, at least among the press. I am quietly watching the show on the floor. They are questioning the Chancellor of the Exchequer Sir Kingsley Wood. The inquisition is about the cost of the war and how it is being paid. So far, Britain is staying out of debt, but Sir Kingsley will not or cannot say how long that will last. I am hearing from my father that New York banks are in a dither about whether or not to loan Britain the money. Dad says it's a sure sign the financial markets are betting on Hitler.

"Did you hear that?" David asks while giving me a gentle elbow in the side.

"Hear what?" I ask. David and Clive have been listening to some friends of Clive while I have been watching Sir Kingsley tap dance around the questions being asked. Answering questions without actually answering them must be a natural talent for politicians everywhere.

"Rumor has it, Neville Chamberlain is on his death bed," David tells me.

This is no longer considered a rumor. Chamberlain has tried to keep it a secret, but a former PM dying from cancer is bound to get out.

"For sure?" I ask.

"Word is he has only a few days left," Clive says speaking across David to me.

I pause for a moment and look out over the floor proceedings. I consider Neville Chamberlain and his place in history.

"I'm sorry about his coming death," I finally say. "He was a decent and honorable man who did what he thought was right."

"He was a damn fool," Clive snarls back at me in a loud whisper. "He should have listened to Winston, and if he had, we wouldn't be in this mess."

I have heard this statement in a number of forms from Clive and others many times. Mostly from people with 20/20 hindsight vision. I lean across David to get closer to Clive, then say, "Clive, the man's dying. Give it a rest. There'll be plenty of time to tear him to shreds once he's in the ground."

David laughs then covers his mouth to stifle it. Even Clive has to smile.

"Point taken," Clive says. "After he's gone, all bets are off."

We stay until one through the Prime Minister's questions which are a bit longer. The news about Chamberlain was the big event of the day. The PM's question period was pretty dull. Churchill can dance with the best of them.

"Let's go find a pub and get schnockered," Clive says.

We are filing out onto the sidewalk and turn toward Westminster Bridge. We are walking past Big Ben when I see her. Across the street near the entrance to Westminster Station, I catch a glimpse of Catherine. I am absolutely certain it is her. She is in a bit of a crowd but wearing the same hat she wore the first time I saw her: the white, flapper hat with a stylish red ribbon and a red rose sewn into it. I stop to stare, and I may have blinked because, as suddenly as she appeared, she is gone.

My friends have not noticed me and are twenty feet ahead of me by now. I hear David yell at me, and all I can do is point as I hurry to catch up.

"Catherine," I say, "I saw her. Right over there."

They both look, then Clive says, "Well, she's gone now. What do you want to do? Go after her?"

We are standing in the middle of the crowded sidewalk forcing annoyed people to walk around us. I am still staring at the place I saw her when Clive asks me this. "No, no, I guess not," I finally answer him. Dejected, I add, "Best to leave it alone. I'm not even positive now that it was her. I just saw her for a second."

David says, "You need to go home. Take a leave. Go back to New York, find an old girlfriend and let her screw your brains out."

"And take me with you," Clive says.

"Let's go get some lunch. I'm famished," I say.

FORTY-TWO

November 6, 1940

Catherine stepped in front of a tall man moving along with her and the crowd. She removed the hat she was wearing as she entered the Westminster tube station. Wearing the hat had been a foolish, impulsive idea. When she put it on, Catherine tried to deny she was doing so hoping to catch Jeff's attention. Having seen him standing still, looking right at her, she became quite flustered and even a bit embarrassed.

As she followed the crowd down the stairs to the platform, Catherine silently chastised herself for her schoolgirl silliness. She wanted him to notice her and when he did, she ran off to hide.

Catherine had hoped she would see him at the PM's question time. Jeff was not a regular at this event, but she knew once in a while, he would attend. Catherine was sitting along the rail of the gallery in the same seat when he first noticed her. In an intimate moment, he had confessed that he may have fallen in love with her that very first time. Thoroughly touched, she had whispered a promise she would cherish that hat forever. Now, waiting for her train to Marylebone, the incident made her feel quite foolish.

The ride back to her current position took barely fifteen minutes. A small crowd exited with her. When she reached the sidewalk, Catherine finally put the hat back on then hurried off to make her report.

November 12, 1940

Catherine was back in attendance at Parliament. Once again, she had used her looks and smile to obtain a seat along the railing. Only this time she was several sections away from her original seat. And instead of a hat that Jeff might remember, she was wearing a dull, plain, brown one, unlikely to be noticed by anyone unless she shoved it in their face.

Neville Chamberlain, a good and decent, if somewhat naïve, man had passed away three days ago. His illness—bowel cancer—had been kept from the public for months. Rumors had leaked out, but his death was still considered a bit of shock.

A funeral service had been held in Westminster Abbey. Due to security concerns, the date and time had not been made public. Catherine had attended with Arthur. As a peer, Arthur had been invited, and Catherine had agreed to accompany him. Today, the House of Commons was holding a service of its own for the former Prime Minister. Churchill was on the calendar agreeing to eulogize his predecessor.

While Catherine waited, as the gallery began to fill up, she found herself recalling the past two weeks. Feeling out of place not being in uniform, more than a touch of guilt crept into her thoughts.

Her time at Uxbridge had been the worst experience for Catherine since Jeff had torn out her heart. Everyone of a lower rank and many of those above her had assumed she used her connections to obtain the transfer. Catherine tried several times to protest her innocence, but no one believed her. As bad as that was, Churchill's visit along with the news she was formally Lady Catherine, all but doomed her. The women turned her into an outcast and avoided her as if she were carrying a plague. On duty, they were professionally courteous, but that was it. Catherine put on her British stiff-upper lip, but she had never been so lonely. Even her roommate, Wynona Graves, became noticeably distant.

Then at the end of her shift on Friday, November 1, she received a reprieve. She was ordered to report to the little tyrant who ran the personnel section, Clark-Hoverfield. To Catherine's total surprise, the arrogant little despot handed her orders to report to the BBC and, after she had seriously disrespected him, he abruptly dismissed her.

Shocked would be a very mild way to describe her. Stunned down to her bones would be a more accurate description. Catherine left the personnel office—although she did not remember doing so—then found an empty bench where she sat for a half-hour. She read over the transfer request and approval order four or five times. It seems the BBC wanted her back. Due to the war, they were experiencing a manpower shortage. Once the shock wore off, Catharine was experiencing significant ambivalence: happy to be leaving and guilty about leaving.

As ordered, she reported to the BBC, in uniform, at seven a.m. the following Monday morning. For the next couple of hours, she made the rounds being introduced to new people and greeting old friends from her previous tenure. Catherine also noticed there did not seem to be a manpower shortage at the BBC. Like most formerly male-only jobs, women had smoothly transitioned, and everything seemed just fine.

At the end of the first day, her boss informed her she would be one of their reporters at Parliament. This meant covering the sessions and generating sources of information. He also told her it was okay to wear civilian clothing.

Within twenty-four hours of her return to the BBC, Arthur appeared in person. How he knew, Catherine quickly surmised. He denied it, but she knew his hand was involved with her new employment. Since that was clearly true, he almost certainly pulled the strings for her original transfer to Uxbridge. Arthur was completely honest and upfront with her. He wanted her back. He was quite persistent, and by the end of the first week, Friday, November 8, she was starting to give in.

Following the sighting of Jeff on Wednesday, November 6, she had time to realize that was over. Catherine also understood that she wore the rose hat so he would see her and chase her. In fact, she had slowly ascended to the tube platform hoping he would come after her. He did not and she had no more tears.

When Arthur asked her to dinner on Friday evening, terribly lonely and still bearing the effects of a broken heart, she agreed. At dinner, she confronted him about the two transfers to Uxbridge and the BBC. Instead of his normal lies, he actually admitted it. At dinner, he had been kind, even charming, the Arthur who had courted her as a nineteen-year-old girl; even more so at Chamberlain's funeral.

"I'm caving in," she quietly said out loud.

"I'm sorry," the older man seated next to her said. "You're caving in?"

"Oh God, I said that out loud, didn't I?" Catherine replied to the man. "I was just thinking out loud."

The man laughed and said, "It gets worse as you get older, especially if you have children. Don't worry, I do it all the time, and only my kids think I'm daft."

Catherine laughed and said, "I hope it doesn't get worse. I'm already bad enough at it."

"Here's Churchill," the man said to her. "He'll speak soon."

***

"May I help you?" Catherine heard the young woman ask as she closed the door behind her.

Catherine turned to face the desk where her husband's assistant was seated. Arthur's assistant was in the uniform of a corporal in the Women's Army Auxiliary Corps. Catherine, with a sincere smile, walked right up to the young soldier, extended her right hand and said, "You must be Claire. We've spoken several times. It's a pleasure to finally meet you."

A flustered Claire Parker jumped to her feet knocking her chair over backwards. "Lady Ashland," she managed to say. "Um, yes, ma'am. I mean, it's nice to meet you."

Catherine extended her hand a little more, and the nervous girl finally realized she was supposed to shake her hand. They did so, then after a moment released each other's hand.

"Please, Claire, don't call me that," Catherine whispered. "Catherine will do just fine. I called ahead," Catherine reminded her.

"Oh, yes, ma'am. Um, yes, you're to go right in. Sorry."

Catherine made a wounded look on her face and said, "Ma'am is no good, either. I'm not that much older than you."

"Yes, ma—um, Catherine, sorry. Please go right in," Claire said as she went to knock and open the door to Arthur's office.

Catherine thanked her as she walked past, then Claire closed the door.

When she got back to her desk, the young woman at the desk next to hers was looking at her. "Smooth," she said. "You handled that well, Claire."

"Oh, shut up," Claire replied. "She's so pretty. Who would've thought someone like that would be married to his majesty, the tyrant?"

"Hello, Arthur," Catherine greeted her husband.

Arthur stood up, came around the desk and took Catherine's hand. He bent down slightly to kiss her on the lips, but she turned a cheek to him instead.

"I'm delighted to see you," Arthur said. "How was the eulogy?"

Catherine took one of the chairs in front of Arthur's desk and he took the other,

"Not one of Winston's better moments," Catherine replied. "Most of the observers were calling it faint praise. 'An English worthy' is what he called him. Even that he attributed to Disraeli. Although, I hear privately, Winston will miss Chamberlain's counsel."

The two of them chatted amiably almost like a normal, married couple for twenty minutes about the House of Commons service. Arthur, ever the arrogant aristocrat, acted as if he really cared. Catherine was unable to tell if he was sincerely interested in what she said or not.

When the subject was finally exhausted, Arthur asked, "What did you wish to see me about, my dear?"

"I've decided I cannot go with you to your parents' home this weekend. It's much too soon for that. I'm sorry, but I need more time."

"Whatever you say is fine," Arthur replied. He softly took a hold of her right hand and said, "I absolutely understand. I don't wish to put any pressure on you whatsoever. It was very kind of you to go to the trouble of coming here to tell me in person."

Catherine pulled her hand back, looked at her watch and said, "I should be getting along. I still have a story to report; my observations."

He gently held her elbow while guiding her to the door. Again, he bent down to kiss her on the lips, and again, she presented a cheek to him.

"Dinner, Friday evening?" Arthur asked.

"Let me see how my week goes. Call me Friday, and I'll let you know," she answered.

"I'll have a car pick you up out front and take you back to the BBC," Arthur said.

"Thank you, Arthur. That would be nice."

As Catherine passed through the outer office, she said to the secretary next to Claire, "Tell Claire it was nice to meet her, and I'm sorry I didn't get a chance to say goodbye."

"I will, Catherine," the woman said.

"Ah, you were eavesdropping," Catherine said with a smile.

"Small office. Hard not to."

Catherine exited the building and found Claire Parker waiting for her. When she saw Catherine, she quickly stabbed her cigarette into a sand filled receptacle by the door.

"Claire," Catherine said, "I'm glad to see you before I left."

"Lady Ashland—Catherine," Claire said, "I feel I must tell you something. Perhaps you know, and if so, then tell me to mind my own business."

"Um, I don't have much time, but you can wait with me for my ride," Catherine replied.

As the two women walked down the front steps, Claire began, "I'm not sure you know, but a few weeks ago a man came to see your husband, an American—very nice and attractive. We all noticed."

Catherine stopped, turned to Claire and asked, "Was his name Jeff? Jeff Bartlett?"

"Yes, ma'am," Claire admitted. "And I'm ashamed to admit it, but I listened in on the conversation he had with Lord Ashland over the intercom system. I've been trying to decide whether or not I should tell you…"

"Tell me, Claire. I won't be angry with you. Please continue."

"All right. This man, Jeff, came to your husband and asked him to use his influence to get you transferred to a safe place. His majesty, I mean, your husband agreed to do so on the condition that Mr. Bartlett break things off with you and agree to never see you again. And well, it took a bit, but Mr. Bartlett finally agreed to it."

"That bastard," Catherine said.

"Your husband also threatened to have you sent to Singapore," Claire further revealed.

A startled Catherine looked at Claire and asked, "He did what?"

"I'm sorry to tell you all of this, but I thought you should know. Yes, he said he would send you to Singapore and make sure Mr. Bartlett would not be allowed to go there himself."

FORTY-THREE

November 12, 1940

Dear Mom & Dad,

Finally, some good war news. At least good if you're pulling for the British, and we better. The British are fighting the Italians in the Mediterranean and North Africa. It probably is not getting the attention it deserves, but it is extremely important. If the Nazis and Italian fascists take Egypt—and they are trying—they will cut off the Suez Canal. By itself, this would not defeat the British, but it would be a serious loss. They are receiving a significant number of men and material through the Suez from their colonies.

It seems the Italians—the Italian people—have little enthusiasm for the war. Apparently, they do not share Mussolini's dream of a modern Roman Empire. The British Army in Egypt, fighting with minimal men and support, extremely outnumbered in both men and material, are whipping the Italians. I am told that the Italian soldiers surrender by the thousands almost at the sight of a British soldier carrying the Union Jack. The Brits are running out of room for all of the prisoners.

Now the really good news. Before the war, Mussolini built up a modern Mediterranean Sea Navy to rival the British and French. Back on July 3, the Royal Navy attacked the French fleet in North Africa to keep it from falling into the hands of the Germans. You probably heard of this.

Better than that, the Royal Navy recently attacked the Italian fleet at their anchorage in Taranto, Italy, using planes flying off an aircraft carrier. I am told it was the first time in history that a naval attack was conducted solely by aircraft flying ship-to-ship. Taranto is located in the heel of the Italian boot if you want to find it on a map.

Using torpedoes and aerial bombs, the planes inflicted significant damage on the Italian fleet. They are claiming that at least half of the Italian fleet was either sunk or badly damaged. We will see. These preliminary reports are usually exaggerated by those involved. I am assured that the attack was, nevertheless, a huge success.

As for London and the bombing by the Germans—it is being called The Blitz—they are still at it. Not every night as before, but they are still at it. Keep listening to Ed Murrow's broadcasts. There is nothing faked about them. He usually broadcasts from the roof of the BBC building while the bombings are taking place. You are receiving real time reports.

There was a service for Neville Chamberlain in Parliament today. Churchill gave a eulogy for him. Not Winston's best everyone agrees. Personally, I thought Chamberlain was an honorable man who tried to prevent a war that he could not prevent. I'll let history be the man's judge.

My life has slipped into a routine of drudgery and boredom. My journalist friends and I file our daily reports which are mostly propaganda from the Ministry of Information. Even the reports of the damage—which I am sure you read—are becoming routine. We still try to help out when we can at places bombed by the Germans. It makes us feel that we are at least doing something, although the luster of being an American is wearing off. The Brits need our help and are not shy about letting us know it.

Time to wander down to the Ministry of Information. I submitted a really good article about Taranto. The censors were quite pleased with me. All is well with me.

All my love,

Jeff

The American Bar at the Savoy is abuzz about the attack on the Italians at Taranto. In fact, it has lifted the spirits of the entire country, or so it seems. When there is good news, the government is quick to release it. David, Clive and I are at a table by ourselves. Although Charlie was not the first person we knew who was killed, his death has hit us all very hard. And Catherine, my friends miss her almost as much as I do. She had that inner something that lifted everyone around her.

David is right. I need to take a leave and go home for a couple of weeks. I am thinking maybe Christmas and New Year's. I have even found myself thinking about my shipboard romance with Jean Butler. She's a sweet girl but that would be a huge mistake.

We are sitting at a table with four chairs. Several of our journalist friends have dropped by and sat down with us. Without a word, they all find a chair and leave the empty chair, Charlie's chair, unoccupied. Gregarious Charlie was popular and well-liked by all who knew him.

Sunset this time of year is about a quarter past five. The windows here in the bar are covered with blackout curtains. My watch reads almost five thirty so I assume it is dark outside. The blackout restrictions have eased a bit. Cabs and buses are allowed to have a little bit of light coming from their headlights. This, at least, allows pedestrians to see them. Accidents have dropped considerably.

"I'm gonna take off," I say. I push my half-full glass to the middle of the table and stand.

"Aren't you going to at least finish your drink?" Clive asks.

"No. Truth be told, I'm tired and haven't slept well lately," I say as I put on my trench coat and hat. "I'm not even hungry. I'll go back to the Ritz, listen to the BBC for a while and go to bed early—maybe have a late supper. I'll see you tomorrow."

There are three black cabs in front of the Savoy. I sometimes feel like I must be wearing a sign proclaiming me to be an American. The cabbies can somehow spot it the moment they see you. Americans are great tippers, and the drivers almost fight to get me as a fare. I take the first one in line.

As I approach the door to my suite, key in hand, like almost every night, I try to remember if I have put the blackout curtains in place. And like most nights, when I get the door open, I wait to turn on a light until I have checked the windows. I stumble around for a minute in complete darkness until I am satisfied. I bang my knee on a chair, curse a bit because of it, then find a light switch. It illuminates the sitting room and causes me to blink several times while my eyes adjust.

"I must admit, you have excellent taste in brandy," I hear her say.

Before I realize who it is, this unexpected voice almost makes my heart stop. I actually yelp a bit and stumble backwards. My right hand has gone to my chest. My mouth hangs open while I try to breathe and stare at her in shock. She is seated on a two-person sofa next to a table with a lamp and a bottle of cognac.

"Although," she says, noticeably slurring her words, "this bottle is almost empty. Better get some more," she says. She tries to stand but quickly falls back onto the loveseat.

"Catherine! You took five years off my life! What are you doing…
Why, you're drunk," I say.

She wiggles her empty glass at me and, with a silly look on her face
and glassy eyes, says, "Yes, I believe I am! At least a little. But you sir,
have some serious explaining to do."

I watch, trying not to laugh as she attempts to put the glass on the table
with the bottle. She misses and it falls on the thick carpeting. While I
continue trying not to laugh, I watch her try to stand.

While she does this, still slurring her words, trying to look angry while
her upper body weaves about, she says, "I am extremely angry with you,
Jeffrey. You have some serious explaining to do."

Catherine is almost to her feet, swaying a bit with one hand on the arm
of the sofa. With a drunken tilt of her head and a fuzzy look in her eyes, she
drops back onto the couch. She looks directly at me as if she has something
else to say. Her eyes roll upward, and she falls over onto her left side. Her
right hand is touching the floor as are both feet. Her eyes are closed, and
her mouth is open. It seems my love is more than a little drunk. Catherine
has passed out cold.

For the past two hours, I have been sitting across the living room from
Catherine. When she collapsed, I gently lifted her up, removed her shoes
and laid her out more comfortably. I also covered her with a blanket and
put a pillow under her head. About twenty minutes ago, she opened her
eyes, lifted her head and looked at me. For a moment, I thought she might
wake up. Instead, she put her head on the pillow and has not moved since.

There is a soft knock on my door which I barely hear. I hear it again
then get up to answer it. I know who it is. I open it and find a young man
from the kitchen standing there with a room service cart.

"Your order, Mr. Bartlett," he says.

"Come in, John, please," I say.

I stand aside while he wheels the cart inside. I have ordered up two pots
of coffee and some bland food. It is time for Catherine to wake up.

When John gets inside—we are in the dining room—he straightens up,
looks around and starts to ask, "What is that—"

I hold an index finger to my lips to quiet him then say, "It seems Lady
Ashland has had a bit too much brandy. She's…" I pause.

"Snoring?" he says.

"Yes, I'm, afraid so. She's in the sitting room on a sofa," I add. I reach in my pocket and find a five-pound note. I hand it to him while saying, "We'll keep that to ourselves, won't we?"

"Mum's the word, Mr. Bartlett. Mum's the word. I must admit I wouldn't have thought her ladyship could be that loud."

He looks at me as innocently as possible. I look back, find another five-pound note and, again, silently hand it to him.

"Mum's the word, sir, and thank you."

"My head is pounding," Catherine says.

She is sitting up on the sofa holding the small pillow on top of her head. I have moved my chair closer to her, waiting patiently for the storm to hit me. I have poured a glass of water for her and hand it to her.

"Are you going to be sick?" I ask.

"No, I don't think so," she answers. "Is that what the waste basket is for?" I have placed a metal waste basket near her feet.

"Yes," I answer her.

"What's this?" she asks.

"Water. Drink it," I say.

Catherine pours the entire glass down her throat, takes a breath, looks at me and says, "Thanks. That helps. I'm still mad at you."

"I know. Do you want some coffee?"

"Oh, yes, please," she answers.

I pour a cup of coffee, add a little milk, place it on a saucer and set it on the table. She tries to pick it up, but her hand is shaking so badly she cannot do it. Instead, I hold it to her lips, and she drinks some of it down.

"Let me get you something for that head," I say.

When I return from the bathroom with aspirin—she is still holding the pillow on top of her head—I pour some more water for her which she uses to drink down the pain relief. It is here that I lose my composure and laugh.

"It's not funny," she says as she throws the pillow at me. I am less than four feet away and she misses.

"It's a little funny," I say. "Are you going to be sick?" I ask again.

"No… maybe… I don't know. I don't think so," she replies. Catherine drinks down more coffee, this time on her own. She hands me her cup and asks for a cigarette.

While I am doing this for her, she finally gets to it. "What were you thinking?" she asks. Before I can answer, she continues basically barking at me, saying, "You grossly interfered in my life and, worse, you almost drove me back to Arthur. What were you…?"

I hand her the coffee and cigarette and say, "I was thinking about how much I love you and I wanted you safe. There. I was being extremely selfish." I sit down in my chair and say, "Are you happy I admitted it? Although I must say, I didn't see you going back to Arthur. Even if I had, I still would have done it."

"Didn't he tell you that's what he wanted?"

"Yes, but I thought you had more sense than that," I reply.

"I was lonely. Everyone at Uxbridge hated me. They thought I used my connections to get transferred."

"Is that where you were?" I ask.

"You didn't know? Arthur didn't tell you?"

"No."

"Plus, I was terribly hurt," she says. After a pause she adds, "By you!"

"I just wanted you safe," I say again, almost in a whisper.

She stands and walks to me, runs her fingers through my hair then sits on my lap. She puts her arms around my neck. I hold her, and we silently look at each other.

"Don't do it again," she finally says.

"I won't," I reply. "I have to tell you something, though."

"If it's about all the women you shagged, I don't—"

"Not a single one. I was as chaste as a virgin nun," I say.

"I didn't sleep with Arthur," she says in response to the inquisitive expression on my face. "Not even a kiss."

"Good. He doesn't deserve it. What I was going to say was how impressed I am at how loudly you were snoring while asleep on the couch."

"I do not snore!" she almost yells and thumps me on the shoulder with a fist.

"Should I bring the room service boy back to verify it?"

"What? You let…? Seriously! Oh my God. I can never come back to this hotel again," she says staring off at nothing.

"I swore him to secrecy. You'll be fine. Your secret's safe. How's your head?"

"Much better. I need to brush my teeth. Is my toothbrush…?"

"Right where you left it. I didn't have the heart to throw it out."

"My clothes and other things?"

"Clothing laundered and everything else also right where you left it. I knew I wouldn't be able to keep my word and stay away from you."

Catherine stands up and says, "Let me brush my teeth, use the loo and I'll meet you in the bed. And you'd better be ready and able."

"Trust me. No problem."

FORTY-FOUR

November 15, 1940

Dear Mom & Dad,

I know it is odd for me to write so soon after my last letter. Don't worry, I'm fine.

This war will be the most destructive of all time. I am absolutely convinced of this. With the advent of the airplane as a weapon of war, there is now no limit to the delivery of destruction. Both sides are doing it, and each is blaming the other. Who started it? The Germans started the war. I will leave it at that.

Cities and civilians on both sides are catching hell. Each side claims they are only bombing war material production sites. I can tell you with absolute certainty, this is nonsense. I have seen the bomb damage to homes and on other 'wartime targets' the Germans have inflicted. I have also spoken to—this would not get past the censors—RAF bomber personnel who admit they are doing the same to the Germans. Even if both sides are truly trying to only target war production facilities, the bombing ability is simply not accurate enough.

Coventry was horribly bombed yesterday. You will recall we visited there about ten or twelve years ago. It was a beautiful city with an incredible, medieval city center and cathedral. The building of the cathedral began at the end of the fourteenth century and finished during the first part of the fifteenth century. The cathedral was completely destroyed and the medieval center wiped out. We cannot replace these things.

Some good news from Greece. So far, the Brits have been correct in their assessment of the military situation. Not only are the Greeks holding their own against the Italians, but the word is also they have started a counteroffensive. Their goal is to push the Italians back into Albania. The Brits are confident they will succeed against the Italians. Their concern is

*the Germans coming to the rescue of their ally, Mussolini. If that happens…
well, we'll see.*

*Personal news. Catherine and I are back together. I am both delirious
with joy and extremely worried.*

*One of Arthur's—her estranged husband—assistants overheard the
deal I made with him. I can't remember if I told you about it. I offered to
break things off with Catherine if he would get her transferred to a safer
place.*

*The assistant told Catherine, and she was waiting for me when I
arrived back at my room yesterday. As you may guess, she was none too
pleased with me. Sort of. We have patched things up, but I am sure I have
not heard the last of it.*

*We received a visit from the German Luftwaffe last night. I have
already made arrangements with my two friends, Clive and David, to do
some rescue work. There will be others of our clique of foreign journalists
to lend a hand as well.*

Don't worry, I'm fine. Catherine is back!

All my love,

Jeff

"What are we going to do about Arthur?" Catherine asks.

I am addressing an envelope to mail my letter. We are seated at the
dining room table where I do my writing. Catherine is to my right, her left
foot on the chair's seat. She is resting her chin on her knee while she smokes
and drinks coffee.

When I finish with the envelope, I look at her, smile and gently wipe
the back of my hand on her cheek. She kisses my hand, returns my smile,
and I am about to melt.

"You're still in a lot of trouble, buster," she says still smiling.

"I know. Dad warned me, women don't forget anything," I say. "I
meant well," I almost plead. "That should mean something."

"It does," she replied. "Now, what are we going to do about Arthur?"

"First, I think we keep a low profile. Do you think you may have been
followed here, yesterday?"

"Oh God, I hadn't thought about that. I was only concerned with how angry I was with you. And speaking of that…" she says, then stands up and goes into the sitting room. A short moment later, she comes back carrying an envelope. She takes her seat and gives me a strange look. "I've been debating whether or not to bring this up. I suppose, given the circumstances, I have no right to be angry, but I can't help it," she says.

"What?" I ask, genuinely curious.

"You did say, how did you put it? Oh, yes, as chaste as a virgin nun. That's redundant, by the way. And actually, I wasn't as angry as I was hurt," she says.

She slides the envelope across the table, and I pick it up. When I open it, I find ten photos of me and an attractive woman together on a balcony. As I look over each one, puzzled, I ask, "Where are these from?"

Catherine says nothing, and then I remember.

"I remember now," I say. "This is a girl I met at a reception for Joe Kennedy at the American Embassy." I look at Catherine and continue, "I was on the balcony getting some air. She came up to me and asked me for a light for her cigarette. She was a very pleasant, attractive young woman. We chatted for a while. I never saw her before, and I haven't seen her since—just a girl I met at a party."

The photos are on the table by now. Catherine pulls one out and holds it up. It is the one where we were kissing.

"Catherine! Really, what you see there is all there was to it. I… Where did you get these? Arthur? Did he give them to you? That bastard. He was there. He was at the reception kissing his general's ass. I'll bet he set the whole thing up."

All the while I am thinking this through and talking, Catherine continues to hold that photo up so I can see it. "You know something?" she finally says. "I think you're right. He did set this up." She looks at the photo again then back at me and says, "Pretty salacious. I can see your hand making its way down to her bottom."

"It is not!" I protest much too vigorously which causes her to burst out laughing.

"You're right. I believe you. Anything worse and there would be more photographic evidence. You got lucky."

"Actually, I didn't get lucky. She left after the infamous kiss," I say.

"What do we do about Arthur? I can't go sneaking around until the end of the war," she says. "And I shan't not see you."

"For now, we do nothing. I have an idea. It may or may not work. I need to meet with someone to find out," I say.

"What?"

"Are you sure you want to know?"

"Of course," she replies.

So I tell her.

"It would be perfect, wouldn't it?" she says when I finish.

"If it can be done."

"Oh, it can be done. Let me think about it. You try your source, and I'll see if I can think of any. I'm supposed to have dinner with Arthur this evening," she tells me.

"Go. It would be suspicious if you cancel now."

"He's going to ask me to spend the night," she says.

"I disapprove, in case you're wondering."

She gives me a look of disapproval that women have perfected over the centuries, then dryly says, "So do I. I'll come up with an excuse. He'll take me home, probably late."

"So stay home—"

"I don't want to," she quickly says.

"We have to be discreet."

Catherine practically jumps out of her chair and onto my lap. She starts kissing me all over my face while saying, "I don't want to be discreet. I want to shag you in Trafalgar Square."

"Yes, that would not be discreet."

We sit silently for a minute then I say, "I really should get going."

"Me too," she sighs. "I'm just… happy."

"Me too," I reply.

Clive, David and I are in a pub a half mile from last night's main bomb damage. It is pushing dinnertime. We are all tired and hungry, smell bad and our clothes are filthy. We have frequented this place several times after helping with search and rescue. Most of the other patrons were also at the bomb site helping out.

More thirsty than hungry, we are each on our third pint when Mike Burns, our naval attaché friend, arrives. So far, I have been able to resist telling my friends about Catherine. I was waiting for Mike. Mike finds an empty chair—we are still keeping a chair open for Charlie—and joins us. The owner, sporting a wooden leg courtesy of the First War, quickly brings a pint for Mike.

"Jeff, what did you want to see me about?"

I look at each of them in turn and say, "Catherine's back."

The three of them were almost as happy as I was. She is every bit as much of a pal, a buddy, a friend as we are to each other. They have missed the sunshine she brings.

Men want to deny it, but they can be, and usually are, as gossipy as women. They want to know all of it: how she found out, what she did, how I found it, everything. I was barely able to close the bedroom door on them. I had to tell them twice about Catherine's drunkenness. They roared with laughter at the description of her passed out, snoring on the couch. It occurred to me I may be able to use this to ward off some of her threats of retaliation for my interventions to get her transferred.

"So, now what?" Clive asks. "His Lordship could still use his connections to put her back in uniform and transfer her to the other side of the planet."

"Well, that's what I wanted to see the good commander about, and you too, Clive. And while we're at it, David can also give it some thought and see what he can come up with."

For the next hour, we discuss what I have in mind. It is agreed we will all look into whatever sources we have to see if we can pull it off.

FORTY-FIVE

November 15, 1940
Piccadilly, London

Arthur Ashland's driver stopped the army staff car in front of the Criterion. The building and street were strictly blacked out and it was barely visible. The doorman opened the backseat door, Arthur exited and held Catherine's hand to gentlemanly assist her. As the doorman, sporting a small flashlight, guided them to the door, Arthur made a confession.

"I'm afraid I have not been completely forthcoming, my dear," he said.

"Given your history, I'm not surprised," Catherine replied.

Because of the dark, Catherine could not see Arthur's crimson face. Having her insult him caused his normal reaction: immediate anger. Realizing he must not act on it, he took a breath before speaking.

"This is not simply a night out for us," he said. "It is a, more or less, mandatory engagement. General Dalton was invited, as was I personally, to dine here tonight and attend the play."

The Criterion was both an upper-crust restaurant and a live theatre.

"What is the play?" Catherine asked while they waited to be seated.

They were standing in the restaurant's entryway. In front of them was an elegant dining room filled exclusively with men in uniform and well-dressed women. Catherine had to keep her disapproval to herself at the number of senior officers escorting much younger women. The war was less of a hardship for some than for others.

Sensing what she was thinking, Arthur quietly said, "Even during war, rank has its privileges." As if the opulence they enjoyed was deserved.

"The play?" Catherine asked again ignoring the chauvinistic comment.

"Oh, I don't know. A Cole Porter musical called *Come Out of Your Shell*. I've no idea what it's about."

"I've heard of it," Catherine said. "I've heard it's an amusing comedy."

In fact, it was a play along with dinner she had been to with Jeff several months ago. And she was tempted to say so and throw it in Arthur's face.

They were seated at a table with three other couples. Arthur's boss, Major General Sir Dalton Floyd, was the senior officer. Catherine was seated next to Mrs. Floyd, a woman she had never met. At first, being seated next to a general's wife sounded like a social death sentence. Within minutes, Catherine found her to be excellent company. Her name was Martha, and she was charming, funny and best of all, irreverent and not impressed with military rank. The two of them hit it off immediately and got along splendidly.

To Catherine's left was a major working in the same department as Arthur. A duller, more intellectually limited and less interesting person would be hard to find. Fortunately for Catherine, Arthur was stuck between two dowdy colonel's wives across the table from her.

The meal itself was bland and the service not up to pre-war standards. Too many men had gone into uniform, especially after Dunkirk. At one point, one of the colonel's wives sitting next to Arthur, grumbled about the food.

Arthur's aristocratic arrogance got the better of him. "You'd think they could at least get decent food for the more deserving," Arthur said.

"Hear, hear," said a chubby colonel, husband of the chubby wife who made the initial complaint.

General Floyd had a mouthful of food and would say something except Catherine beat him to it.

"There is a war on, Arthur," she said. "Others are sacrificing a lot more than expensive meals in fancy restaurants."

The general swallowed, said a brief thank you to Catherine and gave his two subordinates a disapproving look.

The remainder of the meal passed in a bit of an awkward silence. Around them the words 'Greece,' 'Italians' and 'Churchill' were getting louder with each glass of wine. There was no disguising the disapproval of the military for Churchill's aid to Greece's campaign. They were dead set against it. So far, it was uncertain which attitude would prevail.

"General Floyd," Catherine said to the man. The general was seated at the round table two chairs down to her left.

"Yes, Lady Catherine," he replied.

"I'm hearing at the BBC that eventually Winston will get his way and send troops to Greece. I'm curious, what do you think?"

Floyd smiled at her and looked at his wife who was watching him with raised eyebrows. This was a subject he had not broached with her.

"Of course, this is strictly off the record and not for publication. As a soldier, I will do as I'm ordered to do."

"Nicely put, Dalton," his wife said with a smile.

"Why, thank you, Martha," he replied. He smiled back at his wife then looked at Catherine. "I also believe stripping troops from Egypt would be a mistake. We're winning against the Italians there. The Greeks are doing well without our help."

"What if the Germans attack the Balkans?" Catherine asked.

"We'll cross that bridge, if we come to it," Floyd answered.

Across the dining room from where they were seated were several tables filled with RAF officers and women. At that moment, one of the officers, whose back was to Catherine, stood up and headed toward the gentlemen's rest room.

"Thank you, General," Catherine said to Floyd. "That's at least honest."

Less than two minutes later, she saw the RAF officer reenter the dining room. Catherine quickly excused herself and walked off to intercept him. "Hello," Catherine said when she caught up with him.

His back was to her, and the man turned to the sound. Group Captain Robinson's face lit up when he saw who it was. "Catherine! How wonderful to see you," he said.

Tossing protocol aside, they gave each other a hug.

"You look smashing. What are you doing here? How have you been? Come, let me introduce you to my wife," Robinson said.

Knowing Arthur was likely staring holes in her, Catherine kept the reunion short. After meeting Robinson's wife, they chatted for a minute or so then she headed back to her table. Halfway there a thought occurred to her. She quickly turned back.

"Could I have a minute?" she asked Robinson.

"Certainly," Robinson replied.

"I'll bring him right back," she told his wife.

"You'd better. We haven't seen each other in months. I have plans," the woman smiled and winked at Catherine.

"Then I'd better hurry." Catherine wiggled her eyebrows and smiled back.

He followed her about fifteen feet to an open spot in the room.

"When are you going back?" she asked.

"Unfortunately, I'm only here for the day. I came for meetings with the high brass, and I'm leaving tomorrow morning by car. Why?"

"I wonder if I might…" Catherine said as she began to tell him why she wanted to talk to him.

November 17, 1940
Dover, UK

Catherine took her seat in the coach section of the train. She was on the eight thirty a.m. train from Dover to London, Waterloo Station. The train, with its load of foodstuffs, pulled out only a few minutes late to begin the two-hour journey. As the train began her return trip to London, Catherine closed her eyes and leaned her head against the wooden backboard.

Upon seeing her former commanding officer, Group Captain Robinson, this past Friday evening, an idea occurred to her. Catherine wanted to have a private conversation right then, but he did not have the time. Instead, she convinced him to let her visit Swingate for the weekend. Using the BBC as a ploy, he agreed to let her visit in search of a story.

First thing Saturday morning, she called the Ritz and left a message for Jeff, short and to the point: she had been called away at the last minute on an assignment and would be back Monday. She made a vague reference only he would understand to let him know where she was going.

The two days had been a very pleasant reunion, to say the least. Most of her friends were still there doing their part. Catherine was not without a serious bout of guilt that she was no longer with them. She was able to have a long talk with her friend and one-time supervisor, Betsy Halvorson, about this. Betsy assured her no one harbored any ill will toward her. Betsy also told Catherine she would make sure everyone knew the true story about how Catherine was transferred.

Sunday afternoon, the Germans sent over a calling card. Their shore batteries located across the Strait of Dover shelled the nearby Citadel area. It did not last long, and minimal damage was incurred. Later the women heard that there were only three minor casualties.

The train wheels clacked, and the car rhythmically swayed slightly back and forth. The effect of this was similar to rocking a baby to sleep. A half hour out of Dover and Catherine's head gently bumped the window next to her knocking her hat askew. The next thing she was conscious of was the slowing of the train as it entered Waterloo Station.

During the few minutes it took for the little train to come to a complete stop, Catherine woke up and gathered herself. Her one suitcase was in the overhead bin which she retrieved. There was barely a baker's dozen passengers, and she quickly stepped down, onto the platform.

"Hey, lady," she heard a familiar voice say, "looking for a good time?"

Catherine looked toward the sound and broke into a huge smile. Jeff, his hat jauntily cocked wearing a Bogart-style trench coat, was leaning against a support beam.

"As a matter of fact, I am," Catherine replied.

After hugs and kisses, while Jeff carried her suitcase, with her right arm hooked to his left, they headed toward the exit.

"How was your visit?" Jeff asked,

"Nice. Very pleasant," she answered. "I was a little worried about the reception I might get because of the abrupt transfer. But they couldn't have been nicer. I told Betsy, my old supervisor, how it happened. She assured me she would make sure everyone knew."

"Did you get enough for a story?" Jeff asked.

"Yes, sort of. It's so highly classified, what they do. I'm not sure how good it will be."

"Do a 'women-doing-their-part' story. Talk about the hardships, their dedication, things like that," Jeff suggested.

"That's what I have in mind," said Catherine.

By now they had left the station, and Jeff was looking for a cab. Instead, Catherine stopped him.

"Wait, don't get a cab just yet. Give me a cigarette and I'll tell you why I really went." While they smoked, Catherine said, "I saw my former commanding officer, Group Captain Boyd Robinson at dinner with Arthur, Friday evening."

"Okay," Jeff said, keeping his displeasure from showing.

"He's a very nice man and an extremely fine officer and commander,"

"Everything Arthur is not." Jeff said.

"Quite," Catherine said. "Don't be jealous. Anyway, I remembered that he has a cousin, who is also a good friend of his, who is on the staff of Air Vice Marshall Keith Park. Do you know who he is?"

"Sure, he's quite high up."

"Exactly. In fact, Robinson's cousin has been promoted to be Park's Chief of Staff. I told Robinson all about my transfer, including your part in it. He found that to be very romantic, by the way," Catherine said.

"Arthur," was Jeff's one-word reply to get her back on the subject.

"He said he will see what he can do," Catherine said.

"Yeah, but they're air force, Arthur is army…"

"They're all friends, sort of," Catherine said. "My group captain was very angry with Arthur's interference with his personnel. I also told him the story you brought back from Dunkirk: the one about Arthur's cowardice. I thought his hair might start on fire, his face became so red. That did it."

They extinguished their cigarettes in a nearby receptacle, then started walking toward a line of cabs.

"He was very impressed that you and David volunteered to help with the Dunkirk evacuation," Catherine told him.

"His approval can't hurt," Jeff said.

"No, it can't," Catherine agreed.

November 19, 1940
Office of Major General Floyd

General Floyd exited his office into the secretary's workspace carrying several official-looking documents. The women saw him and started to stand up, but as usual, he quickly motioned for them to remain seated. The general rapped twice on Arthur Ashland's door then opened it before Arthur could answer. Arthur also started to stand but Floyd waved him down as well.

"Well, Ashland," Floyd said when he sat down, "you must know some important people."

"Sir?" Ashland replied, making it a question.

Floyd held up the papers and said, "It seems you're needed elsewhere. And I must admit, I envy you. I've been trying to get into combat since Dunkirk."

"Sir?" Arthur said again, only this time the anxiety crept in.

"I have transfer orders from General O'Connor's command. It seems they lost an assistant deputy division commander; killed in action, I'm afraid. Anyway, I have a note here that says they were looking at you for a while because of the courage and leadership you displayed on the beaches of Dunkirk"—the last of this, Floyd was reading from one of the pages; he looked at Arthur and said—"the reason for your medal and promotion."

By this point, Arthur was staring at the General trying to simply maintain his composure. He managed to coherently say a thank you, all the while fighting the urge to flee.

"Um, sir, I, uh, didn't request a transfer. I don't understand," Arthur managed to say.

"Transfers aren't always done by request. The Western Desert Force is doing the only real fighting against our enemies, and they have a need for you, and well, off you go."

"But, um, what about my duties here, to you, sir?"

Floyd dismissed the question with a flip of his hand while saying, "We'll manage. I can fill this slot with any number of officers. This is a huge opportunity. You'll be a brigadier in two years. You'll see. Now, your travel orders. It seems they're in a hurry to get you. There is a supply convoy forming up and shipping out of Portsmouth on Friday. That's top secret, of course."

"Friday? That's two days from now. I'll barely have time to make it, sir."

Floyd stood up and said, "Yes, well, the needs of the army and all. I'm sure you'll manage. Here's everything you'll need: transfer and travel orders. Don't misplace them. Leave your home address with the girls out front. They'll have your personal property delivered there."

By now a thoroughly shaken, almost paralyzed, Arthur Ashland had to stand up to shake Floyd's extended hand.

"You'll be hearing the sound of the cannons roar in a few days. God, how I envy you. Good luck, good hunting, and give the Italians a good thrashing," Floyd said.

"Yes, sir. Splendid, sir," Arthur quietly replied.

When General Floyd returned to his desk, the first thing he did was smile and look at his closed door.

"Somebody up there must have quite the sense of humor," he quietly said to himself. "I would love to know how this came about."

FORTY-SIX

November 21, 1940

Dear Mom & Dad,

Happy Thanksgiving!

First, news from the war. The German Luftwaffe is now not only in London. Instead, they are spreading their terror to other cities, too many to list in a letter. Although, again, the RAF is giving it right back to them. When this war is over, both sides may have some serious questions to answer. Likely that only the losing side will ever have to answer for it.

As to the war itself, not sure if I told you he did it or was only thinking about it. I refer to Churchill sending British troops from North Africa to Greece. Well, he has done it, and the military leaders are throwing a fit about it. They haven't been transferred yet, but Winston is determined to do so.

The generals are worried about two things because of this. First, they are already greatly outnumbered in North Africa. And second, they fear sending British troops to Greece will cause the Germans to declare war on Greece and attack them. From what I am told, the second concern, Germany invading Greece through the Balkans, is the greater danger.

The British in North Africa are being reinforced by colonial troops, especially from India and South Africa. They are also whipping the Italians soundly. I guess we shall see what comes of this.

We received the news that Hungary has signed the Tripartite Pact with Germany, Italy and Japan. This may seem insignificant, but it is not. We are also hearing the Germans are about to convince Romania and the Slovak Republic to join as well. In fact, this will happen in the next day or two. Stalin had better sit up and pay attention to this.

My government sources are telling me that they are receiving information from spies inside Germany. They are quite certain Hitler's next target is Russia. That is why he is pushing to get Middle European nations to sign the Tripartite Pact. He is lining up allies for his war with Russia and probably offering them a nice slice of the Russian land pie for doing so.

How about some good news? Catherine has done it! She used her military connections to pay back her conniving husband. I probably should not tell you this, but he is, at this minute, packing his bags for a sea voyage. He shall soon be seeing the Egyptian Pyramids. Not for long, though. The North African front lines are several hundred miles from there. He will get a close up look at the shooting.

Catherine pulled this off in just a few days. Once she told her old commanding officer what Arthur did to get her transferred, the wheels moved very quickly. It seems her former boss has relatives in high places. Bon voyage, Arthur!

A Happy Thanksgiving, indeed!

Love to all,

Jeff

"What exactly did he say?" I ask. I am on the phone with Catherine. I have just finished my Thanksgiving letter home when she calls.

Yesterday evening, Arthur had simply arrived unannounced at the BBC at six o'clock. He insisted on taking Catherine to dinner. She did not even have time to call me to let me know.

"I don't know if he was more angry or frightened. He told me about the visit from General Floyd and how he was informed of his transfer. I expected it, and he eventually got to it. He point-blank asked me if you or I had anything to do with it. I must admit, it felt wonderful to look him in the eye and lie to him. He has done that so much to me, I almost got goosebumps," Catherine says.

"What did you say about me?" I ask.

"I told him I haven't seen you and I doubted you had the connections to pull off something like this," she replies.

"I almost wish I did, except I'd be too tempted to find him and brag about it. Will he really leave?" I ask.

"I saw him off at the train station. If I could, I would have held his hand and walked him up the gangplank of whatever ship he's leaving on.

"He tried to get me to spend the night with him," she adds.

"How did you get out of it?"

"I told him I was assigned to Ed Murrow's broadcast and couldn't get away. He offered to wait up and I told him no, it was still too soon. He became quite angry. He had calmed down by the time we got back to the BBC. He insisted on meeting Ed Murrow, but he wasn't available. I found an assistant producer who could back up my story. And then, as luck would have it, I ran into Ed, and he invited me to go up on the roof with him."

"And you couldn't turn him down," I say.

"And I couldn't turn him down," she quietly admits.

"Murrow is a well-known, notorious, womanizing dog. He just wants to get in your knickers," I say.

"Won't happen."

"And I am none too pleased you exposed yourself to the bombs up on that roof."

"It's no more dangerous there than anywhere else," she quickly replies.

"I'll pick you up at eight this evening. We're going to the Savoy. The guys are anxious to see you," I tell her.

"Yes, sir. I'll be on time. I want to see them, too. Hey, I love you," she says.

This, of course, melts me like an ice cube in the desert.

"I love you, too. I'll see you at eight."

I am standing in front of Broadcasting House, offices of the BBC, at Portland Place. It is almost eight o'clock, and I am anxious to see Catherine. I am also a little concerned to be about this late at night. The Germans have not paid London a visit for a couple of nights, and something tells me we are due. The blackout, of course, makes the area quite dark. I cannot help but wonder why it is still so vigorously enforced. The Germans seem to have little trouble locating the city with or without the blackout.

"Hey, sailor, looking for a good time?" I hear her voice behind me say.

I turn around and say, "There you are!"

A quick kiss and hug greeting before she loops her arm through mine, and then we start off toward the Savoy. If we do not find a cab, a distinct possibility, we can walk it in under a half-hour. It is a cloudless sky, and the moon phase is about two-thirds full. With the blackout, the moon provides at least sufficient light to read street signs and find our way.

We start off heading south toward the river, chatting about the coup Catherine has accomplished against Arthur. By this time tomorrow, he will be well out to sea on his way to a combat zone. I silently chastise myself for hoping he gets killed.

Ten minutes into our journey, the sirens go off. Less than a minute later, we hear the first bombs explode. They are closer than we thought they would be. For some reason, the sirens sounded later than normal. Somehow the Germans arrived almost undetected.

We have picked up our pace to the point where we are almost running. After a short distance, we are in fact running along the street where the University of Westminster is located toward an Underground station. It is only a quarter of a mile ahead when the closest bombs start to go off. By now the Germans are directly overhead and we are both terrified. Bombs have gone off behind us and in front of us.

Across the street there is a small church. We run toward it when we see four or five others hurry through the front door. There is an elderly man at the door wearing the cassock of a Catholic priest. He is frantically waving at us, and I can barely hear him yelling, "Hurry, hurry, hurry!" as he holds the door open. We get inside, and he closes the door as a stick of German bombs go off a hundred yards from us. They can be counted as they approach, one through seven. The last one, the seventh, blows out several windows of the church as we scurry to our right toward the stairway.

When we reach the basement, the priest right behind us, we find a small, sturdy room with others already there. Eighteen in total, including ourselves. The priest, whose name I find out is Father Donovan, moves about reassuring everyone. There are candles and torches—flashlights—to provide some illumination. The bombs continue to go off around us. Some are close enough to shake the old building, but it seems solid enough to withstand most near misses.

Of the eighteen people, I will learn that including the good Father, there are three older men and the rest, women; no children which strikes me as odd. And no men or women in the same age group as Catherine and me; we are the youngest ones here by at least a couple of decades.

"We should move these people away from the center and up against the walls," Catherine suggests. "They look sturdy and will hold up better than the ceiling."

Being a veteran of several bombings and shelling at Swingate, Catherine is the calmest one here. She quickly takes charge and starts moving people to more solid parts of the structure.

As suddenly as it started, the explosions stop. I use a candle and check my watch. It is 8.25 p.m. The entire raid has lasted barely fifteen minutes, but it has seemed like an eternity while it was happening.

Catherine and I are huddled together along one wall, away from the basement windows. Miraculously none of them were blown out.

"You're a cool one," Father Donovan says to Catherine.

"I've, uh, well, had some experience," Catherine replies.

We introduce ourselves. It is the first time I have spoken to the man who may have saved our lives. His white eyebrows move upward when he hears my American English.

"An American," he says.

By now, everyone in the basement is looking at us. I have grown quite accustomed to it. The look they give me is one that silently says, *Why are you here, you bloody fool?*

"Yes, Father," I reply. "I try to hide it, but it seems everyone notices."

He smiles, then looks at Catherine, then me, then Catherine again and says, "Well, as pretty as she is, even a priest can understand why you're here."

"He might be a German spy," Catherine says. "But I'll get him to switch sides." This remark breaks the tension, and we all share a laugh.

The sirens are off, but no one gets up to leave. These people are veteran bombing victims. They know it is early and the Germans will likely come back. I am impressed with how calm they are. We get into a circle, exchange names, and for the next hour or so I am vigorously questioned. What is a Yank doing here?

About nine thirty, one of the men suggests it may be okay to leave. The Father disputes this, as do Catherine and me. Within a minute, the sirens are sounding the alarm again. "Perhaps I spoke a little too soon," said the gentleman who made the suggestion.

About fifteen minutes later, we hear the bombs going off. The Germans have taken to staggering them. The belief is they are hoping to catch rescue workers out in the open after the first attack. It is coming from the docks which are several miles from us. Being in this tiny little shelter, it is still a very frightening experience.

Catherine and I are holding each other so closely, we are almost one person. This is an unusually heavy raid, and it lasts a while as I nervously look at my watch. I have been through a lot of these raids but have never felt so vulnerable. I think it is because I have never been quite this close to the bombing and the cellar of the church is not very deep. A direct hit would likely kill us all.

All of a sudden, everyone's heads jerk upward and we look at the ceiling. We all hear it at the same time; a screaming, whining sound that is getting louder with each second. We have all heard it before, probably many times. It is the sound of a wounded German plane in a crash dive.

We continue to stare upward as the sound of the dying plane gets closer and closer. I try to calculate the odds of a plane hitting this building then quickly realize how foolish that is. It is going to hit somewhere, and it sounds as if it is coming right at us.

"It's going to hit us," Catherine whispers in my ear.

I squeeze her a little tighter as the screaming reaches its crescendo. We feel it hit the church directly on top of us. The world has literally blown up on us. The cellar is lifted two or three feet off the ground. We are all tossed about, and the far wall collapses down coming close to crushing us all.

FORTY-SEVEN

As terrified as everyone is, me included or even especially, there is no hysteria or panic at all. In fact, we are all lying down, flat on the floor. I don't remember doing it, but I am on top of Catherine protecting her. Miraculously, not a single one of us was injured with anything more serious than minor cuts and bruises.

We are covered with dirt and plaster dust and in the dark with only the flashlights lying on the floor. We are a ghostly sight. It takes a few minutes to get everyone accounted for. Most of us are shocked to still be alive. A few of the women are quietly weeping, but there is mostly calm.

I have been struck by a piece of plaster that hit me on the head. As is true of head wounds generally, it is bleeding profusely. Catherine reaches under her skirt and tears a strip off of her cotton slip and uses it to clean me up. A few minutes later, Father Donovan comes around with a first-aid kit. He has stored it in the basement just for this eventuality. The two of them wrap a bandage around my head. Catherine assures me the wound is not deep. It is then that I look around.

One of the older men, George Foster, has a flashlight and is surveying the damage. He is climbing around the debris of the collapsed wall. Catherine, Father Donovan and I join him. I'm still a bit shaky but not too bad.

"We're stuck," George announces. "We'll have to wait for morning to be rescued, by the look of it."

Father Donovan and I crawl around on the top of the pile of dirt, bricks and rubble. There are three small holes we can look through and see the street. There are fires burning around us. We do not have a good view of the carnage brought about when the airplane hit. We can only see the light of flames and smoke rising up. We also quickly realize George is right. We do not have the means to get ourselves out.

It is still relatively early, a short while past ten p.m. We have no food, water or toilet facilities. But we are alive, and help will arrive. Sooner or later, we will have to improvise some sort of toilet. Modesty will take a hit before we are rescued. If that is the worst of our problems, we will get through this quite easily.

There were a dozen or so candles burning before the plane hit. With the subsequent damage it did, the candles were all blown out. Several of them have been found and are providing light again. That may not sound like much, but it is significant. The batteries for the flashlights will not last until morning. Keeping a couple of candles going providing some light does wonders for morale. Sitting totally in the dark after all that has happened would make the experience much worse. After tonight, I shall make a point of staying out of caves, tunnels and mines as much as possible.

We can still hear planes overhead, bombs and antiaircraft fire in the distance. It is all a long way off, at least a couple of miles. Some poor devils are catching hell.

Catherine checks my head wound and tells me the bleeding has stopped. She retrieves a bandage from the first aid kit and replaces the one on my head. My head wound is the worst anyone has suffered, and it is not bad at all. Catherine and Father Donovan have checked all of the others for their wounds as well—very minor. We were extremely lucky. By eleven o'clock, the Germans have gone, for now, and we are all asleep.

"Hello! Is there anybody down there? Can you hear me?"

I am awakened, along with most of the others, by a man's voice. It is coming from one of the holes at the top of the debris pile. There is also a light being waved around by someone.

"Yes, yes, we're down here!" I yell back as do some others yell similar answers.

I grab a flashlight, turn it on and struggle to my feet. Catherine is right behind me as we crawl up to the hole where the light is. A man wearing a military-style helmet sticks his face in the hole.

"How many?" he asks.

"Eighteen," I answer. "No serious injuries. We're all doing all right, but we're stuck."

"A Yank? What the bloody hell are you doing—"

"Never mind that," Catherine yells at the man. "Get us out of here!"

He looks at me, and I say, "Best do as the lady says."

As soon as the hole is big enough, I practically shove Catherine through it. She is not pleased about going first, and I am sure I will hear about it.

Except for Father Donovan, the captain of this sunken ship, I am last and not because I was showing off my courage; nothing that significant. In fact, it is a bit embarrassing. Being a very well fed American compared to my British hosts, I have to wait until the opening is large enough to accommodate me. And I am on the slender side of average for Americans.

The sun is starting to come up, and there is enough light to see the damage. The beautiful church that had stood for almost three hundred years is gone. The bomber wiped it out and took out three homes across the street. Fortunately, none of the occupants were in them. Unfortunately, they will join the rapidly swelling ranks of Britain's homeless.

There are several rescue workers crawling around the airplane's wreckage. Catherine and I are sitting on an undamaged bench watching them. A short while ago a group of women arrived with coffee and sandwiches. Everyone had a bite to eat and a cup or two of the coffee— possibly the best I ever tasted. I am sure the circumstances contribute to that feeling. After a while most of the others, all of whom live nearby, leave to go home. Hopefully, they have a home still standing when they get there. Father Donovan joins us on the bench.

"I'm sorry about the church, Father," I say.

"Yes, it's sad; a very nice little church. I was happy there and felt I was doing some good serving its congregation," he quietly replies.

"You saved our lives, Father," Catherine says. "You saved us all."

He looks across me at Catherine, smiles slightly and says, "I only opened the door. God saved us. There is no other explanation for what happened."

"Look," I say, pointing at the wreckage.

The rescuers are pulling a body of one of the crew out of the fuselage— or what is left of it. He will be laid out on the sidewalk and covered up next to his two mates already there and covered with blankets. A Dornier, Catherine tells me, has a crew of four. There is one more dead young man to find.

I am not sure what compels me, but I decide I must take a look at the German airmen. I stand up and walk toward them with Catherine on my heels.

"Where are you going and why?" she asks, tugging on my arm.

"Wait here," I say to her, but of course she does not.

We make our way through the wreckage to where the young man's body has been laid down. The two bodies laid out by the street are both badly torn up. Both are missing limbs and barely recognizable. This poor kid—he appears to be, at most, nineteen years old—is mostly intact. His right hand is gone and the lower part of his right leg. Miraculously, his smooth, young face does not have a scratch on it.

A good-looking boy, dark blonde hair and a face that rarely felt a razor; he looks almost peaceful. Seeing the young man like this, it is hard to look at him as a Nazi monster. He looks like some mother's son, which he certainly is or was. A German woman, likely not a Nazi fanatic, will be given the news that her son, the baby she brought into the world, is missing and presumed dead. Will her pain be any less than the British mothers who have and will be given the same news? Of course not. Seeing 'the enemy' like this brings it home. What a horrible, hideous waste it all is.

While we stand over the young German, the fourth crew member's body is discovered. The searchers bring it out of the rubble, and Catherine quickly looks away. His head is missing, decapitated during the crash. Hopefully, as ghoulish as this may sound, it will be found and buried with him. The German aviators who die over England are at least given an honorable burial; a soldier's funeral. We hear the Germans are affording British dead the same courtesy.

We have seen enough. Their dead children will be grieved and missed as much as ours. I put my arm around Catherine's shoulders and lead her away. She is silently sobbing for both of us.

"They're so young," she says as we walk away.

"They always are," I softly reply.

November 22, 1940

I awake with a start, come up and lean on my elbows. For a moment I am unsure of where I am. Catherine is lying beside me facing away and sound asleep. Then I hear it again. The sound that awakened me. It is the telephone. Annoyed, I pick up the extension on the table next to me. I left instructions at the front desk we are not to be disturbed before three p.m.

"Hello," I gruffly say then clear my throat while looking at the clock. It is half past four.

"Are you all right?" I hear David ask.

"Yes, yes," I answer as I sit up and put my feet on the floor.

Catherine stirs, looks at me then turns away, back to sleep.

"What happened last night? We were worried that you might have been caught in the bombing."

"We were," I say. "It was, uh, quite an adventure. But we're both fine. Long night. Why don't we meet you in the American Bar in an hour?"

"Okay, good. I'm relieved as will be Clive and the others," David says. "Can't wait to hear this story."

It is close to six p.m. when we arrive at the Savoy. Sunset was shortly after five, and of course, the blackout is in effect. Catherine is wearing the same blouse, jacket and skirt she wore the previous evening. The Ritz laundry service is still exceptional. Her clothing was cleaned and pressed while we slept.

Along with David and Clive there are at least a dozen others, tables pushed together, waiting to hear our tale. Neither of us has had a bite to eat since yesterday. We order a meal then begin. It takes over an hour to tell it. These people are all journalists and not shy about interrupting to ask questions.

When I tell them about the bodies of the young German airmen, a couple of them make disrespectful, even offensive, comments about them. They were on a mission to kill British civilians after all.

"Don't. Don't say that," Catherine quietly, mildly chides them. She is friends with both men, so it is taken without rancor.

"They were children. The sons of mothers and fathers who will be horribly pained by the news they will receive. Yes," she continues, "the

Germans started it, and we must win. But these young men are no different than our young men, the men we send up to kill them."

This brings a moment of awkward silence.

It is Clive who relieves it. He stands and raises his glass, then says, "May I propose a toast."

By now half the bar is either seated or standing around our conjoined tables. We all rise, those of us who are seated, and raise our glass.

"May God grant us a swift and speedy end to this horror to minimize the number of grieving loved ones of our precious young men and women who will sacrifice their lives for the final victory."

There is a chorus of, "Hear, hear!" all about us.

While I drink to its sentiment, I cannot but wonder how many times the same toast will be made in Germany.

FORTY-EIGHT

November 30, 1940

Dear Mom & Dad,

Hope my letter finds all of you well. Christmas is rapidly approaching, and I was intending on a surprise visit. Unfortunately, the Gazette turned me down. There are others with more senior tenure than me who have beat me to it, our guys in Rome and Athens especially. With them getting a leave, the paper decided I needed to stay. Truly sorry.

News. Two nights ago, Liverpool was struck by what is being called, the worst bombing of the war. They endured a steady eight hours of it. Liverpool, as I am sure you are aware, is a vital port city. They have dealt with the Blitz as much as, if not more than, London. The Germans' primary targets are the docks, but as I have mentioned in the past, aerial bombing, especially nighttime bombing, is imprecise, to say the least.

They suffered a horrible tragedy. Winston Churchill is describing it as: "The single worst civilian incident of the war." An air raid shelter at a local instructional college received a direct hit. It is believed a parachute bomb struck the three-story building and caused it to collapse. There were an estimated three hundred people seeking shelter in it. At last count, over one hundred and fifty dead, and they are still finding bodies: men, women and children.

I need to tell you something. It has been over a week, and I am finally able to write about it. First, let me be very clear, Catherine and I are fine. I received a very minor bump on the head, but that was all.

The night of the 22nd, we were caught out in a bombing. We managed to get shelter in an old, beautiful Catholic church. Along with sixteen others, we rode out the bombing mostly unscathed. We were sheltered in the cellar and well protected. That is, until the church itself was destroyed.

A German plane, shot down by British gunners, crashed into and through the church. It was, of course, quite horrifying. But all of us made it through unharmed, just minor cuts, bumps and bruises.

A wall in the cellar collapsed and it took several hours for rescuers to dig us out. Those with us were mostly older men and women. No children. They have mostly been evacuated to places in the country outside the city.

The worst of it was after we were rescued. Catherine and I watched while search and rescue teams went through the airplane's wreckage. They found the bodies of all four German Luftwaffe crewmen. It was horrible.

Yes, they have been bombing us, and yes, they must be defeated. Seeing their shattered, broken bodies, one in particular, makes you realize what a monstrous waste this horror is for everyone. They are barely adults. Children, really. As are ours. Even Catherine, who as you know has lost a brother, could only feel pity for them. The enemy doesn't seem so hateful when you find them like this.

Sorry, if once again, I have been depressing. When the war becomes that personal, it is depressing.

Again, on the whole, I am fine. Believe it or not, I am still having the time of my life. It is an amazing, incredibly important period of history. And I am certain that sooner or later, we will get in it and win. I would not have missed it for anything. In fact, I didn't know I could be this happy. Of course, Catherine has done that for me. I only hope she feels the same.

Speaking of Catherine, she is working late tonight. I have just finished my story about Liverpool for the paper. I'm off to bed. Tomorrow I will write the story of my (our) experience of being caught in the open a week ago.

Tomorrow morning, December begins. Again, I am sorry I can't get back for Christmas. An early Merry Christmas to all, anyway.

All my love,

Jeff

December 2, 1940

I have arisen early to get started on my church bombing article. There was a telegram from the *Gazette*, requesting it delivered, with my morning coffee. The hotel is still supplied with coffee, but it is getting expensive. I am not a big coffee drinker, but I must have some in the morning—as does my guest.

It is after eight, and I can hear Catherine in the bathroom. She has a touch of influenza and has not been feeling well for a couple of days. From the sounds coming from the bathroom, it seems to be getting worse. I will insist she see a doctor today.

"Morning," I hear her say from behind me.

Catherine takes her usual seat at the table, and instead of coffee, she pours herself a glass of water.

"Still a war on," I reply. "Not feeling well, again?"

"No, and I surrender. I'll see a doctor today. I hate to bother them; they are so busy with war casualties. I know someone I've seen before. I'll call and see if I can get in."

"Good, thank you."

"I received a letter from Arthur yesterday. He managed to get a major who flew back to deliver it," she says.

"So he made it," I say.

"It seems so. He thinks you had something to do with his transfer," she says with a sly smile.

"I'm an American journalist. How could I have pulled that off? Besides, it wasn't me; it was his scheming wife who did it."

"Should I write and let him know?"

"Probably best to let him believe what he wants," I reply.

"He says he's already working on getting transferred back to London. When he does, he will have you sent back to America. He could pull it off."

"Write him back and tell him to pad his war record. It will help him politically. That should appeal to him."

Catherine laughs and replies, "If they don't shoot him for cowardice. I'm famished; let me take a quick shower then we'll get a bite. I'll go into the BBC and make an appointment with the doctor. What are you doing today?"

"Finish this, then go to the Ministry of Information and hang around there," I answer.

"Did you hear the news? Joe Kennedy was finally fired by Roosevelt yesterday," Catherine says.

"That should surprise no one," I reply.

"Southampton was hit pretty hard Saturday night and early Sunday morning," Catherine says.

I am at a loss as to what to say about the bombing of Southampton. The attacks have made us numb because they have become so routine, not just in London but almost every city of significance, especially the large ports. It is considered a small raid if casualties are fewer than a hundred—a number that would have been appalling before this began.

Catherine finishes her glass of water, stands, kisses me and says, "I'll be ready shortly."

***

"Are you sure you're all right?" I ask as I place a hand on her forehead. She feels a bit clammy and looks a little pale.

We are in a cab in front of the BBC building. I will drop her off then meet David and Clive at the Ministry.

"Yes, I'm okay. I'll see the doctor, I promise. I'll meet you later at the Savoy. Around six?"

"See you then," I say. I kiss her and add, "Hey, I love you. See a doctor."

David, Clive and I have an uneventful day. The news about Southampton's bombing raid gives me a story for tomorrow. I sent in my story about my close call in the church bombing. It went by wire, and I have already heard back from the *Gazette*. First, they chastised me for being so reckless, then suggested I keep doing it. The story will be page one tomorrow.

"Here she comes," David says.

We are in the American Bar at the Savoy where, for the past hour, we have swapped our stories with other bored journalists. The only thing of significance we learned today was the Southampton raid was worse than we thought. It is now being reported that almost two hundred were killed, one hundred in an air raid shelter including an unknown number of children.

David is facing the entrance and has seen Catherine coming in. A moment later she joins us.

"What did the doctor say?" I ask.

"I was right. Nothing to worry about. I'll tell you later," she says.

The bar is almost full, and despite the diminishing menu, it is doing a brisk dinner business. The four of us join in—we have given up keeping a chair for Charlie—and pass the next three hours.

The bar itself can and has on many occasions, served as an air raid shelter. The basement of the Savoy is about as likely, or unlikely, to be hit as anywhere else. Mayfair has not been targeted much although a couple of bombers hit it a few nights ago. Several buildings received minor damage. In fact, the street between the Savoy and Trafalgar Square received several bombs leaving damage that has not been repaired.

At nine o'clock, Catherine and I decide it is time to go. We say our good nights, and when we get out to the street, we find the cab stand empty.

"Let's walk," Catherine suggests.

"We may not have a choice," I say.

While Jeff and Catherine are sharing a pleasant evening at the Savoy, Southampton is again targeted for an attack. There is a flight of Heinkel bombers heading south along the east coast of England past Swingate.

Among the squadrons of German bombers, in fact, the very last plane in line, is a Heinkel He 177. The pilot and commander is Oberleutnant Oscar Weber. Usually an easy-going young man, Weber has been in a state of consuming anger. His crewmates, especially his copilot Hans Fischer, have noticed and have tried to find out why. Eventually, even Fischer gives up.

The group they are in is made up of twenty-four Heinkels. They are heading around the south of England to Southampton with orders to bomb the docks.

The first Chain Home Station to report them was Swingate. The RDF scopes picked them up as they were forming up over Calais. On their way to Southampton, they stayed over water flying around southern England.

As Weber's bomber flew past the coastal town of Folkstone, he used the aircraft's intercom to speak to his radioman. "Carl, report to our squadron leader that we are losing oil pressure in our starboard engine. We are turning back."

Unaware that there was no problem with the engine, the radioman simply acknowledged the order.

"What are you doing?" Fischer asked. "There's nothing wrong with—"

"I'm in command, and you will follow my orders. We have a new, more important mission," Weber curtly replied as he turned to starboard and dropped down.

"Where are we going?" Fischer asked.

Weber waited until the aircraft leveled off at two hundred feet before answering. "Gretl died in a British bombing of Berlin a week ago," he tersely said referring to his fiancé. "We are going to kill the man responsible, Winston Churchill. Then we will have peace."

"Are you mad?" Fischer almost yelled. "We will be shot for not following—"

"We will be heroes of the Fatherland," a grim-faced Weber said. "I have been to London several times. I know exactly where the criminal Churchill's residence is. We will bomb it and win the war."

"We will be shot for desertion," Fischer said shaking his head at his friend's foolishness.

When Weber dropped the Heinkel out of formation, the night watch at Swingate immediately reported it. Within minutes after dropping below the RDF signal, the plane's location was no longer visible to British RDF.

Catherine and I have been stumbling along in the dark for about fifteen minutes. I know where we are, but it is not easy going. There are a number of bomb craters we must get past until we get clear of them. Instead of the sirens warning us, the first indication of trouble is the sound everyone is very familiar with. We hear the sirens almost simultaneously with the first bomb blasting.

We are trapped. It is too late to go back to the Savoy. Our only hope is ahead of us. Charring Cross tube station is about two hundred meters ahead. I look at Catherine, and she is looking at me with horror in her eyes. I grab her arm and yell at her to run as we both take off. We have barely taken two steps when the second bomb explodes. It is less than two blocks from us, and it knocks us off our feet. There are five more to come.

Catherine is lying to my left. She struggles to stand and gets to her knees. I yell, "I love you!" then lunge at her from my knees. I push her hard, and she almost flies into a hole left by a previous bomb. I watch her go over the edge as the third bomb in the sequence goes off.

I am still on my knees struggling to stand to jump into the bomb crater where Catherine is. Too late. The concussion hits me and throws me almost a hundred feet. I lie there, face up, as the remaining bombs land and go off past me.

Why are these people standing around me? Who is the man shining the flashlight in my face? Why can't I make out what they are saying? Or are they speaking to me at all?

Suddenly, Catherine appears. She is unharmed and kneeling next to me. I try to reach up to take her in my arms, but I could not. My arms are not working. I cannot comprehend any of this. I must be injured but I feel fine. Oddly, I feel no pain, but I cannot move, and I am beginning to feel very cold. Why are they all looking at me so sadly? Why can't I move my arms or feel my legs?

I look at Catherine, and she is sobbing uncontrollably. I try to ask her why, but I am unable to speak. Still sobbing, Catherine collapses onto my chest, her arms around me, and I try to hold her, tell her I am all right. The man with the flashlight kneels down and with a thumb and finger, closes my eyelids.

"Please don't do that," I try to say, but my mouth does not open, and no words come out.

Suddenly, I am above them looking down. I am floating over them while watching the small crowd standing around my immobile body. It is then I realize what is wrong.

At the beginning of this story, I told you there are three dates I would always remember. The first was May 10, 1940. That was the day Winston Churchill became Prime Minister and, of far more importance to me, it was the day I met Catherine Hartley, the woman I will love for eternity.

The second day of significance is July 10, 1940; the day the Battle of Britain began, the day when Hitler and his criminal horde began to lose the war.

Finally, there is Monday, December 2, 1940; the day I was killed in a German bombing raid.

At war's end, the German war archives would reveal my death was a fluke, as were so many others. The flight leader who killed me was trying to target 10 Downing Street, the Prime Minister's residence. He missed by a good mile.

EPILOGUE

Although the British did not know it, the Battle of Britain was truly over and won by mid-December. On December 18, 1940, Hitler issued a formal order directing the military to begin planning for Operation Barbarossa, the invasion of the Soviet Union. The Blitz would continue until May 10, 1941. For all practical purposes, the British had won in December.

Hitler considered himself to be a military genius, at least on the same level as Napoleon and Alexander the Great. This belief of his would prove to be a great asset to his enemies. Turning his back on Britain to attack Russia was the first in a significant number of huge strategic blunders he would make. A second strategic error made by the little corporal concerning Barbarossa led to a serious delay.

Originally scheduled to begin on May 15, 1940, it was postponed, for what would to prove to be five crucial weeks. When Mussolini ordered the Italian invasion of Greece, he intended to show the Germans that Italy could conquer as well as the Germans. Not only was this proving to be false, the Greeks were, in fact, whipping the Italians. Not wanting his junior partner to be humiliated, Hitler ordered the German army to rescue the Italians.

On April 6, 1941, the Germans invaded Yugoslavia and Greece. By the end of April, both countries had been conquered and occupied. But this set back the plans for Barbarossa to June 22, 1940. The delay, along with other bad decisions by Hitler, would ultimately save the Soviet Union.

December 1941
New York Harbor

Catherine Hartley stood at the portside railing—along with almost all of the passengers—of the SS Serpa Pinto. As with many of her companions, there were tears running down both cheeks. Of course, Catherine had seen the Lady's picture hundreds of times. But to see her in person on her pedestal, arm outstretched, holding the torch, welcoming the world, was almost a dream.

Catherine had flown on a diplomatic plane to Lisbon. From there she had booked passage to America on the Serpa Pinto, a Portuguese ship flying a neutral Portuguese flag. The actual crossing had taken eleven days— eleven uneventful days. Now the ship was gliding past the Statue of Liberty into New York.

During the voyage, she had learned that among the passengers, were three hundred Jews. They were the lucky ones who were able to flee Europe, escape the clutches of the Nazis and, although they did not know yet, survive the Holocaust.

Catherine was on her way to a new job with the BBC. She would be working out of New York for at least a year or longer if she could swing it. During the voyage, she had made acquaintance with several families of Jewish refugees. For the most part, they were a bedraggled group, barely escaping with little but the clothes on their backs. Several of the men, including an obviously highly educated Rabbi from Paris, were certain the Nazis were going to murder all of the Jews of Europe.

Catherine had heard these rumors before and, like most people, dismissed them as propaganda. Even the Nazis were not that horrible. But she had obtained enough material for a series of articles on their plight and escape. Would anyone care?

As the liner slowly made its way toward its Staten Island berth, Catherine again reflected on the past year; the year since the night Jeff died. Too much death. Too much grieving. First, her brother, Tom, then the great love of her life, Jeffrey, and finally, Arthur.

In January, Hitler had sent reinforcements to Africa to prop up the Italians. Only two divisions, but they were being led by a man who was already a legend. Erwin Rommel had turned the tide in favor of the Germans. On April 3, the staff car Arthur Ashland was riding in hit a land mine. The car was flipped over and Arthur, along with two others, was killed. Oddly, when Catherine received the news, she was moved to tears. Too much death. Too much grief.

"Would you mind waiting, please?" Catherine asked the taxi driver. "I'll know in a minute if I need to have you drive me back to the city," she quickly added.

The cabbie, a normally ornery New Yorker, was a little smitten with the pretty British woman and her soft British accent. "Sure," he agreed.

They were parked in the brick driveway of—by Long Island Gold Coast standards—a small, yet stylish, two-story brick mansion. It was a sunny, calm early-winter day. Oddly, no one in the house had noticed the cab parked out front.

Catherine stopped and looked at the door. "Well, you've come this far," she whispered to herself, "ring the damn doorbell."

Within seconds, she heard footsteps coming toward her. A moment later an elegant, slender woman, wearing a Sunday dress with nicely styled graying hair opened the door.

"Yes, may I help you?" the woman politely said.

"I hope so. Are you Abigail Bartlett?"

"Yes, I..." she started to say, then said, "My God, you're Catherine!"

Before Catherine could even say yes, Jeff's mother had almost jumped through the doorway to hug her. Seeing this, the cabbie lightly beeped his horn, returned Catherine's wave, then drove off.

"Wilson!" the woman yelled into the house while Catherine dismissed the cab. "Come here, immediately!" Abigail turned back to Catherine, who had yet to even speak, and said, "This is wonderful. How? Why didn't you call? Never mind, here you are..."

By now Wilson, Jeff's father, was at the door. At first, he shook her hand, then hugged her.

"I decided it was time we met. And I have something to show you," Catherine was finally able to say.

Next to her was a good-sized basket she had set down. It was covered with a small, white blanket. Catherine picked it up by its wooden handle and said, "I'm not sure if we have a future president or prime minister. For now, we'll just settle for being your grandson."

With that Catherine pulled back the blanket to reveal a miniature Jeffrey Bartlett. At the sight of him, Abigail burst into tears as her knees weakened, and Wilson was not far behind her.

While Abigail sobbed holding a hand over her mouth, her husband put his arm around her shoulders and held her. For a full minute, the two of them stood and stared at the baby: shocked, stunned and filled with pure joy.

Finally, Catherine quietly asked. "May we come in?"

"Oh, yes, of course," Wilson quickly replied.

Abigail, still flooding tears and looking down at the baby, said, "Can I hold him? Would—"

"Oh, lord, yes, please take him. I've been lugging the little bugger around for days."

Jeff's brothers and sisters were introduced. Michael, now the oldest, Nancy and Patricia, the two sisters and Greg, the youngest. The girls, of course, could not get enough of their newly discovered nephew, even arguing about who got the privilege of changing his diaper.

The noon Sunday meal was about to be served, and a place was quickly set for Catherine. At one point, Wilson, again fighting back tears, told Catherine that since Jeff's death, today was the first happy day they had.

"Although, you should be chastised for not telling us sooner," he said but with a smile.

"Yes, I am sorry about that. At first, I wanted to wait until I was sure he was healthy and everything was all right. Then time just slipped by. Before I knew it, I had received a chance to come to New York, so here we are. I was told by doctors that I could not have children but… well, here he is," Catherine said.

"You took a chance on us being home," Michael said.

"Yes, but I decided you would probably be back from church and if I timed it right, I could get a meal out of it," Catherine said which brought some laughter.

"Where are you staying?" Nancy asked.

"We would love to have you stay here," Abigail quickly put in.

"Yes, please," Wilson added. "Michael is living in the city. The girls would love to have you, and young Jeffrey here would be a delight. Please."

"Well, I hate to impose…"

"Nonsense. We'll arrange transportation for you to the city. Who's going to watch the baby while you work?" Abigail asked.

"I would hire a nanny," Catherine said.

"Absolutely not," Abigail said.

"You'll spoil him rotten," Catherine said, but she said it with a smile.

"I certainly will," Abigail replied. "We really would love to have you and Jeffrey here. And we certainly have plenty of room. So, please."

"Transportation into the city for your employment won't be a problem," Wilson said.

"Please!" the daughters chimed in together.

"How can I refuse. It would be a big help, at least for a while," Catherine replied.

At that moment, the youngest, Greg, hurriedly came back into the dining room. "Dad, Mike, everybody, you'd better come listen to this," he said.

"What?" Mike asked.

"The radio. The news," Greg said.

With Patricia carrying the little one, they all followed Greg into a sitting room. There was a tall, new Zenith radio in one corner.

"Again," the radio announcer said, "we interrupt our regularly scheduled program to bring you this news from the White House.

"The Japanese navy, in a surprise attack, has inflicted significant damage to the U.S. fleet at anchor in Pearl Harbor. As you may understand, the news is minimal, but it has been confirmed. The Japanese attacked our fleet and airbases in the Hawaiian Islands early this morning Sunday, December seventh. Early reports indicate the damage has been severe and there are large numbers of casualties..."

For the next few minutes, the room was completely silent while everyone listened in shock. It was Patricia, still holding baby Jeff, who broke the silence.

"What does this mean?" she asked.

"It means, we've won," Catherine replied. "You're in it now and we will win. I'm sorry about the terrible news, but civilization will survive."

While Catherine, the Bartlett family and all of America received the news, Winston Churchill was dining at Chequers, the country retreat of British prime ministers. His guests were the U.S. Ambassador Gil Winant and Averell Harriman, President Roosevelt's special envoy to Europe. While the three men enjoyed their meal, the butler came in carrying the radio.

"Prime Minister," the butler said, "excuse me, sir, but I'm certain you will want to listen to this."

The BBC Home Service came on reporting the Pearl Harbor attack. The three men listened with astonishment. When the broadcast reported the attack was confirmed, Churchill leapt to his feet.

"I must declare war on Japan immediately," he said.

"Winston, no. Don't do anything yet. Wait until we see what Congress does," Harriman said.

"I agree," Winant told him. "There will be time. Franklin will go to Congress either tomorrow or the next day."

"Very well. I suppose you're right," Churchill growled.

A few minutes later, Churchill was on the phone. "Mr. President," he said to Roosevelt, "what is this about Japan?"

"It's quite true, Prime Minister. I'll be asking for a declaration of war at a joint session of Congress tomorrow."

After the war, Churchill wrote a multi-volume history of World War II. As to the night of the Pearl Harbor attack, he wrote: "Being saturated and satisfied with emotion and sensation, I went to bed and slept the sleep of the saved and thankful."

On the night of December 7, 1941, Winston Churchill may have been the happiest man on the planet.

On Monday, December 8, 1941, by a vote of 82-0 in the Senate and 399-1 in the House, Congress passed a declaration of war against Japan—and only Japan. There was no vote for a declaration of war against Germany that day.

On Thursday, December 11, Adolf Hitler made the biggest mistake of his life. Without discussing it with anyone or ever giving a reason why, he unilaterally declared war on America. He had been unable to defeat Britain and was stuck in the snow in Russia. Now, in an act that seemed to be a fit of temper, he declared war on the greatest industrial power the world had ever seen—a child kicking over the chess board upon learning he could no longer win.

That same Thursday afternoon, the U.S. Congress, by a unanimous vote, declared war on Germany.

On April 30, 1945, having brought about the greatest catastrophe in history costing sixty to seventy million lives, Adolf Hitler took the coward's way out. Refusing to accept any responsibility for what he had done, he bit down on a cyanide capsule while simultaneously shooting himself in the head.

It took two atomic bombs in August 1945 to convince the Japanese to surrender.

Historical Corrections

Swingate is a fictionalized account of life in London in 1940 during the first year of World War II. It was my original intention to write a historical romance novel; essentially, to do something completely different than the legal mystery/courtroom dramas I normally write. It was never my intention to write a historical book about Dunkirk, the Battle of Britain and the Blitz. There are library shelves filled with outstanding works of these events by lifelong historians with far more detail and accuracy than I could do.

The serious student of history reading *Swingate* will recognize events that, for literary purposes, I simply made up. Almost all of them, however, reflect actual events. Some I did simply for convenience.

A good example of a convenience reason is Jeff Bartlett's trip to England. I have him sailing aboard the SS America in April 1940. While the SS America was a very real luxury ocean liner servicing the Atlantic, it made its maiden voyage to England in August 1940. Sorry, Jeff could not wait that long. I had to get him there in April.

The German submarine, U-48, that Jeff and his fellow passengers observed following the SS America was real. In fact, U-48 was the most successful German submarine of the war. Until it was decommissioned in October 1943, it was credited with sinking fifty-five Allied ships. At the end of the war, it was taken out to sea and scuttled by German sailors.

The sinking of the converted aircraft carrier HMS Glorious by the German battleship Scharnhorst is true and did occur on June 8, 1940. The Glorious went down with twelve hundred of her crew. Tom Hartley, Catherine's brother, is a fictional character and was not among them.

Finally, another example would be Jeff traveling with Churchill to France in June. Winston Churchill did make that trip to try to bolster the French. I could not find any evidence that journalists were allowed to go along. Perhaps there were some; I could not verify this.

Several times I went way out on a limb. Journalists being allowed to go along on inspections of beach defenses would not have happened. Worse, in Chapter 17, Jeff and company were given a lecture about British air defenses, specifically, radar (RDF). This was one of the most closely guarded top secrets the British had. A lecture giving this information to journalists would have been ludicrous, even with the threat of hanging.

The aerial bombings of Dover and Swingate Chain Home Station did occur with regularity. The raid on August 31, during which Jeff was in Dover visiting Catherine, did not happen, nor did the shelling of Swingate on September 14, 16 and 25 occur—or at least, I could find no record of them.

These are just a few examples of the fact-based incidents. They may not have happened on the specific dates I chose, but the bombings and shelling were very real, as were the deaths and injuries that came with them.

Winston Churchill's speeches, as to their dates and times, are factual and accurate. There are voluminous records of these. His visit to Uxbridge and subsequent conversation with Catherine are, of course, fictional.

However, again there is an abundance of instances such as these. Churchill was notorious for dropping in on military installations. Uxbridge, because of its proximity to London, was a favorite. On September 15, 1940, he made a particular nuisance of himself. This was the day that would ultimately decide the Battle of Britain. The war's historical record is replete with these PM pop-ins, almost all of which aggravated the military commanders enormously.

I must give at least some attribution to the movie *Darkest Hour* starring Gary Oldham. In it, Churchill takes a ride on a tube train and talks to ordinary people. I did not intentionally copy this when I had Jeff visit with the people on the bus about their attitude toward continuing the fight. I saw the movie and I may have unconsciously used that scene as a reference for Jeff's discussion on the bus especially with the young girl.

To sum up, I hope the readers of *Swingate* will not be too critical of every detail. Again, it is a fictionalized account. However, I also hope it gives the reader at least a taste of what life was like, the courage, determination and will of a tiny nation who stood up to the tyrannical monster, Hitler the Nazi menace, and ultimately saved civilization. Thank you.

Dennis Carstens

Feel free to email me at dcarstens514@gmail.com with your comments